# PRAISE

"Editors Acevedo and Viola offer an anthology of noirish tales exploring the dark recesses of both real and supernatural worlds... Two sharp, distinctive, and complementary clusters of stories."
—Kirkus Reviews

"In this uniformly good anthology of noir stories, the authors are able to inject some life, of the supernatural variety, into a genre usually rife with clichés."
—IndieReader

"*Blood Business* is as satisfying as a stiff drink after a tough case. Deliciously gritty, and dark as a day-old bruise, these stories will thrill any noir fan."
—Jaye Wells, *USA Today* bestselling author

"In *Blood Business*, duality is a theme but nuance reigns. Honesty won't save you. Virtue is subjective. And what if the only difference between appearance and a reality is what we choose to believe? Cinematic at times, uncomfortably intimate at others, *Blood Business* is a visceral delight."
—John Wenzel, *The Denver Post*

"*Blood Business* compiles an absolutely stunning collection of talent."
—Brian Keene

"Take horror writing at its best and add a crime/mystery spin. Then pair this with psychological depth for the foundation of the special atmosphere and focus of *Blood Business*, where every story is powerfully wrought, filled with satisfying twists, and presented with a flair of originality and surprise not typically seen in crime story collections. For all these reasons, *Blood Business* is a unique, compelling, dark production very highly recommended for fans who like their crimes tinged with psychological depth and horror, and who look for original, unique, compelling productions where every story is a gem and no 'filler' is allowed."

—D. Donovan, Sr. Reviewer,
*Midwest Book Review*

# BLOOD BUSINESS

## CRIME STORIES
### FROM THIS WORLD AND BEYOND

EDITED BY
## MARIO ACEVEDO AND JOSHUA VIOLA

This is a work of fiction. All characters, organizations, and events portrayed in this book are products of the authors' imaginations and/or are used fictitiously.

BLOOD BUSINESS
CRIME STORIES FROM THIS WORLD AND BEYOND

Edited by Mario Acevedo and Joshua Viola
Copyedits by Jennifer Melzer
Cover illustrations by Aaron Lovett
Cover design by Kirk DouPonce
Typesets and formatting by Angie Hodapp

A Hex Publishers Book

Published & Distributed by Hex Publishers, LLC
PO BOX 298
Erie, CO 80516

www.HexPublishers.com

Print ISBN-10: 0-9986667-4-2
Print ISBN-13: 978-0-9986667-4-7
Ebook ISBN-10: 0-9986667-8-5
Ebook ISBN-13: 978-0-9986667-8-5

First Edition: November 2017

10 9 8 7 6 5 4 3 2 1

Printed in the U.S.A.

# CONTENTS FROM THIS WORLD

# CONTENTS FROM BEYOND

*For Ed*

# GARY PHILLIPS

# FOREWORD

WRITERS OF THE HARD-PRESSED AND THE TWISTED KNOW that behind the veneer of normalcy—where trimmed lawns are bordered by white picket fences and the sweet old widow living in the corner house once again wins the church bake sale with her treasured apple-pie recipe—can lie dark and troubled psyches. Didn't those uptight Jamestown pilgrims resort to cannibalism when the food ran out? Piety took a back seat to survival. Given a particular circumstance, aren't any one of us capable of the unimaginable?

Good ole' neighbor Sam secretly lusts for his bowling buddy's wife and one day decides to satisfy his unhealthy desire. Through the cold process of reptilian brain logic, the supposedly meek conclude murder is the only option to accomplish a goal. Or worse, murder is carried out as cavalierly as deciding between sprinkles or candy crunches atop a frozen yogurt treat.

Bad business…blood business, baby.

The nature of our engagements and interactions can be a tricky thing. For each heartbeat of altruism, greed is the selfish counter tempo. For each measure to provide comfort when a confidence is shared, there's the flip side of knowing certain information must never come to light—that money can be extorted to ensure such secrets remains unspoken. The mark is drawn into the con, duping themselves because they itch for something more. They need to feed their hunger and inexorably they fool themselves into believing what they desire is within reach—if only they had the guts to act.

The stories in this enthralling anthology offer a step through the funhouse mirror and into our rubbery distortion. On the other side we see beyond the image and are fascinated by what is reflected. Within these pages you'll find stories that portray the excesses of those who dare to embrace what's inside that mirror to those fleeing to put as much distance as they can from what's been revealed. But Blood Business lets us know escaping our fate is not in the cards. The hand has been dealt and you might just have to wager your life before the night is out.

In these pages there are tales about lowlifes and hustlers, scammers and short cutters...and even a jammed up faerie or two—the sort of individuals who don't populate the environs of everyday society. They operate at the edges, pretending a humdrum existence, but just below the surface they seethe with appetites they can't quite name, that keep them awake past closing time—ready to go on the prowl after their entitled spoils. Or what if the tables were turned, and one of these malefactors was cheated by a bolder thief? There's no righting that wrong through polite means. Hell, maybe it's not about justice, but about getting even and settling scores.

*Blood Business* is the sticky stuff that flows into the abscesses, the voids where theses characters' souls should be. It's a gurgling and coagulating entity that slowly, irrevocably poisons your body and plays havoc on your sanity. This contamination courses through you, quivering in your veins that you are due, and too bad if some chump gets in your way. There's a pulsing along your inner arm and you watch as this clump creeps under your skin like a diseased rat squeezing through a sewer pipe.

*Blood Business* is the thrill you've been jonesing to inject. Roll up your sleeves and get ready to take the hit. You'll find the darkness addicting.

# MARIO ACEVEDO

## INTRODUCTION

NOIR.

Doomed losers. Outsiders. Underdogs. Sinners beyond redemption.

Why should we care about them?

Because these characters allow us to indulge in the forbidden. To wade through the corruption that teems beneath our humdrum existence. We get to part the curtains of decency and reward ourselves with an eyeful of the taboo.

For we love the voyeuristic thrill that noir provides.

Noir is dark fiction. Noir is nihilism. Despair. Menace. Violence. The grotesque. Ruin.

In the hands of a dilettante, the results are cliché. But in the hands of a master, such tropes are both the tools and the medium to craft twisted tales of moral decay.

Noir has its roots in the mystery novel. The detective's search for justice forces him into the underworld of deceit and malfeasance, and this sin stains him. We see in Dashiell Hammett's Sam Spade, for example, a flawed hero whose nobility is illuminated because he stands in contrast to the darker souls he has to pry the truth out of. The hero becomes the anti-hero, but in spite of his defects, he manages to do the right thing.

Then Jim Thompson tossed aside the pretense of a hero trying to do good by society's standards. As the protagonist's world crumbles around him or her, we see them make one bad decision after another on the path to inevitable disaster.

Noir's protagonists creep, lurch, stumble toward self-destruction. Noir is a window into the heart of villainy. The knife is put in our hands so we can spatter ourselves with the victim's blood. We eavesdrop on the protagonist's perverted thoughts, feel their pain as they wrestle with their dilemmas, and yet goad them on to plunge down the wrong fork in the road.

We revel in this because every one of us—no matter how well-adjusted, how gregarious, how cheerfully we greet the world—is trapped within our own minds. No one really understands us. Secret longings and desires percolate into a brew of macabre and obscene what-ifs? We know how easily life can tip the scales, dragging us out of comfort and security and into desperation. We muse about weighing our moral anchor to see how far we can drift beyond the safe haven of propriety and virtue. Give us the Ten Commandments, and we'll smash the tablets and trade the fragments for drugs and sex.

We secretly want to wallow in vice and promiscuity.

We want to lie...to steal...to kill?

In *Blood Business*, we open that door.

Our stories run the gamut of noir. You'll find the unreliable narrator, the delusional criminal, the traitorous partner-in-crime, the smarmy businessman undone by greed, the adulterous husband whose treachery snares him in a dangerous double-cross. A one-time hoodlum is forced to confront his criminal past and thus trips into the web of lies spun by his former homies. A woman's quest for atonement and a righteous life circles back to the abyss of tortured memories. A vignette of stupid criminals careens between the horrific and the humorous, confirming that catastrophe and comedy are flipsides of the same dramatic coin.

But that wasn't enough. We broadened the mix by including stories with a paranormal twist. The supernatural allows us to up the stakes. To make the phantasms of our imagination into monsters of flesh and blood. We make bargains with otherworldy forces, knowing these deals always backfire. To show that even when offered the chance to fly with angels, people prefer to consort with demons.

Such then, is noir. Enjoy then, the company of our doomed losers.

# EDWARD BRYANT

# DOUBLING DOWN ON DEATH
## TWO FATAL FEATURES

## I.
### SUNSET AT THE OASIS

VAULTED AND STARK, BLUED STEEL ONLY NOW BEGINNING TO soften with the approach of twilight. The few wisps of cloud start to glow the precise crimson of arterial spray.

Graeff hunches down in the blind and hefts the thirty-aught. He sights for practice on a dry clot of hardpan. He touches the trigger delicately with less than a hair's weight of pressure. Imagines the sharp report and the hard kick against his shoulder.

Dusk is nearing. The prey takes its own sweet time out there.

He knows they might come down to the water at any time, day or night. But by and large, they all heed the water's call at sunset. It is a reality he counts on. It is a reality that has filled his trophy basement with a lifetime of sharp memories.

Graeff samples the perfectly still air. It smells like heat, tinged with dust. The desert winds will rise with the onset of darkness. But for now, even the beginning twilight shadows seem too dense, too thick to breathe into his lungs.

Good. His prey will be less wary; far too eager to reach

the fresh water that is all too rare in this forsaken back-forty of wilderness.

He stiffens and cocks his head. Graeff hears the sound of small rocks disturbed, two stones lightly clicking together. He carefully and slowly swivels to look up the slope.

No question; they are close. Graeff assumes there are more than one. There usually are. He hopes there aren't too many. He doesn't have all night to take trophies and bury the carcasses. Graeff has promised his wife he'll get back to the city at a civilized hour.

More sounds, louder now. Graeff raises the 30.06 to his shoulder and steadies it carefully. He doesn't need to work the bolt; the rifle has been ready for hours. The butt plate feels snug against his shoulder. He narrows his gaze into the eyepiece of the sight, delicately adjusts the crosshairs, replaces his hand on the polished wood beneath the barrel. This is the time when the rifle feels incredibly light, the beginning of the endorphin rush. Payment will be exacted later.

A head pokes carefully above the rise south of the water. Dark, lustrous eyes survey the oasis cautiously. Graeff holds his perfect Zen stillness. Another head. Good, a male and a female. Not a movement on Graeff's part. Do *not* spook the prey. The male leading, his mate following, both pick their way down the trail toward the water.

They are so close now—and the air yet so perfectly still— Graeff knows he won't need to lead either one. He certainly won't need to use the scope. So he feels the heat in his groin rise up. Point and shoot, and that will be that. Just a matter of pulling the trigger all steady, gently, mercifully.

That's what Graeff does. And so that *is* that—at first.

But then everything goes south all at once.

A chunk of the male's skull bursts out with the first shot, blood spraying a thick mist into the air. He drops to the hard slope, limbs flailing.

His mate recoils instinctively before the second shot, sprawling in the dust with a cry, then scrambling back up the slope. Graeff works the bolt, following her with the muzzle, squeezes the trigger, somehow manages only to kick up dust behind her right heel.

Below her, the male reaches back weakly. Graeff hears the word "—dios—" as the prey collapses, rolling down the slope as if in one final, mad effort to reach the plastic water tank the bleeding hearts from Tucson have placed here in the middle of Satan's own desert anvil.

Make sure the male is dead, Graeff thinks, then track and finish the female. Two trophies minimum for today.

But then one more thing goes wrong.

In the excitement of the kill, he has not been paying enough attention to his surroundings.

"Freeze! Game and Fish, son. Put down your weapon."

Graeff spins and looks directly into the setting sun-dazzle. When he starts to raise the aught-six, he knows instantly it's a bad idea.

Too late.

*Shit*, he thinks.

—the muzzle flash—

The pain.

It all ends…

…until he opens his eyes again.

## II.
### A FAMILY LETTER

DECEMBER 17
My Dear Friends and Family,

I know many of you expected that this year, of all years, we wouldn't send you a holiday letter, what with the Donnie situation and all. But when I thought about it, I realized we hadn't missed a holiday in more than thirty years of mailing out these darned things.

I hope you can understand why this is a time for us to take comfort in trying to keep as regular a routine as possible in all our lives. All of you are the people closest to us in our world and we love you. We have taken comfort in your support and your caring.

Over the past year, admittedly, we've discovered that not everyone has been as faithful as you. Some have drawn away from us, sometimes people we would never have expected that from. But we can't argue. They're doing what they have to do, just as we are doing the same.

I guess when it comes to love and loyalty and support, there's no way to predict which course people will take when the chips are down. Our faith has helped us, of course, but most of our ability to go on getting up in the morning and living all day and then going to sleep and starting over the next day has been a continuing and ever-lasting gift from all of you. I'll admit that I often cry myself to sleep and Jim sometimes drinks himself to sleep. When we do get to sleep, we're usually close but not touching. I'm sorry if that's too honest, but I think candor is probably the only way we'll get through this.

Yes, I know I should mention Donnie somewhere here too, but that's difficult. I'll try, but I can make no guarantees. The thing is, when all is said and done, he is still our son, our only child.

You probably know that Jim lost his job at the realty company right after the final Supreme Court appeal. It was a good severance package, though, and that's what we've been living on. We've cut back on expenses, but we're doing okay. Some friends have helped us out and some have not. It's always surprising. Almost no one from Jim's office has kept in touch.

The same thing's happened with the people at the pre-school where I worked for such a long time. Sometimes I have occasion to go back to the front office, but I feel more and more like a complete stranger. Old colleagues don't meet my eye, and so I do what I need to do and then leave.

Some of you, and I know you mean absolutely well, have suggested we seek professional help. Do you know, we tried that right after Donnie's first trial. I think it helped a little.

Jim disagrees. We haven't gone back to the doctor in quite a long time. The drugs—they just didn't work out. Forget that. Don't tell Jim, but sometimes I go back to the pills the doctor prescribed, though they don't even help me sleep. And sometimes when I drive now, I can't keep my eyes off the big trucks in the opposite lane. And those high bridges off in the distance? I'm trying to drive a lot less. And you know how I used to love to drive.

Have I told all of you about our new cat? Forgive me if I'm repeating. We got a beautiful new boy from our neighbor. Well, actually the woman next door moved to the other side of town along with her kids and left the kitty behind. We hadn't had a cat since Donnie was just a little boy and we had to stop having pets in the house.

So we adopted him. The cat was a young male, gray and sleek and handsome, a real charmer. And such a purr! We could never find quite the right name for him, so we called him Mouser or Killer or sometimes Jim would call him really vile things I cannot repeat in a holiday letter. You have to understand, he was a natural predator, though he always behaved perfectly at home. He used his litter box without fail when he wasn't outside, and he would be graceful and completely loving when he would sleep in my lap.

But it didn't take long before he exhibited the habit that Jim and I tried to understand, but finally couldn't accept. The cat loved to hunt and would bring us mementoes. He would drag back, through the old doggie door in the kitchen, a trophy from the night's journey. We would wake up in the morning and find souvenirs from the cat's victims on the foot of our bed. A rabbit's head, severed at the shoulder. Sometimes just a floppy ear. A disemboweled field mouse. A decapitated robin. Worst of all, once, a dead calico kitten. That was the hardest one for us.

Jim and I told each other that's the way of cats. Isn't it? We talked about it. We fought about it. Finally Jim put his boot down and issued an ultimatum.

I guess I'll have to go along with his wishes. There's no

higher authority in our household. We've asked the vet to put our kitty to sleep.

We will both go along to witness his death. It will be so difficult, but that's the least we can do. It's the right thing. It's the only thing.

I've talked again with Jim about all this, but I know there is no further appeal.

I pray that next Christmas I can pass along better news from us both.

With all our affection from the loving family we still are,
Ruth

# MARK STEVENS

# BONE ON WOOD

NINE MONTHS IN THIS TOWN, SURE, BUT HIS MESSAGES HADN'T changed.

He knew what he needed to do if he was going to whip the troops into shape.

He saw weakness. Weaknesses, in fact, were rampant. They festered. His work spilled out before him. He had a wistful notion that here, out on the eastern plains, things among civilians would be different.

But, no.

Betty Locke sat with a glass of white wine. He pictured the box in the refrigerator—a box of cheap stuff, complete with plastic spigot. He knew it was there. He didn't have to look. He glanced at his phone: 4:10 p.m. Betty Locke tried to put herself together for his visit, but it hadn't really worked.

She wanted his help.

She needed his help.

Odd to get a request for a house call, but so what?

He remained standing; a sign of urgency.

For the third time in three weeks, her son had been disciplined for bullying.

"There's nothing I can do," she said. "I need your help."

He wondered how much her hair coloring cost. Gray roots, ginger coif. A big-screen TV, on mute, played a show about buying mansions.

"Expulsion is next," she said. "If there's another *incident*. It's automatic. Can you talk to the principal?"

Betty Locke married a melon farmer, Alfredo Perez. They lived downtown in a white, clapboard, two-story house. The farm was north ten klicks, out in the country.

"Is Francisco here?" he said.

She cocked her head to think. "I don't think so."

There was a problem right there: houses so big you don't even know who is home. Of course, if you're buzzed at this hour, what did it matter? He thought he heard rumbling upstairs.

"Is he at school?" he said.

"School gets out at three-thirty." She looked down at her wine. "He was here for a few minutes and then ran out again. I think. Sure you won't join me? It's nearly five."

There were no strict rules about it, but he knew the impression it would leave.

"Your boy took a swing."

He let her chew on it. On the TV, the new mansion owners toasted with amber cocktails on a sun-splashed deck.

"Just grazed the kid is what he told me," she said. "And Francisco's eye is swollen. It takes two, you know."

"When will he be home?"

The thought of trying to talk to Francisco, frankly, repulsed him. Francisco wouldn't listen. He was raised to ignore. He was raised to get his way. In other words, he wasn't raised. He was born and waited upon. Francisco played left tackle. His thighs were as big around as a dinner plate. One time, he spotted Francisco downtown, a chocolate milkshake in one hand, caramel something in the other.

"Francisco keeps his own schedule," she said.

"And Alfredo?"

She paused, bobbed her head, squinted. "Where he's from, getting to high school is enough. Alfredo is so proud—all the football recruiters, you know. Of course Alfredo wants him to go to college."

"He's a junior."

"They drive all the way out here. Three at the last game. One from Oklahoma. Hell, we may as well be Sooners down here. Corner of nowhere."

"This is not nowhere." Hadn't they listened? He tried to boost them up, show them he believed that everywhere mattered, everyone mattered.

"You're new."

"Sort of, it's true." He'd heard this argument. "But I was in another town like this one. Across the border in Kansas and—"

And what? He didn't know what he was trying to say

She stared at him, eyebrows popped high.

"There wasn't that feeling of being overlooked," he said. "Small town, sure, but genuine dignity, appreciation."

"Jobs?"

"Not much different than here. You know; a fair amount of struggling, really."

"Good for them, then. Can you talk to Francisco?"

They were longtime members and this was part of the bargain, his end of it. He had a free place to stay, even with the mice and the leaky roof over the spare bedroom.

He cleared his throat. "Can you excuse me?"

In the bathroom, he pissed like a young stallion; loud enough that she'd know his need was real. He made a big deal out of running the water in the sink when he was done. The mirror issued a meek squeak as he pulled it open.

Jackpot.

Oxy front and center. He helped himself to five. No, eight. And half a bottle of Aleve PM, a mini ammo dump of sleep in his palm. And then into his pocket. Oxy in the right, sleep in the left. They would help him take the edge off this cranky, windblown town.

He peeked in their bedroom, a few steps down the long hall. Wood floors squawked. Another giant flat-screen, bigger than the other. In this old house, it looked like the shiny, weird obelisk in that goofy sci-fi movie about the apes and the slow-singing computer. The bed was up as high as his waist. It was so high, Alfredo could stand on the floor while he went down on her. That is, if he wanted to. If Mexican melon farmers did those things. Maybe that's why she drank. The down comforter was a beauty, but it wouldn't fit in his pocket. He had yet to feel warm in the miserable quarters that came with his deal.

They stood at the door. He saw she must need to pluck to keep the eyebrows separate.

"Of course, I'll talk to him."

"Thank you," she said. "He has to graduate. I mean, that scholarship. It's everything."

"She won't tell me the truth."

Johnny DeMuir, the good soldier. The earnest one. The true believer. The straight and narrow wasn't straight enough or narrow enough. He left tithes every week. Checks! $8.50, come hell or high harvest, each week. $8.50! How'd he come up with that?

"But you're sure?" he said.

"I can see it in her eyes," said DeMuir. "Also, a friend saw her car at the Econo Lodge in La Junta. All afternoon."

Odd that he'd been asked on another home visit so soon after Becky Locke, but there it was. Nine months... maybe they were all growing comfortable. Well, not all. What did Johnny DeMuir want for his $8.50?

He tried to look as if he cared. "Are you two getting along?"

Johnny shook his head. Thick sideburns, bushy eyebrows, three days of whiskers or more over a dark complexion. He'd make a decent Fat Elvis. "It's been rough. Can't say what it is. Grown apart, somehow."

"Sex?"

Johnny looked sheepish. They never expected that word from his mouth.

"Not much, not often. Brenda—" He took a breath, shook his head. "You know."

"Do you do things together?" he said. "Fun things?"

"In this town?" said DeMuir.

"See friends, play games? Bowl?"

"Her friends don't like me. I think they're part of the problem. According to her, I'm always wanting to plan for tomorrow. All they want to do is have a few drinks, plug the jukebox at Porky's Parlor."

"Do you get out there?" Already he was feeling discouraged about what reward he might find. Johnny's house was spare like a monk's. "Loosen up?"

"Look, we got nothing in the bank. I mean, not enough to make you feel as if you can go fritter it away on beers and burritos. Not me."

"Have you asked her?"

"About?" said DeMuir.

"La Junta?"

DeMuir sighed.

In the bathroom, he did his best impression of a racehorse pissing on fresh asphalt. The medicine cabinet was lame. Generics. *Good Lord.* Grocery store generics. He didn't believe in them. Two twenties lay folded in half on the bureau in the bedroom, one went missing.

Make it $28.50.

"What should I do?" said DeMuir.

"Do you want to meet; the three of us? I mean, marriages hit their rocky patches and then one day the sun shines and you move on." Hell, he wouldn't be here if his ex could have shown a slight interest in plain vanilla sex. Twice a month was all. With the lights off. He couldn't kiss her below the neck. She claimed it was all any man would "need." How the hell would she know? His ex fussed over the budget, too. Recorded every penny out and in. She'd like Johnny DeMuir.

"You mean *confront* her?"

"Talk it out—in a safe environment."

"She might walk."

He bet, when the time came for a good sob, Johnny was a blubberer. Probably thanked his wife for every roll in the hay. As if it was some great sacrifice. His wife was what, thirty? Thirty-two? And now banging a guy in La Junta?

"She might anyway." A small crucifix hung over the couch

on the opposite wall. He bet his middle finger was longer than the crossbar. What good was it? "Better to get it out, clear the air."

"She thinks we're normal."

He laughed. At least, he smiled and shook his head. "Normal is an average of a lot of things."

"She's gay, I'm telling you."

Third house call in five days. Weird. But again, the thought came to him: Maybe they were taking to him.

"She's how old?"

"Last week." Sheila Judd's bloodshot eyes screamed fatigue. Worry. "Turned twelve."

"And what makes you think—"

"Oh please." Judd cut him off. "I know you're fairly new, but I could never get her to wear a dress. I mean when she was three? No ballerina—no way, no how. And you know, her haircut. You've seen it."

Mrs. Judd kept her long hair straight. She sat pitched forward, as if her belly ached.

"Not just a tomboy?" he said.

"Angie doesn't even notice guys. You can't talk to her about 'em. And look at this."

She handed him a paperback, *The Gravity Between Us.* Kirsten Zimmer. On the cover, two young girls in profile were seconds from a delicate kiss.

"Found it in her backpack, dog-eared at the right spots." Mrs. Judd shook her head. "These days you never know what they're doing. I heard some kids don't think oral sex is sex, for crying out loud."

"It could be exploration," he said.

"It could be it's what she wants. And she'll be miserable. Bullied right through high school. In this town? Are you kidding me?"

He whizzed, flushed, washed up. Scrubbed like a surgeon. The medicine cabinet coughed up the mother lode—fucking Fentora, strong enough for gunshot wounds but dangerous shit, all sorts of respiratory implications, and fresh Vicodin, refilled within the week. He got hooked on Oxy during Enduring Freedom, tried Fentora twice.

"Mind if I get myself a glass of water?"

"There's filtered in the fridge," she said. "The big pitcher. Help yourself."

"Want one?" he said.

"Sure."

Water, hell. He wanted an iced-down whiskey to celebrate. Maybe the worn twenty on the counter by the sad bananas was his tip. It had that look, the way it was left there. All by its lonesome. He didn't really have a fix on Sheila Judd. Up until this visit, she hadn't really stood out. A wanna-be lesbian daughter made her, in a word, *interesting*.

Like the other two in this busy stretch, she expected him to say the right thing, talk to the right person. To fix it.

They all had the power, but they didn't want to do the work.

"You can't kiss it off!"

The podium issued a pleasing pop. A couple of heads jerked to attention in the second pew.

"You can't mail it in!"

There was Sheila Judd—back row. Staring. Two hundred others—staring. They all looked *together*. Like-minded.

"You can't close your eyes and say a few words and call it good. When was the last time you put some passion into it? You get down on your knees because it's *hard*. Bone on wood. Skip the cushy kneelers. Skip the carpet. Put your knee on real wood. Reminds you it ain't easy. You can't get it done between Walmart and McDonald's, in between stoplights and texts. You can't get it done while you're flipping channels on the flat screen. No way."

Betty Locke sat up close—maybe she was coming around.

"You can't do it between pouring the wine and sitting down for hamburgers. You have to make a commitment. You have to set aside time, and you have to de-clutter your mind.

What is the hardest thing you do in your life? Whatever it is, you have to work harder than that. You have to make it a priority. You can't move a mountain or heal a broken situation by being casual."

He shook his head. Blank faces stared back. He ran his fingers over the ridges in the beat-up lectern. How many had stood here, trying to get through?

In Chamkani, where the sun rarely broke the dark clouds, his chaplain's billet was a swirl, never knowing the faith behind the dull, resigned eyes. Here, hell, it should be a snap.

"And now we all need to do this together. We are being given no slack. The elders all know and I've discussed it here before. The electric bill—this is not a joke. We are way past due. And we have the resources, the means. I know it's rough out there. I know times are tough." Who was he kidding? They didn't know the meaning of discretionary. Or income. "But we need to sacrifice, we need to look within, we need to come together, or they will turn off the power! And we know how cold it will be in a month—the rectory, too."

He worked himself into a state.

"In Afghanistan—"

And again he told them a story of misery and explosions and gunfire and the search for meaning.

His chest felt like he'd been running but he'd already done eight miles that morning—four miles out and back along the fallow fields.

"We need to come together!"

His heart worked as if it sought to serve a beast ten times as large.

He waited for breath. His vision went slack and fuzzy.

"You need to pray—collectively—for a healthy—"

Heart doing handstands? Backflips? He tapped his chest. He didn't want them to see, well, weakness.

"We need an angel. We need to find someone who will cover this bill. One time."

In the second pew, Betty Locke turned to her neighbor and whispered something. The neighbor nodded.

Sara.

By this town's standards, she was a cute young thing. He stood, pants unzipped. She sat in the worn old leather chair that came with his tired, drafty office. To stoke his need, he reached down inside her shirt for a handful of her corn-fed breasts, heavy this week.

She didn't look up. He widened his stance, gave her a better angle. Her hair bounced. She worked hard, eyes closed. He gave no signal. He kept Kleenex on his desk and she cleaned him up after he was done. She took care, treated it tenderly. He poured two glasses of wine. She remained in his chair, he sat in the visitor's. He liked to linger, hear about her week. And thank her. He always thanked her, though not profusely. She was an oasis out here in the wilderness and she seemed to understand he was alone. She was the only one who asked about Chamkani.

"I don't know what was happening today," he said. "Something weird was happening today right there at the end. My heart. Very strange. Think you just reset the timer, though."

She shrugged, smiled. "All better now?"

"Dear Lord—"

He'd show them all how to do it right.

He'd locate the money for the electric bill tonight.

Right now.

Eighty-one hundred and forty-three smackers.

He got down on his knees, on the worn oak planks of his bedroom in the drafty rectory. The shag area rug, an old oval, green and matted and limping along on its last legs, was too soft.

He closed his eyes, conjured God. Or Gods. Even now, he wasn't all that sure. The swirl of sullen eyes—death came to some, death came to all, death came.

He worked it. Time grew meaningless. He would find the spot. He shoved all other thoughts to the side. His knees burned. Lights flashed in the blackness, soft bursts. He was here, he wasn't here. He pictured himself with a stack of cash, smiling for a selfie for the church newsletter, squaring up the account.

If only the others were all behind him, doing the same—

His heart.

Here it went again—a mind of its own!

Thumping, grabbing at his insides, clawing its way out. Demanding. Demanding what?

His breath tightened. He gasped, opened his eyes. The lone candle flame spun like a whirligig—impossible—and his lungs begged for a sip of air. He couldn't deliver. He thrust himself off the floor, thinking 911, when the floor flew up and smacked him hard in the face.

"What kinds of issues? I don't know." Betty Locke turned and shrugged.

Johnny DeMuir, her partner on the interview committee, answered by shaking his head.

"You know," said DeMuir. "Small town issues. Everything under the sun, but of course we like to pretend everything is perfect."

Betty conceded that the new candidate had charms—he'd be easy on the eyes come Sundays, for as long as they could pretend to care. The whole town enjoyed the breather for the past three months, sanctimony free. Now it was time to bring in another—if nothing else to have the rectory looked after. Someone with bland platitudes and gentle reminders would be about right. Someone to keep the mice on the run, as long as he didn't try to tell them all about whatever the hell happened in Afghanistan or swipe shit from their medicine cabinets.

"The World Church of God, though, what is that?"

The candidate seemed shy about asking such a basic question. He really could be Paul Newman's brother, around "Cool Hand Luke" days. *Let me know you're up there. Come on. Love me, hate me, kill me, anything. Just let me know it.*

"It's very general." Sheila Judd jumped in. "Jesus. God. The Bible—a good mix of Old Testament and New. As a town, I'd say we don't go for all that mystical Revelations woo-woo stuff. But we're hardly a big enough town for two churches. Because we all like praying together."

"That's right," said Locke. "As one."

# CARTER WILSON

# BLACK AND BLUE

THE MOMENT HAROLD RAISED THE HAMMER ABOVE HIS HEAD, he spied the orange pill bottle in his peripheral vision. Orange, not gray, as it had been last week. Harold's black-and-white world now blazed with color, and the pill bottle glowed against the gleaming white tiles of the kitchen countertop. Then, in the time it took for the claw of the hammer to complete its trajectory and implant itself with a sickening crunch in the top of Judy's head, Harold had a singular thought:

*Maybe I shouldn't have stopped taking my pills.*

But it was too late, and such thoughts were merely dead leaves, swept by the wind to be digested by rain. Transient, useless, and in the past.

Harold released his grip on the hammer and Judy collapsed, the implement lodged in her skull. She thudded face-first on the maple flooring. Two days ago Judy mopped the floor with something smelling of oranges that made the wood look permanently wet. Harold's chest heaved, and he could see his own shadowy reflection in the shiny floor as Judy bled out around his Jell-O—green Nikes. Harold never realized he had green shoes until today.

Judy didn't move, she wore an unwavering expression of mild shock, as if she just learned of the expected passing of a sick friend. Blood pooled in a neat circle around her black and silver hair, which was cut sensibly short, as befitting a woman her age.

Harold wanted to believe this wasn't bad, but even the absence of his medication couldn't result in that much delusion. This was indeed bad. He should have taken the pills, the little gray ones, the pills the doctor told him he had to take every day, even—*especially*—the days he felt fine. Without the pills Harold could have a psychotic break.

He took a step back and watched the blood creep into the spot of clean, shiny floor left behind by his sneaker. The blood looked like melted crayons, he thought. *Judy's head was full of melted crayons. Sunset Orange and Jazzberry Jam.* Colors he remembered ten years ago, back when colors existed all the time.

Harold grabbed the pill bottle off the counter, his fingers shaking as he twisted the cap open. He stared at little oval pills, each one seemingly too small to have any real power, much less keep a broken person glued together. Harold saw the pills were actually blue, not gray. A beautiful, robin-egg blue. He took one and slipped it into his front pants pocket, thinking it was too beautiful a thing to throw away. He wouldn't swallow it, but maybe it would have another use.

*You never were up to snuff, Harold.*

He snapped his head back to Judy. She was face down on her right cheek, one eye cocked open and rolling about unnaturally within its socket, the roving eye of a chameleon. Finally the pupil steadied and aimed right at her boy. Judy smiled on one side of her face, but it looked more like a ghost was hooking her cheek and yanking it back.

*I knew you'd snap some day. About goddamned time. Now I don't have you to worry about any more. Kill me? I don't think so, you burden. You freed me. And you should see the colors here, Harold. It's nothing compared to what you see now. Death is full of unimaginable colors, my dear, crazy boy. You should come and see.*

Harold closed his eyes and used the breathing exercise, just the way that orderly taught him at Bridgewater. She had always been nice to him. Seven years later, the exercise worked at steadying him most of the time. Most.

Calmer now, Harold opened his eyes. Judy was no longer smiling or talking or looking around. Judy wasn't doing anything but being dead.

Franklin, their cat, sauntered into the kitchen. He looked fresh from sleep, and three steps into the room he stretched his long, white legs in front of him, raised his hindquarters to the heavens, and squeezed his eyes shut against a long stretch. Franklin walked up to Judy, sniffed her bare, lifeless feet, then crept around to her face. He leaned in enough for Judy's blood to paint the ends of his whiskers a brilliant gloss of fire-truck red, sniffed a moment or two, then left her in favor of his nearby food bowl, where he picked gently at his leftover breakfast.

Harold looked over the kitchen sink, past the top of the potted dusty-brown herbs that had long since died of thirst, and through the small window streaked with years of grime. It was a sunny morning, no cloud cover except the feathery wisps that rarely appeared past noon. He decided everything around him, at that exact moment, was real. This was not an easy assessment, because the last pill he had taken was six days ago. He had only gone off his pills one time before, seven years ago, and that ended with ninety days at the Bridgewater Institution. But he wasn't going back there. No way. Harold was going to suck in life and hold it in his chest as long as he could.

Harold left Judy and went to her bedroom, where she kept the loaded .38 inside the safe. He knew where the key was. Always did, though she never suspected it. He snugged the gun inside the waist of his jeans at the small of his back. The metal was cold against his skin and he didn't like the feeling one bit. Then he grabbed Judy's cluster of jangling keys and went into the garage, where he slid into the front seat of their twenty-year-old de Ville, the tarnished color of a discarded third-place medal. He knew how to drive but he wasn't supposed to. Then again, he wasn't supposed to be killing either, so he figured God might overlook the lesser transgression.

He eased the Cadillac into the driveway. Sunlight locked onto him through the windshield like a tractor beam, and his skin was suddenly so hot—almost itchy—he had to roll down the window. Mrs. Daniels, who lived alone since both her husband and dog died within a week of each other three years ago, was in her driveway, bending for the morning paper. She clutched her frayed, Barbie-pink robe tight to her chest as she leaned down, and as she rose, she caught Harold's eye.

"Harold, you're not supposed to drive," she said. "Where's your mother?"

Harold didn't want to talk about Judy.

"You were always nice to me," Harold said through the open window. He pulled his seat belt halfway across his chest before reconsidering, then let it spool back into its housing. No seat belt today. "Thank you," he added, then continued backing into the street. As he pulled gently forward, he looked in the rear-view mirror and saw Mrs. Daniels knocking on the door to his house. How much could Mrs. Daniels see if she looked in the front window? Might be able to see Judy's feet, he figured. Maybe even some of the blood. Harold accelerated, and the Cadillac powered down the street like a whale through the sea: smooth, strong, silent.

In ten minutes he was at the pier. The dashboard clock read just before eleven, and since it was a Saturday, the pier was humming with activity. Harold swung the Cadillac into an open parking spot, marveling at his fine luck. He got out, not bothering to lock the car or feed the meter. As he looked up to the sun and warmed his face, he figured that, about now, a policeman was peering down onto Dead Judy.

God, the sky looked *amazing*. It was the sky of childhood, the memory of a day at the beach, of fleeting happiness but happiness nonetheless, and just that first sight of the ocean sky brought Harold back two decades, a time when there was no talk of pills or psychotic breaks. There was only time, sand, and the mosaic of dried salt on seven-year-old skin.

Harold shoved his hands into the pockets of his jeans and wandered along the boardwalk, which was lined with stores full of colorful trinkets. The gun dug into his lower back, cold and unpleasant.

Each of his senses tingled with an almost painful excitement, like snow-cold feet coming back to life in a tub of hot water. He stopped in front of an arcade and became entranced by the cacophony of electronic life and death, the clinking of tokens feeding machines, the violent clacking of air-hockey pucks, back and forth, until the tell-tale goal shot rang loud and true. He took a few steps inside and became dizzied by the bursting lights and colors: kingdom blues, neon greens, Ferrari reds, so many colors he thought his head might just shut down from the sheer beauty of it all. And the best part? There wasn't a gray anything in sight.

He stepped up to a machine loaded with all the classics, some he remembered, some he didn't. He peered over the shoulder of a shaggy-haired kid playing Frogger and became entranced in the rhythmic motions of the small hand throttling an ancient joystick. On the screen, Frogger desperately dodged cars, and he made it about halfway across a teeming highway before a red car unapologetically flattened him. That car seemed to come out of nowhere. Harold's chest tightened, and then he realized he had been holding his breath. He let it out, then he decided he didn't want to be there anymore. Why did that frog even have to cross the interstate, anyway? It seemed like such a pointless waste of energy, and now the thing was dead.

Next door, a quiet t-shirt shop. Harold slowly navigated racks of shirts destined for brief lives on the bodies of tourists (*Any 3 for $9.99!*), some encouraging alcoholism or fornication, but most just declaring the bearer had, in fact, been to this particular Southern California pier (*and loved it!*).

"Help you?"

Harold turned. The disinterested voice belonged to a muscular man about his own age, blond hair spiked into quills, smooth face unnaturally bronzed to a metallic patina. The color of Judy's Caddy, Harold thought.

Harold was going to answer, then realized he didn't have to. Harold never had to answer to anyone ever again. Instead, he reached out to a t-shirt that caught his eye. Easter-yellow, with a rainbow stretched from one armpit to the next. Barreling through the rainbow was a semi-truck, gleaming in a 70's hue, beneath which flowery, bold font asked everyone to *Keep on Keepin' on*.

Harold's daddy had been a trucker, back in what Judy always referred to as *the day*. Back when his daddy barreled through his own life once, maybe twice a year, shared some stories, then kept chasing his own rainbow. All that had stopped a decade ago.

Harold took off his own shirt and didn't even care about his big white belly floundering in front of the sculpted, bronze man. He put the truck shirt on and it squeezed him a little tight, but in a good way, like it was holding everything together. From this angle, he was pretty sure the man couldn't see the gun tucked into the back of his pants.

"Bro, dressing rooms are in the back."

"It's okay," Harold said. "I'm done. I like it."

The man scrunched his face, as if he smelled something past its expiration.

"Fine. That's five bucks. I'll get you at the counter." The man with porcupine hair motioned to the front of the store.

"Oh, I don't have any money," Harold said.

"Dude, quit bustin' my balls, all right? If you can't pay, take the shirt off and take a walk."

"But I like this shirt."

The man squeezed his chin and smirked. He looked like the kind of person who did that a lot.

"Dude, are some you kind of fuckin' loon or something?"

*Loon*. He hadn't heard that word in a long time.

"Yes," Harold replied. "Some kind."

"All right, take the shirt off or I'm calling the cops, okay?" He leaned in. "*Comprende?*"

Harold was going to argue, and then he realized he didn't need to. He never needed to argue again. Harold started walking to the door.

Three steps in this man, this *impediment*, grabbed his arm and spun Harold around. Sometimes when people touched Harold, his entire head would instantly flush with heat, a fire that raged from the base of his neck, up over his checks and spearing his temples. This was one of those times.

"You think I'm fuckin' around, bro? Fuck the cops. Maybe I'll just kick your fat ass. Huh? How about that?"

The man released his grip as Harold felt beads of sweat escaping the pores of his forehead. The man was *really* mad, almost as mad as Judy had been. Harold didn't understand this kind of anger, but the good thing was he didn't have to try to anymore. All that mattered was Harold wanted to keep moving forward, but this man wasn't letting him.

So Harold removed the gun from his waist and pointed it at the bronze porcupine. The man thrust his hands up and stuttered and stammered variants of the word *bro*.

"I just want the shirt," Harold said. He hoped the man would understand. Dying over a five-dollar shirt was as senseless as that frog trying to cross the interstate.

The porcupine said nothing more, so Harold tucked his gun back into his pants and left the store, marveling at how easy that was. If only life was that simple all the time. Heck, Judy would probably still be alive, even.

Harold swallowed a deep drink of ocean air as his face returned to its normal, pleasant temperature.

Outside, the pier buzzed. He picked up his pace as he made his way to the Ferris wheel, which slowly whirled over the surf, seemingly churning the entire Pacific by itself. He counted the line: thirty-one people in all. Harold had stared up at the wheel many times, and he knew the ride itself only lasted about two minutes, but the time-eating part was getting all those folks on and off. He waited behind two teenage girls who stood shoulder-to-skinny-shoulder, elbows bent so they could cradle their phones with both hands and gaze at the gleaming little screens. They giggled, outright laughed, then told each other *shut up!* Then back to their phones to repeat the process. Harold liked to watch them. Harold remembered girls like that when he was that age, back before he started having the thoughts the pills numbed down to little nubs.

Harold made it to his junior year in high school, but his last four years had been at an all-boy school.

The line crept forward.

The one with nectar-blond hair stole a glance back at him, smiled, and Harold's insides clenched to the point of pain. He knew she didn't like him, certainly not in *that way*, and truth was Harold had stopped thinking *that way* many years ago. But this girl, in that one glance, represented to Harold everything he had ever wanted and would never get. He wasn't angry or even sad about it. It was just a bit of a shock, like looking at the entirety of the universe at once and realizing what a tiny piece of softly floating dust you were. Still, he had the Ferris wheel.

"You ask him," Harold heard. It was the one with mocha brown hair. Giggles. "No, you do it," said the blonde. "*No!*" They ping-ponged this argument for a few seconds, before the blonde finally said, "Fine!"

She turned, smiled at Harold, and pulled a strand of hair behind her ear. Her cheeks had just a blushing of red, and sparkling green mascara blazed off her denim eyes. She held her phone up to him.

"Hey... sorry," she said, stifling a laugh. The other one covered her eyes with embarrassment. "But this... I don't know. This thing is going around the Internet. Just... if you don't mind. *God.*" She held the phone closer to Harold. "Just, tell me what colors you think this dress is."

He looked at the image on the screen.

Harold stopped breathing at the sight of *that* dress. A simple dress, which, if he had been asked six days ago, Harold would have said the color of which was a combination of two grays. Light gray and dark gray, or as Crayola might have called them, *Shark Fin* and *Pencil Lead*. But this morning Judy had been swearing at her phone, then had thrust it into Harold's face and asked him the very same question this girl with the honey hair was asking him now. *What colors do you see, Harold?*

But Judy hadn't really wanted a real answer. She knew

Harold only saw the world in the hues of 1950's television shows. She was asking to be cruel, and when he answered her with *actual* colors, she lost her mind. Funny that, being the one to lose *her* mind. Judy couldn't understand Harold being able to see real colors—especially not even the colors *she* saw—and it seemed to scare her enough to smack him. Not hard, but enough to sting. It was as if she was trying to swat a fly.

That was when Harold saw the hammer on the kitchen counter, the one Judy had been using to hang a spice rack. The one next to the pill bottle, its color a beautiful orange rust. Six days ago, Harold would have been numb to a slap on the head. But this morning, numb had been the last thing he'd been feeling.

"Black and blue," Harold said to the girl. "Like a bruise."

A squeal. The blonde raised her fists in triumph, then spun toward her friend. "I *told* you."

"No way," said the friend.

The blonde turned back to him and winked at Harold. "We're special. Most people see gold and white, but only the special people see black and blue."

Special. Harold had heard that word used to describe him many times, but it never felt as good as it did now.

"Thank you," he said.

Then they turned from him and continued with each other, and Harold became just another fleeting memory for people with better things to do than talk to him.

The line advanced, and at the front there was a ticket-taker. His shirt was a glorious red and white, like a barber pole. He asked Harold for his ticket. Harold answered he didn't have one. He watched the girls ahead of him board their cabin, oblivious to the heartbreak happening just behind their back. Harold really wanted to ride the wheel, so he asked this young man as nicely as he could if he could just, please, let him on the wheel. The young man said no. Harold felt the cold, gray steel of the gun against the small of his back, as if reminding him it was there.

But it was the front pocket of his pants where Harold

reached next. He offered this young man the only thing he had left of value in the world. His one remaining blue pill.

The man studied it in Harold's palm, then asked, "What does it do?"

People buzzed in impatience behind him as Harold considered the answer to that very complex question. What, exactly, did little the robin-egg pill do?

"It takes all the colors away," he said. He didn't think it would sound like a good deal put that way, but it was the clearest truth there was.

The man thought about this for a moment, then took the pill from Harold, thumbed it into his jeans pocket, and ushered Harold on board. Maybe this young man was tired of seeing colors. Harold couldn't understand the idea of that, but wasn't going to argue.

Harold sat alone in the slick, plastic cabin of the Ferris wheel. The wheel inched upward as they added more and more people. At the top, a hundred and forty feet in the sky, the pier was a postcard. The ocean stretched out to forever on his right, the pier to his left, the boardwalk and jagged shoreline dead ahead. At last the Ferris wheel was loaded and began its first loop. At the top, he saw police car lights flashing in the distance, *stop sign red and Smurf blue*, accompanied by the baby wail of sirens. Somewhere out there, something bad had happened. Harold vaguely wondered what that thing might be.

Up, then down. Six loops. Two minutes where the world became his very own, glorious kaleidoscope.

Then the wheel stopped turning while he was at the top, and Harold knew his ride was at its end. He drifted above the world, holding the moment deep in his chest. Swaying gently back and forth in the cabin, Harold closed his eyes and imagined walking on a cloud. It would be like walking on a trampoline, he decided, spongy yet supportive, and after a few steps, he found the proper balance in his mind. Cool, thin air licked the tip of his nose.

He opened his eyes and found himself standing on the seat of the plastic cabin, arms wide, knees slightly bent, his weight shifting to counterbalance the gentle rocking. Somewhere in another world, a woman screamed.

Eyes closed again. Harold kept walking on the clouds until he found the edge of a rainbow. *ROY-G-BIV*, Harold thought, each strain of color delivered in Kodachrome brilliance. Maybe his father was down there, down where the beautiful colors ended and the earth began, barreling onward in his semi-truck, chasing things that only existed until you squeezed your hands around them. *Keep on keepin' on.* Harold desperately wanted to see his father again, if only to tell him how he could see the rainbow colors now.

Harold climbed out of the cloud and tried to seize the edge of the rainbow, but felt nothing but the warmth of a promise. He wondered if Judy was telling the truth earlier.

*The colors of death are unimaginable, Harold.*

Then Harold let go. Down he slid, down, down, along the slick colors, those long, arcing strips of brilliant lollipop light that didn't hold him like the clouds did. They offered no support at all. They were just an illusion, and in a final moment of clarity, of an awareness he hadn't known in years, not since before the colors had gone away, Harold realized there were no colors of death. Death was an absence of all light, and without light, all color ceased to exist.

A brief, amazing burst of pain, and then a slow, silky fade into blackness.

Then the great blue sea swallowed Harold, just as Harold had swallowed so many little blue pills.

# CAT RAMBO

## GIRLS GONE WILD

THE QUESTION WAS HOW FAR YOU'D GO TO FIT IN WHEN YOU were the new girl. Faye thought she might be edging up to the line of no. She ran through the math in her head.

For one thing, Heidi was a control freak. They couldn't meet at the downtown Redmond bus stop for example, but had to go to the Microsoft park-and-ride because it was closer to Heidi's house. For another, the way both Heidi and Fuyiko shot their mouths off about their plans in front the small crowd of adults waiting for the bus into Seattle made Faye feel itchy all the way down to the soles of her feet.

"My cousin says there's a shit-ton of cruise ship tourists down there," Heidi said. "Swarming all over."

Fuyiko said, "We can be part of their Seattle grunge experience." She put a hand to her lips, squealed, "My goodness gracious, we were panhandled by street youth, can you *imagine!*"

Faye tried to look like she wasn't with them. It wasn't even as though Heidi, despite her punk Barbie looks, the pink stripe in her hair, or her nonchalant, don't-give-a-fuck drawl, scored that high in the coolness category. As far as rankings in the high school systems went—and despite the fact those rankings could fluctuate radically, according to recent occurrences, associations, and random flukes of social media—Heidi and Fuyiko remained solid high mid-listers. Not quite popular enough to ever hit the top, but enough to give Heidi some delusions and a certain eagerness to take a newcomer under her wing as a potential ally.

Being a new kid meant you could end up anywhere in those rankings, so Faye had chosen a safe strategy by associating herself with this pair. In her last school, she had made a similar gamble and won. Was it going to pay off this time? The equation was starting to slide in the wrong direction. She might have to figure out alternatives, pick someone else to follow.

She stared down at her sneakers and tried to think through the day. Panhandling sounded all Occupy cool and it might even yield money, but what if a cop decided to pick them up and inform their parents? Or if someone saw them and tattled—maybe not even meaning to, just an accidental "oh I saw Faye down by the market, she's getting so big."

The 520 bus pulled up. She followed Fuyiko onto it and stared at the coin receptacle before pouring her quarters into the opening, momentarily choking it before the driver made an impatient noise deep in her throat and pressed a bar on the side, releasing the coins to jangle down into the machine's bowels. She ripped a slip of paper off the pad and thrust it at Faye, who stared, uncertain what to do, before Heidi poked her in her lower back with an exceptionally hard and sharp fingernail. "Take it," she hissed.

Faye did, and stepped away hurriedly. Was the driver looking at her funny?

Behind her the machine beeped.

"Gosh," Heidi said, "I thought I had money on my Orca card. I don't have any cash on me, can I owe it to you?"

"Gosh," the driver said, her tone sarcastic, "you tried to pull this on me last week, sweetheart. Pay or get off."

"But I don't have any cash!" Heidi said.

"Not my problem, kid."

Faye turned around. "I can pay it," she offered, despite Heidi's pointed stare and headshake as the driver looked at Faye.

"Is it going to be another handful of change?" she said dubiously. "It's like you were fountain diving. Go ahead." She waved Heidi forward. "But know your friend got your trip, not your skills as a scammer," she said as Heidi passed.

Heidi tossed her pink-streaked head. "Whatevs." She sauntered after Faye, muttering, "Still didn't have to pay." The driver pretended not to hear.

They found seats near the back and settled in. No one else had come this far past the bus's midsection and so the elevated rear section was their own.

Heidi said, "Did you hear that bitch?' a little louder this time.

"Shut it," Fuyiko said. "You'll get us tossed off the bus. Hashtag chill and cut your losses, Jones."

"She's not going to toss such a nice girl off," Heidi said, sneering in Faye's direction. "*Nice* girls don't get into trouble."

Faye's heart sank. This was going to be a shitty trip, with Heidi sniping at her all the way. Maybe *she* should think about cutting her losses.

The bus shuddered its way down the ramp and swung into the rest of the highway traffic. Fuyiko held up her phone and they all leaned in for a selfie.

"Don't share that," Heidi said. "My parents look at your Instagram sometimes."

Fuyiko rolled her eyes at Heidi. "I'm not a total moron," she said.

"What *do* we say if someone asks why we're out of school?" Faye said.

"Then you lie, dummy." Heidi's voice was so bored it didn't need to contain any scorn to accomplish her purpose.

Stung, Faye said, "Well, don't they have, like, truant officers?"

"You think in today's underfunded educational system, they can afford to have people running around looking for stray students?" Faye wouldn't have thought Heidi's tone could get any *more* bored; she was wrong. To make things worse, Fuyiko was expressively rolling her eyes at both of them now. "It's a nice spring day," Heidi said. "Sit back and enjoy. We'll go make some cash and have fun at the same time. More fun than school, anyhow. Stop freaking out about the bus trip."

"I'm not freaking out," Faye said. "I told you that. I've taken buses before."

"School buses. You said you'd never taken public transit. You're a one percenter," Heidi said.

"You have no room to talk," Faye retorted. "And your mom works too. You guys have tons more money than my family."

Fuyiko slouched back in her seat. "It's tacky to talk about money," she sing-songed. Faye recognized the cadence; Heidi's mother captured it with clinical exactness.

"It's not like we're missing anything important today. In a society that treated us like adults, we'd get to choose which layer of bullshit we were willing to put up with." Heidi's angle of incline mirrored Fuyiko's as she sagged back into the seat. "Like money's everything," she muttered.

They were all silent for a while after that. The sway of the bus as the 90 exit passed was hypnotic. Faye didn't want to be the one starting the conversation again, but Heidi was right. It wasn't as though they were missing anything and they should be able to choose how to spend their days.

And even if they got busted, Faye's dad wouldn't be that upset, even if her mom would be. He was always talking about how important high-school friends were. That was why this had been their last move in a while. He'd promised they'd stay here at least the three years it'd take to finish up, so she could make friends. And that was cool, even though every time he started in on it, he sounded like some sort of preachy Nickelodeon show talking about his two best friends from high school and how they ended up founding a business together after college.

She was glad they settled in Redmond. It was a cool place. The whole Pacific Northwest was cool. And maybe Fuyiko and Heidi would turn out to be part of the whole thing. It would be okay. The bus rolled across the 520 bridge and she watched construction and water lilies and houseboats go past.

"What stop do we get off at?" she asked when she could no longer ignore her inner conviction they'd gone past the right stop.

"Westlake," Fuyiko said. "Two more stops. You excited, Carter? Going to come be a smooth criminal with us?"

You could never tell when Fuyiko was being sarcastic or not, so Faye just shrugged. A shrug was always safe. It didn't commit you to anything.

The Westlake stop was at the corner of Fifth and Pine, and they got off to see the plaza in front of the mall hosting the usual downtown crowd. "Go over to the fountain, that's where people hang out," Heidi said, and led them in that direction. "Those kids are where I want to be, but there's lots of room."

The other kids, though, didn't share her opinion. They were a harder-core group than Heidi and her friends, and, Faye thought, they might actually be homeless, or at any rate a lot more committed to the vagrant look than any of the new arrivals. They had two dogs with them, a ragged ear brown and white pit bull and a small fuzzy white dog of indeterminate breed, as well as a hat with a sign that said "Help us feed our tribe." A scattering of bills and coins were in the hat.

"Fuck off," the nearest one, a thin Asian boy, said as Heidi started to sit down. "Our spot."

"There's enough room," she said.

"Nope, you're going to hurt our take. Piss off, Princess Bubblegum."

She started to say more, but the boy and two of his fellows stood up as the pit bull growled in their direction.

"The cops won't let you hurt us," Fuyiko said with more confidence than Faye felt.

"Bitch, don't tell me what the cops will let me do. Because I can fuck you up before they even notice your skinny ass screaming."

"Okay, okay," Heidi said. Faye could tell she was trying for the same sort of bored tone she'd used on Faye earlier, but her heart just didn't seem to be in it the same way when it was someone who was fighting back. "This is a shitty spot, anyhow."

They went westward down Pike Street, towards the water and the market. Here there were even more people, and Faye could tell the tourists, carrying bags of purchases, snapping pictures of themselves with the bronze pig that stood in front of the market, and talking in a dozen different languages.

"Much better pickings here," Heidi said. "Those kids were stupid, or they'd be down here too. That boy might have been all right looking if he had cleaned up a little." She wiggled her fingers at Fuyiko. "Hey, you know what I want you to do."

"Man, that's chancy," Fuyiko said, but her voice held a juicy edge of happiness.

"What are you talking about?" Faye asked. "I thought we were here to try to panhandle."

"Long as we're going through a nice crowded market, my girl here's going pick us up some pretties while we go through," Heidi said. She was trying to act tough because the kid earlier scared her, Faye thought. Well, it didn't matter. It was Fuyiko's choice.

"Want me to show you how to do it?" Fuyiko asked Faye.

"I'll hang back a ways and watch," Faye said. "Wouldn't want to cramp your style."

Fuyiko grinned. "Like you'll be able to see me do it." She flexed her fingers.

Everything was crammed into the market: stalls of fish, smoked sausage, jams, honey, dried fruit, nuts, and other foods segued into flowers. And then crafty stuff: glass bowls and wooden cutting boards, jewelry made from old silverware or bits of iridescent shell.

She couldn't see Fuyiko's hands as the other girl drifted down the long market aisle, and she didn't want to stare too hard and draw attention to her friend. So at the other side the amount of things Fuyiko pulled out of her jacket pockets surprised her: three rings, two boxes of chocolate covered cherries, a bottle-opener made from deer antler, and a scattering of stickers. She shared them out freely. "Easy come, easy go," she said. "You see something you want, I'll lift it for you."

Faye could see Heidi thinking about that. So she quickly suggested, "If we want to go ask people for money, we should go down near that park. Lots of people standing around smoking there."

They made their way towards the little grassy verge.

"Girls!" someone said behind them and for a second Faye thought it was someone she knew, her heart racing as she turned. But it was just an old bum, leering at them. "Got a dollar for an old guy like me?"

"No, sorry," Faye said politely.

He lurched a step closer. His breath smelled like booze and his gray-white hair stuck in every direction. His jacket was patched with shiny gray duct tape. "That's okay, sweetheart. Maybe gimme a smile? You got a pretty face."

"No." She turned away. They moved away but the man followed them.

"Hey. Hey! Just a smile. That don't cost you anything."

"Here," Heidi said. She tugged them into the safe zone outside the Starbucks, surrounded by tourists. "You guys go in and get me a peppermint marshmallow frappacino. It's too crowded in there." She shoved a couple of bills at Fuyiko.

"That's not enough," Fuyiko said. "You never give me enough."

Heidi added a couple more bills. Fuyiko looked as though she was about to say more, then shrugged and went in. Faye followed her. It seemed a better choice than Heidi or the possibility of the man deciding to come hassle them despite the crowd.

"Crowded, my ass," Fuyiko said as they stood in line. "She just likes to feel like she's being waited on. She told me that's always the best part of vacations for her, being in the hotel and getting room service. She can be such a narcissistic bitch."

It was the first time Faye had ever heard Fuyiko talk about the other girl. Normally she let Heidi lead, but here in the city, a new environment, she was more talkative, funnier. More interesting in a bitchy kind of way. Faye cautiously replied, "She can be a little hard to take sometimes."

"Don't get me wrong," Fuyiko said. "I've known her since third grade and half of the time we've been BFFs. But that just means I know some of the flaws. I know the good stuff too. When my brother died, she called me every night for three months to let me talk about him because my mom and dad wouldn't. So she's okay." She grinned. "High maintenance, yeah. But okay." They came to the counter.

"I'm still short a dollar for her order," Fuyiko said. "Can I borrow it from you, Faye?"

They came back out into the sunlight. Heidi was standing in a different spot than where they'd left her, near a trio of people who were talking. As Fuyiko and Faye neared, she stepped towards them and lowered her voice.

"Hey, I've been listening to these guys and there's something weird going on. I think the old lady is in trouble. She seems all confused, and she's inviting them over because she thinks she knows them and wants to give them some antiques or something. I think she's got Alzheimer's."

Faye tried to hear the conversation behind her. She could hear one man saying to the other, "We could just look, and if it's an actual Hasui watercolor like she's saying it is, we'd pay her fair value, Ron. We wouldn't be taking things without paying, of course." Then a little louder. "Miss Grace, my name's Robin, and I don't know your nephew but yes, we'd come to tea."

"See?" Heidi mouthed. She straightened. "I'm going to step in. They're taking advantage of her. I wanted to wait till you guys were here. I'm going to pretend to know her and that way I can get her away from them."

Without waiting to hear their reply, she marched over to the trio.

The older woman did look a little confused. It was something about her fluff of white hair and her placid blue eyes as she turned a watery smile on Heidi. The two men, by contrast, were hard-edged, clean-cut and dressed like wealthy tourists.

"There you are, Great Aunt Grace!" Heidi exclaimed, with so much conviction in her voice that for a moment Faye felt taken in by it. "We need to be getting you home."

The old woman blinked at Heidi, opened her mouth, then closed it, still wearing an amiable smile.

The taller man looked a little abashed, but the other

frowned at Heidi. "Excuse me," he said. "We were just talking to your great aunt about some art she mentioned having. I've got a gallery in Atlanta, and if she's describing them accurately, there could be a lot of money in it. I'd like to come look at the pieces. She invited us to take the water taxi back to West Seattle with her for tea and to see them."

He looked at the old woman. "They want to come to tea," she explained.

"I'm afraid that's out of the question," Heidi said, clearly emboldened by the lack of protest at her role. "She gets a little vague sometimes, and I'm sure you don't want to stress her and make her condition worse."

"Well, I'd still like to maybe at least see a picture of them." He fumbled in a pocket and handed Heidi a card. "There's my contact information."

Heidi nodded and tucked it away. "Sure," she said. She turned to the old woman. "Are you ready for me to take you home, Great Aunt Grace?"

"You know, I'm having trouble remembering just whose little girl you are…"

"Oh Great Aunt Grace, not again!" Heidi said. She smiled. "Whose do you think I am?"

"Oh, I'd guess maybe Penny or Martha's," Grace said dubiously.

"Can't fool you," Heidi said. "I'm Mary and my mom Martha sends her love. She'll come visit you soon. Come on, let's get you home. My friends and I will get you there."

This was, Faye thought, an unexpected turn. She and Fuyiko exchanged glances, then trailed in the wake of the other two as they headed towards the pier.

Grace seemed pleasantly bemused by the whole thing. Faye wondered if she'd escaped a keeper of some kind, or whether she just didn't have anyone who cared enough to keep her from wandering around wherever her bus card might take her, since she used it readily enough to access the water taxi and pay for her three fellow passengers. She said, "I'm really looking forward to tea, girls."

Her tone was just a touch odd, it seemed to Faye. "Are you okay?" she said.

"My head hurts a little," Grace said. Her hand wavered at her throat, plucking at the crepey wrinkles. "It'll be good to get in out of the sun."

Faye looked up and noticed two other women looking over at Grace. They didn't seem to be tourists. The tiny Asian woman wore stretch pants and a Sounders shirt with a matching visor over her still brilliantly black hair. Her companion was much taller, long graying hair worn back in a single braid, hoodie reading Michigan Women's Music Festival over faded jeans, purple Vibrams on her feet. Her eyes met Faye's for a second before they both looked away.

Friends of Grace's who would know she didn't have a great niece Mary? But surely they would have said something when they had all gotten on the water taxi.

It was okay. They'd take Grace home and get her safely settled.

That *was* what Heidi was thinking, wasn't it? But if that was the case, why was she studying the card the art dealer had given her?

"Look, there's a seal out in the water," someone said, and most of the passengers crowded over to look out the windows. Faye took advantage of the opportunity to grab Heidi.

"What are we doing?" she whispered in Heidi's ear.

"We're taking her home," Heidi said. She smiled innocently, then let the expression turn into something else. "And if we're taking care of her, maybe she'll take care of us. I've been talking to her and it sounds like she's got all sorts of stuff in her house and no one around. They're selling it soon and she says it'll all go to a big garage sale before she goes into a home. So it won't hurt anyone if we grab a few things. If we can find that picture the guy wanted, I bet it'd bring us big bucks."

"This is going too far," Faye said. "Asking people for a couple of bucks on the street is one thing, but you're talking about ripping her off."

"It's a doggie dog world, my uncle says," Heidi said.

"What?"

"A doggie dog world. You eat the other dogs or they eat you."

"That doesn't sound right," Faye said.

"Look, come with us and help us get her to her house. Then you can go home if you like."

"I don't know the buses back."

"I showed you the phone app. If you download it, you'll be set, just put your address in. Or wait for us. I just want a chance to see what she has. What's the harm, Faye?"

Faye hesitated and Heidi pushed her advantage. "I bet she never gets any company. That's why she's out wandering around. She's lonely."

Fuyiko and Grace returned from the windows as the boat pulled into the dock. "Grace says her house is just a couple blocks away, down the street. Let's go."

Crammed between apartment garages, the little house sported a "For Sale" sign that corroborated Grace's story of a sale. It had a sad and abandoned look, like its owner, despite the cement pots of plastic flowers someone placed around the perimeter some time ago, judging by the sun-faded petals. A chain-link fence surrounded the dandelion-fluffed yard.

Grace led them up the cracked steps, fumbled in her purse for the key. "Here it is," she said, swinging the door open. "Do come in, girls."

The house felt unlived in, as though the air had been still for a long time before they'd entered. Boxes towered in a corner, edges tattered; one newer box sitting beside the heap and holding a few pictures. There was no furniture; the floors were bare.

Heidi frowned as she looked around. "What is this?" she said.

"Well, I had to improvise when you altered the plan, dear," Grace said. "Originally, the intention was to bring them back here, let them buy their watercolor very cheaply along with some other radically undervalued treasures, and then be gone long before they got back to Atlanta and discovered they were all forgeries."

Her befuddled tone had fallen away entirely. Raising her voice, she said, "You can come in now, Hannah and Nellie."

The other older women from the taxi appeared in the doorway. "What the fuck is all this?" the Asian woman complained. "What are you doing with these kids? I thought we'd agreed on the art dealer."

"Little Miss Helpful here decided she'd run her own scam," Grace said. "Her pals are along for backup. What was it going to be, girls? Just robbery?" She wiggled her eyebrows. "Or something…darker?"

"I'm glad you're okay," Heidi said. "I just wanted to make sure those guys didn't take advantage of you."

The woman with a braid snorted.

"You're old ladies," Heidi said, her tone challenging. Faye thought it was actually kinda cool Heidi was able to think on her feet still; she herself was at a total loss and Fuyiko seemed equally frozen. "What are you going to do? We're leaving now. Come on."

Somehow now Hannah had a gun in her hand. All Faye could do was stare, terrified, at the innocuous little circle at the end of the pistol. She'd never had a gun pointed at her before. This was a movie moment, surely, happening to someone else.

"I shouldn't have to do this. You *should* be capable of rational thought. Of cutting your losses, kids." Scorn rang in Hannah's words. "You some baby gang, trying to prove yourselves?" She gestured with the gun. "Empty your pockets and toss Grace your backpacks. Jewelry off, throw it in the pile with the rest. Cell phones too."

"We'll tell the police you robbed us!"

Nellie stepped forward. "Chickie, if you say a word, we've got a nursing home's worth of seniors willing to swear to all kinds of elder abuse. That's where we come from. I like to paint and Grace gets bored if she doesn't get a chance to flimflam some nice young man every once in a while."

"Sometimes they try to flirt," Grace said with a smile. "Very nice for the ego at my age. And my goodness, that one knew his Japanese watercolors. He was here hunting for a bargain and I was so ready to make him very happy. For a short time."

Heidi clenched her jaw and opened her mouth twice before she actually spoke, hoarse with anger. "You can't do this." Her voice faltered as she faced the gun. "You wouldn't dare."

Faye's ears rang; it seemed to go on and on as she stared at the hole Hannah had shot in the wooden floor, a splintered star with blackness at its core. The barrel returned to pointing at them. Fuyiko's eyes were shock-wide; Heidi's mouth hung open as she gaped.

"You kids think you're skating on the edge, but you don't understand how easy it is to fall in," Nellie said. "So here's a push. We're doing you a kindness, burning you. Remember this later on, next time you think you're the smartest in the room."

"Or that little old ladies are easy to push around," Hannah muttered.

"I forgot to mention why Hannah's with us. She's got a temper," Nellie went on, with a funny little smile in Hannah's direction. "Sometimes she gets bored and misses the old days when she did a lot more daily shooting. And between the three of us, we've got two centuries of experience in crime. So we know how to cover things up. And how to look innocent. Nowadays people will believe things of young girls they wouldn't in my day. Now everything's girls gone wild and feral teens. But little old ladies? Still harmless." Her tone hardened. "I hate to point this out, but let's be practical—if she shoots one of you, we're going to have to shoot all of you. Loose ends unravel."

Fuyiko laid her backpack on the floor and stepped back.

"Turn out your pockets first," Grace said. "Everything."

Faye and Heidi followed Fuyiko's lead. Faye felt her eyes burning, but she swallowed hard, battling back the tears. How could this day have gone so wrong? What was she going to tell her parents when she couldn't say the truth?

But Nellie had thought of that. "You skipped school, decided to ride the water taxi, then went walking towards the

West Seattle Bridge on Admiral and got jumped by homeless kids. Go back to the ferry and they'll let you call the cops. They'll want to drive you around, look for the kids. Enjoy."

Grace, sorting through the pile and putting most of it in her bulky purse, snickered. Hannah stood, still holding the gun. She looked impatient.

"Don't bother looking for us," Nellie said. "It's been a pleasure, girls."

And with that, the older women walked out the door. They'd left behind Heidi and Fuyiko's backpacks and stuffed everything in Faye's, the nicest and newest of the bunch.

"If you hadn't..." Fuyiko began.

"Shut it," Heidi said.

"No," Faye said. "No one's shutting it." She'd made a decision. Recalculated. She studied the two of them. Fuyiko met her eyes, quirking an eyebrow. Heidi scowled. "They didn't get all bitchy with each other," Faye said. "Did you notice that?" In her head she was rethinking strategies. She'd let Heidi lead. Maybe it was time to try taking that role. New numbers. New factors.

New possibilities.

"I noticed they threatened to fucking shoot us," Heidi retorted but Fuyiko nodded.

"If those three can be scamming tourists at their age because they work together, imagine what we could do," Faye said.

"This is not some twisted after school special. You want us to become some sort of gang, like they were talking about?"

"No," Faye said patiently. "I'm saying that working together, people might be able to find the different senior homes that are easy to reach from here. Maybe walking, but I bet there's a bus stop nearby. And working together after that...well, who knows? But we've got something they don't really have a lot of."

"What's that?" Fuyiko said. "You heard her say they had two centuries of experience!"

"Sure, they have that," Faye said. "And we have something else. We have time."

She moved to the door. "I bet we can talk our way back

onto the bus, if we work together. I'm going to say I left my bag at school in my locker, then 'lose' it on the way home tomorrow with my cell in it. My parents will chew me out but less than for skipping. Or getting held up."

"You've got this all thought through, don't you?" Fuyiko said. "But what do we do once we've found them?"

Revenge was another kind of math, Faye thought, but she shrugged and didn't answer. There was also time for that. She opened the door.

"Ladies?" she said, and beckoned Fuyiko and Heidi to join her.

# MANUEL RAMOS

## NIGHT IN TUNISIA

THE BAND DID ITS BEST TO IGNORE THE ROWDIES IN THE Olympia Bar. The musicians drifted from one standard to another, not that I understood the musical twists and turns. My head nodded and my right foot tapped rhythm. The night was whiskey late, but I didn't want to leave the world I'd stumbled into, a bar new to me

The trumpet player respected the legends who created the music, and he riffed his solo like his heart pumped Kansas City blood. His bald head glimmered in the saloon haze shinier than a polished eight-ball. The rest of the band waited in sweaty anticipation.

One song grabbed me hard and whispered in my ear. I dug the tune but I didn't have time to enjoy it because two men pistol-whipped the bouncer, then the bartender. A lot of shouts and curses and frantic waving of guns. The bar's customers did their share of protesting and cursing until one of them went down in a bloody heap.

Everyone shut up.

The band stopped.

Everyone froze.

The ski-masked pair tore through the place with nervous energy and iron focus. They took our wallets, watches, and weapons and smashed the face of anyone who stalled or tried to run.

I donated fifty bucks, but that wasn't enough. They lifted

a silver bracelet my mother gave me when I finished high school fifteen years ago. She paid a day's wages for engraving: ORGULLOSO DE TI HIJO. I rarely wore it and now it was gone.

I wanted my bracelet back, and I was certain I knew who'd taken it.

"You're joking, right?" Clovis lacked a front tooth. When he talked a whistle hitched to his words. No one liked Clovis' whistle; no one liked Clovis. I visited his grimy house in Globeville because he was the brother of one of the men I believed robbed the bar.

Clovis and I stood in his grubby living room. He hadn't offered me a chair.

"Why would I joke about getting ripped off by Dixon? I'm serious. He has to give me back that bracelet. That's all I want. No trouble, simply my bracelet."

Dixon Hobbs thought he was a ladies man and he bragged about his bedroom scores. He never failed to look dressed up – slacks, silk shirts, clever shoes. He threw money around to impress, and smelled like a pinecone. The guy in the white ski mask from the bar, the one who pointed at my bracelet with his gun, wore expensive pants, a fine sweater, and cordovan wing tips. He left a Christmas tree scent in his wake, along with bleeding men, empty pockets, and a plundered cash register.

Regardless of how Dixon regarded himself, to me he was a lowlife ex-con who hired out as muscle to various shady characters. Loan sharks, bookies, pendejos like that. A brutal mercenary, loyal to no one except the highest bidder. His brother Clovis was only a lowlife.

"Dixon's not into bar jacks," Clovis said. "Don't care what the guy was wearing or how he smelled. Who do you think you are? Sherlock Homey? You got it wrong. Dixon didn't have nothin' to do with the Olympia."

I grabbed him by the left elbow and twisted his arm behind his back. Then I lifted. Clovis doubled over.

"If you don't tell me where your punk brother is, I'll snap your arm off."

"You sonofabitch!" he whimpered. His skinny arm trembled in my grip.

I lifted his elbow another half-inch. He buckled to his knees. "Okay, okay. Stop."

I eased up. He rubbed his shoulder.

"He'll kill you. For putting your greasy hands on me. He never did like your punk ass." I jerked his arm and gave him another dose of pain. "Wait…wait, goddamit! Give me a chance."

I shoved him onto his torn couch and crushed my knee into his chest. My weight sunk him into a mess of flaky Styrofoam, pizza, and cat hair.

"He's been shacking up with Pilar, in Capitol Hill. That's all I know. Ain't seen him for weeks."

Pilar Sepulveda. On the edge. Once a junkie. What a couple: Dixon Hobbs, hardcase enforcer; Pilar Sepulveda, hardass.

I left Clovis groveling on the floor, insisting I was a dead man. I smashed his cell phone but figured he'd warn Dixon somehow. No time to think through a plan. I raced across Denver to the street where I'd once transacted business with Ms. Sepulveda, back when I did crap like that, back when I didn't think I deserved to wear the bracelet.

She answered the door dressed in panties and a bra. She must've expected someone else, maybe Dixon. I endured the view for a minute before I stepped around her and walked in.

"What the hell you want?" She grabbed a robe from a chair and threw it around her bony shoulders and skinny waist.

"I heard you know where Dixon is."

She faked a laugh. "Dixon Hobbs? Get out. I ain't got time for you or anybody like Dixon Hobbs."

I wouldn't try any rough stuff on Pilar. She'd like it too much. I had to appeal to her other appetites.

"I don't want to hassle you, Pilar." I pulled out a vial of coke to help in negotiations. I offered it but she shook her head.

"Really?" I said.

"Job interview tomorrow. Drug test. I've been clean for a couple of weeks, since they said to come in."

The one job she ever had involved escorting men to alleys behind various bars and relieving them of the stress of their long days, for fifty bucks a pop. She might've been sixteen when she started that gig. No drug test required. Maybe she'd straightened out and was about to get hired for something solid. And maybe dreams come true and everyone lives happily ever after somewhere over the rainbow.

Once, I was a tourist in Pilar's Wonderland. I could never figure out what was going on in her head. I placed the dope on her table. She watched but didn't comment.

"I have to talk with Dixon. You can tell him I'm looking for him, that's enough."

"What do you want with him?"

"He took something from me. I want it back. No questions asked. Tell him. He knows how to find me."

I couldn't tell if she heard me. With her hollow eyes and stringy hair she morphed into a nightmare ballerina. She pranced around her kitchen, raised her arms, bent her knees and tried to stand on her toes.

"I took lessons, when I was a kid. You know that?"

"Uh, no-o-o." One surprise after another. "You gonna get a message to Dixon?"

"Why should I?" She stopped dancing, or whatever that was, plucked a pack of cigarettes from the robe's pocket, lit one with matches from the same pocket, and blew smoke in my face.

"For old times? Ain't that enough?"

Smoke caught in her throat and she coughed for several seconds. "What old times?" Her words scratched her vocal chords. "You and I never had no old times." She coughed some more.

"Whatever, Pilar. How about you scratch my back, I'll scratch yours?"

She rushed to the sink, filled a glass with water, and gulped it down.

Pilar was neat, if nothing else. Everything in its place. No dirty dishes, overflowing trash cans, or a pot with two day old coffee. Coat hooks along one wall held a light blue sweater and a heavier maroon and white jacket with a patch across the back that I couldn't read.

"There's something." She paused to let the water take effect. "Not much, but I don't have a ride these days, take the damn bus everywhere. How about a ride to my interview? Pick me up at nine. I got a nine-thirty at this women's shelter in Five Points. For assistant to one of the counselors. I think I'd be good at it. You get me there and I'll hook you up with Dixon. Not that I want to see or talk to that pig. It's your sorry ass that'll be wasted when he gets his hands on you, but if that's what you want, you got it. What'd you say?"

I couldn't believe her about the interview but I agreed to be in front of her apartment building the next morning. Where we went after that was up to her.

That night I returned to the Olympia. I wanted to hear the song again. I found only yellow and black police tape, a padlocked door, and darkness.

From the night before, the cops had my statement and knew I wanted my bracelet returned, but I didn't expect to hear from them.

The song rolled in my memory. I had no clue where to find the band.

Several blocks from Pilar's apartment building I saw flashing lights. Squad cars jammed in the street, parked at odd angles. A uniformed cop diverted traffic. I drove as close as I could. Pilar wasn't at the curb and she didn't answer her phone. I circled the block but didn't see her. My only thought was that she'd been popped by the police. I was about to give up when two uniforms appeared out of nowhere, guns drawn, and ordered me to pull over. When I stepped out of my car, they rushed forward to throw me to the street. I lay on my belly with hands behind my head for an hour, answering the same questions to different cops.

Detective Moreno finally let me sit up. They'd searched me and my car and found nothing they could claim was drugs or a weapon, which meant they had no probable cause to torment me any further.

"Her neighbor called us early this morning, around five. She heard a scream and then the shots. We've been here since. When we saw you circling, we got suspicious."

They'd run my plates, found out who I was and what my record was all about, and concluded that the killer returned to the scene of his crime. Then they surrounded me and dared me to make a wrong move.

I couldn't say that Pilar was one of my favorite people, but she had her moments. I surprised myself when I realized that I already missed her.

Detective Moreno gave as little information as he could. I asked many questions about Pilar Sepulveda's murder, but he remained tight-lipped about those details. He was more interested in my answers to his questions.

"Where was this job interview?"

"Somewhere in Five Points. She said it was a women's shelter."

"And you were driving her because why?"

"She needed a ride. I owed her a favor. Simple as that."

"You know anyone who'd want to kill her? With emphasis. Three shots to the head. She's a mess."

He knew all about Dixon Hobbs and Pilar, but he wanted something more.

"I couldn't say. Guess we weren't that close."

The conversation went nowhere. He didn't believe me, and I didn't care.

He handed his card to me. "Call when you think of something that'll help us find the psycho who did this. Can you handle that?"

I sat on a bench near Sloan's Lake and read the sports section of the *Denver Post*. Patches of gray mud clumped near the weedy shore. Steam from my breath disappeared against the dull autumn sky. Geese that no longer migrated waddled in close formation off to my right. Goose dung spotted the sidewalk. The night of the robbery rewound again and again like a song stuck in my head.

Two men hit the Olympia–sharp-dressed Dixon Hobbs and a smaller man who wore a Colorado Rapids sweatshirt, black ski mask, and black tennis shoes. I never thought of Hobbs or any of the thugs he traveled with as sports fans. Broncos, football, maybe. Soccer?

I remembered the jacket at Pilar's…maroon and white… Rapid's colors.

The Rapids had one game left in their long losing season—the final Sunday in October, a few days away. The team announced open practice sessions all week for fans who wanted to load up on soccer before winter shut it down. I threw the paper in a trashcan, hurried through a mob of squawking geese, and drove to the Rapids' practice field.

Heavy traffic slowed me and I changed routes more than once because of road work. The idea that I wasted time nagged for the entire ride. No way I'd find the second thief at soccer practice. More than once I thought to turn around and forget about my silver bracelet. But I drove on. Forty-five minutes later I arrived at Dick's Sporting Goods Park.

The huge complex must have included two dozen fields. I found the parking lot with the most cars. The team practiced in a field surrounded by a chain link fence. A dozen spectators sat on the grass or leaned against the fence.

The Rapids were in last place and their one bona fide star was injured for most of the season. The listless players practiced as though they'd cashed in for the year.

I walked around the field, looking for the sweatshirt from the Olympia or the jacket that hung in Pilar's apartment. It didn't take long. I held my breath when I saw the sweatshirt, but then I saw another, and then the jacket, and then another jacket. I'd been right and I saw both – unfortunately, numerous times.

When I turned for one last look through the fence nearest the gate, Clovis Hobbs' profile jumped out at me. He wore the jacket. I walked through the gate and stood next to him before he realized the situation. He started to leave but I blocked his way.

"I told you I want that bracelet."

He acted like I spoke a foreign language.

"What the hell, Sherlock?" His words whistled across his teeth. "Still bitchin' about a damn piece of junk."

"Where is it, Clovis?"

"I ain't got it. You talk to Dixon? Why don't you ask him?"

"I'm asking you." I put my hand on his arm.

"Get away from me!" He stumbled backwards and hit the fence.

"You were in the Olympia with Dixon. What'd you do with the loot?"

The soccer fans twisted their necks to stare at us. One or two were on cell phones, calling the police for sure. I pushed Clovis away from the crowd, through the gate and behind a metal shed.

"You need to quit messin' with me," he said.

"Where's the swag? Dixon?"

He let out a deep breath of stale air. "You couldn't let it go?" He repeatedly nodded his head. "That bracelet's cheap. Dixon tossed it. Said we couldn't get nothin' for it, 'specially with all that Mexican on it. Junk. Nothin' but junk. For that, you screwed everything up."

He stopped. A glimmer of awareness flashed across his eyes.

He drew a gun from the inside pocket of his jacket. "How'd you know? I never did nothin' like that before." The shaking barrel of the revolver matched the ragged cadence of his agitated words.

"Easy, Clovis. I wasn't sure it was you. Not until now. The Rapids…gave you away in the bar. And at Pilar's place." His shaking increased. "I only want the bracelet."

He kept the gun aimed at my guts. "Pilar was an accident. Bitch played me and Dixon. I thought she wanted him out of the way. He was trying to cheat me, after I covered his back. Can't say I'm gonna miss him."

I tried to watch the gun and his face at the same time. "I thought you and Pilar…"

"We had a thing for a while. Mostly a dope thing. But she let Dixon back whenever he wanted even though he's always beating on her. I did her a favor. She freaked when I told her it was gonna be her and me. Called me crazy. Believe that? Anyone's crazy, it's her." His eyes faded. "I didn't mean to do it," he mumbled. "It just happened."

Pilar broke his heart so he blew her brains out. Love's a bitch.

"Three bullets in the head. How does that just happen?"

"Fuck you." He moved the gun higher.

I knocked the gun away but he swung back before I made my next move. The gun caught my temple and I fell on a knee, dazed.

A woman peeked around the shed. She screamed. We heard people running.

"Shit," Clovis said. He bolted to the parking lot.

I struggled to my feet and tried to run after him but I couldn't keep my balance. I slid to the grass. Blood smeared my face. When I looked up I saw Detective Moreno clip Clovis from behind and drag him to the ground.

Moreno arrested me, of course. He'd followed me, had coffee in his car while he watched me and the geese at the park. Then he stayed on my tail to the soccer field. He didn't know what was going on between Clovis and me but he made his move when he saw the gun in Clovis' hand.

Moreno filled me in when we waited for the paperwork that would release me.

"He cried like a baby. Then, after he blubbered through how he killed his brother and the woman, he went berserk, tried to ram his head in the wall. He's medicated now. Him and his brother, with the same woman. Made some interesting sibling rivalry."

A secretary entered the interrogation room and handed the detective several pieces of paper. He signed a few before he looked up again.

"You took a big risk to get your things back."

"You're probably right. But I didn't know exactly what I was doing."

"Hard to believe you cornered Clovis because you saw that jacket at Sepulveda's." He slid papers across the table.

"Played a hunch," I said. "Whoever it was, he wore the team colors in the robbery and at Pilar's place. I wasn't sure it was Clovis until I saw him today. But I knew that jacket belonged to Dixon's partner."

"Brothers. You believe that? What a pair."

"When'd he kill Dixon?"

"Night of the robbery. Actually, the next morning, like four a.m. They argued about the split, about the girl, punches were thrown, they drew guns and fired. Dixon went down and Clovis finished him off. In that neighborhood, no one reported the shots. Now he's claiming self-defense. We found the body in Clovis' basement."

I shrugged.

"I have to ask," he said.

"It's your house."

"Why's he call you Sherlock? I think he even said Sherlock Homey one time."

"He's weird."

Moreno nodded. "I thought for sure you were our guy. Didn't connect the woman's killing with the Olympia robbery. Guess I got you to thank for clearing that file too."

I didn't want his gratitude. I wanted to go home. "You find my bracelet in Dixon's stuff? Or at Clovis' place?"

"No. Your wallet, yeah. But we didn't inventory any bracelets as evidence."

"I'll take my fifty bucks. You can keep the wallet."

"No money either. Those clowns blew the money that first night. I think you're out of luck."

I didn't think luck had anything to do with it.

# GARY JONAS

# AN OFFICER AND A HITMAN

DETECTIVE ANDREWS LEANS ACROSS THE TABLE, FIXES ME with a cold, hard stare and says, "How can you kill so many people and have no remorse?"

I shrug. "I used to work retail."

"I'm serious," he says.

"So am I." That's not the answer he wants, but I'm not in a giving mood. "The truth is that if you've pissed someone off enough that they're willing to pay me to kill you, I figure you deserve it."

"Fine," Andrews says, leaning back a bit. "How many people have you killed?"

"Oh come on, Officer—"

"Detective," he says.

"Whatever. I don't notch my gun after each hit, and I damn sure don't report what I make to the IRS."

"Gimme a ballpark figure."

"For the *Psychopath Trading Cards* from Topps?"

"Don't be a smart-ass."

"I'm guessing you're new to this. You've never talked to someone like me, have you?"

"Don't be so full of yourself. I've interrogated killers before."

"I'm sure you have." I start to get up.

"Sit your ass down," he says.

"Or what, you gonna pull a Rodney King on me?"

"Take it easy, all right? I'm not used to this."

I take a seat and look around at the plastic people eating plastic food in the McDonald's restaurant, then look back at the detective.

He hesitates. Looks around. Lowers his voice. "I want to hire you."

I know what you're thinking. *He's a cop. It's got to be a set-up.*

Truth is, Andrews reached me through a trusted referral, and I knew he was a cop before I met him. I stare into his eyes and get the feeling he's legit and really wants to hire me. When you've been doing this as long as I have, you learn to trust your instincts.

"Spill," I say.

So he does. He arrested a couple of bangers who swore revenge. It's the usual—bangers have friends who will murder the detective, his family, and everyone he's ever known. He shows me pictures of his pretty wife and his little brat of a daughter.

"Why are you worried about a couple of bangers?" I ask.

"They're not just a couple of bangers. They're MS-13."

That changes things. Mara Salvatrucha, or MS-13, is a Salvadorian gang notorious for extreme violence and retribution. While they have access to plenty of big time weapons, they'd rather use machetes. Hacking victims to pieces fucks with people's minds in a more visceral way than just shooting them.

"Don't the Feds have a task force devoted to MS-13?"

"We can't prove they're MS-13—no tattoos and they ain't talking, so that makes it a local crime. These assholes massacred and dismembered the family of a witness who was going to testify about another killing. I made the arrest. Long story short, they put word out to have me and my family executed, and since it's not federal, the only protection I have is some buddies on the force who watch my family when I'm working."

"You're saying they've put the word out already?"

"Yes."

I shake my head. "Bit late for me to take them out then." Probably just as well since I don't want to mess with MS-13. Those guys have good memories and they aren't your typical gang members. Most are trained in guerilla warfare.

"I don't want you to kill them," the detective says.

Now I'm confused, so I say, "All right. Who am I supposed to kill?"

He jabs a thumb to his own chest. "Me."

I give him another confused look.

He leans forward again and speaks in a whisper. Most of the customers are parents trying to appease their kids' Mickey-D joneses. With all the screaming little shits, nobody cares what two guys are saying in a booth at the back. "Me and my entire family."

"Excuse me?"

"I want you to film yourself executing me, my wife, and my daughter. Use the recording to get paid for the killing."

"I'm pretty sure they keep things in-house."

"No, they're offering a reward for our heads."

"How much?"

"Fifty large for me and twenty each for my wife and daughter. Basically, I want you to film the execution. I have a friend who will doctor the film. Add the blood, brain matter and such."

"You're kidding me, right?" Just what I need: another loose end.

"No, he works in Hollywood and he's agreed to CG the shit out of it. He said it's easy and while it might be ideal to do a lot of it with practical effects, even without them, he can add muzzle flashes, blood spatter, the whole nine, and he can have it ready in a few days."

"It won't look right. Hollywood always gets it wrong."

"He has the benefit of an actual filmed execution from evidence to work from. We're going to stage ours the same way."

"Why not just have him put your face on the footage of the real execution?"

"It needs to be my house. They've already made an attempt on me there, so they know what my place looks like. Everything needs to look authentic."

I lean back in the chair and consider this looming shit show. "I'm not an actor."

"Daniel Day-Lewis isn't available."

I sigh. "I'll think about it."

"Don't think too long," he says sliding a card across the table. "School lets out early tomorrow and I want my family safe and out of town by Saturday."

"You going into Witness Protection?"

"I hope it doesn't come to that."

I'm kicking back in my hotel Googling MS-13 when Jenny gets back from shopping.

"Hey, killer," she says. She's still amused by the nickname, and if it makes her happy I suppose I can let it slide. "I got us some bullets and burritos."

She sets the box of cartridges on the nightstand and hands me a bag with a foil-wrapped burrito.

Jenny and I have been together for six years. We met when she hired me to kill her husband. She got all hot and bothered afterward, and I reaped the benefits. She's almost as sick as I am, so she ran away with me. She's got steady hands and can film my kills better than anyone. I like to relive the kills a few times before I erase the video files.

"Tell me about the gig," she says and gives me a kiss.

I give her the rundown.

"Sounds like fun," she says.

"If you say so."

"What bugs you about it?" she asks.

"Why hire a hitman to do something an actor could do?"

"Why not? Think about this." She stretches out on the bed. "When I was a little girl, I wanted to be an actress. In college, I worked as an extra on a movie, but it was dreadfully boring. They took forever to set up lights and then we had to keep doing the same damn thing take after take because the lead actor was drunk and couldn't remember his stupid lines and then, when he did get it right, the sound was fucked up, or he missed his mark and they had to do it over. When they finally got it, they had to reset everything for a different angle and go through the whole fucking thing again. I'm amazed movies ever get finished."

"So we pass."

"Not so fast," she says.

"It has to look authentic," I say.

"Fine. So it needs to be a oner."

"A what?" I ask.

"One continuous shot, no cuts. Just like we do it now."

"Okay."

"So we just have to run through it a few times to get it right."

"These people aren't actors either," I say.

"What's your point?"

"They won't be able to pull it off. It'll be obvious that they're faking it. And rehearsing it will make it worse. I really think we should pass."

She frowns. "We need the money."

"There are always other jobs."

"I want this job." Her voice gets sultry hot. "I *need* it."

I consider her and weigh things in my mind. She's great with the camera, and that makes all the difference. "Fine," I say. "But we have to change things up."

"Like what?"

"Simple. We do it for real. That way we can collect the reward money too."

Jenny smiles. "I love the way you think."

I pull out the detective's card and use a burner to ring his number.

He answers on the fourth ring. "Detective Andrews."

"It's Leon," I say, giving him the name he knows me by,

which is Jean Reno's hitman character in *The Professional*, though I prefer *Leon the Integral Version* with twenty extra minutes of him teaching Natalie Portman the biz.

"Are we on?" he asks.

"Yes."

He rattles on about plans and I file the details in my head.

After we hang up I fill Jenny in,

She asks, "So we wait a day or two?"

I smile. "We go now."

Jenny and I wear surgical gloves when we approach the detective's house. I have a clipboard in one hand to disguise the fact that I'm packing a Beretta with a silencer, while Jenny holds her camera in plain view. Anyone watching will think we're there on official business. In a sense we are there on business, but not the kind they think.

My plan is simple. Since Andrews is still at work, I'll ring the bell, and when the cop who's guarding the family opens the door, I'll cap him in the head. Once inside I'll take care of the wife and kid. Then Jenny and I return to the hotel, watch the recording a few times, fuck, nod off for the night and vamoose early tomorrow morning. Works for me.

We step onto the porch, and a big tattooed Latino steps out of the bushes to block our path.

"Go the fuck away," he says and brandishes a machete.

Most folks would shit their pants, but this isn't my first time at the table, and so I'm ready to deal. "You must be the gardener," I say.

He pulls back to strike with the machete, and Jenny, bless her heart, is lining up a good angle with the camcorder. Quick as a magician's trick, the pistol is my hand and I squeeze the trigger.

The banger seems stunned that he's been shot. He staggers backward against the door, which swings open so he falls into the house. The doorjamb is splintered all to hell from when his buddies broke in before our arrival.

Since this asshat is still here, it's safe to assume more bangers are inside.

"Decision time," I say. "This gig is jacked, and as we just whacked one of their guys, we're not getting paid. We can cut our losses and leave, or we can go inside and film something worth playing back."

"Oh, baby, you know how hot I get when the bullets fly."

I motion for Jenny to keep filming.

We enter the house.

A television blares from the back of the house, some action flick with lots of gunfire. The officer who had been guarding the family lies on the living room floor in a pool of blood. One of his hands sits in the corner and a forearm lies in the middle of the floor as if someone kicked it there.

In my peripheral, I see Jenny move the camera around to catch all the details like a documentary filmmaker.

The television shuts off in the middle of a burst of gunfire. Someone screams. I hold my gun ready at my waist military style. I don't want to do the Hollywood thing of having the gun out where I can easily be disarmed.

Past the living room is the kitchen. Red decorates the floor, but it smells like marinara sauce, and as I ease forward I see a spilled pan of spaghetti on the floor next to the stove. To the right is the family room and that's where the action is.

Three Latino men with tons of tatts hold the daughter and the mother down on the sofa. A fourth banger paces back and forth slapping a machete flat against his palm. One of the guys spots me, so I figure the direct approach is needed.

"Hey, assholes," I say.

The leader spins around to see me and Jenny.

"Who the fuck are you?" the guy says.

"Friend of the family," I say and shoot him in the head. One down, three to go.

The other guys let go of the women and dive for cover.

I step into the family room, and with one hand, motion for the women to get out. The detective's wife and daughter don't need to be told twice. They're moving fast.

"Ladies," Jenny says, "stay inside where we can protect you."

I see the heel of one of the gang bangers sticking out from behind the sofa. I put a bullet through the couch and he yelps in pain. When he arcs up, I shoot him in the head.

The other two guys jump into view. One of them throws a machete at me. I didn't even know he had one, so he must have set it down when he took hold of the daughter. I sidestep the blade and it sticks into the wall.

I double-tap blade-chucker in the chest, but the other guy isn't nearly so cooperative. Instead of throwing a knife or rushing me, he dives through the back window. I race over and put a bullet into his back. He doesn't slow down. I fire again and catch him in the head. He slams face-first into the fence and slides down.

I check on those I shot. Two of them are dead. The guy who took it in the chest is still alive, so I put a bullet in his head to finish him off. Can't leave witnesses.

From the front of the house, I hear someone cry out, "What the hell?"

Welcome home, Detective Andrews.

He rushes into the house, sees his buddy in pieces, and his wife and daughter standing with Jenny. And of course, he sees me stepping out of the family room, gun in hand.

"What happened?" the detective asks.

His wife is crying. Through her sobs, she manages to say, "These two saved our lives."

The detective rushes over to embrace his wife and daughters in a group hug and spots the dead men lying in the family room. He nods at me and mouths, thank you.

The family showers us with gratitude and happy, relieved tears.

Pardon me while I go stick my finger down my throat.

All right, sports fans, can you picture me stuck in a house swarming with cops, all of them thinking I'm some kind of hero? That won't happen. The investigators will start digging into Jenny and me, and my good Samaritan act will earn me a long stretch in the big house, if I don't rate a room on death row, so fuck it. I pop the cop in the head, and while he collapses, I ventilate his wife and daughter.

"Damn," Jenny says.

"What?" I ask. "Killing him and his family was the job."

"But we didn't get paid. And you said it yourself, with the bangers dead, we can't collect from them. You're always killing the people who pay us."

I consider that I wanted to pass on this one while she wanted to take it. "There'll be other jobs. There always are."

"We need to get out of here," she says. She's a wildcat in the sack.

"I agree," I say. She has steady hands.

"I should take over lining up our clients." Really steady hands.

"All right, baby," I say. "Want me to carry the camera?"

She smiles at me. "Sounds good." She hands the camcorder to me. "Thanks, killer."

Jenny reaches for the doorknob, and I pop her in the back of the head. Because who am I kidding? Anyone can hold a goddamn camera.

# PAUL GOAT ALLEN

## SLUG

*NOUN: A SLOW, LAZY PERSON; A SLUGGARD.*

The funk in the tiny, upstairs bedroom was overpowering; a stomach-churning mélange of body odor, stale cigarette smoke, Drakkar Noir, and cat piss. The yellowed mattress in the far corner was half-buried beneath piles of dirty clothes and miscellaneous garbage: grease-stained pizza boxes, empty beer bottles, crumpled packs of Marlboro. An expedition of ants explored the topography of a miniature mountain range of crumpled Burger King wrappers on the floor in front of a gray louvered closet door with broken slats. The walls were covered with centerfolds of scantily clad, surgically enhanced women and tattered posters of old '80s metal bands like Mötley Crüe and Slayer. Metallica's "Master of Puppets" thumped from a dust-covered cassette player on an orange plastic milk crate in the corner, next to a rickety table supporting a murky fish tank filled with emerald green water that hadn't been cleaned in years. There was an undeniable dankness to everything in the room; a sense of slow, inevitable deterioration.

Richard Roiche—known to his fellow perverts as Roach—sat in an old swivel office chair missing its wheels, his squat, 350-pound frame hunched over a child's battered wooden desk. He diligently measured out an eighth of a gram of heroin on a set of chemistry scales. A sweat-stained 4XL Syracuse

University Basketball t-shirt barely contained his corpulence and the chair groaned every time he shifted weight.

The teenage girl—Roach didn't bother to remember her name—stood in the doorway of the bedroom with her arms crossed tightly in front of her. Although it was early August and hot as hell, she wore jeans and a long-sleeved sweatshirt. To cover up the minefield of track marks on her arms and legs, he guessed. She was obviously strung out; her hair was greasy and dark rings circled her sunken, glassine eyes. Skels were the lowest form of existence, Roach thought with revulsion as he watched her twitch uncontrollably. Junkies were human vermin and he had no guilt whatsoever about being the facilitator of their eventual deaths. If he was being honest with himself, he considered what he did commendable: doing society a favor by culling the herd of the broken and weak-minded, all while stuffing his pockets with thick rolls of cash.

As the skel stood there shaking, staring at him with despairing eyes, she reminded Roach of the half-starved alley cats he frequently saw wandering the neighborhood.

The doughy, mushroom gray skin around the corners of his mouth pinched as he smiled at her. He stroked his goatee and wondered how large her breasts were under the bulky sweatshirt.

"It's simple, kitty. Since you don't have enough cash for the H, I'll put it on your tab. But only if you suck me off. You decide the deal isn't for you, then hit the fucking bricks."

There was no question in his mind about the outcome of this transaction. Eventually, her lips were going to be wrapped around his stubby member and she was going to be working him like her life depended on it. He rose from his chair, struggled to pull down his black Nike basketball shorts, and settled his bulk back down, making sure to angle himself so that his cellphone—duct taped strategically behind a hole in the closet door—would capture every glorious moment of her soul-crushing degradation.

*NOUN: A TOUGH-SKINNED TERRESTRIAL MOLLUSK THAT TYPICALLY LACKS A SHELL AND SECRETES A FILM OF MUCUS FOR PROTECTION.*

Roach was a 36-year old drug dealer who sold heroin out of his bedroom in his mother's little two-story house in Solvay, a once thriving suburb of Syracuse now in the death throes of urban decay. His mother—on long-term disability for the last three decades after she allegedly slipped a disc while working at the corrugated packaging plant—was seldom home, spending most of her time over at her alcoholic boyfriend's apartment. This meant that Roach not only had the run of the place, he lived there rent free.

But it wasn't the drugs that made Roach so infamous among his tribe of like-minded degenerates; it was his hobby.

Like those pith-helmeted scientists who captured exotic butterflies, impaled them with long pins, and displayed their dead bodies under glass in ornate picture frames for all to see, Roach considered himself a collector of sorts: except instead of insect carcasses, he harvested shame.

For more than a decade, he had secretly recorded countless pictures and videos of women young and old in various stages of undress and compromising sexual positions. Stripping, masturbating, being sodomized by various objects; more than a few were even desperate enough to have sex with the repugnant pusher with his trademark braided rat tail running down his stooped, hairy back.

He loved showing off his collection to his buddies—often even charging an admission fee. "I can get any bitch naked," he bragged. "Ain't nobody who can pry open a clam better than me."

Rumors about the stash of pictures and videos eventually got back to some of the victims, but nothing ever happened to the morbidly obese drug dealer. The day never came when police knocked on his door with search warrants. No enraged fathers or brothers ever came calling to knock his teeth in.

After surviving for so long unscathed, Roach firmly believed he was untouchable; he figured none of his victims would ever want to share their disgrace with anyone about voluntarily doing something so demeaning.

But as far as he was concerned, that was all in the past. None of the pictures and videos of emaciated junkies and two-bit hookers juiced him anymore; the pleasure he received manipulating them into humiliating themselves was getting old. It was too easy; the thrill was gone. He had his sights set on bigger game. Like a trophy hunter looking for the next big rack to mount up on his wall, Roach was preparing to take down prey of mythic proportions: the most beautiful stripper he had ever laid his beady eyes upon.

*NOUN: AN AMOUNT OF AN ALCOHOLIC DRINK, TYPICALLY LIQUOR, THAT IS GULPED OR POURED.*

An aficionado of strip clubs all over Central New York—from Rochester to Utica and Watertown to Binghamton—Roach's favorite nudie bar was a seedy dive in downtown Syracuse called Mounds. For the past few months, he had been going there several times a week to see a new exotic dancer named Amber.

She was the perfect piece of ass: tall and lean with long legs, accentuated by her thigh-high, black velvet platform boots perched on six inch heels. Her tight bod sported a nice set of firm and perkies, and straight jet black hair that hung to her G-string. Her eyes were dark brown, almost black, and she rarely ever talked or even smiled. There was an air of mystery about her, an ethereal quality in the way she moved that enthralled Roach. Sitting there in the upholstered lounge chair—under the garish neon, strobe lights, and flashing lasers—he watched her dance on the stage and in those heady moments felt a kinship with the nocturnal insects that circled his front porch lamp on summer nights. Like those stupid, hapless bugs, he couldn't look away.

Roach dropped a few hundred bucks on Amber every time he saw her, buying time in the VIP Room where he could get special lap dances and the opportunity to attempt to arrange dates with her outside of the club. He tried bribing her with drugs, money, gift cards, concert tickets—swag that would make a lesser skank drop to her knees and get busy. But try as he might, Roach never got anywhere with her; just a cool peck on the cheek after she had gotten him painfully hard and then fleeced him of his cash, leaving him to agonize alone, dizzy with the narcotic fragrance of her strawberry and champagne body butter.

After two months of Roach's begging, the enigmatic stripper finally agreed to do a private, one-hour performance at his house. The price? Two grand. In cash, of course. But no one else could be there—just Roach. And he better keep the deal a secret. She could be fired if management ever found out she was doing side jobs, she said, and Roach readily agreed, although he couldn't care less whether she was fired or not. All he wanted was to get her into his house and persuade her to either partake from an impressive buffet of H, coke, and skunk weed, or, worst-case scenario, if she got all Goodie-Two-Shoes, he'd drop her with a Mickey of his mom's Xanax.

Provided all went according to plan, he was going to be the proud owner of a killer sex tape featuring himself porking a living, breathing goddess. As he fantasized about her and jerked off, he mentally rehearsed in detail what he was going do to her beautiful, compliant body.

His mother would be gone for the weekend so the house was his. It was all going to go down in the living room— the cleanest room in the place—and he had positioned his cellphone on a bookshelf, hidden between a cracked snow globe containing the risen Christ and a vintage ceramic bust of the Virgin Mary.

This was going to be a life-changing experience, Roach predicted, a historic event—bagging and tagging a smoking hot stripper—that would solidify his status as a living legend among his fellow lowlifes, who inhabited the dark underbelly of the 'Cuse. He thought about how much money he could make charging his friends for the privilege of watching the recording. And if the video was good enough, he schemed, he could even blackmail the dumb bitch into doing pretty much anything he wanted.

After ejaculating into a dirty sock, Roach fell back onto his mattress, breathless, euphoric. He fell asleep dreaming of what was about to unfold in less than 24 hours…

*VERB: STRIKE (SOMEONE) WITH A HARD BLOW.*

Wearing an oversized hoodie that obscured her face, Amber hurried to the front door and knocked. A long skirt rustled past her knees. As she waited in the circle of light emanating from the front porch lamp, she discreetly looked up and down the shadowy street, making sure no one noticed her arrival. Glancing down, she noticed on the cracked concrete a pile of dead moths, mosquitoes, and other doomed insects that had accumulated underneath the light. One moth still fluttered feebly on its side, trying to right itself and fly away. She thoughtlessly crushed it beneath her stiletto boot heel.

When the door opened, she was assaulted by a wave of cheap cologne. The pig must bathe in it, she thought as he appeared in front of her like something out of a bad dream. He resembled a carnival clown, wearing a floral print silk shirt that was too small for him, stonewashed jeans, and, inexplicably, cowboy boots. A grin bisected his porcine face as he regarded her like a meal he was about to devour.

After winking at him, she shuffled around his girth with her duffel bag. Surveying her surroundings, she quickly mapped the place in her head: a small living room off to her right, a kitchen and bathroom in the back, a staircase to the left that presumably lead to bedrooms upstairs.

She sauntered up to the pig—she couldn't remember his full name—and whispered seductively in his ear, "Two things right up front. You better be alone and you better have the money, or I'm out of here right now and you'll lose the chance of a lifetime. You wouldn't want that, would you?"

The sweaty clown took a step back, a little intimidated by her abrupt closeness, and raised his hands. "I'm the only one here, I swear. And the money is right here." He pulled a thick green roll out of his front pocket. "See?"

Amber smiled and trailed a finger down his belly. "Perfect. Now go get a chair so I can give you a show that you'll never forget. We only have an hour, right?"

Roach quickly retrieved a wooden chair from the kitchen and carefully—too carefully—placed it in the middle of the living room, right in front of the couch. "How's this?"

Without looking at him, Amber removed her hoodie and skirt to reveal her outfit underneath: a metallic black bikini top and thong, matched with a black choker, thigh-high fishnet stockings, and black velvet boots. "Have a seat, lover boy."

She pulled out a small Bluetooth speaker from her bag and turned on her favorite killing mix: Van Halen's "Hot for Teacher," Pantera's "Cemetery Gates," Type O Negative's "Black No. 1" then Buckcherry's "Crazy Bitch." She always finished them off with that song: it just seemed fitting.

As the music started pumping, Amber began her mesmeric dance, slowly circling him as her fingertips traced over his body. When she was directly behind him, she removed her choker—a black silk sash—and placed it over his eyes, tying it from behind to create a blindfold.

Roach laughed nervously. "Hey now…"

Amber stepped around to his front and straddled him, sitting hard on his lap. Her breasts pressed up against him as she ran her fingers through his hair. "It's part of the performance. You're not turning chicken, are you?"

He licked his lips with a tongue that reminded her of a slimy snail, peeking its head out of its shell. "I just want to see what I'm paying for. That's all."

"You'll see everything in good time," she whispered as she began rhythmically thrusting her hips into his flabby gut. "Trust me."

As David Lee Roth sang about lusting after a sexy boarding school staffer, she unbuttoned Roach's shirt and continued to grind against his lap. His breathing quickened and sweat beaded on his forehead. Still straddling him, she stood and took his hands and began to run them up and down her muscular thighs. "Untie my bikini top," she sighed into his ear and leaned forward so his hands could fumble for the strings.

As his fat hands groped, she took a moment to look around at her surroundings. The house was very similar to others Amber had visited in the past: hog parlors, she called them. Having hunted and slaughtered countless swine over the last few years, she understood from experience numerous truths almost immediately. Her mark was lazy, ignorant, single, and self-absorbed. He lived in filth. He objectified women, maybe even hated them, and thought that he was smarter than he really was. Pigs like him were the lowest form of existence, she thought with revulsion.

This one would make the body count thirteen, and although she wasn't looking forward to packing up her belongings and disappearing—again—it was the price she had to pay for finding redemption in her tortured existence. She considered what she did laudable: doing the world a favor by ridding it of these abusive parasites: like the one—when as children, she and her sister watched in helpless terror—who beat their mother to death.

Once her top was untied, she whispered into his ear again. "Put your hands behind your back."

With his arms stretched behind him, she restrained him with handcuffs. When he began to fidget, she kissed him on the cheek and whispered in his ear, "Sweet dreams, piggy," and methodically removed the tools of her trade from her black bag: a roll of duct tape, a ballpeen hammer, a box cutter, and a propane torch.

*NOUN: A BULLET, ESPECIALLY ONE OF LEAD.*

After receiving a call Monday morning from a hysterical homeowner, Syracuse police were dispatched to a residence in Solvay where they found Roach's brutally beaten, naked body. His hands were cuffed behind his back and his shredded underwear had been stuffed into his mouth. Judging from the maggots crawling from his wounds and orifices, police guessed he had been dead for at least 48 hours. Investigators found a hidden cell phone near the scene that had recorded the murder in its entirety. They also found drug paraphernalia, heroin, and hundreds of computer videos in which countless women were unknowingly filmed in an obscene carnival of degrading positions. One of the victims was a niece of the lead investigator.

The case inexplicably floundered, and the murderess was never apprehended, disappearing like a firefly up into a star-filled night.

# ALVARO ZINOS-AMARO

## MORPHING

ALL THROUGHOUT THAT MISERABLE SUMMER CADMUS Burnett fought the vexing pitter-patter of mice and rats inside his home. The rodent population was out of control. They were abusing Cadmus' grief over the death of his mother, and the size of their infestation was growing to plague-like proportions.

More than anything, it was the rodents' endless chattering that distressed him. Cadmus installed wireless speakers in each of the three rooms of his Santa Ana townhouse and blasted white noise. But within days he developed migraines and tossed the speakers into a garage box.

Next he resorted to wearing earplugs inside the house, but they proved *too* effective, blocking out the only soothing sounds in his life these days—those of his *Pals*.

The scurrying and sporadic squeaking continued on and on, wrecking his nights. Feeling defeated, Cadmus purchased Triazolam and added it his nightly bevy of anti-depressants.

And for a while it worked.

He was able to lumber through the day, and his nights tunneled off into perfect, chemically-induced oblivion, the closest he'd come to bliss since his mother had gotten sick.

In time, though, he became despondent and unable to function without increasing the dosages of the drugs. By September Cadmus was overloading on pills. His pallor had turned to clay, and black ashen rings circumscribed his brown eyes, so that his eye sockets appeared to be sinking into his doughy face. And the rats found new ways to taunt him.

They boggled their eyes and ground their teeth obnoxiously—it was called *bruxing*, Cadmus learned from one of his pet-obsessed students at Mulberry Elementary. More than once Cadmus lost his temper, knocking over boxes and accidentally releasing his Pals. One time, in a rage, he grabbed one and swung it at the rats. But the pesky rodents skittered away, too quick for Cadmus' weakened body and dulled reflexes. He was left only with deep remorse at having hurt his Pal.

*Maybe*, Cadmus thought on a Monday morning, shoving textbooks into his ancient black leather case, *I should just kill them all.* "How would you like that?" he shouted at the rats. "Kill. You. All."

Their beady eyes gleamed and bounced and jiggled in their sockets as they bruxed. And then they darted away, back to their dark places, back to the cozy alcoves and boxes Cadmus had, in more innocent times, so lovingly created for them.

*They know it's an empty goddamned threat*, Cadmus thought.

And it was. If he exterminated the rodents, his Pals would suffer. Many were picky eaters, refusing frozen or even freshly dead rodents. They thrived on live flesh. And Cadmus wouldn't deny them that. His Pals were all he had left. *I will never abandon you*, he thought. They deserved nothing but the best: plenty of pampering and twitching little treats.

"Okay then," he said, and banged the front door.

On the way to his car, a rusted gray Saturn Ion he parked on the street rather than in his cluttered garage, he was intercepted by a busybody neighbor, the bony, sharp-tongued Miss Frust or Fest or Frost or whatever the hell her name was.

"Off to class?" she inquired.

Cadmus didn't stop.

"How are things?" she pressed on, bounding in his direction.

Opening the driver's door, he said, "Better alone," and slammed it shut. Through the rolled-up windows and the roar of the engine coming to life and the blast of the half-working AC he heard her shrill response but blessedly couldn't make out the words. The day at Mulberry passed in a kind of blue haze, leaving no marks or memories in its wake.

On Tuesday morning Miss Fester was at it again, this time cutting straight to the chase with "Is everything okay?"

Cadmus snorted and swung the door of his car inches from her stooping figure. Again, the day passed in a trance.

On Wednesday, the relative peace of his lunch break was interrupted by a most fascinating, singular thought. The notion came to Cadmus minutes after teaching biology class: *population equilibrium.* In order to *decrease* the size of his rodent population, he'd have to *increase* the quantity of their predators. A simple, elegant solution.

"You won't be dancing for long," he said to the rats that evening. "So live it up while you can, motherfuckers." Later he regretted those words, as he found a trail of rat shit pellets stretching from the door of his bedroom to his favorite sleeping pillow.

Thursday and Friday passed by in drug-induced, catatonic glory, and Saturday morning he set out to the local pet store.

The greasy clerk eyed him over. "You sure you know what you're doing?" he asked. "Fifty ball pythons? That's a lot of snakes, dude."

"Been breeding them for years," Cadmus said, fighting the cotton dryness in his mouth. Again he'd forgotten to take one of the xylitol discs designed to counteract the dry mouth resulting from his antidepressants.

"You run a business? Permit to breed and sell?"

Cadmus shook his head. "Hobby."

The clerk looked at him again. "That's a bunch of pythons."

"Love my hobby."

"Yeah? Let me talk to my manager."

The clerk's manager, with his slicked black hair, leathery brown skin and cool demeanor, asked Cadmus the same questions the clerk had asked and Cadmus provided the same answers.

"This will need to be a *special order*," he said. "Considering we're entering breeding season and all."

"Okay," Cadmus said. "By when?"

"We'll call you. Fill out this form."

Cadmus took the form, scribbled down his name and number and left the rest blank. They photocopied his ID.

"How many can I get right now?" Cadmus said.

The clerk and manager exchanged looks. "Cash?" the manager asked.

Cadmus placed ten crinkled one-hundred dollar bills on the counter.

They gave him twenty new pythons, the most he'd ever purchased at once. He stacked the boxes in his car and sat in the driver's seat and breathed quietly. At once his pulse slowed. The Pals' proximity—their quicksand texture in his hands when he reached into the boxes and stroked them—was like a balm on his spirits. Cadmus drove home and hustled them into the room where his mother gasped her final, wracking, sputum-besotted breath. As often happened, merely entering the room was enough to send a heavy curtain of unwanted memories from her last days tumbling over him. He stood, disoriented, for a moment a pawn of the past as much as an instrument of the present. *You did everything you could for her*, he thought. *Remember how she looked in her final moments*, he told himself. *Peaceful*. But that was a lie. She had looked gaunt and vacant, transported to a meaningless realm by the morphine. And how had she looked in her coffin, at the funeral? Cadmus couldn't remember. His brain hadn't been working properly, and the events of the weeks immediately following her death vanished to him, lost in the fog of pain. But he'd made a vow to pick up the pieces, to resume his life. *So do it*, he thought. *Stop standing around here and get on with your project.*

He visited three more stores, collecting over a hundred more python Pals. He also bought new cages and incubators, Rubbermaid boxes with damp moss for the females to lay their eggs, paper towels, water bowls, hide boxes, the works.

By sunset he was back home. Placidly he walked from room to room, surveying his snake empire, marveling at each morphology and the possibilities suggested by interbreeding the pythons. On each box he affixed a hand-lettered label, covering the stores' impersonal fonts. *Fire Ivory*, he wrote, and then *Coral Glow*, and *Asphalt Pastel Spider*, and *Red Stripe*, and *Caramel Albino*, and *Circinus* and *Blade* and *Matriarch* and *Fusion* and *Cypress* and *Aurora* and *Sapphire* and *IceFyre* and *Bamboo* and *Sirius*, becoming intoxicated by the words, each name writhing in his mind like a living thing.

Once all the boxes bore his neat cursive labeling, he yawned, exhausted, and tried to remember what else needed to get done before going to bed. Something important; after all, it was the reason for bringing all these new Pals into his life. But try as he might he couldn't recall. *Fuck it.* He shuffled off to bed.

The following morning Cadmus made a stunning discovery. Second after second passed, and he realized he could no longer hear the mice and rats.

It was utterly quiet.

"Where did you go?" he asked, peering along the furniture and shelves. And now he remembered what he had forgotten to do the previous night, of course: to gather up rodents by the dozens and feed them to the pythons. Perhaps the rodents had somehow realized this and had fled en masse?

"Is that it?" he asked. "You all took off in the night, sensing impending doom?"

They had not. Moments after getting out of bed he saw their familiar troops with their bulging eyes and waving tails, traipsing and dallying about, oblivious to Cadmus' lethargic presence. They were everywhere, gnawing, excreting their skinny pellets of feces wherever they fucking pleased.

Except that he couldn't *hear* them.

He banged his fist against the wall and rattled a nearby shelf. Rats scattered in all directions, and he knew such panicked movements would have been—*should* have been—accompanied by frenzied sounds. But there was only blessed silence.

A curtain of isolating peace had descended upon Cadmus.

He trembled with relief in the dawn light that crept through his living room shades.

"I can't hear you," he mumbled. "I can't hear you."

By breakfast, he found himself discarding the previous day's plan. Now that the noise problem had been solved through some mysterious, internal compensating mechanism, there was no reason to punish the rodents. They were just fueled by instinct, whereas he, Cadmus Burnett, was a rational, civilized man. *The thing to do*, he thought, *is buy* more *rodents, a new population I haven't become attached to, and use the newcomers for food. Now that I've adapted to my old friends' sounds, they can stay.* In a gesture of rapprochement, he reached forward to stroke the tail of a nearby rat that seemed to be coveting his cinnamon cereal box. "Here you go," Cadmus said, and spilled cereal on the chipped tabletop. The rat grabbed two flakes and scampered off.

Five hours later, Cadmus returned home with fresh rodents and supplies. As he lay the babies in their boxes, having to pile the cages four high per shelf, he discovered a concentrated pile of rat excrement behind his bedroom door and his gorge rose. He could taste foul cinnamon bile from his half-digested breakfast coming up, and he held his breath until the nausea passed. "Son of a bitch," he said, retrieving a brush and dust pan, and cleaned up the mess.

He made similar discoveries in the other rooms, and each one churned his stomach like the first. After having cleaned up the third such mound, he gave up and retired to bed.

That night he dreamt of his mother, as was often the case. In the first of several dreams he came home after a particularly taxing day of teaching, and she let him know that dinner was ready. They sat in the living room, watching one of their favorite shows, and Cadmus told her that the chicken pot pie she'd prepared was delicious. "That's not chicken," she said, and laughed. "It's your favorite—brown rat." In the following dream he complained to his mother of a horrible toothache. "Let me take a look, dear," she said. He opened his mouth impossibly wide. "Nothing to worry about," she assured. "Just your new fangs coming in." The dreams rolled on and on, and when Cadmus finally woke up in the early morning, he was no longer in his own bed, but in the room where his mother died. Her presence clung to the very air. Memories of her final hospice days at home under his care remained jagged sharp; the lung cancer that consumed her faculties hollowed out Cadmus' insides in equal measure. Her body's emaciation had been perfectly mirrored by his spirit's depletion. Just thinking about it was intolerable. Cadmus shoved the recollections aside, though he was too late to stop tears. He blinked a few times and stared at his surroundings. He was twisted on the floor with one arm under his head and the other stretched behind his back. His cheek was pressed against an old newspaper, with a trail of rat dung leading up to his nose.

Bizarrely, the smelly pellets did not repel Cadmus.

In fact, he sniffed again and discovered that another miracle had occurred.

The smell was gone.

He rose, careful not to look in the direction of the bed where his mother died. Then he popped a stimulant. Moving briskly despite the cramps in his neck and shoulders, he started his work week with renewed zeal. First the detestable sounds faded from Cadmus' reality; now the vile odors performed a similar disappearing act. His brain was rewiring. *I'm changing*, Cadmus thought. *Morphing. It begins with the mind, and goes on with the body.* He stretched his arms as far out as they would go, rotated his head to each side until the pressure was unbearable. Despite the pain, he told himself he was feeling more limber already. And all week he didn't run into that busybody, Miss Feisty, which further buoyed his spirits.

During the weekend he discovered that rats had shit inside his cereal box, but he forgave them at once, was even thankful— for it allowed him to discover that his sense of taste had now also evolved, shielding him from their unpleasantness. Sound, smell, taste—soon sight and touch would follow, and he would be able to stare at a rat and see nothing at all, pass his hand right through it.

He smiled.

Free of distraction now, Cadmus cared for his Pals. With all the recent purchases he was unsure exactly how many snakes, and of which types, he had, so he undertook a survey of the complete python population. About halfway through he was overwhelmed by dryness in his mouth and cold sweats, and downed several more pills. The interruption caused him to lose track and so he had to start again. After an hour, feeling itchy and grimy, he decided to take a short break and sat on his living room couch, a striking *Mojave Diamond Russo* in his lap. When he woke it was four in the morning and the snake was out of sight. He scratched at his face, finding something unfamiliar there. A beard? When had he stopped shaving? But he liked how it felt. Promptly he returned to his slumber.

Sunday morning he arose feeling queasy, on the precipice of a deep, yawning mood chasm. A stray *Vegas*, somehow outside its cage, coiled on the kitchen table. Cadmus watched it open its mouth, a grotesque displacement of its jaw; snakes usually yawned to re-align their jaws after meals, but ball pythons sometimes did it for no reason. Before Cadmus could grab the python it slithered away. *Did that just really happen, or did I hallucinate it?* Cadmus wondered. Perhaps his senses would now fabricate things that didn't exist, in order to offset some of the realities they were weeding out for him. They had to keep busy one way or another, didn't they?

Cadmus took double his recommended dosage of antidepressants, washing them down with expired milk that dribbled down the tufts of his unkempt facial hair. Then he remembered that this particular type of medication made him sleepy, so he gulped down a couple of caffeinated pain-relief pills. But those burned a hole in his stomach, so he added an antacid, and fearing the combination would still be somniferous, he swallowed some Dextroamphetamine. Wearing yesterday's clothes, he drove himself to the closest pet store. Wandering through the brightly-lit aisles, emptiness gnawed at him until at last he reached the pythons.

"Hey, don't I know you?" one of the clerks said.

"Nah."

"Yeah," the clerk said. "You were here a few weeks ago. Placed a huge order. And almost wiped out our stock of ball pythons."

"Must have me confused," Cadmus said, stroking his beard.

The clerk disappeared and returned with a piece of paper. "Cadmus Burnett," he said. "Says so right here. We have a copy of your driver's license on file. You're fifty-three. Live in Santa Ana. We tried calling you. Like seven times, man. You acted like you really wanted the snakes."

The clerk's words seemed to Cadmus to *drip* with accusation; a speech given only with the aim of rattling Cadmus' cage, of *unnerving* him. But of course the clerk couldn't know that Cadmus no longer had *nerves* of that kind. He had shed them. One of the changes wrought by his transformation, with more sure to follow.

"My mom and I started together," Cadmus whispered. "1.3.2 that first week. I remember it like it was yesterday. Poor mom. She couldn't even get out of bed at the end."

Now the manager was standing beside the clerk and a second clerk had been called in. "Mr. Burnett," the manager said, "do you mind telling us what you do for a living?"

"What's one point three point two?" one clerk muttered to the other.

"It's ratios man," the other clerk said. "1.0.0 is one male. 0.1.0 is one female. 0.0.1 is one unknown. Like that."

"Mr. Burnett, what is it you do?" the manager asked, stepping forward.

"That first egg," Cadmus said. "Like magic." Then he sagged, arms limp at his sides. "Morphing is just a hobby. For fun. My mom's legacy." The thought of the hundreds of pythons and rodents waiting at home stung him in his side, like being prodded with a stick, but it also flooded him with excitement. He leaned forward to hide his unexpected arousal, but it was hard to stand still with all the chemicals coursing through his blood.

"*Fun*," he repeated, grimacing.

"Mr. Burnett," the manager said, "I'm afraid I'm going to have to ask you to leave our store. We take animal cruelty very seriously here. It's a crime punishable by law. I can't *prove* you've done something wrong, but let's just say you're acting strange, and I don't appreciate your evasions."

Cadmus' mouth opened, and it felt like the movement of his jaw went on and on and on, reminding him of that *Vegas* yawning on his kitchen table. His arms jittered. "Cruelty? You don't understand. I would *never* hurt them. *They're my Pals.*"

Brow coated with sweat, he trotted out. Inside his Saturn Ion—had the paintjob always been this bad?—he focused on breathing and reached inside the glove compartment for a pill. The pouch was empty. When had he taken the last one? He stared at his grimy hand. Was that rat shit under his fingernails?

He laughed and cried a little. "The Pals are getting lonely," he said. "They need you around, Cadmus. And they want new friends."

Nine hours and four hundred miles later he had acquired fifty-seven new ball pythons. The last purchase wiped out his savings. *Whatever*, he thought. A voice from inside told him that wherever his transformation was taking him, he wouldn't need money.

He stayed up all night relabeling and organizing his new Pals. The boxes no longer fit in the three rooms, so he had to use the bathroom. He checked humidity and temperature. Not ideal, but it would have to do. The sliding doors didn't close all the way, but he would use the shower stall anyway.

When morning came he staggered to his car, drained from the riveting wonders of the night. He shivered. When had it become this cold? What month was this?

As though in slow motion, a human-like figure approached.

"Mr. Burnett," the figure was saying, "I think we should talk."

She approached, only to stop and gag; a hand shot up to cover her nose.

*Loon*, Cadmus thought. *The air smells of flowers.* He coughed, which hurt. *Did I just think that or say that?* he thought. "Flowers," he said. "Flowers, Mrs. Ferese."

"My last name is *Farrell*," the figure said with some indignation.

A second human-like figure was beside Miss Fresca now. "There's a stench coming from your house," it said. "Unless you convince us that everything's okay right now, we're calling the city."

Cadmus realized he'd forgotten his textbooks inside the house. He lurched towards the front patio, a vague smile on his face. The human-like intruders trailed behind him.

When he pushed the door inward, they retched and then puked on his lawn.

Cadmus was about to ask why, but by the time the door had opened all the way, he knew the answer.

He fell to his knees, gagging.

All the sensations that had been imperceptible to him assailed his senses simultaneously, coiling through his system like lightning.

The human-like creatures tried to help him up, but all he could do was keel over and embrace the darkness.

Weeks later, newspapers would report the discovery in his home of the remains of his mother in her bed, and two-hundred and ninety dead snakes and one-hundred-eighty-two live ones. Some of the dead snakes, they said, were little more than skeletons, much like his mother. Others, they claimed, were covered with flies and maggots. Cadmus questioned all of this; it made no sense. Mom had had a funeral, hadn't she? He couldn't remember it, but he was sure he hadn't just let her rot away at home. Had he? *Could* he have? It was so hard to focus on anything from that period; like trying to read fine print through cataracts. He stayed by her side, day after day, tending to her needs, trying to soothe here. *And when those needs ended?* Had he continued to diligently sit by her bed, oblivious to the necrosis, the gases, the leaks of her decomposing flesh? He simply couldn't remember. The reporters also said there was an infestation of rats and mice in the house; they suspected rats had eaten part of his mother's remains. *No*, Cadmus thought. He *never* would have let that happen. He cared for her. *About* her. Was diligent, obedient, responsible. But what *if* the rats had done it behind his back? He shouldn't have trusted them. They weren't loyal, unlike his Pals. Reporters further claimed that many of the rats had been left in bins so long that they had started eating each other. Well, if Cadmus couldn't hear or smell them, how was he expected to be attuned to their eating cycles? Served them right, as far as he was concerned, for disrespecting his mother's body.

When asked by his defense lawyer what his state of mind had been at the time all this had happened, Cadmus said, "I will never abandon you."

The lawyer asked him about his mother, but Cadmus had nothing to say.

"I will never abandon you," he repeated at the trial.

"My client's depression was *paralyzing*," his defense attorney said, "tragically causing him to allow the advanced decomposition of his mother following her death, and to neglect his family hobby, which just happened to involve reptiles."

As Cadmus watched television footage of crews removing his Pals, he mouthed the words "I will never abandon you" one last time, and he knew his morphing was complete.

# MARK STEVENS AND DEAN WYANT

# THE PLEDGE

THERE ARE A COUPLE OF WAYS TO ENTER THIS WORLD. FOR THE most part, it's one.

Departure routes? The count isn't complete.

New ways to exit are being dreamed up every day.

Desma wondered when she might stop thinking about her father. She stared into the face of the insurance agent, but she pictured her father. She kept imagining a conversation with the man who had let her down so hard.

Conversation? *Hardly*. She would be the one screaming in his face.

The insurance agent's lips moved. The words carried an earnest flavor. The performance was Oscar-worthy. The message dripped with sincerity, but he didn't care. Not really. He'd move on to the next loser. She saw his lips move, but didn't hear the words. She gazed at his inert eyes but he avoided eye contact. No surprise. Nothing new.

He kept yammering about creditors. Assets. Debts. Forfeiture. She didn't need every freaking detail. What was worse? Her father's chosen exit from Planet Earth, a.k.a. Planet Disaster, or the mess he left behind? The nothing?

The straight-as-an-arrow evangelical pastor, serving a genteel mix of hard-working parishioners in one of Denver's close-in, overlooked neighborhoods, had embezzled his way to the point where the only reasonable way out was for him to light the fire first and shoot himself second. The only sensible thing to do was to let everyone else sift through the ash of what he'd left behind and see if they could find a scrap.

Nothing but dust.

He embezzled from Living Hope Assembly of God for years. He started early, the forensic accountants had figured out, and turned it into a fine art. He'd been ratted out by his long-time assistant, a glum housewife who could no longer live with the double-whammy guilt of the theft and tending to his sexual needs during their adulterous affair. Yes, that too.

Desma's father killed himself just before she got back from her first and only tour of duty. He timed his exit so he wouldn't have to say anything to her, so he didn't have to face his daughter and try to cobble together a lie that would make a difference.

The insurance guy wasn't going to say it, but she knew.

The arson investigators would confirm it soon. The fire was deliberate. Desma only hoped he'd made it painless, somehow, for her mother and for their pup, the ageless Basilio. The Mexican parishioners treated the dog like a member of the family—*king*—and the regal Basilio accepted their affection with grace and patience. He didn't deserve to die in a fire.

All gone. Father, mother, Basilio, property, assets, nothing.

She ushered the insurance man out. That is, she stood and held the door open. He might not have been done talking, but she was done listening.

"I'll be in touch," he said.

Whatever. She didn't want to be *touched*. He didn't have a pocket full of magic cash that would cover the motel lease—another month's worth was due—or take care of her needs for the next year. When she left the Army she should have followed up on all their offers—job training, résumé building, all that crap. Something to do with the GI Bill benefits. But she wanted nothing to do with anyone in uniform after what she'd done, how things had ended up. The men who came home in a box because of what she'd done.

Desma flopped on the dingy bed.

Soft, smoggy Denver light filled the room. A stiff, faded

yellow drape filtered the dead October sun. The room's brightest hours, midday, evoked a sad pallor. She swore the room's vents were positioned to inhale exhaust from passing cars. The bedspread carried a whiff of cat pee. The heater under the window clanked and whirred, its thermostat a joke of technology. Meaningless. The bathroom was a place she spent as little time as possible. The fewer minutes inside, the lower risk of contracting an as-yet-undiscovered third-world disease. She'd spent a few bucks at the Dollar Store for Pine Sol and cheap bleach. Desma figured it had to have made a difference, even if nothing looked better.

No insurance money. No job. A damaged face.

And, alone.

She left one war to fight another.

Walking equaled escape and salvation. The only problem? Walking equaled the need for calories. She grew hungry more quickly. Maybe it was her military metabolism. She enjoyed moving. And at least she wasn't exiled in the motel room, alone.

But hungry meant food and she needed money for that. She was running short. She was running nowhere. She had nothing.

Thanks to dear old dad. *Betcher* bottom dollar. Yeah, right.

Was this beat-up dollar her last? Should she have saved money on the bleach? Was it time to go full Ramen? Nineteen cents a serving, those little silver metal packs of chemical who-knows-what, *Asian* something?

She pictured the line of creditors the insurance guy described, pictured them pecking for scraps off the carcass her father left behind.

She had no job. She owned a hard-to-look-at face. Mangled. Scarred. Could she interview with her face turned? Maybe? Could she find a job over the phone?

The fresh air might clear her head. Denver changed so much in the two years she'd been gone—one year in country after one year of basic and advanced training at Fort Gordon, Georgia.

She thought about Chris, the guy she dated when she first returned. He cut hair. He made enough that for a few weeks she felt normal. She allowed herself to look ahead, a luxury. She'd shown him the empty lot where her house burned to the ground. She showed him the church the parishioners were scrambling to rebuild. He seemed sympathetic and said the right things.

The lift didn't last.

Chris had tattoos up his arms, down his back. Sinister shit. He didn't seem to care about the disfigurement to her face and chest. He claimed we were "all disfigured" in one way, inside or out. He said the right things. It turned out he wanted to disfigure her some more. He had money. And coke. And weed (but who didn't?). For a few weeks, it was fun. But every day revolved around when they'd do it, at least once and maybe more. Chris was lead dog. She fell under his shadow, under his wing. But drunk or high, he grew dark. And then darker still.

Was she desperate? How desperate? Not enough to endure the humiliation. Following the third time with the rough stuff, she kicked him out of her life.

If he would've hung around, she knew she'd kill him.

She knew how.

Did he think her face meant she knew pain? That she wanted more? In the Army, she'd grown inured to death. She would never reconcile the effort that went into organized killing in Panwar Province with everything she'd been taught by her pastor-father. Logic didn't cut it. All she knew was that she was one of millions who had been sent to war over the millennia, more often than not in the name of some god. She'd given her pledge "against all enemies, foreign and domestic…" The Army said kill. Allegedly, the Bible said don't. But it wasn't the enemy that took the lives of her five fellow soldiers. It was her mistake, inching the ASV forward when the supply convoy stopped to fix a flat tire. After all the training, she'd gone too far. A lax moment and five men got blown up and somehow, she survived. She dragged the guilt around like a lead ball and uranium chain. She would live with the reminder forever on her face.

She walked to Riverpoint on a cool fall day, low clouds fitting her mood. It was once overlooked, almost trashed-out. Now the downtown stretch along with South Platte had gone glitzy upscale and brimmed with moneyed hipsters. She watched the skateboarders at the park. She drifted down near the ritzy coffee shops, the fancy walking bridge with its towering structure that led the way to LoDo. She eyed a sad homeless man on the corner of Little Raven. His tattered cardboard sign read *Anything Helps* in smudged letters. Anything helps—indeed. She would never go there, sink that far.

Would she?

She wandered, fended off the hunger. If she stayed in her sad room, she could count on precisely nothing happening. Out here, you were a pinball.

Getting slapped around but at least moving.

She could feel people pulling away, keeping their distance. Was it the camo military pants? The heavy boots? She wore a big gray baseball cap, a few sizes too big and the bill pulled low to shadow her face. Did she smell? No; she wouldn't tolerate *that*. Everyone else had a purpose. Even the joggers and the lunchtime walkers, you could tell. They walked with purpose. They had direction. A goal. They had bank accounts and a place to go. They had things. They had stuff. They had routines.

She spotted an empty black metal bench, felt the urge to take a load off.

She tipped her head back, closed her eyes. The Army taught her the power of a positive mental attitude. She had done so much more in boot camp, and beyond, than she ever thought possible. If she kept her spirits up, she'd get her life back on track. In Afghanistan, she had considered herself in charge of morale among all the Joes. That is, until the day she screwed up driving over the moon dust, the dust of Afghanistan. She wouldn't let her father's bullshit smother her options. She'd find a spot. She'd find an exit plan from this entire nothing.

She needed to find that positive center.

A tiny, muffled cough caught her off guard. The sound was soft and gentle, almost cute. But from where?

She hadn't noticed the plastic stroller tucked up against the side of the bench.

Desma stood, looked around. She was alone. Slumped in the stroller seat, a pint-size baby keeled to starboard, his face jammed into the side of the fabric seat. A blue blanket wrapped his tiny torso. A white knit cap covered his head. His eyes were closed and his minuscule fists were scrunched up by his chin, a little boxer pose. A fighter. Like herself.

"What the—?"

Desma sat back down, her arm protectively now on the stroller's handle, giving it a little back-and-forth motion. The baby coughed again, the little mouth opening like a bird.

"And here I thought I didn't have anybody, what about you, little fella? What the heck?"

Again, Desma stood and looked around. The path nearby snaked under a bridge and she stepped away from the stroller, looked to see if she could spy anyone in the shadows. Nothing moved.

Desma sat, stared off, a spot of strange pride blooming inside. She was meant to be here.

"I knew someone would find him."

The voice came from smack behind her. Desma woke up startled and on guard. Had she dozed off for a moment?

The stranger was thin, scrawny. Her face was sunken, and Desma knew the look immediately. The dead eyes, a blink or two from desperate.

"That's Carlton." Such a fancy name for a little kid. The mother hid her shape under a few layers of coats and clothes. A sour stench hit Desma's nose. The woman's hands shook.

She was strung out, tense. She was distracted by a pink cell phone. Desma moved away from the stroller and the woman grasped it by the handle to rock it back-and-forth.

"How old is he?"

"Almost two months. Good sleeper, but he needs to sleep less and eat more, so little you know? You live around here?"

Desma sighed. "Yeah. Sort of."

"Sorry to ask, but what happened?" The woman pointed to her own face but meant Desma's.

"Roadside bomb. I'm the lucky one."

"Sorry," she said.

"I've seen worse."

The woman's phone squirted a tone.

She answered in a flash. "Yes?" She stood and turned, walked a few steps off. Desma couldn't make out much in the way of words.

The woman came back. She looked at Desma, eyes pleading.

"Just watch him for a few minutes?"

Carlton burped.

"Well, I—"

"You been doing it already. Only another few."

"You know, I—"

What else did she have to do? Desma shrugged.

"Where do you live?" said the woman

"Little motel by Chubby's. Other side of the highway."

The woman walked a few paces. She stopped and turned. She held up three fingers and then popped up a fourth, but kept her thumb tucked in.

And then let the thumb go.

"I'll buy you a hamburger when I get back," she said. "Or a burrito. I know a place, smothered. So good. Swear to God. We can talk. I'm meeting somebody. I need. You know."

The woman fanned her hand out flat, let Desma see it quiver. Why would she think Desma thought it would be okay?

Desma nodded. What was the worry?

Better to watch the kid than have it exposed to that. "Sure."

"Good burger place. Real deal. Thanks." The woman

turned her back, long coat nearly dragging. She didn't look back.

Desma watched her disappear down where the path ducked under the bridge. Maybe the baby sensed the mother's absence.

He woke up, fidgeting and crying.

Desma picked him up. The smell told her everything she needed to know. How many minutes had it been? Eight? Ten?

The baby's bottom was heavy. She foraged through a gray canvas bag hanging from the stroller. Bottle, can of formula, wipes, Pampers, powder. It wasn't the first diaper she'd changed. Babysitting neighbor kids as a teen, orphans in Iraq, her grandfather with Alzheimer's when he lived with them in his last six months.

She placed the baby on the bench, took care of business in the bright sunshine. The used diaper went in the trash. She brought Carlton to her neck, gave him a gentle nuzzle, put his soft hair on her neck and felt his small body twist and squirm. The baby's presence stretched time. The baby filled her heart. In country, the word *mother* faded. War gave little reason to think about the future. *Mother* meant nothing. She had come home with a soul of bricks, heavy and complicated. Driving over the IED was her fault, inching forward. She should have disobeyed the voice commands coming over her headset. Everything. Her fault.

The sweet smell on Carlton's head was floral and medicinal at the same time. Desma returned him to the stroller. It would be weird to be caught nuzzling the baby.

She stood and stretched, spotted the woman's phone in the pink-shelled case on the ground. The battery was almost dead, the screen cracked with a distorted photo of the mother looking healthy and smiling. A guy stood next to her in the grainy picture. He sported a wan smile and a green hoodie.

Thirty minutes.

What the hell? She held the half-full bottle for Carlton and he sucked it down and sucked it dry, then fell back asleep.

One hour. Sunlight faded. She tried the phone to see if she could fire it up; couldn't get past the passcode.

A name from the phone would help—

But she couldn't get in.

Desma fiddled and paced, growing hungry herself. Promised hamburger, hell.

Sunlight started to fade.

A fire station? A hospital? She remembered something about the laws for dropping off unwanted newborns. Police? She didn't want to deal with them, not sure why.

A church? No fucking way.

What happened to Carlton's mother?

Desma had a sinking feeling.

This was the plan all along.

Back at the room Desma worried over things that hadn't occurred to her before. Spiders, bed bugs, dust. Did babies need water or only formula? Not water from this tap, no way. Responsibility for someone else felt foreign.

With one hand, the baby in the other arm, she sat on the bed, untied and removed her boots. She dropped onto her back, Carlton quiet on her chest. The pacifier twitched.

She put her arms around the baby and scooted to the middle of the bed, felt the weight of the day pull her down.

Loud knocks shook the room. The baby cried. A chain on the door allowed her to peek out. She cradled Carlton in her arms, still bawling. Two people. The landlord and Chris.

Both unwanted.

"No kids, Desma." The landlord was fat and toothless.

"Babysitting."

"Rent is due."

"I have a few days."

"One." He never looked her in the eye. "Twenty-four hours." He walked away.

"Babysitting?" said Chris.

"What the fuck do you want?" She put her face closer into the gap by the chain, to see what other trouble lurked.

"Talk?"

"Not a good time." She shoved the door closed with her foot.

"Desma." She heard him through the door. "What the hell are you doing?"

His kick against the door rattled her bones.

The people she wanted to notice her, to give her a chance, did nothing of the sort.

The ones she wanted to leave her alone refused to give up.

The baby was wet. Desma changed him on a clean towel on the bed. *Clean* was relative. Carlton's eyes seemed to take it all in. He looked worried. Five diapers remained and they would go quickly. She'd need more. How? With what money? Another knock on the door. Softer.

"Damnit, Chris." She put Carlton back in the stroller, strapped in. She cracked the door open. "I told you it's a bad—"

The chain broke. The door flew wide. Wood splinters splayed from the frame. Desma fell. Her head slammed the nightstand.

She rolled, her head in searing pain. She tried to focus. She balled herself up, prepared for another blow. The motion around her was all a blur. She caught the flash of his green hoodie, black jeans, and dark running shoes. Shards of orange flashed on the shoes. She fought to her knees, but it wasn't easy. The man steered the stroller through the doorway and Desma grabbed her head. She'd felt that pain before. Her vision went foggy. She couldn't focus. She felt herself being pulled down, and under. She couldn't fight back.

Who was on the bed with her? Desma propped up her throbbing head.

Chris.

Shirtless. Shoeless. Jeans.

She shook him awake.

"What the fuck?" she said.

"Covered your rent for another week," Chris said.

"Where's Carlton?"

"You're welcome. Who?"

"The baby."

"Gone."

She sat up too quickly. Dizziness. She struggled to put her boots on.

"I stopped drinking," he said.

"I don't care."

Desma returned to the park bench where she first met the addict, where she found Carlton. She ate a fast food burger, ninety-nine cents, and drank black coffee that another customer had left on the counter. She hadn't eaten in two days.

Who the hell did he think he was? Sleeping on the bed? Paying her rent? He said he'd cleaned up for her. He pleaded his case in a gentle way. Could people change that fast? She didn't trust him, but she wasn't unkind.

Where was Carlton? She stood and hefted the backpack onto her shoulder. Everything she owned fit in the black canvas pack.

Tears came.

Desma *never* cried.

Not once over there, not once through it all. But now? Of all times?

She threw the cup and burger wrapper into the trash and walked in the same direction Carlton's mother headed the day before.

She walked for hours. Headed north to nowhere. The sun dropped behind the western peaks. She knew only one thing for certain: She would not go back to the motel.

Chris might still be there. Fuck him and his rent.

All in all, not a bad first night on the streets, she thought.

*I can do this.* The words became her mantra. Responsible only for herself.

Other than a guy blowing his partner in the bushes earlier, she had not been interrupted. They never noticed or didn't care. Swaddled in her sleeping bag, she listened and was secretly glad someone was getting some pleasure, getting something, getting something they wanted.

The sky to the east turned from black to purple.

Morning. After crawling out of the bag, she rolled it up as tightly as she could.

Then she saw him. On the west side of the park. The green hoodie, hands in the pockets, jeans and black shoes. His face remained hidden inside the hood.

She had to pee. Bad. She made her way to a port-o-let the joggers and vagrants used. She was neither, right? This was all temporary, right? Wasn't it? She considered going back to the motel. Realized that bathroom probably wasn't any more sanitary even after the bleach.

She kept her eyes down, away from Green Hoodie. She tried to ignore the stench and the cold seat. But it was a spa compared to the shitters she had to clean during latrine duty. She held the door open with her foot and kept watch.

Done with her business, Desma trailed him across the park. Her backpack and sleeping bag might tag her as one of them, but most looked away. She kept her distance, but she kept him square in her sights. He turned into an alley, oblivious.

She followed.

He skirted the edge of downtown. He stopped to chat every now and then. Talk or hustle or something. He knew people, or pretended. Fist-bumping and shoulder slaps.

Green Hoodie headed up toward Five Points, skirted the key crossroads by a block. He made his way to the back yard of a serene old Victorian mansion under renovation. A towering scaffold was propped against the face of the structure. A few workers milled about. A third-story window was open to load in dry wall. A big long dumpster took up space where two cars could have parked on the street. An old sink sat idle in the cool sunshine. A weathered roll of carpet sat on the sidewalk next to a chunk of sad, yellowed linoleum. An old motor home squatted down at the end of the driveway that ran up alongside the house.

Green Hoodie pulled keys from his pocket and unlocked the door to the RV deal. He stepped inside.

Desma waited.

She shoved her hands in her pocket.

And waited.

A shout tore through the quiet. And then a yell. She heard a crash like furniture being knocked over.

She edged closer between the house and the RV.

A steady *whump-whump* came from inside, the unmistakable sounds of fists on flesh.

A baby cried.

*Carlton.*

Desma dropped her pack. She grabbed a broken board from the scattered junk on the ground. One end of the board tapered so she could grasp it in one hand like a baseball bat. She put a foot on the little metal step and pushed the door open.

She stepped up. And inside.

Green Hoodie straddled Carlton's mother on the floor. The mother's arms were pinned under her back and butt. Hoodie's knees jabbed her forearms. His closed fist floated high above his shoulder. The hood had dropped and for the first time Desma saw his face.

Young. Bald. A black swastika looked shiny on his neck.

Desma shook her head. Fucking idiot Nazi wanna-be. The Nazis turned the symbol ugly. In Sanskrit, the original, it meant good fortune. Something she'd learned in country.

Desma had the feeling again—she was meant to be here. Fortunes were about to change.

The woman kicked. Carlton cried, sitting in the stroller. A syringe lay on the bench in the kitchen nook, beside a spoon and a lighter.

Desma pushed over a chair.

She swung the board at the top of Hoodie's head. Connected. The board cracked. Or maybe it was his head. A gash on his skull gushed blood. He rolled over. His arm dropped.

Carlton's mother scrambled to stand, a look on her face trying to put the pieces together. Hoodie slumped to the floor. Blood pooled. His Nikes twitched.

Carlton's mother wiped at her face. Blood ran from a busted nose and split lip.

"Get him out of here." She pointed to her baby.

"I got no place."

"Your motel?"

Desma shook her head.

"Pretend he's yours."

"Your phone is in my backpack outside. But the battery's dead."

"Leave. Take Carlton. I'll tell them I did it. Self-defense." She dragged herself to the stroller, pulled something out of a bag. She pushed the stroller over inside the tiny space.

"Take him."

She pointed a small semi-auto. Clicked the safety off.

Desma stared, right into the dark hole at the end of the muzzle. Not the first time.

"I'll shoot you. I'll tell them you killed him. So I had to shoot you before you killed me. Drugs, you know?"

Desma heard the gunshot from the street. The sound didn't surprise her. She turned to see a lick of flame at the window, smoke starting to pour out. Another fire, another clench of anger in her gut, another life taking a left-hand turn. This time, for good reason. She left the stroller, sprinted back to the door and tossed the pink phone into the open door. She started reciting her line for the cops: *I found him at a bench at Riverpoint.*

Desma waited, hidden, until dark.

She locked the wheels of the stroller at the door of a fire station on Broadway. She rang the doorbell and walked off down the street, her head down.

She was thinking about good fortune and all the ways that people chose to leave the planet.

# SHADOWS WITHIN SHADOWS

DESMA DECIDED TO KILL HERSELF ON TUESDAY.

And then she bumped into Andy.

At first Desma thought he had passed out. It wouldn't be the first time. Then she looked into his eyes and knew better.

Death only looks one way.

"Andy," she said, still in denial. He was right-side up, half in a puddle of restaurant backwash and dumpster drippings. The loss stung her gut. Yesterday's trash. "What the hell?"

Desma hadn't cried in years, but one lone tear formed and her chest tightened of its own volition. Hell, she'd seen enough dead guys, she'd been in a war, but she thought of Andy's corny jokes and his killer recipe for ramen and wild ramps. He knew a wild patch of edible weeds and other plants down by the Platte. He always traveled with a small bottle of Sriracha. Made everything better, including the alley pickings.

Andy was on his back, right leg hitched in an awkward fashion. His thick parka, too warm by miles for a September night, bunched up around his shoulders. The side of his head looked smashed and wet with blood. He was stuck in a frozen backstroke, reaching up and over his head.

What the hell? LoDo was quiet. The Rockies were out of town. It felt empty when baseball was away.

Pots clanked. A man laughed. Somewhere, a band muddled their way through "Peace Frog."

Two guys in white aprons stepped out from a back door,

lit something. Beards, heft, health. The source of the laugh. Closing time or almost.

She went to them, pointed back to Andy. One pulled out a phone to call 9-1-1.

"Fuck," said the other.

"You have a phone I could borrow?" she asked.

The way he looked—he'd already taken a scared little step back—she might have asked for a month of free meals. Round face, one well-tatted forearm, plump like a dumpling.

"Borrow?"

"Before the cops come," she said.

They were smoking weed and it smelled divine, skunky-sweet. There was good stuff to be had.

She waved him over.

"Here." She pointed. Andy still hadn't moved. She caught herself again, choking back the feeling. Nobody was pals out here on the street. Not really. Trust could fuck you.

"Ain't enough light for the phone," he said. "Flash doesn't work." The weed cloud surrounded him—and garlic. The restaurant was The Jenny Rogers, one of the first brewpubs in town.

She grabbed an empty beat-up box next to the dumpster. She always carried matches. A mini-bonfire erupted in seconds, but it wouldn't last. The kid had his phone ready. "That enough?"

The prints were a mess on the sloshed-up sand from the puddles, but she saw four diamonds in the tread on one.

The flash fire faded.

"What should I do with these?" Restaurant boy had three shots and scrolled through them. These gizmos came out just after she'd been back for a year, still trying to piece everything together from what she'd seen, what she'd done. Then her father, the pastor, had been caught after decades of embezzling from the church accounts—fingered, so to speak, by his long-time assistant, an otherwise plain housewife he'd been screwing for years. She finally had enough of the guilt and the secrets. Desma didn't need the details. Her father exited the planet by setting their house on fire. He took her mother with him and their proud poodle, too. Her world melted to nothing.

To this.

"E-mail 'em," she said. "F-D-U-P at gmail."

"What are you gonna do?"

God, she wanted a hit of weed. It smelled like heaven and it would take her away.

"Don't know," she said. "Depends."

The cop fought the stench.

The alley was rank, no question, but wouldn't kill you.

"You say you found him?"

Officer Feldon looked bored.

"About tripped over him," Desma said.

Two cop cars idled at the end of the alley, electric blue-and-red fire. Radio squawks would wake any sleepers, maybe the dead. It was 3 a.m. Telling the time was no problem when your feet recognized every gutter and you could read the day by how fast the rats scurried—and where they were headed.

"You happen to be here and he happens to be your friend?"

"Someone I know," said Desma. Headlights from the squad cars caught the worn tips of Andy's shoes. "Knew, I mean."

"Acquaintance?"

"A lot of us know each other."

"Us?"

"Us out here."

She didn't need to explain homeless to a cop, did she? Andy's shoes remained too still. He'd grabbed for her once and she'd barked "no," and he'd kept things platonic ever since. Operation Enduring Freedom and Operation Desert Storm—it was all the same when you were back home. Everyone got along, no matter what you'd done. Andy had spent a lot of time talking to himself. Not anymore.

*Fuck.*

She wanted to see those feet jerk to life, watch him roll over and stand up.

"All you know is Andy?"

"First names are plenty out here."

Officer Feldon took notes.

"That ring, I'm telling you. Must have been that," said Desma.

"How did you get hurt?"

"What?"

"This?" He pointed to his own puffy pink—healthy— cheek.

"IED," she said. "Parwan Province. Know where that is?"

"Afraid not," he said.

A radio on the cop's hip squealed and he reached down to adjust the volume. He waved with his flashlight to the end of the alley, gave a head bob to follow. She didn't want to leave Andy, but was used to orders—it was in her bones.

"M.E. is here," he said. "Busy night."

Were they going to leave Andy there? Flat on the ground? Alone?

"Is he a user?" said Feldon. .

They were walking; she was a step behind.

"What?" said Desma.

"You know."

"No. He got fucking robbed." She heard her voice go up. "You think—"

"Did he shoot up?"

"Check his hand," she said. "The ring is fucking gone. You can see the circle of white skin."

They reached the blazing squad cars, those brooding SUV-shaped deals with front grills like war machines. One of the waiting cops laughed. She didn't know why.

The scene swelled. A crime scene truck, another cop car, brewpub extras. A few street faces, too. Soon, she was elbowed to the outer ring. A television news truck pulled up. The guy who climbed down fought off a yawn and trudged to the back of his van.

Desma started at dawn, upriver.

She knew what she needed to do. She knew who to look for, listen for—a certain rumble through the camps where she visited but never felt as if she really belonged. They paid her no attention. Her fused-up face, her left check expressionless as a slab of porcelain, one thick chunk of cold scar, didn't prevent some men from checking her out. There were always men looking for someone to do them a favor. Or someone to protect. Or someone to show off. Could they tolerate the messed-up eye? Her nightmares? Her insomnia? She'd grown to love the night and its indifference, shadows within shadows. Sleep was a joke, a fantasy.

She stayed by herself in an abandoned maintenance shack up by the Coliseum. She lived apart to avoid complications in camps. She lived apart to not make a show out of staying in shape. She wanted to kill herself because she saw no end to the downward spiral, hadn't seen a glimmer of hope in years, but staying in shape was one of the good things she brought home from the sand and the war. Wandering into the thicket of grubby men and hard-bitten women reminded her why she needed a solo lair. She was no better than any of them, but she preferred to operate alone, to avoid risking anything again like what happened in Parwan Province. She'd been the driver, the one who caused all the pain. Two guys didn't get to come back home, one on his fifth fucking deployment, because she kept inching forward. She'd been so sure. And she'd been so wrong.

She'd met Andy the first time near Commons Park so she wandered into the camp nearby with her head down, per usual.

"Seen Vic?"

To Big George, an old-timer with shoulders like Frankenstein. She'd seen Vic buddying up to Andy once. Or trying.

"Last night." Big George didn't have to think. "Coming back from somewhere."

"How's he doing?"

A minuscule shrug. How was anybody doing?

"Where you been?" said Big George.

"Nowhere, really."

Big George had a protective streak.

Desma didn't trust it. "Tell Vic if you see him."

She tried not to be too obvious, to draw too much attention.

Curly-haired Elsa, the mumbler.

Skinny Jack, toothless.

Buddy, the Star Wars fan. He was bipolar and a tweaker.

A young Trans girl stood with her hands on her hips, snapping bubble gum, tall as a tree it seemed. She wore the saddest flip-flops, the toes of her big feet black from all the street grime. She went by Terri, and she might have been sixteen. She liked to talk about the guys she'd blown, the cash she'd scored, and how her family kicked her out when she came out to them. They had lost a son and a daughter on the same day.

Sloop-nosed "Uncle" Reilly, one of the few who hadn't abandoned basic pleasantries.

Tiny Mary with her crosses and her repeated invocations. She was known to say things like, "Luke six thirty-five, look it up."

And sad Joe, who liked to lecture about his days as an MP in Qui Nohn Airfield. He cocked his head to stare at you with his one eye. The other bore a black triangle that always seemed fresh.

"Two lefts don't make a whole pair," said Joe. "You'd see funny."

"I'm not donating today anyway," she said. "Not an issue. Seen Vic?"

No cops would ever go to this trouble. Desma felt revved—a mission.

"Yeah."

"Where?"

Joe rolled his head around as if he was looking for a constellation. All he could see here was the black underbelly of the thumping bridge. "Am I supposed to keep track?"

"Just asking," said Desma.

"Said he'd be back, but said it with a smile."

"A smile?"

"It's relative."

"Back from where?" said Desma.

"Big Daddy's."

A pawn shop down on Broadway, couple miles.

"Any cops come around?"

"No. Why?" said Joe.

"Andy turned up dead."

"What?"

She appreciated the genuine concern.

"Damn," said Joe. "Just died?"

"Killed."

"Fuck. And Vic?"

"Think he knows something, that's all. You sure no cops?"

"Down here? You joking?"

"Just checking." Desma gave a flash of a smile with the side of her face that worked.

The walk to the library took an hour. She waited her turn for a computer. Up here, top floor, nobody paid attention to each other. The computer room was its own strange camp. Sniffles, muffled coughs.

She logged into her email, paid for the paper copies of the prints in quarters and pennies. They came out good—knife-edge sharp. They were only partial footprints, but still.

The cop shop HQ was a few blocks away. Fortresses didn't scare her.

"Witness?"

The woman at the desk had gear strapped to every pocket flap and every inch of belt space. She had a giant handgun on her hip. With her bare hands, Desma knew she could snuff the life out of the cop before she got her piece out of its holster. When you used your hands to kill, the key was to strike hard and follow-through.

"He'll know," she said. "The dead guy the other night behind The Jenny Rogers."

She held up the copies of the prints, but didn't unfold them.

She sat out in the chilly sunshine while she waited.

Forty-five minutes went by. She sat—nothing else to do—and thought about Andy.

Officer Feldon pulled up along Cherokee Street, waved her over. He stood between her and his squad car—*don't get too close.*

She waved the papers, opened them up this time. He took them, with disdain.

"How'd he die?" she said.

He flipped through the pages. "We took our own pictures," he said. "Did you touch the body? Mess with the crime scene?"

"How did he die?"

He massaged his teeth with his tongue, lips closed. He stabbed a finger in one ear and wiggled it hard. Maybe he was digging for brain cells.

"One blow to the head. Skull shattered. He was pretty frail."

*Jesus, of course.*

"Vic," she said, pointing to the papers. "Tell pawn shops to watch for that ring."

He handed back the copies.

"Thanks," he said and turned to go.

"What? Where are you—?"

She knew she was hard to look at, but really?

"I'll tell the pawn shops." He circled around to his driver's side door. "Don't worry."

"He's probably on his way back right now, pocket loaded with cash."

"Vic who?"

"Told you, we're not big on last names."

Officer Feldon shrugged. Sighed. "Where does he live?"

"All over the place. What, you need an address?"

"For starters."

"You have other leads?"

"We're working on it, okay?"

"I know the camp where he'll be coming back—" God, she wanted to kick and scream, throw a fit, not let him jerk her around. "You can wrap this up. Couldn't you guys use some good news? A quick, what do you call it, resolution?"

They parked along Speer Boulevard, good view of a long stretch of the sunken creekside path, eight feet down. Officer Feldon scrunched as far over on his side as he could squeeze, windows down. She hadn't heard so much beeping and radio static since she wore a uniform. She hated being so close to any driver's seat, but it would be worth it.

"I'll give it an hour," he said.

Joggers, bicyclists, roller-bladers, walkers, strollers, lovers, a fucking unicycle, groups of runners, no Vic. They didn't talk. He worked on his computer.

"Got a bad feeling," he said.

Fifty-three minutes had passed. This time, she watched every minute flick by on the digital clock on the dash.

"Wait," she said. "Please."

"If you find him, call me back."

He pointed to a stack of business cards by his laptop on the console, loaded in a clip.

"Call with what?" she said.

"You'll figure it out."

Ten minutes after Feldon left her standing on the curb, still watching the path, Vic materialized like a ghost. She had been willing it to happen and pictured his presence so many times; she had to blink to make sure he was real.

He walked high, strode hard. He sported new boots—canvas with laces that started down near the toes and crisscrossed half way up each shin. A thousand crosses. He stared down at them as he walked. New footwear gave you a lift. She knew.

He didn't notice her.

She followed him, her anger rising.

"Hey, asshole," she barked.

She didn't need to say it very loud for him to hear, but he didn't look up.

Desma swung her body over the lip of the high retaining wall, dangled from her fingertips and let herself drop. She was twenty feet behind him on the sun-shot walkway and she knew it was too bright. Not here, not now. "Hey, asshole," she said again, her blood churning. Vic didn't look around.

Under the bridge, Vic lingered and, goddamnit, smiled. He pointed to his boots. Desma didn't recognize the guy he was talking to. Most of the gang was up working the streets, no doubt, but she didn't care if the whole world watched, she had to do this.

"Hey, asshole."

"What the hell—"

Vic whipped around but the turn only added to the velocity of her flying four knuckles, curled down and moving up. They caught their mark and she heard the snap and squish of his throat, square on the larynx. She cupped both hands and popped his ears with simultaneous blows and he stood shell shocked but of course had no real idea what that was, his ear drums throttled. A knee caught his balls full bore, and the blow to his temple cracked with conviction, and she had little doubt of the blood starting to pool and the pressure starting to build, inside.

"Feldon."

Desma heard his voice through the phone. They flagged a guy on a bike on the sidewalk, asked to borrow his phone. Terri did the talking, Desma listened.

"Down near the hospital, uh-huh," said Terri. "Other side of the creek." Terri waited, studied her fingernails and blew out a breath. "I don't know when."

"Who found him?" said Feldon.

Terri held the phone so Desma could poach in. Their ears touched—Terri's left and her right. Terri's ear was soft and delicate.

"I said I don't know," replied Terri.

"Your name?" asked Feldon.

"I think you need to come get him. There's a bunch of people standing around down here, right off the bike path. You

know, it just doesn't look very good. You know, for the image."
She waited, listened, scratched behind her ear. "Yeah, image of
the city."

Sirens followed and so did a parade of beat cops, a
paramedic. Pulse check, etcetera. Head shakes. A sheet. The
M.E. A body bag. Zip, zip.

Desma drifted to street level, using a ramp down the
way, and circled around, above the scene. The cops worked
quickly, the definition of short shrift. Feldon found Terri. She
wore brand new canvas boots and, with the added lift, looked
Feldon in the eye. Almost. Terri shrugged a lot. The M.E. asked
a question of Feldon and Terri took the moment to turn and
duck back through the gathered throng, head down and away.

Desma sighed. Speer Boulevard was jammed—a gaggle of
emergency vehicles, rubberneckers.

She crossed the street between bumpers, drivers checking
their phones and worrying about their commutes, and what
the hell was the hold up.

Desma dropped Terri's nasty old flip-flops in a dumpster
in an alley behind the houses on the fringes of the country
club neighborhood. Daytime was giving way to night and she
was a long way from home.

# SHANNON BAKER

# IT DOESN'T MEAN ANYTHING

THE SURF LICKED AT NIKKI'S BARE CALVES. SHE REACHED A finger under the elastic band of her bikini bottom and tugged, blessedly covering only half of one smooth, sun-kissed cheek. She twisted her slender neck to me and flashed a sly smile acknowledging my complete attention.

Balancing in the foaming surf, I pulled off my fins and splashed toward her. Blazing sun reflected painfully off the white sand of the beach, so I kept my eyes on the tanned beauty in front of me.

She leaned in to me, licked salt from my lips and wiggled her tongue into my mouth to begin a deep and promising kiss. When our lips parted, she cooed, "Oh, Trevor. Did you see that blue and pink fish?"

It felt like a gift I'd arranged just for her. "That's a parrot fish."

She hugged me. "I love you so much."

I couldn't care less about her words, but that tongue, and ass, and the tits smashed under her buoyancy vest and tank, were worth the travel expenses. I helped with her fins and held her arm as we walked from the ocean and across the sand to a pile of rocks. "I knew you'd love diving in the Caymans."

She squealed. "Everything is wonderful. The smell of the salt and the way the sand is all hot. The sun on my skin and your awesome condo. And you. The love of my life."

It might sting to find out I was the love of the weekend, but she was young and would move on. Kind of like a puppy who is happy to be with whomever feeds her.

The good thing about diving here, with a girl like Nikki, was water warm enough we didn't need a wetsuit. Watching Nikki kick through the water, scissoring her legs—man, that was pure art. Erotic art. Close to porn, actually.

I shrugged out of my vest, resting the heavy aluminum tank on the sand. Always the gentleman. "Let me help you."

The pink tip of her tongue dabbed at the crust of dried salt on the corner of her mouth. She gave me another teasing smile. "Please."

I unzipped the front of her vest and before I eased it from her shoulders, I let my palm rub against those firm, young breasts, nipples erect from the ocean breeze. She reached up and kissed me again.

I held my breath, sucked in my belly, and lifted her tank as if it weren't a strain. I settled it against the rocks and…

I let out a yip. Maybe more like the scream of little girl. I jumped back, embarrassed, even as the chills chased themselves up and down my spine.

Nikki leaped from the rock. "What?"

I pulled off a nonchalant chuckle. "Crabs."

"Huh?" She spun toward the rock and took a step closer. She bent to search between a crevice. "That?"

I stayed put. "Not that guy. There was a much bigger one but he scuttled away. Startled me, that's all."

She puckered her full lips. "Is mighty Trevor afraid of that little ol' crabbie?"

I couldn't blame her for making light of the danger. With age comes wisdom. I'd had twenty, okay, maybe thirty, more years than Nikki to learn a thing or two. "Crabs seem pretty harmless until they crawl all over you. Then they can devour you in minutes."

Her smooth forehead bunched into wrinkles. "Really?"

Always time to enlighten and enrich. "I saw a documentary about Amelia Earhart. They theorized she'd crashed in the

Pacific and washed up on a deserted island only to be eaten by crabs."

Nikki's eyes widened. "No shit?"

I shivered despite the tropical sun burning my back. "They put a pig out on the sand and set up time-lapse cameras and showed how the crabs came in, all sizes, small as your fingernail to as large as a terrier. The carcass was crawling with them. Within six hours the pig was completely gone. Vanished. No bones, no blood."

Nikki blanched and even turned a little green. "That's creepy."

"They're delicious though." I swaggered a little, never admitting I hadn't eaten a bite of crab since I'd seen the film.

She gave me a wicked grin and crossed her arms as if she were chilly, pushing her fleshy tits together and stretching the scanty string bikini down to reveal dark areolas. "I can think of better things to do than talk about crabs."

No need to tell me twice. I grabbed my vest and tank and scooped up my fins. "I'll take this to the pickup and come back for yours." That's the difference between a girl like Nikki and a woman like Janice. Nikki didn't analyze and question me the way my wife did. When I'd told her about the documentary on Earhart, skeptical Janice reached for her iPad and looked it up. She argued with me about Amelia Earhart and debated whether crabs would actually leave no trace. Nikki didn't give a shit about crabs. She moved right on to the fun.

Most of the time I appreciated Janice's brain. She's a great wife. Without her I'd never have grown my business to such a success. You couldn't ask for a better mother to our kids. Smart and funny. Everything, except a twenty-something's body and libido. God-damn, there was a lot to like in an air-brain with a great chassis.

Halfway up the beach I glanced back to make sure Nikki waited with her gear. She sat on the rock with her legs crossed, one bare foot swinging. As she stared across the water, I hoped she was thinking of me instead of those crabs.

Good girl. I didn't need a witness to see me swallow my blue pill.

After dropping my gear, anticipation thrumming through me, I trotted from the pickup to the rocks to collect Nikki and her equipment.

Her tank sat strapped to the black vest, her fins lay next to it, her mask rested in the sand twenty yards away. I scanned the beach. An expanse of white sand. The road lay fifty feet away, beyond a few scraggly tropical trees. The only other cover was a patch of jungle not more than a few yards deep between the beach and the pickup.

"Nikki!"

Maybe she went for a swim. I squinted into the surf. Making sure no crabs scrabbled around my feet, I climbed onto the rock to get a better vantage. "Nikki!"

There's that moment when something is off a little but you hold on to the hope that everything is going to be okay. You take the first steps to figure it out and then it builds from a ripple into a crashing wave. At that instant you realize something is wrong. Really wrong.

Did she swim out and drown? Where? What? Nothing came to me. I jumped from the rock, spraying sand on the fins and tank. I spun around, the sun blinding me, and it felt as though someone sucked the air from the beach.

I sprinted for the little bit of jungle and crashed through the wide, waxy leaves of the tropical trees, roots and rocks bruising my feet through the bottoms of my dive booties. "Nikki!" I broke through the other side onto the road, looked left at my pickup, right at an empty curve of asphalt.

Sweating, head pounding, mind racing, I panted. Where was she? A tinny bell sounded above the ocean breeze. It was my cell phone ringing from the pickup cab. The rubber of my booties slapping on the hot macadam, I raced for the phone, reached through the open window, and answered.

A low voice growled, "We got your Nikki, Loverboy. You want her back, it's eight hundred thousand in cash. By noon tomorrow."

I reeled, breathless, and gasped until I managed to say, "What? I can't. Wait. That's…"

A heavy breath whistled from the caller. "I'll call and tell you where to drop the money."

I braced my hand on the pickup and scalded my palm on the hot metal. I lurched back and retreated off the road into the sand. "I don't have that kind of money. Not here."

"Then find it." The gruff voice mangled my jingle. "1-800-We Sue 4U." The jingle—plastered on billboards strung all over Houston, on posters on bus-stop benches, and even in TV commercials—had been Janice's idea. It made me a household name. But who would have thought it'd make me a target for ransom here in Cayman?

Eight-hundred thousand? No way. "I can't get it by tomorrow. Not cash. Not on this island."

"Then say goodbye to the girl. And hello to headlines. CNN, FOX, Greta and Nancy Grace."

My knees buckled and I dropped to the sand. This couldn't be happening. Why me? I didn't do anything wrong. All men had affairs. It wasn't even an affair. It was only a few short days.

A brief vacation from being Houston's earnest family man. The attorney sitting with his adoring wife of twenty-five years and their Texas University children, Kimmy and Jay. A master at facing the camera to tell the world he believes in playing it fair, but when it can't be worked out, he's the one to call.

I couldn't lose it all. Not over a little tail. All I wanted was some fun on the side, and now my life was smashed to pieces.

When my head cleared I pushed myself from the sand and thumbed my phone, drawing up my Cayman account. We only stayed in the condo several weeks a year and rented it out the rest of the time. The location and upgrades made it easy to get top dollar. Janice and I kept an account on the island which was used for rent deposits and to pay for expenses. Janice kept the accounts, of course, but I was certain revenue far exceeded expenses.

I tried a password and got denied. I tried again. Denied. Shit. Damn.

Reason finally caught up with my racing heart and brain. I needed to calm down. The password would be in the safe in the condo, encrypted with Janice's code. Her sentimental streak combined with her practical side created a string of possible passwords you could only figure out if you'd been married to her as long as I had.

On the drive back to our condo in the tony canal area on the north side, I had to pull over to toss my guts on the side of the road. Despite shaking hands and pouring sweat, I was finally able to make a plan. I'd get the cash from our Cayman account. Pay the ransom, fly Nikki home, replace the Cayman account with money I'd socked away, and be a faithful husband for the rest of my life.

When I burst into the condo, the air conditioning smacked me full in the face. I ignored the swaying palms and ocean view from the balcony window, turned my head from the tangled sheets Nikki and I had left a few hours ago, and with shaky fingers, I punched the combination into the safe's buttons.

After retrieving the password I pulled up the bank site and entered Luvo7!99!, Janice's code for our July 1991 wedding. I blinked at the small screen of my phone and dropped to the cold tile floor. $236,421.16.

That was all? What happened to the rest?

*God. Oh God. What the hell would I do?*

Could I get any from my credit card? Not nearly enough. How about wiring from the States? That much money in cash would raise questions.

Restless with panic, I jumped up, dropped my ass on the sofa only to jump up again. Pacing. Pacing. How long until noon tomorrow? Grasping and desperate, each idea worse than the last.

I rested my forehead against the glass of the balcony door, already cooling with evening, fighting the urge to cry. Janice would leave me. My business would be ruined. The kids. Oh God, Kimmy and Jay would never speak to me.

And Nikki. Of course. Nikki would not return home to cut hair in Houston.

A rattle sent a jolt of electricity through me and I spun toward the door. The bright brass knob turned and the front door inched inward. It stopped, along with my breathing and heart.

In a whoosh, it banged open to a broad butt. Janice straightened and tugged the handle of a roller bag big enough to hide a body. She twisted around, waddled in, and grinned so that her first chin folded into the one below it. "Surprise!"

I must have looked like an opossum on a moonless night with a car bearing down on him. I couldn't move.

She left the bag and hustled across the tile to throw herself into my arms.

Shit.

My arms automatically circled her, the softness of her middle-age, familiar roundness pressed against me and for an instant, I felt relief. She was here and it would be all right.

Comfort vaporized in the too-cold air. I couldn't tell Janice. She wouldn't understand. Blood drained from my face and I felt myself go icy cold.

Janice jerked from my embrace and stared into my face. Her hazel eyes widened in alarm. "Trevor? Honey, what's wrong?"

She knew me so well. How would I hide this? But I couldn't tell her. "Nothing. Tired from diving."

She tilted her head and studied me. "That's not it."

Tremors started in my gut and pushed toward my throat. To my horror, tears sprang to my eyes. I dropped my head to my hands. "Nothing."

"Oh my God." Her arms clamped around me and she patted my back. "What is it?"

By now I couldn't stop the sobs. She led me to the sofa and lowered me onto the cushions.

She pulled my head into her big, pillowy breasts and rocked back and forth, patting my back and murmuring meaningless words until I got myself under control. After a time I sat up and rubbed my hand across my eyes.

I was going to confess as I'd always known that I would. "I've always loved you and I always will."

Her face wrinkled in confusion. "What's this about?"

I spilled the details of meeting Nikki at the salon and bringing her down here. The ransom, the bank account, the whole nine yards. All the while Janice paled more and more, so by the time I drew a breath she looked like plaster.

And like plaster, when the final blow hit, when I said, "It doesn't mean anything, I swear," she shattered into a million shards.

Janice wasn't the type to throw china or break vases. She'd never destroy anything with the slightest value. Screaming and crying, she slapped my arms and chest a few times before retreating into the master suite and slamming the door.

Broken with shame, I didn't move from the sofa while the sun set and the lights of Cayman's bustling nightlife glittered through the patio glass. The full moon spotlighted the original oils on the wall, then the bronze sculpture on the coffee table and eventually created a wedge along the tile floor, pointing toward the front door like it was showing me the exit.

Maybe I dozed a second. I opened my eyes to Janice silhouetted with first pink blush of dawn behind her. "You know, I recommended you go to the salon. I hate that I had any part in you meeting Nikki. She's Donna's daughter. Did you know?"

*Donna's daughter?* Shit. Donna and Janice had gone to high school together and remained lifelong friends. "I never meant to hurt her. Or you."

Janice held up a finger. "We need to help Nikki for Donna's sake. And we need to keep this from the media."

For the first time since I saw Nikki's gear abandoned in the sand, I drew in a refreshing breath. "I'm so sorry."

I rose to hug her. She stepped back and planted her palm on my chest. "As for you and me. I don't know."

Tears pushed at my eyes again. "I understand."

She swallowed and blinked. Cleared her throat. "As soon as the bank opens we'll go together and transfer money from Kimmy and Jay's trust."

My hopes vanished. "We set it up so we can't touch it."

Her hand went to her hip as it did when she lost patience. "Only if one of us dies. That was your idea. You were afraid if you died and I remarried, my new husband would get your money instead of the kids. If both of us sign, we can change the way it's set up."

"But that's money for Kimmy and Jay." I tried to sound reluctant, but I was too relieved to carry it off.

She brought out her finger. That meant serious business. She pointed it at my chest and pounded with her words. "Exactly. That's why you're going to replace it with the money you've been stashing away."

"How did…?" I sputtered.

Finally she quit jabbing my chest with her fingernail. Her hand fell back to her hip. "I've been doing the books since we got married. I'm not stupid."

I should have known. Sharp-eyed Janice was well aware of my skimming off the family business. "You never said anything."

"It made you feel secure to have your pin money and that was fine by me."

Pin money? I probably had a cool million socked away. Nikki's ransom would eat into it but I'd still have some left over.

She snatched a pad of paper and pen from the kitchen counter and shoved it at me. "Give me the routing number and pin and whatever I need to transfer money from that account."

I didn't take the paper. "I'll do it."

"Uh-uh."

I wanted to argue, but she had that look. You live with someone for twenty-five years, you know when you've lost. I returned to the safe for the number and pin and handed them over.

No one raised an eyebrow at the bank and we were back in the condo with the cash when my phone rang at noon.

The gravelly voice spit at me. "There's a sunken fishing boat thirty yards at a heading of 73 degrees from the rock where you were yesterday. Leave the cash under the hull in an hour."

"But…" He hung up.

I relayed the instructions to Janice. She insisted on going with me and I shouldn't have agreed. But I wanted her at my side. Grim-faced, she packed the cash in a dry bag while I got fresh tanks and all the gear.

Once I got going—between my nerves and the effort of pulling the bag behind me—I was quickly sucking the air from my tank. Janice was a slow swimmer and I worried we wouldn't make it to the wreck before the hour was up. She had the headings and could use a compass, so with renewed urgency, I pumped my fins against the water and left her behind.

I checked my air, 1500 psi. Half of the tank gone. I wouldn't need as much going back and I could always surface swim if I got in trouble. But the wreck should be here. Even with the clear visibility, frustration built as I strained to see further and only caught sight of more angel fish, blue tangs, and the thousand little gray and silver fish that swarmed around me.

There. I spotted a dark blob on the ocean floor. My dive computer read 65 feet deep with 1300 psi. I glanced back, wishing Janice would hurry and catch up.

Fishing boat wasn't an exaggeration. The inverted husk couldn't have been more than twenty feet long. The bow rested on a coral head with fans and columns in vivid purple spouting around it. Brain coral the size of Janice's Viking oven propped the boat off the sand bottom. The boat had been abandoned long enough for coral to cover the hull, and striped sergeant-majors fiercely protecting their patch of violet turf.

Worried about my air, I darted to the space under the bow. I pushed the bag under but it wouldn't go in. I pulled back to look. A large rock blocked entry. I wedged the dry bag against it and shoved. Little by little it moved. But with my increasing anxiety and the hard work, I knew I was depleting my air too fast. I glanced from under the boat. Where was Janice?

When I had shoved enough I was halfway in the darkness, I decided the bright yellow of my dry bag couldn't be spotted by other divers. I pulled my feet under me to turn around.

A blow, like a kick on my butt, accordianed me. I jerked my head around. The boat slipped off the brain coral to entomb me.

Had Janice banged against the boat and upset it? I positioned my feet under me and flexed my legs against the boat to flip it upright. It didn't budge. Fumbling, I unzipped my vest pocket and pulled out a flashlight to read my gage. 800 psi, at this depth, about ten minutes..

I shined the beam around the edge of the boat and noticed it was buried in the sand. Looking for an escape, I struggled with the rock that blocked my entry. I managed to nudge it aside enough to let me aim the flashlight to the other end of the boat.

On the edge of the beam and tucked against the hull a small diver's whiteboard caught my eye. I reached for it and a sickening wave of fear and defeat rolled through me. That's when I knew this wasn't an accident. If I'd had any doubts about what was happening, the words in Janice's hand made my fate clear.

*I'm sorry. It doesn't mean anything.*

I'd loved Janice since I first saw her. Together we'd conquered the world, raised two kids, grew a fortune from scratch. She had to know how much I loved her. I'd devoted my whole life to her, done all I could to keep her happy.

But I'm no saint, and I'm not the only man to need a little variety. I thought I'd been discreet with my dalliances over the years. But, as she'd discovered my secret bank account, it now seemed clear Janice wasn't blind to anything.

My heart went cold when I realized she had used Nikki to bait me into this scheme. My soft-hearted wife had teeth like a shark, and she had sunken them deep into my soul. She tricked me into not only signing over my private account, but the kids' trust as well.

She, who knew me so well, understood I wouldn't have the courage to pull the regulator from my mouth but would stay here, breathing in and out, bubbles seeking the several holes on top of the hull as I hoped for rescue before my air ran out.

Two cables snaked through those holes to a metal cage

at the stern of the boat. The slack tightened on the cables and my heart leapt at the prospect of salvation. But the cables only lifted the door of the cage and a squirming mass of legs and claws tumbled out.

The mass dissolved into crabs. Hundreds of crabs. A carpet of crabs. Crabs that began crawling toward me.

# THE GUESSING GAME

"LET'S GO OVER THE DETAILS AGAIN," I SAID, ELICITING A grunt from Nathan and an exaggerated sigh from Screamer, who occupied the back seat.

"Why?" Nathan said.

"Because I hate improvisation."

Screamer sighed again, and then began spouting off details. I listened, staring at the road ahead of us—the same road we'd been on for an hour. It felt more like an hour and a half.

"Jacob Leeweather, divorced, one teenage girl—"

"Who *won't* be there, right?"

"Shouldn't be. His wife has full custody and they live in another state. School's in session, it's not spring break, and it's a Wednesday. No way we'll be seeing her."

"Is Leeweather dating?"

"Unknown."

I rubbed the bridge of my nose. "Okay, what about the house?"

"2,000 square feet, split-level, no basement. Nice secluded street. Seven neighbors, none of them too close."

"Pets? Dogs, specifically?"

"Not as of last month."

"What else?"

"Nothing."

I craned my neck back and found Screamer smiling at me.

He was okay. I'd worked with him on a couple of jobs. Nathan I knew much better, enough to know he was solid if unlikable. This was the first time all three of us had been together.

The car Cartwright gave us didn't have shit. No stereo, no radio. That wasn't unusual. He knew a lot of things about the people he employed, and little details didn't escape his attention. He probably realized we had irreconcilable tastes in music and gave us this car specifically to avoid... problems.

I settled back into my seat. "Sounds like a simple job."

"The details Cartwright gives us are never very interesting," Nathan said.

"They're not supposed to be trivia. They give us the information we need to do the job right."

"But aren't you ever interested in other things?"

"What other things?"

"Like the color of the paint in the kitchen," Nathan said. "It's funny what we find out about people sometimes."

None of us spoke for the next few minutes. It was Nathan who said, "The bedroom curtains: red or blue?"

"Huh?"

"What color do you think the curtains in the bedroom will be? Red or blue?"

"Couldn't they be yellow?" I said.

"Sure, if that's your guess. I say blue."

Screamer said, "Who has curtains anymore?"

"So you're guessing no curtains?"

I looked at Nathan. He stared straight ahead, both hands vised on the wheel as if he alone kept it attached to the steering column. He was grinning.

"What the hell are you talking about?" I said.

"For curtains, we've got blue, yellow, and none. What about the carpet in the living room: brown or white?"

Screamer immediately said, "It'll be wood." He sounded excited.

I saw Nathan glance at him in the rearview mirror. "Contrarian. What about you?"

"I don't know," I said. "I don't give a shit."

"So we have wood and we have shit brown. I'll go with white. Let's go to what started this. What color in the kitchen?"

"Light green," Screamer said. "Definitely light green."

Without looking at me, Nathan said, "Well?"

I crossed my arms at the chest. "Red."

"Goldenrod," Nathan said.

Screamer hunched his long body forward, sticking his head between Nathan and me. "This is fun. Cartwright didn't say anything else about the house. Let's guess on it."

"What about it?"

"Like will it be mostly brick, or lots of siding, or stucco, or—"

Nathan snickered. "Stucco. Just because I like the word."

"Do we know when the house was built?" I said.

"No. Probably pre-1960."

"Then I'd go with brick."

"Siding," Screamer said. Then he laughed.

Nathan nodded at me. "Your turn. Give us something to guess about."

"What's the point?"

"It's passing time, isn't it?"

I inspected my watch and was surprised to discover several minutes had slipped by in a wink. But there had to be something more valuable to this sudden game than wasting time, and I told them so. "Each guess earns us a point. We'll total the points up when we're done."

"What's the winner get?" Screamer said.

"The losers will have Cartwright fork over half their fee to the winner."

"*Half?*" Nathan said, shaking his head. "Hell, no. I've got a kid to feed."

"I'm game," Screamer said. "Yeah. Let's do this. So I said no curtains, wood floor, green paint, a wife, and siding. Nathan, you guessed blue curtains—"

"Jesus Christ," I said. "How can you remember all that?"

"Same way I remembered Cartwright's report. I've got a photographic memory."

I turned around in my seat. "You weren't reading those details off of something?"

"Didn't have to. I saw it once and that's all I need. I remember what I hear, too."

"Bullshit."

You'd look at Screamer and picture his brain as a single marble rattling around an otherwise empty mason jar, but the son of a bitch proceeded to reel off everything we'd guessed so far. Nathan actually let his hands leave the wheel long enough to applaud.

"Don't doubt me again," Screamer said.

"Just make sure you don't forget anything from here on out. I don't want to miss taking half from both of you bitches."

"Nathan, you in?"

He said he was.

Screamer said, "Chimney—yes or no? I say yes."

"Sure," I said.

"No."

"How many electrical outlets in the kitchen?"

"Three."

"Five."

"Six."

Nathan said, "Gun in the house? I say yes—a pistol."

"No. Cartwright said he's a liberal douchebag."

"It's not fair to guess if you've got insider information. The gun guess doesn't count."

Screamer said, "Sure it does. I guess he has a shotgun."

I said, "How many pairs of black shoes in the closet? I say four."

"Two."

"One."

Screamer said, "Total number of bathrooms? I guess two. And *no*, Cartwright didn't show me a floor plan."

"One."

"One and a half. How many rolls of toilet paper in the whole house?"

"Five."

"None. He ran out yesterday and he's been too busy to get more, so he's using paper towels."

"Fifty. He shops at Costco."

We chuckled at that.

"How many trees in the front yard?"

We all guessed one.

"Fine," Nathan said. "What type?"

"Maple."

"Yeah, Maple."

"What the fuck?" Nathan said. "Are you two suddenly playing for a tie? Honey-Locust all the way."

I said, "How many paintings on the walls, *total?* I say nine."

"Six."

Screamer didn't answer right away. I looked back at him. "What's the hold up?"

He said, "Do photographs count?"

"Sure."

"Because you said paintings."

"God damn it, anything framed and hanging on the wall."

"Okay. Sixteen."

"I'm changing my guess then," Nathan said. "Because you *did* say paintings. What was my answer before, Screamer?"

"Six."

"Make it twenty."

I glanced at my watch again. We'd be at Leeweather's house in under twenty minutes. Time had been a dried up old cunt for the majority of the trip, but the guessing game really lubed it up good.

"Leeweather's hair color?"

"Can't guess that," I said. "We know what he looks like."

"Well, I don't," Nathan said.

"I haven't seen his picture either. Guess Cartwright gave you special treatment."

I smiled. "I *am* the man with the hammer."

"Gray," Nathan said, "with a hint of black."

"Brown," Screamer said, "but actually a wig."

"You're both wrong. He's Jean-Luc Picard all the way."

"How many sex toys will we find in the bedroom? I guess two—a dildo and handcuffs."

"One—just a dildo."

"Agreed, only a dildo. But longer or shorter than twelve inches?"

"Longer," I said.

"Longer," Screamer said.

"Less," Nathan said. "Black or white?"

We laughed and everyone guessed black. Then we guessed whether Leeweather used the dildo on himself exclusively. Then we guessed boxers or briefs (Screamer said panties). We guessed on a whole boatload of other shit, whether they could be verified or not. Then we found ourselves pulling up into Leeweather's driveway. We hadn't thought to guess on it. It was gravel rather than paved.

"Got the cash?"

Screamer showed me the briefcase Leeweather would be expecting. "Look, we can already start adding points. There's a maple tree in the front yard. You're already down a point to us, Nathan."

"Plenty of time to make it up."

"Don't get out yet."

"Is something wrong?" I said.

"No," Screamer said. "But there's got to be more stuff to guess on. Let me think."

"We've guessed on at least thirty things now. And it's not like we're actually going to stick around to see who was right."

"We're not?" Screamer sounded hurt.

"It was just a game to pass time."

That's when Nathan surprised me. "Like hell. We're talking *half* here."

"What happened to the kid you have to feed?"

"He'll get fed a lot when I take half from each of you. Let's go."

We got out and went for the front door. I wore baggy cargo pants, the type with generous pockets along the legs. I rarely wore a belt but I needed one now against the hammer's sagging weight.

I heard voices from inside. Sweat broke out on my forehead.

"It's the TV," Nathan said, his voice now a whisper.

I closed my eyes and grinned. *Yes.*

"Plasma or LCD?" Screamer whispered. "I guess plasma."

"Plasma."

"LCD," I said.

We tried the storm door. It wasn't locked. Screamer came around to hold it open. Then we rang the bell. There was immediate movement from within. Footsteps. "Shit," I said, remembering I didn't have the briefcase. I snatched it from Screamer. Another few moments passed. We were probably being stared at through the spyhole. I raised the briefcase and smiled, Cartwright's friendly courier and his protection. Next came the sound of locks being worked. We hadn't guessed on the number of locks on the front door. That was okay—there were just two, the knob and the standard deadbolt. About what anyone would figure, though I could imagine Screamer guessing something cartoonish, like seven separate locks.

Just before the door cracked open, I shifted the briefcase to my left hand so my right could sneak into my right pocket. My fingertips caressed the head of the ball-peen hammer before moving to grasp the shaft. I had the tool out and brandished seconds later.

There was shouting as we bum-rushed through the opening. Screamer and Nathan pulled guns. The door opened to a small foyer and there was a staircase before us. Nathan pointed his gun straight up, like some SWAT guy. Screamer aimed his gun down the hallway. That left me to confront Leeweather, who'd been thrown to the ground, just as planned. As I shut the front door and tossed the briefcase aside, he cowered against the wall, hands over his face, blubbering about being betrayed by Cartwright. He really might have guessed such a thing was bound to happen.

"Lower your hands so I can see your face," I said. Then: "No—*wait*. Guys: eye color. Blue or brown? Honest to God, I don't know. I guess blue."

"Brown."

"Green," Screamer said.

"Okay. *Now* lower your hands."

I had to kick Leeweather to convince him. He stared at us. His eyes were very wide and very, very brown.

"Fuck me," I said, and swung the hammer. Like I'd told them, Leeweather was a *total* Picard, his head smooth and particularly egg-like as I cracked it. The first blow brained him so hard he slumped forward, his body's only remaining movement centered in his arms and hands, which jerked like someone plugged him up to a car battery. The center of his forehead had a bloody dent in it. I knew I had to hit him at least one more time. I didn't mean to pause, but I did and caught Screamer's eye. I could tell he was about to have us guess how many blows it would take. I don't know why the idea made me queasy.

I moved before Screamer got a chance to speak. (The right guess would have been five). Screamer and Nathan swept through the house while I cleaned the hammer head on Leeweather's shirt. They both returned. "Looks like no one else is home," Nathan said.

"Then let's go," I said.

"*What?* Are you forgetting about the game?"

"Like I said, Screamer, it was just to pass time. We can't hang around."

"You said *half.*"

I sighed. "I don't want half. It was a joke."

Screamer's hand closed over mine as we both reached for the doorknob. "Mighty generous of you—assuming you win. But I've been doing some counting while I went through the house. You're down three points to me, and five to Nathan. We've still got more than twenty guesses to confirm."

I looked at Nathan for support but he wasn't giving it. "You're the one who said half."

"Unbelievable," I muttered as Screamer took the lead, moving through the house, calling out guesses I didn't even remember. We entered the kitchen. The walls were yellow.

"That's a point for Nathan. He said goldenrod. Now let me see. One, two, three...."

"What the hell are you doing?"

"Counting the electrical outlets."

"We had a fucking guess about the number of electrical outlets? I don't remember that."

"Four. Damn. No one gets a point."

"Wait a minute," Nathan said. "Open the cabinet below the sink."

"Why?"

"The garbage disposal has to be plugged into something."

Screamer opened the door and squatted. He let out a gleeful holler. "*Five.* Point for me."

The game intensified as we moved room to room. The lead changed several times, and suddenly my point total started building. I thought I might have the game won after all, but I hadn't reckoned on how many guesses we'd actually made. Screamer remembered them all: how many bedrooms, how many closets, how many toilets, how many towels and washcloths—even how many rolls of toilet paper (six). Screamer and Nathan pulled well ahead of me. Screamer was up one point when we entered Leeweather's bedroom and to search for sex toys.

All we found was a black, ten-inch dildo.

"I believe that puts me ahead of you by one point, Screamer," Nathan said, slapping the dildo over and over again into his open palm. "Excuse the gloating. I'm just feeling cocky."

Screamer's eyes bulged in his flushed face. "We're not done yet."

Nathan grinned. "No? We've been through the whole house now. What the hell else could we possibly have guessed on?"

"Don't you remember—boxers or briefs?"

I groaned as we returned to the foyer. They looked at me, and I said I sure as hell wasn't going to inspect a corpse's underwear. Screamer shoved me aside and knelt. His broad back blocked my view. Then his shoulders shook, and he erupted into a fit of laughter. Such a thing was tough to interpret when it came to Screamer. It could mean disappointment and bitter irony or supreme triumph in equal measure. Nathan's hangdog expression told me he'd lost.

"Well, which is it?" I said. "Boxers or briefs?"

"Panties," Screamer said, standing and whirling upon us in a rush of glory. "That makes us *even!*"

"Son of a bitch," Nathan said. "What do we do for a tie-breaker?"

"Nothing." Screamer looked at me. "He owes us *each* a half."

I laughed at the ridiculousness of the assertion. "That'd leave me with nothing."

"You're very good with numbers," Nathan said.

"How is that fair? *I'm* the one who actually did the killing."

They were unmoved.

"Look, guys," I said.

Screamer pointed his gun at me. "We're not leaving until we have an agreement about what you owe us."

"Nothing was said about a tie. If anything, you should each just get fifty percent of my half."

"Half of a half isn't half," Nathan said. And now he too aimed his gun at me.

I remembered Leeweather's final gasps about betrayal. I didn't want to be in his place saying essentially the same thing anytime soon, but I also damn well couldn't afford to lose my entire fee. It wasn't that I'd rather die than settle up on a bet, it's that I likely *would* die if I didn't get at least half of my payment. I was overdue on loans from people who'd been sharpening their knives for some time now.

There wasn't any point pleading with Screamer and Nathan for compassion. There also wasn't any reason to play along. We'd be driving straight back to Cartwright, and they'd demand my fee from him on the spot.

"Okay, fine," I said, and started for the door. Nathan lowered his gun first, and when I saw that I whipped the hammer out and tagged him in the wrist with it. He yelled and staggered back. I should have kept going for the front door and took my chances with the night, but momentum turned me around. All I had was the stairs, and I launched myself forward. In my mind's eye, my back was a huge target. Screamer fired, but the slug hit me in the left calf. Hobbled, I turned the corner and kept going.

I escaped into Leeweather's bedroom and shut the door, locking it. Moments later the knob rattled. Then the whole door shook as both Nathan and Screamer tried to kick it open. But the door was good, sturdy oak, and not your typical hollow core Home Depot shit. I had some time.

Not much, though. The window revealed a straight drop. No chance there. I really had no options at all. Already bleeding on the carpet, I might as well let them kill me in the open. It was a better fate than being shot cowering in a closet. As I looked at the unmade bed, however, I noticed something was off. I pushed the mattress back and found a shotgun tucked between it and the box spring.

It was loaded.

Damn. I'd been awarded a point earlier when we couldn't find any evidence of a gun in the house. I had no idea which of them had guessed Leeweather would have a shotgun, but I could tell them the tie had been broken after all.

Then Nathan said, "Make this easy on yourself, asshole, and open up. What are you going to do? All you've got is that fucking hammer."

Guess again, I thought, taking aim at the door and waiting.

There were other ways to break a tie.

# STRAIGHT TO THE TOP

"Get in."

Mallard was shoved into the backseat. Weasel Face, the goon who manhandled him, climbed in beside him and shut the door. He rapped his pistol against the tinted glass partition in front of the passenger compartment. Right away, the engine started.

"Guess I shouldn't bother with the seat belt, right?" Mallard asked. He knew Weasel Face was Mr. Robert's number one thug and this ride wasn't for fun.

Weasel Face didn't look at him. "Keep making jokes, smart guy."

"You're going to use a gun, right? A gun's a sure thing."

*Son, only suckers bet on a sure thing.*

"Not this time, Dad," Mallard said softly.

This remark drew Weasel Face's attention. Whatever the man's real name was, Weasel Face still fit better. Jesus Christ, what a pointy mug.

"Are you calling me your dad?" Weasel Face pressed.

"No."

"Then why the hell did you say it?"

"I always talk to my dad when I'm in trouble."

"Talk to him?"

"It's just a thing. When my dad and I can't talk in person, I talk to him in my head."

Weasel Face raised his eyebrows. "Daddy going to leak out with your brains, then?"

*Changed my mind, Son. From the sound of things, definitely bet on a gun.*

They sat in the back of a black Lincoln Continental. 2017 model, must have cost around $45K—a good quarter of Mallard's gambling losses this month alone. The driver had the radio on a Top 40 station.

"Is this Ariana Grande? I don't want to die to this. I want to hear real music," Mallard said.

"What's real music to you, Mr. *Duck?*"

Mallard considered the question and realized he couldn't think of an actual song. He knew only the soft, stereotypical vibraphone notes found in the background of casino high-roller tables. Christ, what he'd give for about five minutes of that ambience now. It might actually calm his nerves.

When Mallard didn't answer, Weasel Face said, "You know what's real music to *me?*"

*Jesus, this guy. Four to one odds he actually says—*

"The screams of your victims?"

Smiling didn't help Weasel Face's expression.

"Executions are like guitar solos to me. Some deaths, they just go on too damn long. Think of Neil Young and 'Down by the River.' It's overindulgent. I appreciate guitar solos that capture everything in two minutes. Slash is a good example. He solos, it's done and the song moves on. That's the kind of scream and moan I like. If I want to hear Neil Young, I shoot the kneecaps first."

"And if you want to hear Slash?"

Weasel Face pointed to his stomach.

Mallard pressed his lips together. "Where's our game?"

"There's a little spot up in the mountains I like."

*What is it with psychopaths and little spots up in the mountains?*

"I don't know, Dad."

"Quit talking to yourself like that, Duck. It's fucking

creepy." He tapped the muzzle of his pistol against Mallard's chest. "And I don't like creepy."

Mallard went quiet. He stared out the window. The glass was tinted, making the night even blacker. The ride was smooth, but as the Lincoln wound its way up the crooked mountain roads, the constant side-to-side motion made him queasy.

"Oh God," he said.

"What?"

"Mr. Roberts shouldn't have bothered taking me to dinner before sending you after me."

"He's a gentleman. Even treats you to a last meal."

Mallard hunched forward. "That last meal is about to be all over the backseat."

Weasel Face twisted toward him. "Don't you dare."

"Or what? You'll kill me?"

"I'll go Neil Young on your ass."

Mallard hunched forward. "Spill my blood all you want, but my guts are about to spill themselves."

Weasel Face leaned forward and tapped on the glass partition. It cracked open.

"Pull over," Weasel Face said to the back of the driver's head.

"There's no side to pull over to. We're halfway up the mountain."

"You want to be the one to tell Mr. Roberts his car's covered in puke?"

The partition closed. The car veered right and slowed.

Mallard made a retching sound and clutched his stomach. His peripheral vision caught Weasel Face inching away.

*The psychopath is squeamish. Who knew?*

The car stopped. Weasel Face locked gazes with him. "Get out. I'll wait."

"You're not worried I'll run?"

Weasel Face gestured toward the back window. Mallard saw endless darkness beyond the bloody glow of the brake lights and understood at once.

"You going to puke or what?"

"I think if I just sit here the nausea will pass."

They waited. The music must have become too much for even Weasel Face, who beat on the partition again.

"Change that shit," he ordered when the glass lowered. "An old guy like you should be into the Beatles or something."

The glass rose again. The music changed a few seconds later.

"Eagles," Weasel Face said. "That's more like it."

"I don't know them."

"Seriously? What the hell *do* you know?"

"Poker."

Weasel Face laughed. "You must know poker like you know the Eagles. Who taught you?"

"My dad."

"Does he exist anywhere besides your head?"

"He lives in New Jersey. Taught me to gamble in Atlantic City."

"Must have been a shit player, or you wouldn't be in this predicament."

Mallard forced a laugh. "You think I owe Mr. Roberts *money?*"

"I've never killed anyone yet who wasn't up to their neck in debt and excuses."

"So says Mr. Roberts."

A trace of suspicion entered Weasel Face's expression. "You saying Mr. Roberts is a liar?"

"How many guitar solos have you taken working for him?"

"Six."

"Bet they were all Jews like me."

"Maybe one was."

*You hear the note of caution in his voice, Son?*

"I hear it, Dad."

Weasel Face frowned. "Sure you're not schizo?"

"I don't know."

"What happens when you talk to your dad in person?"

"I don't. The dad in my head's a lot nicer than the real one."

"You're a strange duck. Maybe I'm doing you a favor."

"Some of what's between my dad and me is my fault. He taught me poker and craps and roulette and all of that when I was just ten. He taught me well, leading me to think he's this expert. And when I ask him about it, he tells that he sits on the State of New Jersey Casino Control Commission and he's got all of these connections and he's Mr. Big. Meanwhile we're living in this fleabag apartment. But I'm a kid at the time, what do I know? Then comes the day I stroll into the Borgata with some friends. It's my twenty-first birthday. First time I'm there because I'm legal, and who comes out of the service elevator pushing a mop bucket and wearing this janitor's outfit?"

"Your dad? That's hilarious." Weasel Face slapped his leg.

"We saw each other. Don't know whose face was redder. Don't know who was in more shock. And after that he hated me. I tried to tell him I didn't care. But it didn't matter. He'd been exposed as a fraud and couldn't deal with it. He felt like a failure."

"He was mopping the floor in a goddamn casino. Sounds like a loser to me."

"I wouldn't mind being in his shoes right now, cleaning the shit off some linoleum."

"You going to throw up or what?"

Mallard glanced down at his stomach. "No, I think I'm good now."

Weasel Face smacked the partition and shouted, "Let's go!"

*You're doing fine, Son. I believe in you.*

"Thanks, Dad."

The car accelerated.

Mallard took a careful glance at Weasel Face to guess what he might be thinking. A man doles his thoughts out before him like a deck of cards. The trick was getting him to play the right one.

"What was that shit about the Jews?"

"Sorry?" Mallard said.

"Don't play dumb. You asked if I'd killed any Jews. What if they were?"

"Mr. Roberts likes his Jew boys. Up to a point."

"What point would that be?"

"Puberty."

Weasel Face stared at him. Mallard shrugged and added, "Guess I was an exception to the rule."

Weasel Face's eyes darted back and forth like someone trying to see something that wasn't there.

"You're full of shit. I haven't been killing boys," he said.

"No, you've been killing men who helped him get boys. The men who figured they could make a nice penny turning it back on him for blackmail."

"Mr. Roberts isn't like that. Word would get out."

"It can't, thanks to you. What do you care anyway?"

"I've got standards. Mr. Roberts could be a faggot. Doesn't bother me. But a pedo? Fuck that."

Mallard chuckled. "Would you keep working for him if what I'm saying is true?"

"Don't know."

"So there's no problem killing gamblers in hock to Mr. Roberts, but there's a moral issue with greasing his humps? That's progressive."

Weasel Face scowled and slapped the partition. It lowered.

"Pull over."

"Why?" the driver said.

"I'm wasting this guy right here."

"But we're ten miles from the spot."

"I don't care. Pull over!"

The glass rose again.

*Shit, Son. This round's taken a bad turn.*

"Look, I'm sorry," Mallard said. "Dad just told me I shouldn't have lied to you."

"So you *are* lying about Mr. Roberts?"

"Of course I am."

"I knew Mr. Roberts wasn't fucking boys."

Mallard made an exaggerated sigh. "I can't say how happy I am for you."

"Happy?"

"You passed the test."

"What test?"

"Mr. Roberts doesn't like idiots. He put us into this situation to test your loyalty. But you need to call him now, okay?"

Weasel Face just stared.

"Go ahead," Mallard continued, adding a slight chuckle. "Seriously. Mr. Roberts is expecting it. He doesn't really want you to kill me."

"This guy," Weasel Face muttered toward the partition, as if the driver could hear. "Can you *believe* this shit?"

He rapped on the glass. This time it lowered about halfway. Mallard watched the driver making eye contact with Weasel Face in the rearview mirror.

"I'm still trying to find a place to stop. There hasn't been a shoulder."

"Then never mind. Just get us straight to the top."

"Yes, sir."

The partition closed again and the Lincoln accelerated, pressing Mallard into his seat. He swallowed. "You're going to call Mr. Roberts when we get there right? To confirm what I said?"

"Mr. Duck, you're just how Mr. Roberts described you."

"Oh?"

"He said you talked your way out of this trip a couple of times before and that you'd try talking your way out of it tonight. He said I shouldn't listen to a word. You're pretty good. But in this world, there are only two kinds of speech that get results: the whisper of cash and the shout of a gun."

*You got to know when to hold 'em, know when to fold 'em—*

"Jesus Christ, Dad. That's so cliché," Mallard said.

"So what's your dad really do? The one who's not in your head."

"He's a delivery driver."

Weasel Face laughed. "I guess that's a step up from being a janitor."

"A small one."

They were both thrown when the car suddenly jerked left. The glass lowered. "Sorry about that. Deer in the road."

"Watch what the fuck you're doing. You don't want to get Duck killed on the way to his execution, right?"

The partition closed again as Mallard watched Weasel Face settle back. "What if I told you I just lied about my father?"

"Wouldn't surprise me at all."

"What if I told you that Mr. Roberts is my father?"

Mallard backed up his assertion with a stare. He threw everything he had into it, Poker Face versus Weasel Face.

*Interesting play, Son. Mr. Roberts' garbage man isn't about to believe something so audacious at this point. But he might if you'd played the card earlier. You had him going just a little bit with that pedophile shit. You made it real enough in the guy's head to get him stirred up. At least for a minute. So tell me what that says about this guy?*

"He's got a button to push."

*Hell, everyone has at least one button. But this guy, he—*

"Doesn't trust Mr. Roberts."

Weasel Face said, "I trust him to pay me a lot for what I do."

"What if I could guarantee you more money?"

"Reality check, Duck. You're in this situation because you couldn't repay the money you owe Mr. Roberts."

"That's not true at all."

Once again Weasel Face proved that smiling added no charm to his looks. "Go on, tell me another story. Make it fast, though, because we'll be reaching the top soon."

"I owe Mr. Roberts about a hundred grand. But that's chump change to a man like him. He wouldn't have me killed over it. It's not that I can't pay him back, it's that I'm not going to pay him back. Big difference."

"Dumb strategy."

"The problem was with tactics, not strategy. Owing someone money and finding a way to not pay it back is always worth the effort. I figured a man like Mr. Roberts would have some incriminating shit *somewhere*. So I got a buddy to help me run a phishing scheme on him. Totally worked. If his

Gmail account was his asshole, I'd have been his proctologist. I was up to my elbow in his private stuff."

"Yeah?" The excited lilt in Weasel Face's voice proved a pleasant surprise.

"Let's just say what I found would have him behind bars sharing a foot-long with Subway's Jared."

Weasel Face shook his head in disgust. "Not the pedophilia bullshit again."

"You can believe it or not. The point is I was looking for blackmail material and I thought I had it. Enough to cancel out my debt. The thing is I'd discovered too much. One ace would have been enough for my purposes. I came at Mr. Roberts with a handful of them, and in life it's possible to overplay a strong hand."

"You thought he'd do everything you wanted?"

"Between relieving my menial debt or going to jail, I figured he'd fold. Instead he called your ass."

"Texted, actually," Weasel Face said.

The road leveled out. The Lincoln slowed and stopped.

*Running out of cards to play, Son. You may have to try Roulette instead.*

Mallard laughed. "Yeah, Dad. Russian roulette."

"Need a revolver for that." Weasel Face jabbed his pistol. "This here is a Beretta, an automatic."

The partition descended all the way and the driver said, "We're here."

Weasel Face and Mallard got out. Weasel Face pointed his gun and motioned for Mallard to walk into the darkness.

"Get moving," he said.

"Dad was just saying I should have gone for roulette rather than poker. But it's a boring game," Mallard said as he walked away from the car.

"Wouldn't know. I don't gamble."

"Not even a little?"

"Not on nothin'. Not even the ponies."

Mallard looked up at the sky. A magnificent star field capped the world up this high. For just a moment, he thought he could raise his hands, spread his arms and take flight into the universe.

"That's a shame," he said, looking back at Weasel Face.

"Why? It's just wasting money."

"Oh, it's so much more than that."

Mallard saw a trail ahead of him in the moonlight and followed.

"That's good," Weasel Face said. "That's just the direction I want you to go. Nice acoustics up here for a guitar solo."

"Much more," Mallard continued. "Gambling is tension, and in the space of that tension you feel yourself wrestling with implications of fate and self-determination. *Luck* is the most powerful aphrodisiac in the world. It's the greatest prize."

*Keep talking, Son. Get it all out. Maybe you'll bore him to death and he'll forget to kill you.*

"That so?" Weasel Face said.

"Do you know what Napoleon used to ask about his generals?"

Weasel Face chuckled. "So now you're a history major?"

"He'd ask, 'Is he lucky?' Isn't that amazing? All the possible skills for a general to have, and Napoleon only cared about luck. But what it really says—"

Mallard heard footsteps behind him, closing space. He couldn't see exactly how much land he had ahead of him or where he might flee, though of course Mallard knew he wasn't running anywhere. Not at this point. But he kept walking.

"What it really says—"

"Well, spit it out, Duck. Tell me what it says."

"The illusion of being in control. No one ever is. Even a man like Mr. Roberts. We're all losers who think we have our hands on the steering wheel. But it's the road that determines whether we turn left or right, or keep it in the middle. The road was there before we were born."

"How very philosophical."

Mallard smiled into the dark. "The casino graduates a thousand doctorates a day."

"You can stop right there," Weasel Face said.

Mallard did. He stared up at the stars. Not a bad parting vision if it came to that.

"Any last words?"

*I'm never going to let you down, Son.*

"Just that I wished you'd gambled at least once. Because for all illusion, there comes a moment—a round—when you realize you *are* in control. When you know you've played your hand perfectly even if it wasn't your strongest, and everyone's in, and your hole card is the ace of all aces, and all the money is yours."

Mallard flinched when the gun fired. Weasel Face was right about the acoustics. The sound echoed magnificently, and worked such a strong effect on Mallard's mind that he felt the impact and collapsed to his knees.

He was still kneeling when the hand appeared before him.

He took it and was pulled to his feet, just as his father had done for him ever since Mallard could remember.

"Don't know which of us played that better, Dad," he said, and started working out the audio receiver in his ear. It was a pesky little thing that had been driving him nuts since he inserted it before dinner with Mr. Roberts. Weasel Face was crumpled on the ground, blood spreading beneath him.

Dad grinned and spoke into a little microphone concealed on his jacket. The words piped out of the receiver clearly—

"I did, of course," he said.

"But I was the one whose life was on the line," Mallard said.

"Well, I was the one who had to sit up front listening to you describe me as some sort of asshole. I got so pissed I almost ran the goddamn car off the road."

They looked down at Weasel Face.

"If that dumb bastard had any experience in the casinos, he'd have known the greatest threat comes from the employee who's been turned or compromised," Dad said.

"In an odd way, I think he was too personally loyal to even consider the idea. I really don't think he could have been bribed. Noble, I guess," Mallard said.

"More like stupid."

"It says something about the quality of men Mr. Roberts hires."

Dad raised his eyebrows. "Oh yeah? He was dumb enough to hire me as a chauffeur. Sorry, Son, but this guy's HR department isn't running any detailed background checks. Which is mighty lucky for both of us."

They started toward the Lincoln and Mallard gave a final glance at the stars. If they were just a little bit flashier, he could imagine himself inside some dome-capped gambling resort. He said as much to his dad.

"Get your head out of the clouds, son. Keeping your feet planted on the ground is the surest way to keep them from being planted under it. Got it?"

"I got it."

"Good," he said. They got into the car, Dad behind the wheel. He turned the ignition and the Lincoln started almost noiselessly. "Now let's go kill Mr. Roberts."

CPSIA information can be obtained
at www.ICGtesting.com
Printed in the USA
LVOW12s2330271117
557815LV00001B/121/P

9 780998 666747

# BLOOD BUSINESS

## CRIME STORIES FROM THIS WORLD AND BEYOND

EDITED BY

## MARIO ACEVEDO AND JOSHUA VIOLA

# CONTENTS FROM BEYOND

# CONTENTS FROM THIS WORLD

# EDWARD BRYANT

## BITTEN OFF

IN MY PROFESSIONAL LIFE, SOMETIMES THE SKY CLOUDS UP and pours. I sometimes bite off more than I can chew. I just didn't know that yet, but had just come from a meet with an old friend with Homeland Security. Too early in the day for crises, but he was in a big hurry, having been shanghaied into an emergency call-up to tackle the Z-class ultraMRSA epidemic, which the Feds now admitted to everyone but the public was crafted by man and showed no sign of slowing down.

"Let's see if I got that straight," I said. "It's a staph bug that gets into the tissue and cannibalizes its host faster than antibiotics can root it out. And even surgery doesn't keep up with it."

"That's about it," said Jake from Homeland.

"So why me?"

"Nobody I know is better at finding stuff out. Especially weird shit," Jake said. "God save my soul. And we're desperate." He mentioned my retainer.

"I'm in," I said. "Where do I start?"

"We know it's food-borne and blood introduced. CDC's figured out the first wave of victims shopped at natural grocery stores."

"Aha," I said. "Tofu."

"Not funny," said Jake.

I took the hint. It was time to leave.

But I had to ask. "Lone wolf or terror cell?"

"Pick one," said Jake. "Or both."

Even though my business card bills me as an independent public relations consultant, I still use the same office I worked out of as a P.I. As a matter of fact, I still work for some of the same clients I had as a gumshoe. That's "private investigator" for those of you who are too new school to know what I'm talking about. A dick with a piece but no badge.

My office is a fourth floor walkup in the old brownstone that used to house the grand Navarre Restaurant right in the heart of downtown. The steep, creaky stair flights serve as my exercise program as well as screening the health and announcing the approach of prospective clients. Not to mention bill collectors. Only process servers seem to have the stamina to make it all the way to my door without wheezing to catch their breath. The process servers I recognize by their natty silhouettes against the frosted glass of the door. If I remain quiet and perfectly still, eventually they go away. My office door pane holds an offshore drilling platform's worth of oily nose prints.

I always try to be in the office by a civilized hour—noon.

This morning I unlocked the door at 11:55 and poured more water into the Mr. Coffee. Unfortunately I had to use yesterday's filter and grounds. Or maybe it was the setup from the day before. What the hell. I slapped on two caffeine and one nicotine patch. I'd pretend it was a dark Brazilian blend and call it espresso.

While it perked with the guttural chugging of an aged sump pump, the carafe slowly filled with a fluid the evil shade of brown rarely seen outside a hazardous materials dump.

I checked for messages. Business had been a tad slow of late, other than the get-together with Jake from Homeland. Nothing on the answering machine other than a heavy breather who sounded in desperate need of a rescue inhaler.

Didn't think he (if it was a guy) would be calling me much longer.

The caller ID log noted half a dozen hang-up calls from the pay phone at Crazy Sid's, a dubious strip joint on East Colfax.

And there was nothing in the fax tray other than an incredibly obscene—not to mention racist, sexist, ageist, weightist, and intellectually pretentious hand-sketched cartoon from my insomniac old P.I. partner, Ray. I scanned it, tried not to snicker, then slipped it into a manila folder and filed it with all the other potential blackmail materials adrift in the bottom desk drawer.

Finally I fired up the ancient Ohio Scientific desktop and checked my email. There was only spam, and not a very high grade of that. Punching the delete key was like a five minute session of the most boring game of Asteroids ever. But at least I didn't have to think much, and that was good. I don't have that much higher cerebral function to spare, lord knows. Really, I mean why purchase Canadian Viagra and Indonesian knockoffs of Cialis online? If a live woman came with the order at no extra charge (and with free shipping), then it might be different.

The gray-market painkiller solicitations were a little more tempting. My right foot ached like hell, neuropathy notwithstanding. After the doc took off my pinkie toe, the one that was supposed to go "wee wee wee" all the way home, I begged unashamedly and he prescribed just enough Vicodin to run out about three days before the pain did. I've always suspected him of being a closet sadist.

Then I heard the steps on the stairs… Light and brisk—that wasn't the pattern of my usual lot. I perked up, even if Mr. Coffee didn't. Didn't sound like a collector, so I slipped the latch and retreated behind the desk.

The presumed and devoutly hoped-for client tapped on the frosted glass. The shadow on the pane at first suggested a slender macrocephalic. Then I realized the woman was wearing a hat. Unusual, these days.

"Come in," I called, rocking back in the old wooden

swivel chair. The spring groaned when I brought my brogans back flat on the floor when she appeared. I started coughing uncontrollably and acidic black coffee sprayed from my nose. I don't usually greet new clients in such a fashion, but this was clearly a special moment.

I admit it. As she entered my office, I stared.

"Are you Mr. Harker?" she said. I had never heard my name uttered by more perfect lips. They were full and shaded with the vivid crimson of fresh blood before it oxidizes to brown. Those lips framed a generous mouth and teeth shining white with the albedo of newly flensed bone.

I blotted the coffee on the front of my shirt with a paper towel without looking from that face. "It's Jack," I stammered. "Jack Lee Harker. Call me Jack."

She stopped in front of my desk and stared down at me, smiling, one hand resting on her hip, elbow akimbo. "Pleased," she said in a husky contralto. "I'm Lilith Janick. I am delighted to meet you, Jack Lee."

I would have been happy had the conversation just stopped there for a time. I couldn't help myself. I stared at those brilliant, deep emerald eyes alight with what I suspected were both intelligence and allure. Her nose was lightly freckled. Her hair curled down around her shoulders, a shining red that complemented those lips. Her nails were long and immaculately manicured, lacquered the same shade as those brilliant irises. I kept eye contact, knowing if I dropped my gaze much below her face I'd either turn to stone or say something truly unfortunate.

I believe she knew exactly what I was thinking, and I suspected she was gaining some mischievous delight.

"May I sit?"

I chivalrously lurched to my feet and pointed to the least decrepit of the two threadbare client chairs. "Yes, of course, please sit, Ms. Janick."

"Lilith," she said with a dazzling smile, gracefully sitting, and crossing her legs with a whisper of silk.

"Well, uh, Lilith," I said. "How may I be of service?"

Lilith smiled the kind of smile that just turns up the ends

of the mouth. "I won't hedge," she said. "I represent a group that's interested in helping improve their public image. We have already researched your life and career—particularly when you worked as a relatively unsuccessful detective."

That stung.

"We believe you possess a tolerance for diversity in the community."

"Actually," I said, "I can rarely afford to turn any client down."

"Your modesty is endearing." Lilith said.

"So," I said, "is this a particularly challenging group to represent?"

"I fear so," she answered.

"So it would be harder than, say, making sympathetic fascists, gay hillbillies, Tourette's syndrome talk show hosts, mass murderers paroled on a technicality, or day-care pedophiles?"

Lilith considered. "The pedophiles might be a bit more dicey."

Swell, I thought. I'd have to earn my money. "You might want to go with a larger firm with more staff and resources," I said.

"No, you're the one I—we—want. You're hungry. That's a good thing with us. Very good indeed."

I thought about that. I asked the obvious question. "So who's the group?"

"Later. I'd like to set up a meeting," Lilith said. "Might you be available ten o'clock tonight? River Edge Cemetery. The central tombs."

I stared at her. "A historic boneyard in the middle of the night? Are you nuts?"

"Are you superstitious?" she countered.

"No," I said. "But it's a little too melodramatic for words."

"It's what we want," she said, great seriousness in her voice.

"And if I dig in my heels?" I said.

Lilith smiled wider. "Jack Lee, how's your present cash flow?"

She had a point. I already had a job offer today but God only knew when the retainer might flow through the federal pipeline. "Okay," I said. "I'll be there. Ten tonight. Promptly."

Lilith stood, so I did too. "I look forward to seeing you then," she said. She turned toward the door but hesitated. "One final question."

"Shoot," I said.

"This isn't business," said Lilith. She cocked her head. "Do you ever get personally involved with your clients?"

The questioned stunned me into silence.

Then she turned through the doorway, closed the door behind her, and was gone.

I kept staring, her image burning in my imagination as her steps on the stairs diminished. Finally I shook myself back to reality and started making a mental shopping list beginning with extra batteries for my old eight-cell flashlight.

On the way home from my local hardware store, I decided to give the government a break so I stopped for an unpaid look-see at Green Acres, a natural foods market I'd driven past maybe a thousand times without stopping. What I found was not unlike my usual supermarket with a few significant differences. Most of the brands were unfamiliar and the prices were generally higher by about twenty percent. The produce looked great, but tomatoes and fruits and such weren't as uniform as I was accustomed to. It all looked more like it had just come out of an actual garden.

I paid special attention to the meat section. It was a cursory survey to see if I could spot psychotic nutballs or crazed terrorists plunging syringe needles into plastic wrapped bison chops or turkey breasts. I could see this was a security nightmare. My understanding was that the deadly contaminants didn't have to be massive. Not finding any obvious evidence of a an insane criminal conspiracy, I grabbed a take-out cup of expensive, dark-but-freshly-brewed, avowedly organic, fair-trade coffee from a Starbucks clone in one corner of Green Acres, and headed home.

Still, something niggled at that dark spot in my mind as I walked through the store among all those stacked and binned

products that promised good health. I had a feeling, no, *I knew* I had to come back to this store.

Ten at night and the iron gate to River Edge was, of course, not only closed but chained shut. I found a section of the two centuries-past brick wall that had crumbled, so I just walked ten feet down, stepped over the pile of bricks and into the nineteenth century graveyard.

River Edge was dead silent—no surprise there. In the background I heard the murmur of the river and the hum of the Interstate beyond. The city lights glittered on the near horizon.

I visited the cemetery in daylight, so I knew exactly where the central tombs were.

Some of the city's most prominent citizens were planted there the century before last. Some of the older families still buried their dead there. That brought a perk of generous grants for the upkeep of this beautiful but decaying old location.

I wasn't overly noisy as I approached the central tombs, but I didn't want to announce my arrival until I was ready. Some habits die hard. That's why my trusty .38 special was fully loaded and tucked into the shoulder holster beneath my windbreaker.

I saw the flicker of what I took to be candles set on the stones ahead.

Then I saw the figures—maybe a dozen—gathered around the flat surface of a ground-level crypt. I also saw a dismembered body lying forlornly on the stone table.

I was close enough, even in the flickering glare, to recognize the face of the inarguably deceased.

"Christ on a crutch!" I gasped.

"Actually a recently dead city councilman on a spit," said Lilith Janick's voice from a point behind my left ear. I jumped and reflexively reached for my gun. Arms like steel bands grabbed my elbows and held me motionless.

"Not to worry, Jack Lee," Lilith said, moving into my range of vision. She wore a dark hooded robe, but I still saw her

emerald eyes glittering in the night. "Nothing will happen to you. We just want you to watch for a bit."

The other hooded figures dipped to the stone table and began devouring the deceased city councilman. It wasn't so much like feral wolves feeding on a gutted moose as it was the ravenous but exceedingly polite guests as a traditional Hawaiian luau. True, the eaters did tear the joints loose with their fingers, but then they scrupulously licked those fingers clean, and chewed with their mouths closed.

When the councilman was gone and his bones picked clean, the diners policed the area. The separated bones went into a clean burlap bag, the candles were snuffed, and Lilith, licking her lips a final time, came back to me and said, "Sorry to sup without extending you an invitation to partake, but I suspect that would have been an empty gesture."

What could I say? I nodded.

Lilith leaned unexpectedly toward me and kissed me full on the lips. I realized it was fulfilling a fantasy I hadn't quite admitted to myself yet—well, other than the smell of corrupted flesh that flooded my nostrils. The politico had, I recalled, died two weeks past.

"Sorry," Lilith said, drawing back. "You're so darned cute I couldn't help myself." She sighed and added, "You came to talk. We'll talk. But first I need to floss. And if you need a snack, I can get you that too." She glanced at the guys still securing my arms. "Take him to the Apple Tree," she said. "I'll be along directly."

I started to lick my lips, then thought better of it. I really wasn't hungry at all. But, heaven help me, I wanted her to kiss me again.

The Apple Tree was a rustic all-night diner across the river from the graveyard, through the trees, and closer to the Interstate. While we waited for Lilith, I sat tightly wedged between my two caretakers on the side of the red vinyl-clad booth facing the front door. The big guys doffed their robes and handed

them to a confederate back in the graveyard. Aside from being on the WWF large side, both gentlemen were dark-eyed with square jaws and Slavic features. I introduced myself but no one reciprocated. Nobody said much. No one ordered.

After about ten minutes, Lilith came in, accompanied by an older man and woman dressed in dark formal clothing. Everyone had ditched their robes and looked like normal folks out for coffee and a piece of pie on a typical Wednesday night in late August.

The older woman slid in first on the other side, then Lilith, then the older gentleman. When all were settled, Lilith leaned across the table and planted another sensational kiss on me. I felt her tongue run lightly along my lips. Her mouth tasted sweet and a bit minty.

"Better?" she said.

"Uh, yes," I had to answer. "Much."

"Flossing is half my life," said Lilith brightly. She sighed. Then the conversation got serious. Lilith introduced the couple bracketing her: her mum and dad. Mr. and Mrs. Janick. The silent bodybuilders on either side of me were her brothers, Vlad and Phil. I tried to take this all in with equanimity.

Then came the killer.

"My family has always held back in the cultural shadows," Lilith said. "Even in the old country. But this is the twenty-first century. We want to come out of the closet, as it were. Out of the tomb, actually. We want effective public representation." She stopped and the silence lengthened uncomfortably.

"Okay," I said. "Specifically now, who am I representing?"

The parents exchanged glances.

"Ghouls," Lilith said. "We're an extended family of ghouls."

"Ghouls," I repeated, sounding foolish in my own ears. "Like, uh, cannibals?"

"Don't be silly," said Lilith's mom quickly. She sounded like anyone's mom from suburbia. Well, perhaps suburban Bratislava. "We kill no one for food."

"We scavenge," said Dad. He sounded even more old-world.

"Ghouls eat only corrupted flesh," said Lilith. "For ages

we've evolved to be biological opportunists rather than active predators."

After a moment I said, "I see some major image challenges here. I've got to think about this. You know, consider the options?"

"But you will do it?" said Mum. I noted the hope in her voice.

What the hell, I thought. "I'll try," I said. "There are plenty of challenges in this project. But I still think you need higher-powered help."

"No," said Lilith. "I have faith in you." I watched as she unstrung the tangled gold chain from around her neck and handed me the large, ornate pendant. "It opens," she said softly.

I took my cue and unclicked the pendant. I stared at the contents. A chill ran through my gut. "Is this what I think it is?" Inside the pendant was something black and dry and a bit withered.

She nodded cheerfully. "It's your toe, gangrene and all," Lilith said. "I claimed it from the surgical waste at the hospital. It's what I then used to track you down. It's a talent of mine. I simply couldn't bring myself to eat it."

"I wouldn't either," I said fervently.

"No, what I mean is, I can tell this is nearly a holy relic. Ghoul senses are quite acute. With this sample I can tell what kind of gentle person you truly are. My sense of taste, my brain, my heart, all tell me you are a truly righteous man."

I wasn't quite sure what to say. I remembered my mother's long-ago advice for almost any social situation. "Thank you," I said. "But it tells you I can solve your family's problem?"

She nodded solemnly, then flashed a smile that could pool a tallow candle. It gave me an amazing sense of well-being and confidence. Maybe I *could* do this thing.

"Still no guarantees," I said, pulling back. "But I'll try. Give me a few days. We'll talk."

All the Janicks exchanged glances and smiled. The brothers Vlad and Phil even grinned. Then everyone raised their hands above the Formica table top, crooked their fingers, and waited

as though anticipating the downbeat from the maestro. A slight nod from Mr. Janick and they began to drum. It was amazing. Each had an individual rhythm, but all were complementary, weaving in and out, augmenting and then diminishing to a triumphant crescendo. Jazzy, I thought, with a touch of New Orleans funeral. Tough nails. The subsequent silence deafened. I just stared. At the far end of the diner, a young couple started tentatively to clap, then trailed off. I think they were genuine tourists. The ones I took to be Apple Tree regulars just sipped their java.

The waitress had been hovering discreetly to the side. Finally she came up to the table and said, "Who all's ready for pie and coffee?"

I sincerely hoped nobody ordered baby back ribs.

Pie and coffee it was.

I realized I was glad to order coffee I hadn't brewed myself.

But I passed on the pie.

The next morning I called Lilith and she seemed glad to hear from me. I asked her to meet me for what else?—coffee and gave her directions to Green Acres.

She had already arrived when I got there and was seated at a table down by the produce section. I looked briefly to the side where a young man with swarthy skin, squinty eyes, and curly black hair was busily stocking bins with fruits and vegetables and fungi. Only a glance and I discounted him as a menace to society.

Lilith and I exchanged smiles that lasted slightly too long for polite decorum. "Question," I said.

She inclined her face quizzically.

"That thing last night at the Apple Tree," I said, "when you all drummed on the table with your nails? What *was* that?"

"You didn't like that?"

"I've never heard anything like it."

She laughed. "It's the sound of approval from my people. Our nails are important to us."

I said, "Do you spend all your time with flossing and manicures?"

Lilith said, "I know that must make us sound vain." Her voice turned serious. "The nails. Do you know my people served an important role in your Civil War?"

"How so?"

"They volunteered particularly in the surgical corps and served as doctors and nurses. Strong, durable nails were essential."

"Why?" I suspected I knew the answer.

"For scooping.'"

I decided not to order lunch.

"I think I've got a strategy." I told her. She looked pleased and nodded encouragingly. "Fortunately," I said, "I've finally listened to my friends and upgraded from my vintage 400 baud acoustic linked modem. I'm amazed not only by what I can find on the Internet, but how fast I can find it."

"Even I can see the wisdom in that," said Lilith. "And I have learned to call the digital gestalt something other than the Interweb."

"The hook," I said. "Ready?"

She nodded, her expression eager.

I said, "'Give the gift of meat.'"

Lilith raised an eyebrow.

"Well first we leave out the grave robbing and all that sketchy stuff. The plan is to present ghouls as the greatest humanitarians of the twenty-first century. Maybe even the third millennium. Not to be overly modest."

"Okay," said Lilith, "and that would be done how?"

I practiced my upbeat voice. "First I thought about ghouls taking a green path—you know, becoming an acceptable alternative to conventional burial or cremation. In short, to preserve arable land and thus to help solve world hunger."

Lilith chimed her charming laugh. "Well, a solution to global *ghoul* hunger."

"Yeah, I know, I know," I said. "But human burial customs carry a lot of historical baggage. That's when I tried a different

tack." I smiled my most significant smile, and she picked up on it immediately. "I'm neither as naive nor as outright stupid as I know I sound."

"Thank goodness," she said. "I was starting to worry."

I realized I was smiling a bit too much. Too much like the Cheshire Cat. When things come together, while it's not a moment of blinding satori, the binding together of synchronistic bits is mighty satisfying. I could see the picture coming into focus and Lilith was the catalyst. Almost there…

"You devil," she said, grinning. "You borrowed from your life. Type One diabetes? The long-term side effects? Neuropathy? Limb amputations? Gangrene?"

"That's part of it." I couldn't help but stare at her gold pendant. I knew my absent pinkie toe was still inside.

"Will our lives be sustainable on so limited a food source?"

I shook my head. "Practically speaking? Probably not. But think for a moment. What's this year's hot pandemic?"

She looked blank.

"Mersa," I said triumphantly. I spelled the acronym out. "MRSA. The nastiest of the staph infections. It's an opportunistic and highly aggressive bacterial infection that spreads like wildfire, and it's deadly. There are some great antibiotics that are highly effective, but not invariably. And timeliness is critical."

Lilith looked like she was waiting for another shoe to drop. Actually, I knew, it was an army boot. "So?" she said.

I said, "Pardon me while I violate national security." I gave her the rundown on my recent meeting with Jake from Homelamd. "The epicenter of the aggressive outbreak of the new staph seems to be right here in River City. The bug is called Z-class ultraMRSA. It's hugely opportunistic, aggressive, and looks like it's ready to gobble up the human species."

"And you got a juicy new assignment," she said. "So what are you doing? All I really know is you're slurping gallons of decent coffee in natural grocers."

"I will share a secret."

She cocked an eyebrow. "More secret than the prospective end of the world as we know it?"

"I'm *quite* lucky," I continued. "I admit it makes me lazy."

"Ah," Lilith said with a beaming smile. "You are the lazy crocodile. You lie on the warm sandbank with your sharp-toothed jaws wide. The prey walks past with little suspicion and those jaws snap shut. You earn your living. The mad terrorist is thwarted. My commission to you is completed. And this all snaps together how?"

"The pattern is still weaving itself," I said. "It's not all neat and tidy. But it's coming along. We're almost there. Be patient."

"I'm not a patient woman," said Lilith. "There's an old cartoon by a man named Callahan. Two vultures perch on the lone branch of a dead tree in the desert. One bird says to its fellow, 'To hell with this patience, let's go out and kill something.'"

"I sympathize," I said, "but I must again counsel a bit more waiting. The synchronistic little bits are circling in closer and faster." We both stared down philosophically at our cooling mugs of coffee.

I looked up and surveyed two Green Acres employees grooming and restocking the store's lush shelves of fruits and produce. "I was going to mention," said Lilith sunnily, "that neither of my parents is opposed to intermarriage."

Now that, I thought, is *not* random.

Time to close the deal. "Don't you believe I can work miracles?"

"You are adorable," she said. "Before I know it, Jack Lee, you'll have me eating out of your palm."

That one I had to think about.

I'd been hoping just for a kiss.

∴∴∴

The following morning we again rendezvoused at Green Acres in the crisp mid-morning. I had not yet told Lilith that my faithful, synchronistic dice seemed to be lining up. You sound a little too full of yourself if you casually inform someone you really want to impress that you're expecting to save the world before lunch. I entered Jake from Homeland's direct number on speed-dial and arranged my new Smart Phone on the table

right beside my steaming first mug of Wake Up Little Susie brand elephant-processed South Asian coffee. Lilith hadn't wanted to try it yet, but I figured why the hell not? I sensed a big payday coming up soon.

I looked over at the fresh produce and saw the staffers restocking the shelves yesterday were nowhere in evidence. Now there was just a single white guy with no store apron, slightly older, cheerfully spritzing the intact new pyramid of pineapples. The pointed leaves at the top of each fruit shined like fresh cutlery. The new guy looked absolutely normal. He had brown hair, bright blue eyes, and wore an utterly bland expression. He didn't meet my eye but smiled.

"Time," I said just loud enough for Lilith to hear as I picked up my phone and thumbed the speed-dial key.

"Just one?" Jake said without salutation.

"Yep," I said.

"Keep your position. If things go south, just keep your head down 'til the shooting stops."

"All will go fine," I said.

The circuit went dead. I reached across the table and put my hand across Lilith's. I thought I could hear helicopters and looked up, expecting to see battle-armored commandoes rappelling down ropes through the morning-lit skylights. Instead the market doors burst open and in rushed a crowd of efficient guys in what appeared to be hazmat outfits, some with guns and others with what appeared to be medical gear. Two large men grabbed Mr. Normal's arms while a third held a gun to his head. A fourth plucked the spritzer from his hand and stuffed it into a plastic bag. A couple of techs slid something akin to a Christmas tree storage bag over the pyramid of pineapples and snugged it tight at the bottom. Then a woman with a megaphone ordered us all to vacate the premises. With a great deal of mumbling, we all followed orders. I took Lilith by the hand and used my other to grab the mug of Wake Up Little Susie. I wasn't about to abandon a coffee serving touted to be a peak experience of my whole caffeine life.

All manner of law enforcement types were in the parking

lot dividing bystanders into small groups. Jake from Homeland came up to us and said, "Take off. I'll catch up with you later." As he turned away he looked back and flashed a grin at us both. "She's cute."

Lilith raised her chin and kissed my cheek. "Are dates with you always this exciting?"

"No," I said honestly.

"But the world is saved?"

"The hardest work starts now," I said. "The press releases, the media conferences, the internet memes, endless interviews, and all the photo ops, all the—forgive the phrase—viral campaign. Part of my agreement with Jake from Homeland involves crediting your family with this whole event today—and that's important because this whole terrorist event has reached a point of criticality where this new plague is going to multiply exponentially. Only the ghoul population will be able to stop it. Are you ready to woman up?"

"Yum," Lilith said.

I took that as a yes.

ALYSSA WONG

# A CLAMOR OF BONES

THREE MONTHS AFTER I DUMPED WHAT WAS LEFT OF DETECTIVE
Callaghan's body into the San Francisco Bay, Jun phoned in
with another job for me. "There's a girl," he said.

There was always a girl with Jun. "Okay," I said.

"Ming Ho Yu's daughter disappeared last Monday. Yu tells
me the San Francisco PD did a cursory investigation, but I
mean, it's Chinatown. You know how it is with gwailo and
anything south of Broadway. If it's not in English or for sale,
they couldn't give less of a shit."

"So you want me to find her," I said, and flipped the
contents of my frying pan. My lunch was almost ready, and
the scent of fried lapcheong and fresh, steamed rice filled my
tiny apartment.

"I do," said Jun. "Yu is a big player on the city council.
We find the kid—or convince him we do, whatever—it'll be
a big windfall for us." He cleared his throat. He was always
smoking those shitty knockoff Marlboros smuggled over from
the mainland. "Anyway. Dead or alive, make sure we get her."

I knew the Yu girl. She was ten years old, if that. Last Lunar
New Year, she'd smiled at me through the parade crowd, gold
foil flowers in her hair. "You got it, boss."

"There's just one thing." Jun paused. "I don't like it, and
you're not gonna, either."

"Tell me," I said.

He did.

"Are you fucking kidding me?" My lapcheung was burning, but I didn't give a shit. "Who the hell put him back together?"

"Look, the real problem here," said Jun, "is that when Ming Ho's kid went missing, so did a shit ton of the money in Callaghan's bank account. The money belonging to the Elder Brothers." *The reason we had you murder him* went unsaid but not unheard.

"Well, shit," I said. "I didn't know dead men could make cash withdrawals."

"They shouldn't be able to. And therein lies the issue." Another crackling breath through the phone speakers. "We had a deal, An Mei. Assuming you're not lying to me about sawing Callaghan into chunks like you did the others—"

"I'm not," I said.

"—then either some other deadtalker is encroaching on your territory, or Callaghan wasn't as much of a corpse as you thought he was. Fix it, or the Elder Brothers will."

Fucking hell. I hung up the phone. I'd have to take lunch to go.

He was still where I'd left him, thank god.

"So what's this I hear about you and the Yu girl?" I said to the pieces of Detective Callaghan. I'd called him up by tugging on the fine strings of power I'd left hooked into each bit of him. They were the same strains of power that kept his pieces motoring slowly across the floor of the San Francisco Bay like disconsolate crabs. I'd figured it would make finding bodies harder if they kept shifting locations after being dumped. The magic, plus the concrete bricks shrink-wrapped to each body part, kept the evidence from resurfacing at inopportune times.

This was not one of those times, and Detective Callaghan was in pretty rough shape. I had carefully laid each piece on the pier in rows, but some parts were lost causes. The fish had gotten to him even through the shrink wrap, and the flesh of his fingers and toes, along with the soft tissue on his face, were gone. The skin that remained had a blistered, cracked texture.

Cold Pacific water and a dark environment helped preserve him a bit, but…I frowned. Something didn't feel right.

"The Yu girl," I repeated, and tugged on the strings of power again.

This time his voice filtered through my consciousness. *Go to hell.*

I took a delicate bite of lapcheong from the Tupperware on my lap. It was still warm, thankfully. Detective Callaghan stank, but that was nothing new. "Someone said they saw you walking around with her a week ago. Which is funny, because last I saw you, you weren't going anywhere."

*You did this to me,* he snarled. I shrugged. I'd done a good job of it, too. *Bitch. Cunt.*

As he ranted, I held my chopsticks in my teeth and picked up one of his arm segments. The plastic had been carefully wrapped just as I'd left it, but it looked newer and cleaner than it should have been for having spent three months underwater while wrapped around a corpse. Too new.

"Someone's been digging you up, huh?"

Silence. Bingo.

I put the arm down. "Really. Who was it?" I peeled the plastic wrap from the arm and peered more closely at it. My power was there, but someone else's threads were definitely there too. Thin as floss, pale, pulsing. Unfamiliar, but I'd never been good at reading other deadtalkers' power. "I swear to god if it was Chen I'm going to ruin every one of his shipments for the next six months."

*It wasn't one of your kind*, said Detective Callaghan. A sneer curled through his voice. *None of you tattooed Chinese thugs.*

"Huh." No one I knew well, then. "Someone you recognize?"

*As if I'd tell you.*

I chewed my lip and snapped my Tupperware shut. Fair enough. "You won't have to. I'll figure it out eventually. In the meantime, why don't we go for a walk?"

His voice sounded wary as I tucked my lunch away. *What do you mean? Wait—*

I plucked one of his remaining finger bones from the soggy mess that used to be his hand. After wiping it gingerly on a paper napkin, I put it in my purse. It fit nicely in the smallest inner pocket.

The rest of Detective Callaghan went back into the bay. *Fuck you,* he snarled. *This is sick. Let me go.*

I rolled a leg segment unceremoniously into the water. It sank obediently beneath the waves. "Let's go downtown," I said. Maybe I didn't know the deadtalker who had raised Callaghan from the bottom of the bay. But maybe someone I knew might have an idea of where I should look if I wanted to find them. And when it came to gossip and magic, I knew just the people to bribe to get the answers I needed.

Two hours before opening, the White Dragon was appropriately quiet. Only Jeremiah was behind the counter, and Lan was sweeping the floor beneath the pool tables. Jeremiah's sleeves were rolled down, but Lan's tattoos pulsed and glimmered with power when he waved me over.

"Yeah, I saw Callaghan with the kid," Jeremiah said when I asked. He frowned, scratching the buzzed patch of hair behind his ear. "I thought you took care of him back in January."

"I did. Somebody didn't like my work, apparently, and thought it'd be cute to dig him up again." I plopped down on a seat and waved Lan over. I wanted him to be in on the conversation too. "So I got two things to ask you."

"Hey, I didn't fucking touch him." Lan held his hands up. "You know I don't fuck with your territory, An Mei. I stick to the Tenderloin."

"I know it wasn't you." I dropped Callaghan's finger bone on the bartop. Jeremiah grimaced.

"Do you have to, An Mei?"

"I'll wipe it down later," I said. "Lan, take a look at this. Does the signature feel like any you've seen?"

Lan picked up the bone and squinted. Callaghan hissed.

"Huh." Then Lan licked a wide stripe across it, from joint to joint.

"Jesus Christ, you deadtalkers! That's disgusting."

"No, no, I got it!" said Lan, his eyes bright with excitement. "I *have* seen this. A couple of stray cats over by Main Street were wrapped in power that tasted just like this. Whoever done this, they're young. Strong, though."

I scrubbed Callaghan's finger bone on my shirt and tucked it back in my purse. The dead detective was muttering again, but I ignored him. "How young are we talking?" I asked.

"Maybe twelve? I put a puppy back together when I was that age." Lan sighed. "He fell apart a few days later. I wasn't very good at it yet."

I'd started young, too. But like Lan, who was twenty now and had spent a couple years wandering the streets until Jeremiah took him in, I hadn't come from a household that wanted a child who played with corpses. Deadtalking was rare, but nearly every one I met fled home as a kid and survived, like a feral animal, in alleys and on doorsteps until one of the tongs scooped them up.

"So we're looking for a kid," I said, thinking about the Yu girl and her bright smile, and the soft, proud look on her father's face as he lifted her on his shoulders so she could watch the lion dance during the Lunar New Year parade. Would he still be proud of her if she started bringing dead things home?

"I'd bet money I don't have on it." Lan held out both hands, fingers crooked. "So, if you're done with that bone?" he said, a bit too hopeful.

"Let's not get carried away. Second question." I turned to Jeremiah. "You said you'd seen Callaghan and the Yu girl. What else did you see?"

"It was after one in the morning. I remember thinking it was way too late for a little girl to be out." Jeremiah grunted. "Then I saw the corpse walking, and I figured I'd better mind my own business. They had a pretty, dark-haired girl with them, too."

"Another kid?"

"No. About Lan's age. She looked like she was one of those Pacific Hill types, the kind with rich parents and not enough hobbies to keep her busy."

Callaghan stirred uneasily in my bag. Interesting.

I slid a folded fifty over to Jeremiah, who still looked sour. "A shot for each of you, on me."

"It'll take a bottle of whiskey to disinfect the bar," Jeremiah grumbled. "And his mouth."

"Fine, whatever. Keep the change."

As I sauntered out the back, Callaghan finally spoke up. *That man's spit is still on me.*

"Maybe they'll have fancy antibacterial wipes in Pacific Hill." There were hundreds of pretty, dark-haired women living there. How was I going to narrow down that list?

*Thank you*, said Callaghan, *for not giving him my finger bone.*

I snapped my fingers. "Wait, Jun might still have your wallet!"

*Don't bother*, said the dead detective. He sounded tired. I'll tell you where to go. *A favor for a favor.*

That gave me pause. But I didn't interrupt him as he recited an address in Pacific Hill, and when I hailed a cab and repeated it back to the driver, I could almost feel Callaghan nod beside me.

It was a posh-ass house. If it hadn't been, I would have been disappointed. The woman who opened the door was pretty, dark-haired, and very harried-looking. "You're late," she said.

"Excuse me?"

But then there was the muzzle of a pistol pressed into my stomach, and the look in the woman's eyes brooked no argument. "Get inside."

I did.

The Yu kid was seated at the granite-topped bar in the kitchen, sipping a vanilla Coca-Cola through a striped straw

and looking perfectly content. A kitten wobbled around the bar on unsteady legs. It was definitely dead.

"Huh," I said. *Callaghan, you asshole.* "What's all this about?"

"You have something I want," said the woman. She settled into a high-backed chair upholstered in cream leather. It looked expensive and also rather comfortable. "I hear you're the one who cut up my husband."

Oops. "Someone's got loose lips," I said.

"He told me himself." She waved a languid hand at the Yu girl, who was petting her reanimated kitten. "I heard a knock at my door and found him standing there, with this child. He pushed his way into the apartment, slurring something about a Chinese woman named An Mei who murdered him."

"I'm surprised he knew my name." I hadn't known there was a SFPD case file on me—I'd been careful—but this night was full of surprises. "So how did he end up back in the bay?"

"Well, I couldn't have him dripping that mess on my carpet. And when he fell apart again, it was quite a shock. I had to have the rug completely replaced."

I folded my hands and regarded her. It felt improper to compliment her on her poise while she had a gun trained on me. "So why do you still have the kid?"

"I didn't know where to put her." The woman glanced at the Yu girl, and for a second I imagined her gaze softened. "She couldn't get the information I wanted out of James, although not for lack of trying. And I couldn't let her go after she helped me sink him back in the bay."

"Well, you could," I said. "You could let both of us go, and I'll take her home, and we'll all pretend this never happened."

"Cute." The woman narrowed her eyes. "I've already lost a good rug due to James' shenanigans. No, you're staying. I wouldn't have put him back where he came from and kept the girl if I didn't think someone would come sniffing around for answers. It's a good thing it was you, or I might have lost another rug." Her finger traced the groove right above the trigger. "I want information, and James has it, and I hear you

can get it for me. But you'll need a body part." She nodded at the counter. "Show An Mei what you've been working on, sweetheart."

As I walked over to the Yu girl, she beamed up at me. "I've been working really hard," she announced. The kitten stared with empty eyes.

There, on the counter in front of her, next to the bottle of vanilla Coca-Cola, was a severed, waterlogged finger. So that was why he'd been missing so many of them.

*Why do people keep taking my fingers?* Callaghan said.

"Shut up," I muttered, scooping it up. It was clever, really. His wife was clever. I really wanted to know her name.

*Rose*, said Callaghan. *I bet you're wondering.*

I dropped the finger on the table a little harder than necessary. "I can't guarantee answers," I told Rose. "But if I get them, you'll let us go."

Rose smiled, and I could tell we both knew that was an empty offer. "Ask James for his bank account information. Not the joint one; I cleaned that out. The one he didn't think I knew about."

*Goddamn*, Callaghan said, and it could have been disgust or admiration in his voice.

I turned to the Yu girl. "Kiddo, go play in the living room. Or—is there a bedroom?" She nodded. "Okay. Take the kitty and go to the bedroom."

Rose let them go, the pistol steady and familiar in her hand, never wavering from the center of my chest. I pulled Callaghan's finger from its bag and lifted it to the light. It was soggy and disgusting.

And then, deliberately, I licked it.

Rose made a sound of disgust; at the same time, the lines of deadtalker power went bright in my head. Lan was right: You could feel everything like this. My power, the Yu kid's, and Callaghan's voice, all through it—*Rose, Rose, always using me, even after I was dead. Rose, with her beautiful laugh and long curls and weak ankles*—

I flung the finger at her face. She yelped, and for that

moment, her guard was down. I lunged for the pistol, my elbow cocked and ready to meet her hip, to throw off her center of gravity.

She was clever. But I was faster, and in the end, that was what counted.

"It really is too bad about the rug," I said as I walked the Yu kid and her dead kitten back to my Chinatown apartment. "I don't think the fish in the San Francisco Bay are going to appreciate it very much."

*You framed me,* complained Callaghan. I had, using what was left of his finger to leave a few choice prints in the apartment: on the doorframe, smeared across the knife block, on the handle of the refrigerator.

"You set me up first," I countered.

*You murdered me and threw my pieces into the bay,* he shouted.

I stuffed my hands in my pocket. "Right. That…yeah." We walked in silence. "It wasn't anything personal," I finally said. "If you wanted to know."

*That makes me feel so much better.*

"I think it's nice they'll finally be together," said the Yu kid. She still had her bottle of vanilla Coca-Cola. I'd made sure she brought it with her. "The lady and her husband sleeping in the water."

"Just promise me you won't wake them up again, okay?" I said.

She nodded, eyes bright but canny.

"Pinkie promise."

She looked a bit put out, but she grudgingly locked her pinkie with mine.

"Now remember, you have to tell your papa about the lady who took you and her boyfriend who took her. Don't tell them anything about the deadtalking."

"Why not?"

I sighed. "You'll understand when you're older."

*Your own people don't like it?* Callaghan said slowly. The Yu girl glanced at my purse.

"Is that true, Ai Mei aiyi?"

I looked at her. She was just a child, but she'd brought a dead man back to life long enough to cross district lines. That was adult power, with adult ramifications. She deserved the truth. "Yeah. So wait until you're grown and out of the house. Better yet, never tell anyone. Never get caught." She deserved so much more than the life so many deadtalkers had gotten.

The kid regarded me, then nodded. "Okay. Take care of my kitten."

I ended up putting the kitten in my purse with Callaghan and delivering the girl back home myself. Her father scooped her up and hugged her so tightly that she squealed, and the tears in his eyes were real. "I'll never forget this," he said.

"Just be good to her," I said before I left. Jun would be pissed when he found out I'd found the kid and hadn't told him, but he'd make sure we got paid in the end.

The sea air at the edge of the pier was cold and sharp. I picked up the kitten and set it gently in the water. "Sink," I ordered, and it did, its breathless lungs offering no resistance. Then I took out Callaghan's fingers.

*Wait.*

I glanced at the fingers. "What is it?"

*It's…* Callaghan huffed out what could have been a breath. *It's cold and shitty and boring at the bottom of the bay.*

"Maybe you shouldn't have tried to poach the Elder Brothers' money back in December, then. You might still be in one piece." I peered at him. "Wait. Are you saying you want to stay?"

The silence was enough of an answer.

"You do!" I said gleefully. And just for the hell of it, I tossed the rotting finger back into the bay. Callaghan yelled.

*Fucking hell! Are you even listening?*

"You know you had that coming. You just almost got me killed."

*Being dead is fucking terrible, but it's not as bad as you might think,* he snapped. *You should try it sometime.*

"I can wait," I said, but my brain was ticking. There were disadvantages to holding onto Callaghan, but then again, he was right. Being bored was awful. Besides, I was getting used to his company. "I don't know. Maybe you should keep the kitten company for a couple decades."

*God, you're awful. Shut up and put me back in your purse,* said Detective Callaghan. I grinned and slipped the bone into my bag. It fit perfectly.

# PATRICK BERRY

## DIVIDED THEY FALL

SHE WAS A HOT LITTLE NUMBER FROM THE POSITIVE SIDE OF town. Everybody called her "Perfect Ten," and I could see why. She had a set of curves that just went on and on. But when she came sashaying through my door that night, I knew right away she was trouble. I knew, but I let her come anyway. That's the price I pay for being irrational.

"Are you 3.14159268…" she began in her sultry voice, but I rounded her off. "No need to make a production out of it," I said, cracking the seal on a fifth. "The name's Twenty-Two Sevenths. Private Investigator."

She stretched herself provocatively across the plane of my desk. "I want you to investigate a murder for me."

I poured myself four fluid ounces, bisected them, then added three more. I had a feeling I was going to need it. "Someone's number came up?"

She nodded. "You probably heard about it. It's all over the line. Zero."

I felt a chill travel up my axis. Sure, I heard about Zero getting long-divided; who hadn't? According to the newspapers, there hadn't even been a remainder. But even the coppers thought it was probably the work of some radical. Why would a rational number try to divide Zero?

"Forget it, toots," I said brusquely, subtracting another ounce from the glass. "The cops are swarming all over that

case, and besides, the divisor was probably just some simple root. What's it to you, anyway?"

Wrong question. The tears started flowing at an exponential rate. "He was...special to me," she sobbed. "Oh, I wouldn't expect you to understand, but he was...different somehow. My better half, if you want to put it that way."

I drank my rye in silence. It was hard to believe, a two-digit gal like her hooking up with the likes of Zero, but the world of mathematics is a strange place. "I still don't see why you need a detective, doll. The police'll solve it sooner or later."

She let out a contemptuous little laugh. "The fuzz don't care about Zero. He was nothing to them. Anyway, their investigations are textbook stuff. They check the common divisors, they move on." She leaned close. "Listen. Zero was into something big. The last few weeks I saw him, he was hanging around the Denominator."

I bolted upright in my chair. "That's impossible. Zero's not allowed anywhere near there."

"I'm giving it to you straight, shamus. *Now* will you take the case?"

I reduced the whiskey to lowest terms. A voice inside my head was telling me to stay away from this one—if Zero really *had* been hanging around the Denominator before his death, he probably created problems no one in the world could solve. But my irrational nature got the better of me, as it often does.

"Yeah, sweetie," I said, grabbing my .45 from the top drawer. "Stay positive. I'll be in touch."

Five minutes later I was at the Denominator, a seedy bar on the low end of town. It was mostly a hangout for the zero-to-one crowd—small-timers looking to hook up with a high-rolling numerator and make it big. I wasn't a frequent visitor, but I wasn't prohibited the way Zero had been. What could he have been up to?

I entered and looked around. I was shocked to see Twenty-

One managing one of the roulette tables; he stood out like a sore thumb in that crowd. I sauntered over and dropped a fiver on number 7.

"What have you heard about Zero lately?" I asked him.

Twenty-One spun the wheel and regarded me sourly. "That's just what I've heard—zero," he said. The ball stopped on 21. "House number," he added smugly, collecting the fiver.

"I heard he was hanging around here last week. Maybe looking to divide and conquer."

"You heard wrong," Twenty-One shot back. "I haven't seen him. Besides, I'm not crazy enough to make fractions with Zero. Who knows what the result would be?"

I shrugged. "Maybe infinity. You looking to get high, Twenty-One?"

"Push off, three-point-whatsis." He idly cracked his digits.

"You don't mind if I question some of your little friends, do you?" I gestured contemptuously toward the fractional values, who glared at me but made no move. I was bigger than all of them put together. "I'm sure they'd remember a visit from an integral value like Zero. Don't you think?"

"You're wasting your time, hawkshaw. Zero wasn't interested in division." He gestured for me to lean closer. "I hear what he really liked was multiplication. The dominance thing, you know? He was into kinky stuff—the FOIL method, x-intercepts, Pythagorean triples. A real pervert. If you're going to talk to someone, try Thirteen. He knows all about that stuff."

I could see he was trying to get rid of me, but I decided to play along.

"Thanks for the pointer," I told him, and left.

Thirteen's last known address was the Four Points Hotel, but when I arrived and asked for him, the manager told me he was long gone. "We took out his entire floor," Four said brusquely.

"Any idea where I could find him?"

Four shrugged. "You might try the bakery. It's the only place he can find employment."

Four proved to be right. I found Thirteen working the bakery counter, dispensing his peculiar version of a dozen to all the lucky buyers. I wondered if management knew. Then again, if they'd hired him in the first place they had to expect some oddness. "I need help," I told him.

"Take a number," Thirteen said, gesturing to the dispenser on the counter.

I flashed my additive identity card. "Twenty-Two Sevenths, P.I. I'm working on the Zero murder."

Thirteen gave me a dirty look and abruptly began shutting up shop. "There's no real answer to that one," he said dismissively. "Besides, who cares if Zero's gone? Even alive he never amounted to anything."

"The word is," I continued, "you know something about it."

"Oh, is that the word?" he retorted. "Well, you got word problems, Sherlock. Zero and I weren't buddies."

"You had your differences?" I asked, making sure he picked up on the double meaning.

He grimaced and ushered me out, locking the door behind him. "Even if we did, it doesn't change anything," he said curtly. "Do the math."

I decided to level with him. "Look, Thirteen, I heard Zero was hanging around the Denominator before he died. I don't know what that means—*nobody* knows what that means. But I have a feeling we don't want to find out."

Thirteen raised his brows. "The Denominator, eh? Twenty-One's new hangout."

I was surprised, though I shouldn't have been; news traveled fast on the number line. "Yeah. Twenty-One's value must have dropped a bit, to be hanging around that dive."

Thirteen laughed at my naiveté. "Your mother must have simplified you when you were small. Twenty-One's not down and out; he's got friends in high place values. If he's hanging

around the Denominator, it's because some significant figure wants him there."

"Oh?" I said, trying to sound casual. "And who is this significant figure?"

"You wouldn't believe me if I told you," he replied, walking off toward the lower end of town to find his on-again off-again sweetheart, Negative Thirteen. It was the oldest story in the world: He kept trying to meet with her, she kept canceling. Alone, I found a seat on the corner and tried to get the numbers to make sense: Ten…Twenty-One…Four…Thirteen…Zero. By any reckoning, it was quite a combination.

The whole thing was getting too complicated for me. Could I really count on Ten? Was it just bad luck that I'd gotten nothing out of Thirteen? And what was Twenty-One's game? At first he'd claimed to know nothing about Zero, and then he'd practically rattled off all of Zero's properties. It just didn't add up.

The cold press of a .32 in my back interrupted my thoughts. "Come on, Sir Cumference, let's go for a walk," a voice said.

I felt a giddy moment of relief when I realized my captors were badge numbers. It was only the coppers; at worst, I would be thrown into a cell for a while. No long division, like poor Zero. With my digits, it would be a long division indeed.

A police vehicle waited nearby. My escorts shoved me into the back seat and slammed the door. A dim figure in the passenger seat twisted to face me. It took me only a moment to recognize Thirty-Eight, Special Investigator of the Number Line Police Department.

"Quite an honor," I said. "The NLPD's finest."

Thirty-Eight smiled and waved a thick text at me. "Careful we don't throw the book at you, wise guy. We could, you know. We've collected a good bit of scratch-paper work on you." He showed me the text, which turned out to be my police file—a sordid history at best. I winced as he read through some of the high points: "Six violations of the Order of Operations…

two violations of Cramer's Rule…three violations of the Law of Cosines. And we've got proofs on all of them. You'd do best to show a little cooperation here."

I shrugged. "So what do you want?"

"You're off the Zero case as of now. It's closed."

As I've said, news travels fast on the number line. "So you've found the solution?"

"Yeah, it was Eighty-Six. We got a confession and everything."

It was hardly a surprise; Eighty-Six was a notorious assassin. Still, something didn't quite compute. "You got him in custody?"

"Nah, he's dead. One of Zero's conjugates got to him before we did and ran a prime factorization on him."

"You said you got a confession."

"Yeah, well, Eighty-Six doesn't factor well. One of the pieces was still able to talk. So we asked him about the Zero murder, and you know what he said? 'I did it.' You can't ask for better proof than that."

The answer came to me all at once. "You missed an angle, flatfoot," I told him. "The real divisor is still at large."

He gaped at me, and I smiled. Suddenly I was running the show. "I'll cut you a deal, copper. I'll deliver him to you—but it has to be done *my* way. Not by the formulas. Plus, my police file gets erased."

He didn't look happy about it, but what choice did he have? "All right. What do you need to finish this thing up?"

"Gimme a piece of graph paper and I'll show you." I pulled a pencil stub from my pocket and took him through all the critical points. He balked a little, but not much. In the end, you can't argue with figures.

Thirty-Eight offered me a police assistant, but I preferred to work with known quantities. I got on the horn and explained the situation to Three, an old buddy of mine. We've always been pretty close.

Fifteen minutes later I met Three at the Denominator. Twenty-One gave us the fisheye as we entered. "You're becoming a real unpopular figure around here, gumshoe," he said ominously. "Careful you don't get erased."

I acted as if I hadn't heard. "Maybe you can help me, Twenty-One. I'm looking to extract a root."

Twenty-One smirked. "You need help with roots? That's simple."

"No, not simple roots," I said with a hard-edged smile. "Complex."

Twenty-One abruptly lost his composure. I sat and watched him squirm. "Who says one exists?" he said at last.

"*You'd* better say so, oddball, or my friend over there is gonna test your divisibility."

He started to sweat. "Look, Twenty-Two Sevenths, I'll level with you. Zero *was* here. He was helping us with a few divisions—but only as a place holder, I swear it."

"For Gauss' sake," I said in disgust. "All right, Three, lay into him. Seven times."

"No!" Twenty-One shrieked. "Okay, I give up." He pressed a button underneath the table and a section of wall swung outward ninety degrees. A mysterious figure stepped out, holding a .44 pointed straight at me.

"Hello, *i*," I said.

"Ingenious, twenty-two sevenths," *i* said. "How did you figure it out?"

"A few critical numbers," I replied. "Eighty-Six, in particular—he wasn't dead when you left him. He even told the police about you, but they didn't take his words mathematically enough."

"A crucial error," *i* conceded.

I regarded him curiously, this imaginary nemesis. "Why did you do it, *i*? What did Zero ever do to you?"

"Nothing," *i* said. "It was what he could do *for* me that mattered. I was tired of being imaginary, and he was my ticket to the real world. One quick multiplication."

I saw the light. "But you can't have more than one Zero on the number line, so…"

He nodded. "So I canceled him out. But no loss; I'm ready to take his place. No one need ever know."

"That's where you're wrong," I said and brought an arm down on the .44, hard. A quick uppercut to the jaw completed the exercise; he went down like the graph of $e^{-x}$.

The coppers entered the equation on both sides and took care of the rest. I took Three back to his proper coordinates, then headed uptown toward Ten's place.

It was high time for a little one-to-one correspondence.

# ANGIE HODAPP

# JANE DOE MUST DIE

I STOMP THE BRAKE AND CRANK THE WHEEL TO THE RIGHT. The Dodge Charger fishtails around the corner, siren wailing, tires cutting a wide arc across the icy snowpack. My heart hammers. I glance at the dash. It's 11:42 PM and only 18 degrees, but sweat beads on my forehead, plasters my shirt to my chest. How much time do I have? Minutes? Seconds?

Am I already too late?

Up ahead, a police cruiser sits in front of 645 Clover Street, its reds and blues flashing in the frigid night. I can make out the portly silhouette of Officer O'Dell, whose call woke me from a whiskey-induced slumber about ten minutes ago. He stands on the driveway beside the couple who owns the house. They're hunched inside thick down coats, gesturing wildly. *What the hell is going on?* O'Dell is holding out his hands. *Calm down. We're going to take care of this.*

God bless O'Dell. He worked with my old man, before my old man got himself killed in the line of duty. Now he works with me.

I brake next to O'Dell's cruiser and launch myself out of the car. "How much time do I have?"

"Few minutes." O'Dell turns back to the couple. "Mr. and Mrs. Jacobs, this is Detective Michael Preston. He—"

"We didn't hear a thing." Mr. Jacobs starts toward me, his flannel pajama pants bunched over his snow boots. His voice comes out in a high-pitched rush. "We went to bed at

nine. I got up for a glass of water, and there she was. We don't know how she got inside or how…who…" He swallows, looks as though he might be sick. "Jesus, what kind of sick bastard would do something like that to her?"

O'Dell lays a hand on the man's arm. "Let Detective Preston do his job."

I brush past them, catch O'Dell's raised eyebrow. He knows I've been drinking. Maybe he can smell the whiskey coming out of my pores. Maybe tomorrow I'll care.

I glance back at Mrs. Jacobs, who mutters, "Why haven't you called an ambulance?" She's hugging herself, trembling. If I weren't racing the clock right now, I might take a moment to feel sorry for her. She and her husband only bought the house six months ago.

Six months might be a record for this place. I doubt that "phantom crime scene, complete with unidentified female murder victim, intermittently and without warning manifests in kitchen" ever makes it onto the list of property disclosures.

I push the thought back and shake my head. Dammit, why tonight? On a night I've been drinking? Like anyone on the force, I need—no, I *deserve*—the occasional pull. But I'm a third-generation detective on a fifty-year-old cold case that'll be damn hard to solve if I'm not straight every time the crime scene makes an appearance.

Unfortunately, it only makes an appearance maybe once every year or two and never on any kind of schedule. The longest it's ever stuck around is thirty-two minutes, and because the whole thing's an apparition anyway, I can't bag any physical evidence.

Pulse pounding, I crash through the front door. The house is dark, but a winter moon shines through the kitchen window, casting the scene before me in ghostly silver light.

Jane Doe, murdered here August 23, 1966, lies dying at my feet.

She stares, as always, at the ceiling. Her pale eyes are wide and glassy and fixed on something only she can see. Long black hair splays across the white linoleum. Blood flows from

the stab wounds in her chest and neck. It drenches the front of her flowered dress and spreads beneath her, a hellish shadow creeping across the floor.

I fall to my knees, each breath tying a painful knot in my chest. I know better than to reach for her. If I do, she'll disappear.

"Who did this to you?" I ask as though she can hear me, as though this time will be different and she'll turn to me and speak.

Her lips move without sound. Her bloodied hands flutter as though she is trying to usher to mind the words of some forgotten prayer.

"Give me a name." Is it her killer's name I want, or is it hers? Fifty years of detective work, and none of us ever found out who she was or why she was here. The house had been long abandoned by 1966, and no one matching her description was ever reported missing.

I lean closer, taking in every angle of her heart-shaped face. In the moonlight, her thick lashes cast spidery shadows across the soft curves of her cheeks. Her skin is as fine as porcelain, her lips like the petals of a rose.

"Give me anything," I whisper.

A drop of blood slips from the corner of her mouth, traces a dark line toward her ear.

The sight of it sends an aching heat through my core. A shameful brew of desire and self-loathing simmers in me like poison. The frustration I feel when I look at her is agony.

I want her.

She is all I think about. She is exquisite, even in death. *Especially* in death. She comes to me in my dreams, and I hold her in my arms and feel her breath against my cheek as she whispers my name, her eyes full of longing and promise. Some wicked, unnatural force has bound me to her, and I don't understand it. Would I break free, even if I wanted to? I know I'm too far gone. I want her. I want her because no other woman will ever be as beautiful, and because she is a mystery I can't solve, and because she has ruined me.

This is the seventh time I've seen her, the seventh time I've knelt at the crossroads of violence and lust, wasting what little time I've been given *wanting her* more than *wanting to help her*. Some rational part of me knows beyond doubt that only justice will lay her soul to rest. Yet since the first time I saw her, I've learned nothing new about her murder, nothing new for her case file that my grandpa or my dad didn't already put there.

Beneath the hem of her dress, pulled tight across the tops of her thighs, a slender leg bends. A bare heel kicks feebly at the floor.

I clench my jaw. That kick—it's the start of the end. In seconds, she'll arch her back, fight to draw her final breath. Then she'll lie still, posing exactly as she did for the original crime-scene photos my grandpa snapped fifty years ago.

The scene will disappear. She will disappear with it.

Tonight, for once, I resolve to do the right thing. I'll do my job, even if it means abandoning her before the end.

I lurch toward the back of the house. Her killer's footprints—streaks of blood too smeared to reveal useful particulars about the size or type of his shoes—lead to the door. I push it open, stand there in the doorway gasping cold night air.

Beyond the porch, the back yard is quiet, starlit, and blanketed in snow. But superimposed over this is another yard—one of high, late-summer corn and August sunflowers as big as dinner plates.

I blink, trying to distinguish one image from the other. Where did the killer go after fleeing the house?

Movement. To my left.

I tense, peering into the darkness. The scene is fading.

Movement again. A figure, tall and lean, running toward the cornfield. Moonlight glinting off a knife clutched in a fist.

Whiskey fogs my brain, but I plant a hand on the railing and vault over. Land hard. Stumble. Recover. "Stop!"

To my astonishment, the figure stops.

Turns.

Looks me in the eye.

I stagger back. On instinct, my hand goes for my piece. I blink sweat from my eyes, then open them wide. The scene is gone. The specter has vanished.

My world is reeling hard and fast, some out-of-control carnival ride gone spinning off its rails. The killer isn't a man. The killer is a woman.

And I know her.

Sleepless, I toss and turn. Sometime after 3:00 AM, I'm sober. I'm closer to understanding why my grandpa didn't close the case. Why my dad didn't either.

At first light, I drive to my grandma's house. She's shoveling snow from the driveway—something most women her age hire the neighbor boy to do.

My grandmother isn't like most women.

Even at eighty, she cuts an imposing figure. Nearly six feet tall, strong and lean, her posture as straight as it ever was. She's healthy as a draft horse and just as capable.

Capable, it turns out, of murder.

I get out of the car.

She leans on her shovel and waves. "What a nice surprise!"

I don't reply. I can't find the words.

Just like that, she knows. I see it in the shadow that crosses her face.

"Come on inside," she says. Her voice is wary.

I follow her into the house. She shucks her snow boots and coat in the front hall. Then she leads me to the kitchen.

The kitchen is—has always been—yellow and white. This morning, its sunny cheer is lost on me. It feels as cold and gray as the January morning pressing against the frost-etched windows.

Numb, I sit at the table and stare at the sunflowers printed on the oilcloth. I've eaten a thousand Sunday dinners at this table. A thousand times, I've recited the prayer my dad made

us all say before we ate: *God bless this meal, and God bless the hands that prepared it.*

My grandmother opens her ancient Frigidaire. Removes a basket of eggs. Sets it on the counter. She scoops a spoonful of lard into a frying pan on the stove and lights the burner beneath it.

I find that I'm watching her hands.

"Fifty years I've been waiting for this day," she says. She cracks two eggs into the pan. "For so long, I didn't know who it was standing there, watching me run away from that house. By the time you were born, I convinced myself I imagined it. Chrissakes, it was the hottest August on record, and there you were, a ghost of a man standing knee-deep in snow. Who could explain such a thing?" She picks up a spatula and pushes the eggs across the pan. Her movements are listless, halfhearted, as though her years have finally caught up with her. "The older you got, the more certain I became that your face and his were the same. Not that I got a good look, mind you, but it was good enough. Everything was so vivid that night. The stars, the smell of the corn—everything was *heightened*. It's all still bright as day in my memory."

So many questions stick in my mind, but they are like flies in honey. None seems capable of unsticking itself.

I finally choose one and pick it free. "When I yelled at you to stop, how could you hear me?" The question I am really asking is *Why can't the girl hear me?* But if my grandmother suspects my obsession with Jane Doe, she doesn't let on.

"Blood, maybe. We're kin, after all. When you figure out how exactly, let me know." She goes back to the Frigidaire, removes a half-carved roast on a platter. She peels away the plastic wrap and slides a large knife from her butcher block.

A cold shiver rakes my spine. Her butcher block, I realize, is as old as everything else in this kitchen. So are her knives.

Jesus. Which one did she use?

"Your grandpa was never unfaithful again." She pulls the knife through the roast. Once. Twice. Two thick slabs of meat

slump over onto the empty half of the platter. She stabs them with the knife's tip and drops them into the pan with the eggs. They pop and sizzle and spit.

The smell of it turns my stomach. "Grandpa was the first on the scene. How did he know…?" I can't finish. The smell makes me gag. I swallow bile.

"Because I told him straight away what I'd done, and I told him where he'd find her. In that abandoned house on Clover Street." She pauses. "Where they'd been trysting."

*Trysting.* I bite back a bark of manic laughter. The word strikes me as absurd, far too chaste to have been spoken by an old woman holding a knife while confessing to murder.

"I had four babies at home," she continues. "How would I have raised them if he'd run off with her? You have to understand, Michael. In those days, women were left with nothing when their husbands strayed. Nothing but shame and cruel whispers and a public-assistance check that left them hungry a week before the end of the month. I decided right quick that no baby of mine was going to be raised on the dole. I did what I had to do."

I feel dizzy, but I manage to keep it together. "That's why he kept the case for himself. He made sure the murder wouldn't be tied back to you. Or to him."

She nods.

"What about my dad? According to the case file, he saw the crime scene nineteen times. He put in some new detail now and then, but you…you were right outside, practically in plain sight. He had to have seen you."

She slides the contents of the frying pan onto a plate. "I don't know what the case file says, but I do know that every single time your dad stood over that woman's body, he did nothing more than watch her die. You see, your dad was six, almost seven, when I…" She trails off, clears her throat. "Your dad knew about her, even met her a couple times because your grandpa had underestimated the ability of a child so young to comprehend what was going on between them. But your dad knew. Just six years old, but he told me what I needed to

know." She sets the plate in front of me and eases herself into the chair at the head of the table. "Your dad joined the police force to keep that case cold. To protect me."

I glance at the oily eggs, the glistening meat. I push the plate aside and look at the woman sitting across from me.

She is my grandma. Over the years, she has read to me and tied my shoes, has walked me to school and kissed my scraped knees. She has loved me fiercely since the day I was born, and I have loved her back. But I feel myself pulling away from her. In this moment, I cannot be her grandson. I am only a detective listening to a criminal's confession.

A sudden, sickening thought tears through the back of my mind. I am also a man who harbors a wretched lust for the ghost of a long-dead woman—the same woman my own grandfather desired so many years ago. He and I were lured by the same siren call, and something in our blood, some twist in our DNA, awoke and came running. She is a ghost who, now that I know the truth of her murder, may never reappear.

I could be sure of it. I could lay Jane Doe's soul to rest right now by clapping handcuffs on my grandma's wrists, reading her rights, and marching her toward her reckoning. Justice would be served.

But if justice were served and I laid Jane's soul to rest, her ghost would be gone from this world for good. I'd never see her again.

I swallow hard. "What do you know about that house?"

My grandma cocks her head. Her eyes narrow as though she suspects there's more to this new line of questioning. After a moment, she says, "There are reasons it was always being left abandoned, even long before I ever did what I did. Same reasons all its owners since keep turning tail and moving back to wherever they came from. In my day, folks always called it haunted, but anyone who might have known how it got that way is long dead."

A cold sweat crashes over me. It rolls back, sucking away my ability to reason, and with it any sense I ever had that I'm an honorable man with good intentions.

That house. It's the key to everything. It might even be the key to my salvation.

I stand so fast I knock my chair to the floor. I stumble down the hall.

"Wait."

I pause, my hand reaching for the door.

When she speaks, her voice is low, almost taunting. "Do you want to know her name?"

I close my eyes. In the darkness, I see Jane Doe's parted lips, a single drop of blood slipping from the corner of her mouth.

"No," I reply. "No, I do not."

I am sitting on the kitchen floor at 645 Clover Street. It is a mild evening in late spring. A cool, dusk breeze drifts through the open window, bringing with it the smell of roses. On the floor to my right sits an uncapped bottle of Jim Beam. To my left lie the fluttering pages of my signed purchase agreement.

I have no furniture, and after emptying my bank account for the down payment and closing costs, I can't afford to buy so much as a lawn chair. This morning, I quit the force because it was quit or get fired. Too much drinking. Too little sleep. Too many mistakes.

Too much ruin.

I haven't seen Jane since the night I discovered who killed her. I've told no one what I know. Her case is still as cold as her body, which lies in a pauper's grave in the cemetery at the far edge of town. I've visited that place, many times, but I feel nothing when I do. Her spirit is here, in this house. In *my* house. I have to believe that means I'll see her again.

Until then, I'll be right here waiting.

JOSHUA VIOLA

# OUTSORCERY

THE SLUG SMASHED INTO THE BACK OF PAGEY'S SKULL AND knocked him facedown into the ground. Then a brutal kick to the ribs flung him onto his back and he saw his assassin.

Bet he's not even twenty, Pagey thought.

*This* is how little the Don respects me, by sending out a kid on his first whack? A boy out to make his bones? Well fuck him sideways, then. I'm *glad* I took all that money.

The kid smirked at Pagey as he brought the gun's muzzle to his lips and blew away the smoke.

Smug little prick.

Pagey said, "Who the hell do you think you are—Billy the Fucking Kid?"

Seeing a presumably dead man talk must've spooked the shit out of the kid. Spooked him so bad, he reflexively pulled the trigger. Unfortunately for him, the barrel was still aimed at his own face.

Unable to move just yet, Pagey nevertheless heard the kid's body drop dead beside him, and he really wanted to shake his head. Young assassins these days were all so high-strung.

Amazing anyone gets whacked at all, he thought, and grinned at the bright blue sky overhead.

A moment later, Pagey's wound closed and feeling returned to his limbs.

Bada, Pagey thought as he picked himself up, bing!

Pagey slouched at a small table in a dark room, his gaze following bizarre, ritualistic drawings on the ceiling and walls. Several bookcases crammed with old tomes and artifacts loomed over him. This place always reminded him of that cartoon where Bugs Bunny pretended to be a swami.

He started whistling the Looney Tunes theme.

A large woman entered through a beaded doorway and joined him at the table. Her heavy face bore tattoos of slithering snakes. A bone necklace hung below her throat.

"Hello, Pagey," she said.

Pagey straightened himself and smirked. "There she is, my little miracle worker."

The woman rolled her eyes. "I see you've returned unharmed—just as I promised."

"I gotta say, Juma, I'm feeling pretty damn good for a guy who got his brains blown out today." He pointed to the back of his skull.

"Would you like to make the arrangement permanent?"

"You better believe it! This immortality racket is great."

Juma held up a warning finger as she brushed dreadlocks from her eyes. "I told you, I cannot save you from dying. You signed your own death warrant when you stole from your employers. I can't stop them from attacking you."

"Right, right," he said, barely listening. "Whatever they do to me, happens to them. I remember. I took a bullet to the head and don't even need an aspirin. I feel like the fucking Highlander over here. There can be only one!"

Juma frowned. "God help us if there were more than one of you, Pagey."

He smiled. "You know you love me."

Her expression softened a little. "All this trouble over dance lessons?"

"If my little girl wants to be a ballet dancer, then I'm going to make sure she's got the best teachers money can buy. It's her Sweet Sixteen present, after all. You should've heard the Don

when I asked for the money. He told me to send her to Arthur Murray like he did his own kids. 'Don't get above yourself, Pagey,' he said. 'I've had this talk with you before. You ain't better than me and you never will be.' All that after the work I've done for him? After all the loyalty I've shown? Hell, thirty-five grand's hardly a scratch in their monthly take."

"It seems they noticed your embezzling quick enough."

"Yeah, well, cooking the books isn't as easy as icing some babbo, I guess. What can I say?"

"You could have just asked me to cook up a spell to make her a great dancer."

Pagey's eyes widened. The color drained from his face. "No, Juma. I know how your magic works. She'd dance well for a day and end up a quadriplegic. I won't risk it with her—not after Carol's death. You got that?"

Juma nodded.

"I'll take the consequences for myself, but not her," Pagey said.

Juma leaned forward and took Pagey's hands. "Magic's repercussions are always a tad unpredictable. But this promise I will make, the death your associates plan for you will not last. Whatever method they employ against you will fail, and their own intrigues will rebound against them tenfold."

"How long will the spell last? Two weeks?"

"What's special about two weeks?"

"It's when all the Families are gathering. My Don's hosting it for the first time in years. He'll want his house clean by then. That means my head on a platter, just to show the others he knows how to deal with a rat, no matter how valuable I've been in the past. The next fourteen days are going to be rough and I—"

"Forever."

"What?"

"You ask for two weeks. I give you forever. As long as these people come after you, you will be protected."

Pagey nodded. "I like the sound of that."

"Then let us draw up the contract?"

Pagey extended his arm and barely winced when Juma

slashed his palm with a stiletto and sealed their bargain in blood.

Pagey's mother gave him the nickname when he was a boy because he always had his nose in a book. She would have preferred the Bible, but unfortunately for her his reading tastes dipped into esoteric topics like alchemy and black magic. It was nice to think of a world where you could whack someone from a distance by uttering a simple chant or brewing some leaves in a pot. But he never really thought any of it was real until he happened upon Juma and her shop.

He already made his bones before meeting her, but Juma's magic made him a bit of a legend in the Family. It worked like this: the Don gave him someone to kill. If it was an easy job, he'd do it himself. Sometimes there were complications, though, and that's when he needed Juma's help. She charged a hefty price, but her magic always did the job and, of course, Pagey got all the credit. Just a simple bit of outsorcery.

The first time he ever actually used her services for personal matters was two years ago, when Pagey's wife was threatening divorce. He didn't want to be known as *the divorced guy*. The Family looked down on that, but even the Don couldn't talk his wife out of it. Desperation drove Pagey to see Juma, and she promised the divorce would never happen. She also gave him a firm warning. Meddling with strangers was one thing. When magic was used for reasons closer to the heart, there could be unforeseen consequences. That was just the way it worked.

And Pagey found that out fast.

His wife was run over by a semi-truck the next day. She was sunbathing on the beach when it happened. The rig careened out-of-control from the highway, plowed through the sand, and flattened her. Made the newspapers and everything.

After that, Pagey was a believer.

After that, Pagey knew there was magic and then there was *magic*.

Pagey was met one afternoon by two hoods he knew well, Willie the Can Opener and Neil the Jackknife. Both goons with a capital G.

About time I'm getting a little respect around here, Pagey thought.

He walked sandwiched between them, his hands in his pockets as they went to a ten-story building the Don owned downtown. There was a hole in the roof and several other structural problems. Willie and Neil told him all three had been asked to check it out. That was a hoot. As if any of them knew a goddamn thing about building maintenance.

Pagey couldn't help feeling a thrill of anticipation as he tried to guess how they were going to off him. Would Neil attempt to gut him like a fish? Maybe slit his throat? The garbage bag-over-the-head trick was a good one, employed by Pagey himself a few times.

Or hell, maybe they'd simply club him to death like a seal.

"The roof's got a bad leak and the Don's getting pissed," Willie said as they made their way up ten flights. When they stepped into the breeze, Pagey knew what the plan was. "Seems like the contractor's been cutting corners."

Neil laughed. "Hope not. Or he's going to get some of his own corners cut."

*God* was Pagey getting bored. He almost said, *Shit, fellas, I'd rather jump to my death than listen to any more of your bullshit.* He took several bold strides to the edge of the roof.

At least they chose a classic, tried-and-true hit, he thought. They must really respect me.

The sudden shove between the shoulder blades pitched Pagey over.

Hitting the alley hurt a hell of a lot more than taking a bullet to the back of the head, but he was surprised to find how quickly he could get back up. Just in time, too.

The building started to collapse, and a few minutes later Willie and Neil were splattered about his feet like ripe melons.

"Wow," Pagey said, stroking his chin. "Talk about cutting corners. I guess the contractor forgot to use quality steel."

Pagey kicked and thrashed as Mickey the Skeptic shoved his head into a toilet bowl. Mickey screamed, "This is what you fucking get when you steal money from the Don, Pagey!"

Drowning actually proved to be far easier than getting shot or being thrown off a building. But the toilet smelled just awful, and all Pagey could think was, Jeez, Mickey, couldn't you have given it a courtesy flush?

Mickey didn't even bother to take Pagey's head out of the bowl. He just left him there once his body went limp. Pagey waited several minutes before pushing himself up. He scrubbed and dried his face before leaving, hoping his car would still be in the lot. It was. He got quite the chuckle when he drove home and the radio broke the news that a sinkhole had opened up, swallowing a car. Its single passenger drowned in a sea of raw sewage.

Guess they can call you Mickey the Septic from now on, Pagey thought, and honked his horn in triumph.

With three days before the Families were to meet, Pagey knew the efforts to off him were really going to heat up. He could just imagine the Don's frustration that his little traitor was still alive, so there was no doubt the next effort was going to be overkill.

But a steamroller?

*Now that's some classic Looney Tunes shit.*

He didn't know the four guys who kidnapped him that night and hauled him off to the construction site on the edge of town. The Don had more than a few bodies planted here—the real troublemakers—and Pagey couldn't help thinking he'd gained a measure of respect at last.

Figuring it had to be the last attempt made on his life before the gathering, Pagey felt a little flamboyant. It didn't help that he'd been dosed with enough heroin to off a racehorse.

"Seriously, fellas," he said, slurring his words as he dropped his trousers. "A shotgun straight into my asshole. Really wedge it up there. Don't even bother with lube."

The four men looked at each other. "Can you believe this guy?"

Juma's words echoed through Pagey's mind—*Their own intrigues will rebound against them tenfold*. The idea doubled him over with laughter and he fell, clutching his stomach.

"Get the little freak into position," one said.

The men had West Coast and Southern accents, and he guessed they were heavies who worked for the other Families, all in town extra early just for him. One grabbed him by the ankles and dragged him into a ditch. Then they announced he'd be pressed flat and have hot tar dumped over him.

"Maybe they'll call it the Pagey Malone Memorial Parking Garage."

A fat guy pulled up in the steamroller. Its lights were glaring but nowhere near as bright as the guy's smile. He shifted and jammed his foot against the gas pedal, the engine shuddering as it approached. Pagey's body went flat as a pancake. Being crushed was a strange sensation and he felt an intense heat surge through him. Or maybe it was just the heroin.

With as much as they'd shot into him, it was hard to believe they had any leftover for themselves. But they must have, because the driver OD'd on the spot, leaving him dead with his foot wedged on the throttle. The other guys somehow never saw it coming. Maybe they were too busy gaping at Pagey's body as it began to reform itself. Regardless, the steamroller pressed them into a uniform thickness less than most books Pagey read.

But then, Pagey always liked thick books best of all.

Nothing happened for the next couple days, but Pagey didn't have any illusions about being left off the hook.

They made their move the night the Families gathered. Everyone was dining in a private room. Being the paranoid

fucks they were, the heads of the Families brought their own chefs, their own food tasters, and assigned their own people to act as servers.

Being a waiter wasn't the job for a made man, Pagey thought, and he realized this humiliation was probably the only reason he was allowed to attend at all. No one spoke to him, least of all his Don, who stared intently at him the whole night. The last few weeks had been a strange game of pretend. Sort of cute and old-fashioned in a way. Pagey was supposed to act like he had no idea he was on a hit list, and the Don acted like he hadn't heard so many of his best guys had met bizarre, inexplicable fates trying to wipe Pagey out.

As the gathering was winding down, the Don himself approached Pagey as he filled a wine glass.

"Need you to get my car," he said.

"The Rolls?"

"A night like this, what else am I going to be riding in?"

The Don's words were slurred a bit, which surprised Pagey.

"Everything okay, sir?"

"Just peachy. I want you to drive me home. Mosso's been hitting the flask. He's denied it, but I saw it and took his keys. Here."

He tossed Pagey the keys.

Mosso was the only driver the Don ever trusted, and Pagey, like everybody else in the Family, knew Mosso didn't drink, do drugs, or fool around.

Which told Pagey how this one was going to end.

And wow, he was getting more respect than he'd ever believed possible. *The Don wants me out of the picture so bad he's willing to sacrifice the Corniche?*

Pagey found the car in the parking lot. He got in and put the key into the ignition.

Bada bing—

He turned it.

Bada bang!

The car exploded. A million fragments of Pagey flew through the air.

In an instant, his body fused back together, just in time to feel the pain of landing hard in the parking lot. But all in all, he just had a few bruises.

Which was a lot more than could be said for the Family members inside the restaurant when it blew a minute later. Police and fire investigators blamed a gas leak. Forensic scientists couldn't find more than an occasional limb, torso or head in the remains, and the reporters and editorial writers said the explosion was the biggest disruption to organized crime in a century.

Guess it's all over with at last, Pagey thought. He could look forward to just living his life now. He'd do it pretty well, too, since he had a good idea what death felt like.

Pagey knew where the records were kept, where the cash was stowed, and in the confusion following the blast, he got his hands on both, and set himself up nicely.

Very nicely.

He wouldn't have any worries, and neither would his daughter. Not even expensive ones. He soon began looking to see if there was an even more expensive dance studio for his daughter to attend.

After all, Sweet Sixteen was just around the corner.

Pagey was smoking a Gurkha on his new leather chesterfield in the grand foyer of his new home when the door behind him opened. Smiling, he knew just who it'd be.

"How were dance lessons, sweetheart?"

"I hate it. I don't want to be a dancer anymore, so I quit."

"*What?*" Pagey said, dropping his cigar on the sofa. He jumped up in a burst of rage. "Do you have any idea what I went through to—"

Pagey's daughter removed a katana from a display of weapons mounted on the wall and pointed it at him.

"I think I've got a different career in mind, *Daddy.*"

"Please, honey," he said, taking a slow step toward her. "Put the sword down. You don't know what you're doing."

She tightened her grip on the haft. "Sure I do. Before he died, the Don offered me a chance to make my bones by taking you out. I decided not to, but now that he's out of the picture, you're the only one standing in my way."

Pagey frowned. "What are you talking about? In the way of what?"

His daughter closed the distance between them.

"The chance to become the head of the new Family."

She moved closer.

*Their own intrigues will rebound against them tenfold.*

Pagey raised his hands. "You don't understand, honey! You need to put the sword down. You can't kill me."

"Of course I can, but I'd appreciate it if you move a little to the left. Don't want to get any blood on that lovely sofa."

If he could keep her talking, Pagey thought he might be able to convince her to drop the katana. And if he couldn't do that, maybe he could get close enough to disarm her.

"You don't have to do this. Everything I have is already yours—"

Pagey felt cold steel slice his chest.

And a moment later, quite à propos of nothing, ten bloodthirsty ninjas broke in through the windows, and Pagey's daughter's dancing days truly were over.

# STEPHEN GRAHAM JONES

# DO IT ALREADY

November 2

NICHOLAS IS A WUSS, BUT HE WON'T SNAKE HIS MOM'S CREDIT card if I don't do this, so here I am, right?

A year ago, when we'd had tenth grade Business together with Mr. Jordy, we'd had to team up on a workable model for a company that "filled a niche everybody knew was there but nobody was capitalizing on." Our pitch was that, in crime shows, how when you go see the bad guy, and you make yourself bulletproof by stashing an incriminating letter with a trusted friend, to be mailed in case of your disappearance? For a fee, we would be that trusted friend.

It was solid thinking, Mr. Jordy said, but it would also mean consorting with criminals, and painting a big bullseye on our place of business, and we would probably have to hire full-time legal aid to keep us from drowning in subpoenas. Not to mention how thorough the background checks of our employees would have to be, as we'd of course have to guarantee that we were, in fact, "trusted."

We got a B, and he said that was a gift. What he wanted us to do, he explained to the whole class, was to come up with a business model so foolproof that he'd be tempted to quit teaching, and ride our golden idea out into the real world.

This is that real world, Mr. Jordy.

I wrote a script for this feed, see. If there's not an update

within forty-eight hours of the last update, then the .htaccess file eats itself, and takes the password with it, letting all the prying eyes in the world see this record of what we've done. Because Nicholas insists. The wuss.

I haven't told him the password.

For all he knows, I'm just importing chat-trails of game sessions in here, or pasting my History and English papers up for the world to see.

Why Nicholas insists, it's that he thinks what we're doing is illegal, like that Peeping Tom who was hiding inside portapotties at the festival grounds last year, a tarp pulled over him, one hopeful eye peeking out.

That's not us.

And anyway, that guy, his crime *was* his punishment, right?

Nicholas's idea, it's that if I journal up our whole adventure online like this, it'll vindicate us, should this end up in court.

The reason it's me helming the keyboard, it's that A) Nicholas' connectivity at his house is hopeless, as he has to jack into his neighbor's wifi, and B) I'm the one always writing everyone's English papers for them, for cash.

His idea—no, what he wants me to do here, it's clean up our little project. Whitewash it into some "boys will be boys" thing, and use a lot of science, so it sounds like it was *that* kind of curiosity. Like building trebuchets (fourth grade) or water rockets (second grade) or chemical bombs (freshmen year— copper etchant and aluminum foil).

If we were actually going to get caught, sure, maybe I'd be saying this started in advanced physics, that what we were really interested in, it was optics and lenses and refraction. Not the female form.

But this .htaccess is never going to time out.

November 4

One time at church, the youth pastor had all the kids herded around her feet like sheep, and she said how sometimes you can pray for a thing, but then get all frustrated because it

doesn't happen right then. You don't always get what you want right away.

It was supposed to be this big lesson about how you pray anyway, about how God's not on our timetable, I don't know, but this one four-year-old, he stabbed his hand up into the air, said that was because of *shipping*, see?

He was right.

Shipping sucks.

Nicholas took my paper-writing cash and logged into his mom's laptop, where her cards were all stored in autocomplete, and he ordered it for us.

Now we're in the standstill that comes before delivery. But I had to log on. Updates or no updates, I've got to be in here saying something, I guess.

So, hm.

I know: What are we getting in the mail, right? Enquiring minds and curious officers of the court want to know.

It's a peephole reverser. Fifty-five dollars—forty-nine, really, but six for shipping.

Online, it looks like one side of a pair of those small binoculars. Nicholas said it looks like a range finder. Not because he's a golf-nerd, but because he's an archery nerd. It's what happens when you're neck-deep in the Big Brothers program. It's like Boy Scouts, just, without the real dads.

I don't have any papers to write tonight. It's not paper season.

So, Nicholas. I'll talk about him, since he's not here.

Three years ago, when he was twelve, his dad goes back to the Chinese food place they always get take-out from, and he just keeps on going, never comes back. One night the summer after freshman year, over stolen beers at the pond, with a thousand ducks watching us, Nicholas told me that his dad had been pissed about how the Chinese food place was always shorting them a single fortune cookie. They knew there were three plates—Nicholas, his mom, his dad—but every single Tuesday when his dad got dinner on the way home from work, every single Tuesday it was the same thing. *Two* cookies.

Though his dad drove to the Chinese food joint, that was

just because he was already driving, coming home from work. It was walking distance from the house. So he'd loosened his tie, waggled his eyes to Nicholas like saying how he didn't mind, this was the kind of thing you're expected to do when you're a father, and he walked out, never came back.

Had he been violenced away?

That was the thinking, at first. On the radio. On the news. In Nicholas's mom's eyes.

What Nicholas told me that night at the pond, though, it was that after his dad had stood from the coffee table, he hadn't fastened the styrofoam lid over his Chow Mein like he was always adamant about, even if he was just going for another beer from the kitchen. It wasn't to keep the heat in so much as it was to keep a fly from landing, barfing up its stomach juices.

Nicholas said, after the door shut, he'd reached over, protected his dad's food from all the flies the world had, but it hadn't changed anything.

"Maybe he got that cookie," Nicholas said, breaking it up with a gulp of warm beer, "maybe he got it and read it and it, it told him not to come back. That if he did, something worse would happen."

"Worse?" I'd said.

"Than him not coming home."

After he told me this—it even included his voice cracking a couple of times, the wuss—I shrugged like that was nothing, and made a story up about *my* dad: When I was a baby he'd tried to drown me in this aboveground pool we used to have. Because the neighbor's teenage daughter was always documenting him on video—ever since the accusations she hadn't been able to prove—he'd worn a mask of some sort when he did it. A mask with a long snout, and whiskers.

He hadn't held my baby head under the water or anything, I told Nicholas, trying to make this real. Just, he'd acted like he was playing with me, fake-scaring me with the mask—I shivered, hugged my arms, told Nicholas I still saw that snout some nights, in my sleep—and then when he stepped away from the edge of the pool, he'd left me there.

I didn't remember it, I told him. All I'd ever seen, which I had to sneak around to see, was the shaky bedroom-window video recording from the neighbor girl next door, that got my dad sent to jail. At which point we'd quit keeping up with him.

I said I hoped he'd been shivved by now.

"My dad too," Nicholas said, the cast of his face fake-grim.

I studied his profile against the blue-black sky, and that was when I told him about the yoga convention, which I'll get to tomorrow, if our package still isn't here.

NOVEMBER 5

This is why need the peephole reverser.

It's my mom's fault.

She's been the head maid at the La Quinta by the interstate since my seventh grade. On nights where she had to cover for some no-show—this is back when she was having to impress the new management—she'd bring me, let me do my homework in the lobby if it was empty, or up in the supply closet if a conference was happening, or it was a weekend.

By freshman year of high school, I had the run of the place, pretty much, and not remotely enough homework to keep me in one place for very long.

In trade for cokes, I'd run mail and left-behind driver's licenses up to the rooms for the front desk, and the cokes would hype me up enough that I'd have to walk the halls jittery, bouncing on the balls of my feet.

Where it happened was on the fourth floor. The top floor.

I was plugged into my earbuds, my head bobbing with the beat, not really paying attention, when I walked into wall of yoga pants and girl-sweat and slow-motion hair of all colors.

Time slowed down for me. There were minutes between each beat of the song in my ears. And my finger was *pumping* that clicker on my mental camera.

Because I was so oblivious, and had momentum, I would have zombied into the front two or three of the group if they

hadn't touched my shoulders, guided me between them like passing me back.

It was a yoga convention. A yoga reunion. Yoga pants and yoga bodies forever. It was like wading into a sea of women's magazine covers.

According to my mom, during what she didn't realize was an interrogation, they used the Sierra Room for their yoga. Twice a day, same week in November, every year.

"It's just fancy stretching," my mom said to me, bored, tired, two hours left on her shift.

Moms don't know anything. Not about being fourteen.

I was there the next day as well, walking the halls, collecting the pizza boxes guests always tilt up by the doors.

Specifically, I was on the fourth floor. Again.

They were in every room on the east side.

"For the sunrise," my mom explained, disgusted.

She wasn't helping.

Or, she was: now (then) I was seeing them rolling out of bed in whatever they did or didn't wear, when sleeping alone. Rolling out and sweeping the curtains open, breathing in the sunlight, luxuriating in it. Doing some casual, warm-up yoga in it, the kind you do when nobody's watching.

It got me a lot of miles, that.

But not enough.

After a while, you want more.

And, goodbye cruel world: The doorbell just rang!

NOVEMBER 8

So I forgot. Sue me, Nicholas. It's not like anybody copied this while it was live.

The password's back in place, don't worry.

I had other things to think about. Like saving your life when your mom found that charge on her card. You actually let it email a receipt to her? *With* the shipping address on the invoice?

I'm working with amateurs.

Because this company's the kind that, if they had a magazine, would have to put a belt of brown paper around it for store display, at least "Peephole Reverser, Guaranteed!" wasn't in the email. Just a model number.

Small favors and all.

Because I had a new pair of actually-good headphones still in the blisterpack, I on-the-spot saved Nicholas's life: They were a gift for my mom, for vacuuming at work. Surprise.

My mom misted up, Nicholas's mom pursed her lips in whatever the opposite of censure is. That's an SAT word, for anybody listening.

It helped the story that Nicholas still had the cash.

Business transaction: complete.

Now on with the crime.

NOVEMBER 8

The yoga convention crowd is nothing if not punctual.

The lie we told my mom earlier this afternoon was that Nicholas needed the hotel's free lobby wifi for homework.

We staked out the registration desk, our laptops propped open like shields. Like ramparts we could look over.

The yoga women didn't come in one by one, but as a single body, almost. Emphasis on "body" there, if you didn't notice.

I looked through the side window to see if a bus dropped them off or what, but there was nothing pulling out, and I had more interesting places to be looking.

The peephole reverser was in the right-side cargo pocket of Nicholas's army pants. We'd already tried it out, too. On rooms we saw on my mom's chart were empty.

The lights were out in those dead rooms, but still, instead of the blur of looking backwards through a convex lens, the reverser was correcting all that away. There was the blocky shape of the foot of a bed. There was the side of the television set. There was the desk-shadow and chair, just beyond.

"Worth every penny," I said to Nicholas, and he just nodded.

Because this was a project we were supposed to be working

on for World History, it was both forty percent of our final grade *and* super-complicated, Mom agreed to let us camp in the lobby after her shift was over. I had to give her a ride home first, though. My new headphones were around her neck.

The second time she looked over at me, when I was sure it was there on my face, what we were really planning, I blurted out that I was feeling sorry for Nicholas. Because of his dad leaving and all.

She told me I was good friend. And, that of everybody, of course it would be Nicholas I would be drawn to, wouldn't it?

I asked her what she meant and she shrugged like she'd said too much. Then two streets later she looked over once, again, and said Nicholas's dad, he was probably on a beach somewhere. With mine.

At which point I clammed up.

My face wasn't giving anything away now.

I'll make up stories about him all week. But that doesn't mean I want the truth.

I dropped her off, waved bye, promised to be in as soon as I could.

Our plan—the lie, it's that, while waiting for an animation to render, we both fell asleep right there in the lobby.

I'm writing this right now mostly to stay awake, I guess. If I don't, the lie'll be true, and, if it gets true, then we might sleep right through sunrise.

NOVEMBER 10

Caught it.

No: *caught it*. Italics can indicate how out of breath I am.

Genius that I am, I'd set a reminder to log in here. Dummy that I am, it gave me one minute to make it to my room, log in. Less than a minute really, since it took a few seconds for it to register, what this "Do it already" reminder was for.

Now that I'm here, though.

The net result of this whole operation? A) I bought my mom a gravy pair of headphones, and B) we're out fifty-five

dollars. Evidently people who sell peephole reversers online, their customer relations departments don't have phones, just chat sessions tied to the email account used to purchase.

And, I say "we," but it was my fifty-five dollars.

I should just delete the .htaccess file myself. There's nothing illegal here. We may have intended something in the general area code of a crime, but the joke, it was really on us, wasn't it?

I still don't want to talk about it. But I can't stop seeing it, either.

Maybe vomiting it up here will get it out of me.

Let me start over, pump a little of the old drama in:

All we wanted was a glimpse of one of those perfect bodies, backlit by the morning sun.

In the chill before dawn—you can feel it in the halls of the fourth floor, because the hall opens to the stairwell, and guests are always propping it open to smoke—we were casing the doors on the east side.

Which one, which one?

The blond? The tall one with the French braid?

We were so the opposite of sleepy. I've never been so alive, I don't think. This was the dream.

Nicholas reverently (a word he doesn't actually know) pulled the reverser from his pocket, and we executed one more walk-by of all the doors, finally chat-rouletted ourselves to 412.

Our bulletproof plan was that, whatever door we were looking into—they went all the way to 432 on the east side—we were going to have a pizza box already leaned up against the wall beside it. And we were each already carrying pizza boxes. And one of us would always be watching both ways, up and down the hall.

Nicholas paid four of my fifty-five dollar bills back to get to be first.

We were both holding our breath. He leaned in like over a microscope in Biology, and then he dialed on the focal-thing, and then he kind of grunted, looked over to me, a question there in his eyes.

"What?" I said.

His face was pale.

With delight, I figured. With amazement.

I palmed the reverser away, held it up to the peephole as quietly as I could.

It was just a room, like we'd seen before. The curtains were drawn so the sun was coming in, but otherwise—and then a form shadow-blotted across that window.

I smiled, not breathing, just waiting for Downward Dog or Mountain Pose or one of the others I'd been studying, and that was when she—*it*—seemed to sense me watching, and turned her head sideways.

Because her head was the last thing I'd been interested in, I hadn't clocked it.

I should have, though.

There was a long snout. And, in profile, round ears way at the crown.

When the face cocked its head over like looking back at me—by that time I was running, taking the stairs four and six at a time, passing Nicholas by the second floor, our pizza boxes abandoned.

We hid behind the dumpsters, our breath rasping in and out, our eyes wet, and when we looked up at each other, it was Nicholas who finally said it: What had I seen?

I asked him back what *he'd* seen.

He turned. He ran.

November 12

The second day of Nicholas not being at school.

His mom calling my mom. The police talking to me. My mom talking to me after that.

I didn't know. Truly.

But then I did.

After my mom left for her late shift, I left too. Not for the hotel—I'm never going there again, no matter what—but for the pond.

Nicholas was there. Floating face-down, about fifteen feet out.

A thousand duck eyes were watching me from the darkness.

No, *two* thousand, for a thousand ducks.

This is why I'm the paper-writer. I get the details right. I remember that things have to make sense.

What finally made sense of Nicholas being out there, dead, drowned, it was that, sitting there hugging my knees, trying to decide if I could anonymous-tip his dead self in or if I should let him get reported the natural way, I started noticing the trash blowing around my feet.

Strips of paper.

Fortunes.

I picked one up, like I was compelled to read it, to intone it out aloud, but right when I started to be able to see the thin pink letters, I backed away hard instead, stumbling, my palms smearing in the green duck shit.

Reading that fortune was what pulled him into the water, wasn't it?

I'm not stupid.

I walked all the way home, my hands deep in my hoody pockets, and I didn't look behind me even once. Because I knew I'd be running if I did.

NOVEMBER 12

Suicide.

We had a school assembly on it today. Because of Nicholas.

The yoga convention still has one more night.

It's been on my mental calendar all year.

I'm not writing this all down for Nicholas anymore.

I'm writing it down because my fingers are already shaky, and this keeps them doing something. I'm writing it because I just called the hotel and asked for room 432, and when the phone was picked up in there, there was just breathing. And then a hang-up.

November 12

Mom's coming home. Early.

What I told her was that it was Nicholas. That I couldn't stop thinking about Nicholas.

To be sure I had all her attention, I told her it was me who found him at the pond.

What I didn't tell her was what I can't stop thinking about. What I can't stop thinking about, it's stepping into the hall and there being a yoga woman there, in Downward-facing Dog. She's lurching her way down to me, her hair loose, hiding her face until it's not. Until I have to see that her head, it's twisted around backwards.

It'll be stupid, once Mom gets here and I don't tell her about it.

To prove it's stupid now, I just pounced out into the hall with my old t-ball bat waggling behind my ear, because t-ball beats yoga.

There was no woman there.

But there wasn't for Nicholas either, was there?

What Nicholas got, it was fortune cookies left in his path, in his day, in what was left of his life.

What I got was, at the end of the hall behind me, a bare foot shuffling across carpet. A thick, pink, dry-scaly tail dragging into the bathroom all at once. Just the tip, whipping in. My throat dried up with certainty. I knew exactly what this was: the story I'd told Nicholas, about getting nearly drowned as a baby. The story I'd made *up*. The story that wasn't real.

But I'd thought it. I'd said it out loud. And now something was completing the picture. A man with a rat head, he needs a rat tail.

"Dad?" I said, shaking my head no, falling the other way, crashing into the living room, the t-ball bat cocked behind me because I'm a writer, not a fighter.

Next one of Mom's brass saucepans hanging from the ceiling over the island in the kitchen—it didn't quite rattle, but

it shivered in that metallic way thin pans can do. Like a cymbal you want to grab, to make it quiet.

Something did quiet it, all at once.

"*It was just a story!*" I screamed, trying to make it forceful. Trying to insist. "It was a lie! I made it up! He just left, like dads always do! And we didn't—I didn't…we didn't see anything."

I was kind of sobbing by the end of it, I guess. I can say that now.

The pan didn't make any more noise. But when it settled down, quit rotating on its hook, I did look past it for an accidental moment. Long enough to see a reflection in the darkened kitchen window, a reflection of the other side of the refrigerator.

What it was was a darkness where eyes would be.

Long, pale whiskers splayed out below that.

And then nothing.

And then everything: headlights washing across the front window; the garage door creaking and cranking, shaking the whole house. Getting stuck halfway up, like always, when leaves blow in and cross the sensor.

"*Mom!*" I screamed, afraid to move, afraid to do whatever it was Nicholas had done.

Which was when the stupid doorbell rang. I flinched so hard I nearly fell down, and then I rushed to the door, was twisting the deadbolt when it hit me: wouldn't Mom just duck under the half-up garage door like always, come in through the utility? And, wouldn't she have a key for the front door?

Not if the car was still running, I told myself. Not if she still wanted to pull into the garage.

Shaking my head no, I leaned forward, looked through the peephole. Into a fisheye. Into a *rat*-eye.

Which is why the door of my bedroom is barricaded now.

Which is why I'm writing this.

Was that even Mom I called, earlier?

I'm sorry, Mom.

I don't know how you're going to find me.

I don't know what ritual or observance I interrupted at the

La Quinta, either. I just know that they're not what they seem. They're more. They're everything. And they reach into your head with their thin claws, and what they pull out, it's what they use against you.

Nobody just called my name down the hall.

It wasn't a man's voice. A dad's voice, one I've been imagining my whole life.

And he's not wearing a mask.

And we don't have a pool.

Last time, in my story, the girl next door had raced down the stairs of her house, dove in with her cheerleading clothes still on, pulled my gasping, coughing self out.

I love you, nameless girl. Faceless girl.

Come fast, please.

In case you don't, don't worry—I'm not going to be sitting at my laptop when my door crashes in.

Rats and fathers, they don't understand about computers, won't be able to hear an .htaccess file already timering down on a server a continent away.

I'm sorry, Mom.

Leave your headphones on as long as you can.

Somebody show this to her, please.

# JEANNE C. STEIN

## LUNCHTIME

MIKE WOLF KNEW SOMEONE WAS WATCHING HIM. HE FELT IT the minute he pulled the Porsche to a stop on the dirt road. Yet all around him the meadow stretched to the horizon, gently rolling land with no trees large enough to hide behind, no clumps of bushes high enough to conceal even a small child.

He shut off the ignition and shrugged. He was getting paranoid in his old age. But was it paranoia? Being a land developer in a county where the locals were fighting tooth and nail to keep him out was enough to make anyone paranoid. He endured late night hang ups, anonymous threatening notes, and frivolous lawsuits designed to keep him tied up in court for months. Amateur efforts at intimidation. He'd battled them all.

And won.

Now all that was left was this morning's meeting with Lloyd Baxter. The final holdout. Lloyd said something about lunch, but looking around, Mike wondered if he misunderstood. Unless Lloyd packed a picnic, there wasn't any place to eat out here.

Besides. There would be no time for lunch. Mike patted the trunk of the car. Would be a tight fit but unless he agreed to his terms, Lloyd would never have to worry about lunch again.

His gaze swept the meadow and he imagined the single family houses that would soon replace all this—grass. That's what everyone was fighting for…acres of grass.

Didn't the stupid, shortsighted locals realize what development meant for the town? Jobs. New families. New businesses. A Walmart, for Christ's sake.

Oh, well. Most of the members of the town council who didn't bend to bribery came around pretty quickly when the intimidation started.

Should have tried that first. It would have been a hell of a lot cheaper than the friendly nice-guy approach.

And then there were his competitors. Five or six other developers who thought they could undercut his bids. It only took greasing a few palms to make sure he was always the winner. And when that didn't work... He smiled. It's amazing how motivating a rock through a window or a slashed tire could be. Or an anonymous threat to a loved one. One by one, the others dropped out, leaving the prize to him.

He pushed open the car door, climbed out. Glancing down at the Rolex that sparkled on his wrist, he saw Lloyd was fifteen minutes late.

*Goddammit.*

He timed it so *he'd* be late. Just enough to let Lloyd know who was boss.

Still, he couldn't shake the feeling he was being watched. He scanned the meadow again. Nothing. The roadside. The only thing that caught his attention was a curious mushroom, round, about four inches in diameter, growing just at the edge of the road. He wouldn't have noticed it all were it not for two black orbs on top that curiously resembled human eyes.

He bent over for a closer look.

The "eyes" looked back.

And blinked.

Wolf jumped.

"What's the matter, Mike?"

Wolf jumped again and whirled around. "Lloyd. Where the hell did you come from?" He looked toward the Porsche, parked alone in the road. "Where's your car? How did you get here?"

Lloyd laughed. "Which question would you like me to answer first?"

Wolf shook his head. They were miles from town. Lloyd couldn't have walked all that way. And he was impeccably dressed in a suit Wolf guessed must have set him back a grand or two. No sweat stains or wrinkles to indicate he'd jogged or ridden a bike, even if such a thing were possible. "How did you get here?"

Lloyd ignored the question. He moved to the mushroom Wolf had been observing moments before. He knelt down and petted it the way one would a small pet. Wolf watched the mushroom-thing curl to embrace Lloyd's touch and heard a sound uncannily familiar to a cat's purr.

"What the fuck?" Wolf said.

Lloyd looked up. He grinned. "It's very simple. My little friend here wants me to give you a message."

"The *mushroom* wants you to give me a message." Wolf snickered. "This is a joke, right?"

"It's no joke." Lloyd stood. "I'm afraid the meadow wants you to cancel plans for the development."

"The *meadow* wants?" His eyebrows jumped. "Lloyd, my friend, I think you've been eating too many mushrooms. Or smoking the wrong kind of grass. Our meeting today was a mere courtesy. The papers have all been signed, the contracts let. The bulldozers will be here Monday morning to start grading."

"Aren't you forgetting something?" Lloyd faced Mike. "You can't do anything without my okay."

Mike took a step forward. "That's what this meeting is all about. You are going to have a change of heart." He reached in his pocket and withdrew a sheet of paper. "Today. Now."

"And why would I do that?" Lloyd shook his head. "You have a chance to save yourself, though," he said. "But only one. Get into your car, drive into town and tell the city council you've changed your mind. The ground is unsuitable for building after all. Unstable."

This was too much. "Unstable?" Wolf exclaimed. "The only thing unstable in this meadow is the nut job standing in front of me."

"Are you sure?"

Wolf felt the ground shift beneath his feet. "What the—?"

Lloyd's expression softened. "I'm sorry. I did try to warn you. The *Jinni* live here—have lived here for hundreds of years."

Wolf danced and bobbed, trying to keep his balance as the ground roiled under him. "Jinni? What the fuck's a Jinni?"

A fog emerged from the grass and surrounded him. In less than a heartbeat, the fog congealed into tangible shapes, transforming into round mushrooms with those unworldy black eyes. The mushrooms changed shape, becoming wraiths. Male and female. Small people dressed in leather tunics, gossamer wings sprouting from their backs. Their humanoid features were marred by one striking detail—teeth—pointy, sharp, evil looking teeth. They grinned with malice.

Was this a nightmare? Wolf cast Lloyd a look of growing alarm. "What the fuck are they? Fairies?"

Lloyd let out an exasperated breath. "Not fairies. Fairies are simple-minded, simpering creatures that let people walk all over them. That's why they are dying out. We are Jinni. Masters of our own fate."

Wolf stared incredulously at Lloyd. "You're a Jinni?"

"Only half Jinni. My mother was a human. The human gene is always recessive in such a match. For most things. I grew much taller than is normal for my kind."

A dozen pairs of feet took a step closer; a dozen set of sharp, shark-like mandibles snapped with hunger.

Wolf tried to step back. He would turn and outrun whatever these gruesome creatures were. But his legs refused to move, and his blood turned cold. "No. Lloyd, keep them away. I'll go!"

Lloyd shook his head. "Too late, Mike. I gave you a chance to leave. You've seen them now. No one leaves after seeing them. It would be too risky. The secret of their existence must be kept." He sighed. "I must say you've gotten farther than

any of the others who've tried to disturb their home. It was a mystery to me at first, how you did it. But then I learned your secret. You didn't exactly play fair, did you?"

Wolf scowled. "What do you mean?"

"Don't be coy, Mike. My contacts told me what you'd done to eliminate your competition. Not exactly kosher, right? All the time you complained about what was being done to dissuade you, you used the same tactics against them. And more. Breaking kneecaps, Mike? Threatening families? What are you, a gangster?"

Legs weakening, Wolf struggled to stay on his feet. What was happening?

Lloyd continued. "You wanted to win. And you did. You got the others to pull out before it got to—" He waved a hand. "This. Too bad you were so persistent."

"This is crazy! You can't do this! People will come looking."

Lloyd shook his head. "No. You'll be reported missing. The development will be put on hold. In time, your body will be found in your car, the victim of a terrible accident. Body burned beyond recognition."

Wolf could no longer keep his balance, and he toppled to the ground. The eyes of the Jinni flashed in eagerness and they advanced another step toward him. "Lloyd!" he begged. "Help me."

Lloyd's lips pressed together. Then he smiled.

His razor sharp teeth flashed. "Wish I could, Mike," he said. "But I can't. It's lunchtime."

# JASON HELLER

## NUMERAL ELEVEN

IT'S HALF PAST FOUR IN THE MORNING AND I HAVEN'T EVEN had the chance to let my cup of joe from Manny's 24-Hour Deli scorch the back of my throat and here's Officer Dipshit, handing me a plastic baggie holding a severed foot.

"What do you make of it, Detective Okereke?"

I sip my coffee, leaving a ghost of last night's lipstick on the styrofoam. Not that my lipstick rubbed off on anything other than a shot glass. I wasn't in the mood to chat up anyone anyway. I'm still not on the mood for chatting. Too bad Officer Dipshit can't get the hint.

My breath steams in the dank air. The alley reeks of diner grease and human shit.

Like many things, I've learned to live with it.

CSI is pulling apart the dumpster next to us. Its innards are being strewn about and sifted through like it's a corpse getting stripped by vultures.

What do I make of it? The foot in the bag? I couldn't answer the rookie's question, even if he wasn't a rookie. Fuck, I don't know if I'd tell my best friend about this. Or even my girlfriend. Not that I have one. Esther left last week. Finally had enough of my midnight spasms, my spring-wide-awakes in the middle of the night, clawing and kicking and gouging and screeching.

"Detective?" prompts the rookie. His rosy, razored-clean cheeks radiate goodness and earnestness and kindness. Why

he became a cop, I'm clueless. Not that I'm in the mood for caring.

"Stand clear, Officer…"

"Anderson."

"Officer Anderson. Give me some room. This isn't a bullshit TV cop show. I'm not going to stand here having a Socratic discussion about the case in this stinking alley."

He scowls. Or maybe it's a pout. "I know who Socrates is, you know. I went to college."

"Good for you. Maybe you should've been a professor."

He takes his pout and trudges off toward the nearest CSI. I exhale, deep and long. Didn't want Professor Anderson to smell the whiskey on my breath. I just closed down Patrick's an hour ago. Been there all night. Patrick loves me. I'm a novelty, he says. Not the black-girl-at-a-white-Irish-bro-bar kind of novelty. The homicide-detective-at-a-lowlife-scum-hangout kind of novelty.

I'm daydreaming. Trying to avoid thinking about the thing in the bag.

I'm still holding it.

My spine turns to ice.

I walk a few steps over to the mouth of the alley, trying not to hobble, and hold the bag up to the cold light of the nearest streetlamp.

My heart squirms.

Sure, it's a severed foot. Sure, it belongs—belonged—to a child. Sure, the CSIs are searching for the rest of the body right now, even as I stare, petrified, at the only piece of the victim they've found.

But I can't tell them the truth.

They're not going to find the rest.

I'm not scared because it's a foot. Or even the foot of a kid. During my decade on the force, I've seen worse. Way worse.

But this foot?

My guts shudder. It's not nausea. It's *recognition*.

I know this foot.

I know it.

The skin is brown. The toenails are painted purple, chipped from playing shoeless outside. The plum-colored nail on the big toe has a pink decal stuck to it. A tiny cartoon octopus, smiling and trailing bubbles.

The sight of the octopus suckerpunches my memory. There's a scar. *The* scar. Right across the top of the big toe, from falling off a new bike while riding it barefoot on Christmas morning.

I squint, mentally measuring the blob of flesh in the bag. The size is right. Exactly right. This girl must have been about nine. Nine and a half, to be precise. Birthday of January seventh. Only this girl wouldn't be nine and a half now. She'd be thirty-seven. And a half.

I think in numbers when I think of it. One number in particular.

Eleven.

I shove it out of my mind like it's a rat that's crept in. Twenty-eight years ago. Think of that number. Twenty-eight years. Yet the foot is perfectly preserved. Doesn't bear any of the telltale signs of being frozen and thawed. And the amputation wound is still jagged. Messy. Glistening with barely coagulated blood.

My own left ankle, where flesh meets prosthetic, starts to tingle.

I take another sip of coffee. The shot of whiskey I tipped into it on the way over from the deli slices down my gullet like a hot knife.

Patrick's opens at seven in the morning. A little over two hours from now. I'll need to go there. Not just for info. For a drink. Maybe six.

The thing is, I know this foot.

Or at least I used to.

"You look familiar," Patrick says as he slides me a shot I didn't ask for.

"I might have been in once or twice." I shrug, mumbling from around the lip of the glass. It goes down like liquid

sandpaper. Some godawful song by some godawful Celtic punk band is playing on the jukebox, all slurred shouting, seesawing fiddles, distorted guitar. The place is empty, which is a rarity for sunrise. Patrick put this shit on the jukebox just for me. Fucking sadist.

Patrick sighs through his silver moustache and pours another. "Remind me, Okereke, why you insist on drinking the cheap stuff?"

"Same reason I buy generic prescriptions." The second shot goes down even rougher. I cough and wipe my mouth with the back of my hand. Lipstick's pretty much gone by now. I wasn't lucky last night, but you'd be surprised how often I pick up chicks from an Irish bar full of wannabe Boondock Saints. Not that it's the main reason I come here. It's just that Patrick's is the only bar within stumbling distance of my apartment. That, and it closes at four in the morning and opens at seven.

"If it's a thrift thing, ever consider hitting up the LQ and drinking at home?"

"Isn't it bad business to point your regulars toward a cheaper product?"

A smile opens up beneath his mustache. Not a mocking one. A warm one. "Maybe I'm a lousy businessmen. Or a lousy pharmacist."

I hang my head to hide my own smile. Fucking Patrick. Not sure what it says about me that my bartender is one of two people in the world who can crack me. The other just walked in the door.

Mike.

From the corner of my eye, I scan her. She lets the heavy oak door of Patrick's swing shut with a gentle thunk. A hood is pulled up over her head. A shock of filthy pink hair, like cotton candy that fell into a mud puddle, juts out from under it. Her jeans have holes. Her sneakers are falling apart. Her jacket hangs off her like she's a scarecrow. I couldn't imagine being that skinny. Wouldn't want to.

She shuffles past me and bellies up to the bar. If you can call it a belly.

"I knew you'd be here," she whispers.

"*I* knew *you'd* be here," I say.

A grin peeks out from the shadow of her hood. "Causality. A circular thing, is it not?"

Every time I think I'm too full of my own bullshit, Mike reminds me that I'm not always the least human person in the room. She sees right through things. Right through me. I never had to tell her about my past. The first time we met, during an investigation into a string of street murders five years ago, she told me she was going to become my informant. That I needed her. That she knew about my history. She could read it in my smell, in the slump of my shoulders, in the slant of my hips. She said I carried my trauma around with me like a swollen gland the size of a Buick. Quite a poet, Mike. A sick fucking magic junkie poet, but still. After that, we became friends. Not that I'd cheapen it by calling it that. Something cleaner and harder and purer than friendship. Not that I'd ever let her know that.

Not that I'd need to.

I motion for Patrick to pour her a drink. He makes her usual. A Roy Rogers, heavy on the grenadine, with extra cherries.

"You know, that would taste better with some booze in it," I tell her. "Or with a sandwich on the side. Sometimes I think those are the only calories you get."

She pops a maraschino in her mouth, drops the stem on a coaster, and nods at my empty shot glass. "Ditto."

As long as I've known, as much as she knows, Mike is the only name I've ever been able to get out of her. Not that I call her by name often. Or vice versa. We've got a strictly economic arrangement. I settle her tab at Patrick's once a month, and she feeds me the word from the street. I only have one rule: nothing about me. No looking into my past. She already knows enough. I'm not out for vengeance or closure or completion or any other shit like that. I am whole. Right now, as I am. Not human, but whole. All I want is to put a plug in the pain every once in a while. When I solve a case, when I keep a killer from

doing it again, I can almost sleep for a few days. The Podiatrist? I don't give a shit about him any more than I give a shit about the victims of the killers I catch. I'm not doing anything for them. They're beyond help. I'm doing it for me.

That means a lot of after-hours investigation. Mike's tab isn't cheap. But the info she provides sometimes feels downright... magic. Impossible stuff that no one could possibly know. She chalks it up to being invisible, just another druggie in the alley, a fly on the wall. I don't ask too many questions. Or any questions, really, beyond who-what-when-where and the occasional why, if I'm feeling lucky. I've broken at least three big cases because of the scoops she's coughed up. I care as much about her methods as I do her meth habit.

The last of her cherries goes down. "You're here about the foot. In the alley. Washington and Eighty-Sixth." It's uncanny sometimes how she doesn't even need to ask.

"Believe it or not, I already know more about that fucking foot than I want to. I actually have another question for you. What do you know about the Podiatrist?"

I may not know Mike well, but I've known her long enough to tell when I've thrown her. She stiffens for a second before relaxing back into her usual junkie slump. That's Mike. The most laidback meth-head you'll ever meet.

"You can't be serious."

"You're right. As usual, I'm here doing standup comedy."

"You've got to be able to stand up to do that."

Amputee jokes. Classy. I let it pass.

"Mike," I say with a pause, trying to add some weight to the question, "I mean it. What do you know?"

"About the Podiatrist? The serial killer?"

I'm surprised at how steady my voice holds. "He never killed anyone."

"Oh, right. He just mutilated them. Dozens of them. Until some of his victims escaped." For a second I forget that she doesn't know about the Podiatrist. About my past with him. She only knows that I suffered as a kid, and that I lost my foot,

and that if she ever used the word "suffer" around me I'd snap her forearms off and feed them to her. In a sandwich.

That's when her eyes roll back in her head. All whites. Dead white, no veins, inhuman, like boiled eggs. She does this sometimes. She doesn't mind doing it in front of me. Patrick is at the other end of the bar, but it's not like he'd notice anyway. He turns a blind eye to the weird stuff Mike and I drag in, so long as our tabs stay paid.

Her eyelids flutter. She's moaning something. Her fingers are twisting the stems of her cherries into strange shapes, like symbols.

Her eyes snap back. Her pupils are dilated. I smell something metallic in the air, like busted batteries.

Like I said, I don't ask questions.

"Middlefield," she whispers.

I feel like I've gulped a bag of rocks.

"What did you say?"

"Middlefield. One... One-Eighteen..."

Suddenly the jukebox stops. A last wisp of fiddle echoes in the air.

"Hey, what the—" Patrick growls from the other end of the bar. "Goddamn power went out."

Mike's eyes lock mine. "One-Eighteen Middlefield Circle. That's the place. The address. Where he took you. Where he kept you. Where he..." She glances down at my left leg.

"*He* didn't do anything to me. He did *nothing* to me. He didn't fucking *touch* me."

Mike goes on staring. "This whole time. I never knew. You had to steer me onto that line of possibility. Onto the circle. Circularity..." Her voice drifts off. Then she jumps in her barstool. Her stare goes wide. You're *her*. The girl that got away. The girl that—"

"I think we're done," I hiss through gritted teeth. I slap a twenty down on the bar and get up, leaving Mike sitting there with an unreadable look on her gaunt, scrawny face. "Keep the change," I yell to Patrick.

"I always do," he hollers back as I storm out the front door. "Unless you pry it out of my cold, dead hands."

Middlefield Circle is exactly as I remember it. Which is funny, because I never remember it. I never think about it. But my memory of the place must have been sloshing around in there somewhere. As I pull up to the small house marked "One-Eighteen," it's as if I'm ten years old and back at the shrink, trying hard to keep the demons stopped up.

I get out of my car. Don't bother to lock it. What's the point? Middlefield Circle is a graveyard. Has been for a while now. Tree limbs dangle in a state of decay. The asphalt is like rubble. A few curtains are drawn shut here and there as I do a three-sixty in the fading daylight, but most of the surrounding houses are empty. Some are boarded up. The housing crash didn't help, but this neighborhood had already long been on the decline.

Wonder why.

The screen door is unlocked. So is the front door. I hesitate for a second before pushing it open. Why am I here? What am I doing? Oh, right. I reach into my jacket pocket and touch the plastic. Slick and warm. The thing inside. The foot. It's still warm. I have no idea how. I'm hoping there might be some answers here. At the very worst, someone's copycatting the Podiatrist, and somehow found the foot I lost that day, twenty-eight years ago. Then somehow performed some master taxidermy on it so that it seems as fresh as if it'd just been cut off.

I slip it out of my pocket and peek at it again. That's the real thing, all right. No need to send this to lab for DNA analysis or whatever the fuck they do on cop shows. No budget for it even if I wanted to.

I'm still standing in the doorway, the door half open. My ankle aches. I wish I could say I started drinking to numb the pain, the friction of leg meat against prosthetic foot, but that'd be a lie. I think I tried to give that excuse to Patrick once,

when he was cutting me off after a shot too many, and he just laughed at me and took my glass away.

Next time I see Patrick, I need to remember to call him an asshole. Lovingly, of course.

I hold my breath for as long as I can, thinking that some kind of unholy smell is going to hit me. It doesn't. Just disinfectant. Sterile. Institutional.

Maybe that's worse.

The kitchen is a wreck. Linoleum curls up from the baseboards, mottled and yellow, like diseased skin. The sink's been removed.

I remember why. He did things in that sink.

I push it out of my mind. My other jacket pocket has a flask. I pull it out, take swig. Booze is an antiseptic. I feel clean for the three seconds it takes for the whiskey to make it to my stomach. Cleansed in alcoholic fire. Fuck, that's what it's been like since???

It's dim, but I don't try the light switch. It takes me a second to remember why. It's an instinct. The light switch is bad. What it meant when I heard it. What I was able to see when it was turned on. What was about to happen once the room lit up.

The hallway catches a few shafts of the sun's last light. The floor doesn't creak or groan so much as sigh as I walk across it, my limp causing a slight drag across the floorboards, like a drawl. The wallpaper is dingy, streaked with moisture, speckled with mildew. Still, all I can smell is the disinfectant.

Clean. Inhumanly clean.

Like a doctor's office.

No. More like a showroom.

The basement door appears in front of me. A simple door. Hinges, knob, frame. I walk through doors every day. Sometimes there are bad people on the other side. People with guns, even. I have one of my own, I remind myself, patting my holster. My training screams at me to draw it. But I don't. I won't hide behind a gun. Not here. Not now.

I reach for the knob, but my hand freezes. This isn't fear I'm feeling. I know fear. I swallow it down and drown it in bile

and booze. No, this is something deeper. Like some invisible force is grabbing hold of my backbone and trying to yank me away.

I let it. This is insane. I shouldn't be here. This isn't detective work. This is self-sabotage. I should know. What do I think I'm going to accomplish here? Part of it is the drunk in me, making me impulsive. More so than usual, I mean. I've learned to live with those regrets. Or at least ignore them until they fade to a dull throb of guilt, just more background static to help shroud the sharp bits.

This is as sharp as it gets. Being here. About to go into this basement. I don't want this sharpness.

I'm not here to solve a violent crime. I'm here to commit one. Against myself.

Again.

I turn. The grip on my spine pulls me toward the door. Maybe it's survival, or some other kind of sense. The same sense that made me do what I had to do. All those years ago. To get away. Before he could do to me what he did to the others. The people in the basement. Some kids, like me. Some adults. Grownups, old people. Babies. All naked. All with mouths taped shut. All squatting in their own filth, whimpering, eyes bulging in horror, trying to communicate with those bulging eyes.

Chained. To the cold cement floor.

By their feet.

Being carved up, but by bit. While the others watched.

I can't take it. It's flooding back, like a burst dam inside my skull. I'm halfway down the hall when I hear something.

"Okereke!"

It's muffled, but there's no mistaking it.

"Okereke! It's me. Anderson! Oh god."

Anderson. The rookie? What the fuck's he doing here? Did he follow me here? If so, how did he get into the basement without me seeing him?

Then he screams.

I'm down the stairs before I even realize I've opened the basement door. My pistol's drawn and held low. It's one thing

for me to be crazy and head in without my finger on a trigger. It's different when someone else is at stake. Even the rookie.

My head is swimming. It's like the air has suddenly turned into a soup of antiseptic gelatin and I'm trying to inhale it.

I see Anderson. He's on the floor. Chained. A shackle leads from his ankle to a bolt in the cement. Ancient stains scar the floor, splashed in squiggly patterns that look like some kind of alien algebra.

Anderson's naked. Just like we were. All twelve of us. It had to be twelve. The number was important, he always told us. The Podiatrist. That stupid, fucking meaningless name the media came up with so that the public could easily wrap their heads around something that no simple cutesy euphemism could ever define or contain.

His sweaty body gleams pink in the glare of the bare bulb hanging overhead. The light is on. I try not to shudder and fail.

"Okereke…I'm sorry," he gasps. "He made me. He said he knew you were coming, he got it from someone named Mike, squeezed it out of her brain, and he made me…"

He turns his head toward the light.

Anderson's shoulder is hamburger.

His arm is still attached. But meat and fat and bone glisten in the glare of the bulb, and his right arm is dangling by a few thick strips of muscle. He's holding it to his torso with his left arm, cradling it, as if he were a mother who had just given birth, reluctant to let the umbilicus be cut. The flesh is charred and crudely cauterized, like meat seared on a grill. That must be the only reason he's still alive. Barely.

I hold back puke. That's the thing. The Podiatrist, he didn't just take feet. That's what most people think, but it's not true. He took random parts. From all over. Carved them out. Made a ritual of it, chanting, cutting intricate geometric shapes. Always left them alive, though. I must have gotten here while he was halfway through his…business. He didn't have time to get all the way through Anderson's arm. Probably burned the wound shut so he could come back and finish. Maybe that's what this is all about. Finishing what he started.

The media called him the Podiatrist because of me. Because of what I did. Because of how I escaped. Me, nine and a half years old. With the rusty piece of metal siding I found in a dark corner of the basement. The way I sawed and screamed and sawed and screamed until I was free, I was free, I was free...

The next thing I know I'm trying to break Anderson's shackle. With my bare hands. I'm yanking on it. I'm clawing and kicking and gouging and screeching. Then I'm shooting at it. Bullets ricochet off the cement. Anderson cringes and I hear him whimper something about calling for backup.

A small part of me wants to listen. But I can't hear it over the roar coming out of my own throat.

Something stops me. Another voice. One I know. One I thought I'd never hear again. Fuck that. One I always hoped I'd hear again. Because how else was I going to gut the sonofabitch?

"Numeral Eleven," the Podiatrist says. His voice is many voices, many languages, calm and loud, soothing and cacophonous. Just like before. "I never thought I'd see you again. Of all my disciples, of all the facets of the Trapezohedron, you were always the one I coveted the most. Do you know how much it pained me to see you forsake me? Tell me, Numeral Eleven. Did you receive my gift?"

Trapezohedron? What the fuck? I don't have time to turn the weird word around in my mind. I turn. There he is. A man in a suit. Impeccable, expensive. But instead of a head, a cluster of nodules and apertures and bladders and cilia squelch and squirm in impossible configurations.

Trembling, the air like jelly in my lungs, I point my pistol at that hideous mass of grayish flesh. "You mean this?"

Three shots ring out. Then it's silent for the longest second of my life. The Podiatrist does something with the organs of his face that might be a smile.

It hits me. He didn't used to look like this. What did he used to look like? A man? Did I ever see his face?

I try to clear my head. My heart hammers. Of course I

can't kill him. All these years, in my head, I've never been able to. Why here? With something as primitive as a bullet?

I lower my weapon. Anderson's finished whimpering. I think he's passed out. I know I need to get him to a hospital. But things like hospitals and doctors and bars and dumpsters and jukeboxes and cherry stems all seem so distant, so flat, so false, like shadows on a wall. This is full. This is real. This is the only thing that was ever real.

"Am I…were we…just numbers? Parts of this…whatever the fuck you just said?" I suddenly realize it's the one question I've always wanted to ask, even if I've never actually put it into sentence form before now. "Is that all we were to you?"

The bundle of voices coming from his head buzzes. "You don't understand. You're one of my disciples. One of the facets of the Trapezohedron."

That word again. "You said that already. Fucking nonsense. Gibberish."

Something like frustration twitches across the alien landscape of his face. "Trapezohedron. The Conveyance. You were meant to part of it. You are sacred! Sanctified. Chosen. Blessed. Instrumental."

He's babbling. "For what? Why? I never wanted to be!"

"Didn't you? You didn't? It's so confusing. I'm confused. Causality, linearity, I…it is not my native atmosphere."

I don't know what he means. He seems puzzled, like he's trying to figure out a math problem that's beyond him. I want to ask him, press him, scream every question at him that I've ever had, that I've ever buried deep in my bones to keep myself upright. But I can't. A trap door opens up. In my mind. A hole gapes. Inside it is…chaos. Shards of worlds. Geometry that doesn't add up. Tunnels through empty space. Impossible flesh. Every molecule in my body wants to pour itself into that hole. To follow that scrap of meat that the Podiatrist took all those years. I feel myself leaking away, cell by cell. I grit my teeth and steel myself to keep from falling. From falling apart.

The Podiatrist. This *thing*. It doesn't belong here. I shouldn't see it. I mean, I shouldn't be *able* to see it. And it

shouldn't be able to see me. The fact that we *can*, that it's *here*, is a dislocation. An abomination. Not to me. To the universe.

What does Mike always say about causality? And circularity? My brain screeches like a jet engine.

Mike. Anderson said something about Mike.

"What did you do to her?" I keep my voice cold even though a scream coils right behind it.

"The female? I harvested what I needed. To draw you here. It needed to happen here. Causality. All these decades, moments, rushing streams, crystalline time... It was so difficult. Has it been long, Numeral Eleven? Since we were here last? You look so strange. Your silhouette. You displace more air."

Mike. It hits me like a needle in my chest. Why Mike? Why couldn't she see this coming? But I know the answer. She was blinded. By caring. Maybe even by love. I don't know. All I know is she's never walking into Patrick's again, never chewing cherries and cracking bad jokes and...

I can't tell if I'm shouting or crying or whispering. Maybe, like the Podiatrist, I'm talking in many voices at once, speaking in tongues. "You did it all for this?" I hold up the bag, my foot, the foot of a girl who never got to play shoeless ever again. Who never got to know what the absences of pain felt like. Who couldn't keep Esther. Who couldn't keep Mike. Who's even gonna lose this goddamn fucking *rookie*.

"No. It was more than that." His head pivots left then right, as if scanning the basement, as if accessing the apparitions of twenty-eight years ago. "You wanted to go home, didn't you? Back then?"

My jaws clench. "Of course I fucking did."

"So did I." His immaculately clad shoulders slump. "The sacrament. I must take it from you."

"This? My fucking *foot*? I don't know why you gave it to me, just to take it back. But that isn't going to happen. I'll die first."

"But you can't die. It won't work if you die. And it won't work if you surrender it. Or...leave it behind. Like you did the first time."

I choke back tears. That's it. That's the thing I could never forgive myself. Not for being stupid enough to be kidnapped. I was just a child. Not for escaping and leaving the others behind. I was just a child. No, I could never forgive myself for leaving a part of myself behind. For having the courage to sever a piece of me, but not to carry it along.

I glance down at Anderson. He hasn't passed out, but he's delirious. Still clutching his arm. The arm that's hanging by a thread.

I try to clear my head. I've got to get out of here. I've got to get *him* out of here.

I look inside the bag. At the brown skin. At the big toenail painted purple. At the pink decals, the tiny cartoon octopi, smiling and trailing bubbles. At the scar, right across the top of the big toe, from falling off a new bike while riding it barefoot on Christmas morning.

I thrust it in front of me.

"*Take it.*"

The Podiatrist recoils as if I'm handing him a death itself.

"No! It won't work! I can't return that way! Each facet must be taken, stolen, torn away, never given. The Trapezohedron will collapse. I'll be stranded here, an infection in this tissue of physics, contracting and contorting, this maddening tissue…"

He flickers, like a flame that's begun to gutter.

"Eleven," he begs. It's almost a sign of familiarity, the way he drops the "numeral." Intimate. Pitiful. "Take it back. Take it and hide it. Hide it so that I might steal it!"

I thrust it at him again.

He flickers again in a shimmer of thickened air and is gone.

Before I can take a deep breath I'm on my phone, calling for an ambulance. I take off my shirt and tie up what's left of Anderson's shoulder. When I'm done, my bra is slick with his blood.

The rookie swims back up into consciousness.

"What…what was…"

"You're hurt. In shock. You imagined things. Hallucinations. Let them go. Trust me."

He gets angry. His eyes flutter open. "Why? Why did you wait? Why were you standing there? Talking?"

I don't have an answer.

Anderson's getting hysterical now. His state of shock must be passing. Wish I knew the feeling.

"Damn you! What am I going to do now? What am I going fucking do? My arm. Oh god, my arm." He grabs at the thing, screaming in pain, in loss. I try to tell him they might be able to save it. Honestly, I don't care. I can't. If I do, it's all over. If I cared, I wouldn't be here right now. I wouldn't be standing.

He grips my arm like I'm the one who just killed him. Like it's my fault.

"*What am I going to do now?*"

Empathy and pity have been scoured from me. All I can be is an asshole. I want to tell him, "Become a professor." I want to comfort him. I want to run away from him. From this. From everything. But I know there's no running anymore. The Podiatrist is still out there. Maybe he always was and always will be. Maybe I messed up his only chance to leave and never come back. I don't know. All I know is I'm still a number, a variable in an equation, and that's its own kind of damnation.

"What'll you do?" I say as I hear the first siren. I start counting them. I think of numbers. And causes. And effects. I think of how much of our lives we spend counting the bits of ourselves we leave behind. I think of this rookie, this kid, and the kid I was. Or wasn't. My skin crawls as I hold him, slick and quivering. "What we all do, rookie. What we all do."

# BETSY DORNBUSCH

# A ROSE BY ANY OTHER NAME

MISTER MAGIC SAT HIS FAT BUTT DOWN ON THE CHAIR opposite me in his home office, laid a hand on each squatty thigh, and grunted a command to his troll goons. It made my blood run black. Even though I don't speak Trollish, I've had enough unfortunate experience with them to know when things aren't going well. Never mind I owed Mister Magic several thousand gold pieces and my pockets were empty. They knew. They checked.

"Why am I here?" I avoided the gazes of the two trolls manhandling my wings. You meet their eyes, they take it like a challenge, and feathers take months to grow back.

"Devin, Devin, Devin." Mister Magic's sigh painted my name in colors I didn't like. A feather started to give in my right wing. His sprite enforcer, Pricillian, flittered around my face.

I wished I could give her a swat that would send her into next week. Sprites hate time travel. But I just sat and sweated.

Figure of speech, of course. I'm Faerie and we don't sweat. Faeries do tend to cry when stressed though. I was hexing my eyes dry. Blinking would be hell to pay in ten minutes. I stared at the roses on his desk. Their sultry scent made my hands tremble.

"We've got trouble." Mister M leaned forward, all bad breath and cyanide-laced concern. "THHievery."

I leaned back out of range of his spit. "I've walked the streets two weeks." I hardly get any sleep when I'm on roses. "Dragons haven't come round. No leprechauns either."

Pricillian snorted and I caught her drift. Leprechauns are squirrelly little dudes, and I've hardly been sniffing around alleys for lep-scat. I avoid them when possible. Rotten tricksters, leps.

"I'm not talking about missing gold," Mister Magic said.

Pricillian swatted me on the nose with her wing. "Mister M isn't talking about gold."

My wings started to flex, but I thought better of it with the troll claws digging in. However this party went down, I guessed flying would be crucial. I made myself meet Mister M's watery eyes. Behind him was an oil painting of flowers on flower wallpaper—a reminder of the illegal trade that made him so very rich. Human taste in decor really is awful.

"Magic," he whispered, glancing around like someone would hear. "Devin, someone took my magic."

Served the old jerk right. He'd stolen it in the first place. "That's…terrible."

He mopped at his bald head and ran a sluggy tongue over flaccid lips. "You're going to find it for me, Devin."

"Will it erase my debt?"

"It'll keep you alive so you can repay it."

I flew a couple of inches off the sidewalk because my brain was all tied up figuring how I got to be in charge of getting Mister M's magic back. Pricillian floated near my ear, talking ten leagues a minute. I've never been able to keep up with sprite-chat. I stopped flying. My Doc Martins hit the ground with a thud. "Wait. They did it when he was awake?"

"One minute he can conjure a pot of tea and the next he's asking me to boil water. Steam and feathers do not mix." Pricillian managed to preen a wing mid-air, but looked over her shoulder and darted back to me.

I sighed, wishing losing the sprite was that easy, but she had a good sniffer. She was old-blood, from a solid family. Came from serious gold, too. I heard she got mixed up in a bad pollen racket and Mister M bought her debt.

"Why did you stop?" she asked, feathers ruffled in annoyance.

"I'm thinking," I said, walking again.

"Ah, don't want to trip over your tongue."

Or maybe Pricillian just liked getting paid to be a bitch. I ignored her as I turned the corner into the Firefly. Pricillian fluttered nervously over the counter as I ordered from the barharpy.

"Beer for me. And a blueberry for my…" I cast a glare at Pricillian. "Business associate."

"You want petals in that, Devin?"

I shook my head. "I'm working."

The blueberry arrived on a chipped saucer. Pricillian hovered for a second before ripping into it with her barbed tongue. She curled her lips but it couldn't have tasted too bad because she kept at it until the skin lay there like a deflated balloon.

I scanned the Firefly. Centaurs liked to hang out and lord over everybody like they used to in high school, reliving the old football days, outnumbered by their women. Today was no exception. Even Harry Starling was there wearing a high school sweatshirt. Guy needed to get a life.

A unicorn drank from the trough at the back, accompanied by a young blonde, probably his virgin. Must be slumming from uptown.

Phillip molted in the hearth, surrounded by scraps of flaming feathers. Damn phoenix needed to get on with regenerating already. He'd been at it a week.

A faun nursed his glass of soggy newspaper down the bar. He had a broken horn and a black eye.

"Did the attack happen at Mister M's house?" I asked Pricillian.

"In his back garden," she answered, still worrying the scraps of the blueberry.

I didn't answer because Celeste had just walked in. People tell you not to date a succubus because you'll never get over her, but until it happens, you just can't really know how bad

it is. They even glow a little, which attracts us winged folk like pixies to a jig.

She walked past me to the back, all curves and glowy pheromones, and went straight to Harry Starling.

I coughed to get my heart started again. It took some doing. Pricillian pounded me on the back, which tickled and made me cough worse.

Harry clip-clopped to the bar to order a drink. Her favorite. Ground bone tea with a splash of faerie tears. First clue she wasn't meant to be mine.

"Hey, Devin," Harry said. "I didn't see you there."

Tough to see me around his ego. "Are you dating Celeste?"

Harry glanced back, his profile Romanesque, his hair glossily molded into curls. "I am."

"She usually goes for magical guys," I said, my eyes narrowing.

"It's my charm, I guess."

"Where were you two nights ago, around dinnertime?"

"What? None of your business." Harry shook his head, but his flank quivered. Had I struck a nerve? Hit upon the truth?

I edged closer, trying to sense if he had magic. "Go around Mister M's place about then? Steal some magic?"

"You know what? You're crazy, Devin. It was amusing in high school but now it's just sad."

"Like you're doing much better, day drinking and wearing a football jersey in bars."

"I wear one a lot. I'm the high school football coach."

Of course. That's how it goes with centaurs. They're like leps. They turn everything to gold. "Oh yeah? Why aren't you there now?"

The unicorn and his virgin made their way for the door, carefully not looking our way. Probably anticipating a fight. Phillip pushed back further into the hearth. The faun was too wrapped in misery to notice us. Celeste shook out her long black hair and gazed at me with contempt.

"It's summer. There's no school." Harry rolled his eyes and trotted away, tail swishing like he was flipping me off with it.

I curled my lip and downed the rest of my beer. My eyes hurt worse now, lids scraping over them.

"He's a lot bigger'n you," Pricillian piped up. "You shouldn't taunt him like that."

I couldn't even summon a snide tone. "Can't find out anything unless you ask."

"You won't find anything but a bad attitude and a warm beer."

Mister M said blood was good for the soil, and it must be true, because his garden bloomed like crazy. Nobody was being tortured there today, though. All was still and oh-so-floral...I breathed in the scent of roses and my eyes slid shut in a moment of rapture.

Pricillian slapped my cheek a couple of times with her wing. "Wake up. *Focus,* you big loon."

I'd need to explore it on a grid, which made me grit my teeth. Fae aren't much for squares. Corners get to us. A spiral, then. I walked toward the middle of the garden, a grassy spot with a tinkling fountain, and started walking in ever expanding circles, eying everything. Sniffing. Listening. Running my fingers over plants. Magic echoed faintly. "Anything disturbed or different?"

Pricillian drifted alongside me. "How would I know?"

I sighed and kept walking. It took a while. Pricillian made herself useful by shouting every time I stalled out in front of roses. About halfway I found a big flattened spot in the grasses and flowers. Looked about the size of a small bear. Or Mister M's butt. On the next circle, though, I stopped for real, squinted, and knelt.

A divot of grass had been torn with a sharp, curved edge. Lingering magic brushed my fingertips when I touched the dirt.

"What?" Pricillian flew down to perch on the edge of the hoofprint, blocking my view and probably contaminating

evidence. I brushed her away. She flittered off, scolding. I ignored her, ignored even the intoxicating scent of roses.

Mister M didn't hold with any hooved creatures. Really, we all just tolerated them because we had to. But he *really* didn't like them and had enough power and money he didn't have to pretend to.

I couldn't help but think of the coincidence of seeing Harry at the Firefly.

"I know what you're thinking," Pricillian said. "That unicorn. They don't come down here often, eh?"

"What? No. Forget them. Spoiled rich kids slumming. It's Harry I've got my eye on." The more I thought about it, the more certain I was right when I'd seen Celeste with Harry. Centaurs aren't magical. They're really just big, dumb jocks. But if Harry figured out how to steal magic, that'd be very attractive to a succubus.

I finished looking around the garden, drew in one last deep breath of floral air, and told Pricillian I was going home to think. I meandered alone through the streets to my windowless, back alley basement room. I hated the place, more indebtedness to Mister M, but it gave me a private place to crash. I had every intention of warming some stale petal tea on the hotplate and having a nice nap, but someone slammed into me as soon as I stepped inside the door.

I shoved the door at my attacker, but mostly missed because it was darker than a ferryman's soul in my room. She—I determined from the furious screeching—came at me again, raking claws down my face and bare chest. The fresh cuts stung with blood. With no time to work a drying spell, my eyes squirted tears. I growled and thrust myself forward with my wings against the doorjamb and tumbled into her, grabbing at everything. I got hold of long hair and yanked. She screamed like a banshee. My mind sifted through memories of lovers to find one who might attack me. Celeste because I harassed Harry?

The thought was enough of a distraction, slowed me down

or some shit, because she broke away. I couldn't get to her quick enough, scrabbling in the dark with my hands and wings stretched out like a fool. I heard a curse in a sweet-sounding voice, and a really loud metallic clang. Pain slammed through my skull.

The weapon was my toaster if the storm of crumbs was any indication. Then things went blacker on the inside of my mind than even inside my room, and it was a damn relief.

I woke with a groan and a murderous instinct. My mind clutched at the idea of a revenge attack from Celeste, but my hand also clutched several long blonde hairs. Not Celeste, then. My head felt like marbles were rolling around in there, but this investigation had just gotten personal. I hauled myself to my feet.

Night had fallen and the Firefly was quiet, thank the gods. I tried to think through who was here and who'd left. The faun still, with a new glass of wet paper. Looked weedy, like it was recycled. I shuddered, but once you're hammered, it doesn't matter what you drink.

Harry and Celeste made out by the jukebox. I leaned on the bar, ignoring them blearily and sipping a rose-and-tonic. I thought over the day. The full bar earlier, the people there. It was a less crowded now. Fewer centaurs. And the unicorn ditched out when he'd heard me talking to Harry, running scared like maybe he thought a bar brawl was coming on, virgin in tow...

I uncurled my fingers, heart hammering. Six golden hairs wound around my petal stained hand.

His *blonde* virgin, who might just have clocked me with my, er, toaster. But why would they need magic? Unicorns are more magical than everybody.

The regular barflies had shown up. Usually they were good for information. I beckoned Pip over and she landed on my forefinger.

"You don't look zzo good, Devin."

"I feel worse. Hey, you see a unicorn around here?"

"Nonezz so I notizzed."

I couldn't hide my disappointment. "Oh well. Thanks."

"I'm zzurprizzed you're here, with Mizzter Magic doing zzo poorly."

"It's why I'm here. I'm trying to find out who stole his magic and—"

Pip twitched her multifaceted eyes. "Magic? Nooo. I'm talking about hizz coma—whoopzzy daizzy!" She flew up as I bolted out the door.

Honestly, dying couldn't happen to a nicer guy. But I had to go. He'd hired me, for one. And, um…he hadn't killed me when I owed him a lot of money? Anyway, I liked to think old Mister M had *some* affection for me.

Two goons flanked the pale, wrinkled petal boss. He looked like someone deflated him and put him away wet. Pricillian sat on Mister M's pillow, wings drooping.

"He's dying, Devin." Then she perked up slightly. "The last thing he said before he went under was to take you out if he goes before you get his magic back."

Right. Affection. I had to get that magic back and quick. Except I had no idea where the unicorn was, or his virgin. I sure as hell wasn't going to bring it up with Pricillian. They were shit for suspects, and all I had were five blonde hairs and a partial hoof print to go on.

"Where'd Mister M get his magic?" It was common knowledge he took it.

Pricillian ruffled her feathers. "None of your business."

"It's for the case. It might be important."

One of the trolls grunted. "Some changeling traded it for his knees."

I stared at them. I knew why the unicorn and virgin stole the magic.

The garden was different at night. All intoxicating smells and rising magic. I entered cautiously, cursing my damn pride

that kept me from asking for help. But then, who would I ask? Pricillian was useless in a fight, and a unicorn could handle a couple of trolls. They wouldn't leave Mister M's side anyway.

At least the unicorn wasn't a pegasus too, but it'd take some quick wingplay to avoid his horn. I crept out to find a place to hide and watch, thinking of that long dagger on the unicorn's head.

Which, before my next breath, pressed against the center of my back between my wings.

The blonde virgin stepped from between the flowers. "You should have kept your wings to yourself, Devin."

Shit! They knew my name and everything. "Look. I know you took the magic but—"

The horn pressed deeper. Maybe best not to lead with an accusation, then. "Mister M is dying."

"Love always requires sacrifice," the virgin said. "And he deserves it. He's done horrible things."

Well, yeah, he'd even done some of them to me, but… "Mister M—"

"You know his real name is Eugene Puce, don't you?" the virgin said. "He was a banker from Cincinnati."

I wasn't about to admit I didn't. "How do you know?"

"I'm his daughter. Charmed my ma into bed and then up and left. Took me this long to find him."

"That sucks." It really did. "So this is revenge, then?"

"No. Like I said. For love." She looked past me at the unicorn. Her expression softened a little.

I eased forward. The horn followed. "So you're going hooves?"

"Yes. Consider the magic my inheritance. And all this."

The extent of her intention finally dawned on me. "You're going to take over the whole operation."

She looked around at the garden. "We have to eat somehhhoww." She blinked as a neigh dragged out the word.

"I bet you don't know the first thing about petal pushing."

"We'll learrrrhhhn."

I quirked my brow at her. "You'll need smart people

around you. People who know the streets." People who could actually speak in words.

She scratched at her forehead. A glint of horn was already protruding from her skull. "You applying?"

"You keep the goons from my back; I'll keep the riff-raff from yours."

She brayed a laugh. "Like you did with Mister Puce?"

"I found you, didn't I?"

She shook her mane as her neck lengthened. "I found you first."

Damn toaster. "I'm a good enforcer and you know it. We have a deal?"

She pursed her horsey lips, considering, and reached to shake on it. Stared. A hoof; a gleaming, silver hoof. I shook and she dropped to all fours, snorting.

The horn at my back eased off. The unicorn trotted around me to nuzzle the virgin's neck.

I grinned and plucked a rose. Time to celebrate young love and my new job. "Roses are red; violets are blue; somebody ends up dead; it might as well be Eu…gene."

# AARON MICHAEL RITCHEY

# SHOE

WELCOME TO MY NIGHTMARE. OTHERWISE KNOWN AS TUESDAY.

The first rule of being me? Don't leave the basement. The second rule? Stay high.

As long as I'm stoned, I can peer through the veil between our world and the supernatural to see the realm of ghosts and demons. So I smoke my daily dope. I want to see what's gonna eat me.

While some might call my walk-out basement a prison, I prefer the term *underground kingdom*—a paradise of linoleum, carpet remnants, a sofa, two La-Z-Boys, and my bed. Dark red curtains cover the glass patio doors. On the walls hang four decades of movie posters and three decades of video game boxes.

Normally I'd be kicking pixel ass on my Shockbox, but my entire kingdom is in jeopardy.

I draw back the curtain of the patio doors to look for Gussy, out on bail, which I paid. One million dollars for first degree murder, though he's innocent. He isn't coming over to thank me. No, something else is going on.

Autumn twilight murks up the evening, casting shadows over the clique of demon girls standing on the yellow sea of my dead lawn. They look like girls I went to high school with— same heavy make-up, same highlights, same short skirts and straining sweaters, but these girls have lawn-clippers for

hands. Fangs bristle from red painted lips. They have eyes the color of open wounds.

One sees me and raises a hand-clipper and snips them open, closed, open, closed. The blades squeak, stinking with the rusty smell of blood.

I gulp at the idea of castration. The sigil I drew to keep demons out of my house hums softly. Several bottles of Axe body spray stand under it. I test them on the demons. *Black Chill* seems to act as demon repellent, however odd, while *Black Temptation* seems to be demonic cat nip.

Mackie, the ghost of a 1970s housewife, hovers over my left shoulder, freezing me to get a look. "Looks like Asmodeus is still mad. Sucks to be you, Shoe."

I'd saved a nice young virgin from the sacrificial dagger of a devil cult and in the process pissed off a prince of hell.

"It's all so high school," I mutter.

"I wished I'd gone to school more, but you know, I had other things to do. Fucking flower power, man." Mackie floats around in regret.

Same as me sometimes. Fucking high school. Luckily, those years are far behind me and now I rule my own domain where I have all the sexual activity I want thanks to www. pornblister.com. Mom brings me food to keep my ass fat. Video games and video streaming complete the picture.

I have everything I want since my access to the spirit world made it easy for me to get rich. For example, I knew Netflix stock would split weeks before their CEO did. Also, the Jefferson County sheriff's office pays me a hefty monthly stipend as their "special services consultant," which means I help them solve the impossible cases.

As long as I have my ghosts and Gussy, I never have to leave, which keeps me alive since everyone in hell hates me.

Speak of Gussy, he comes marching around from the back gate and up to the patio door. He doesn't see the demon teens, but he sees me and his eyes turn furtive. I slide open the doors, an *oh-shit* on my lips.

While I love Gussy, his taste in clothes is highly questionable. Lately he's replete in blue leather—from boots to coat—a very bright sapphire color, matched with a dark silk shirt and even darker pants. We lock eyes.

I see the terror there. A second later I know why.

Two horrendously huge men appear beside Gussy. They shove him into my basement room and then bustle inside. They are works in contradiction, tall, big, in suits with ties. Black lipstick and mascara match their dyed black hair. Piercings decorate their faces like grenade shrapnel.

The warding sigil screams and gleams a neon light, and then goes back to its normal hum.

Some kind of supernatural something just burst into my kingdom. But which soul hides the stowaway?

Both men try and throw arms around me. But I'm roughly the size of Jupiter's largest moon and manage to slip away from one. The other trips me, sending me to the floor. Cold steel presses against the back of my skull.

I piddle myself, but only a little.

This shouldn't be happening, not in my underground kingdom. I shouldn't be under attack by suited, mascara'd gangsters. Liches or revenants, maybe, but not mortal men.

A knee knifes my kidneys. A Russian accented voice says, "You shout, I kill you. Then I kill woman upstairs, your mother I am thinking."

I sold a bit of my soul to keep Mom safe from the demonic world, but the living go by different rules.

Mackie gets in my face. Her real name is Candace McKenzie. She died in 1975 from a heroin overdose and left behind a husband and two young children. She's bell-bottoms pretty if you can ignore the pasty white skin and the marble-black eyes.

"Who are these guys?" I ask her.

The guy kneeling on me responds. "You don't need to know."

I don't correct him. My straining, pounding heart reminds me of every nacho-cheese thing I've ever eaten.

Mackie answers. "Boiko and Bondar. They send a lot

of spooks my way since they kill so many people. Big-time enforcers. Dang, Shoe, seems like everyone hates you today...."

Her voice is going hazy, which means my head is clearing. I need a bong hit, and pronto, or I'll be on my own.

One of the goons hoists me onto my ass. Sweat drips down my face.

"Boiko," I sputter, "which one of you is Boiko?"

One of them gives me the fish eye as he slips a Glock into an underarm holster. "Me. How did you know?"

"I know things. If you don't kill me, I can help you. I swear. Like I knew your names. I just need to smoke more dope."

Both laugh.

Boiko curls his lip. "Look at you, fat and disgusting. You live with your mother. You do the drugs all day. And you say you know things. I don't believe you."

Gussy stands decked in blue leather, visibly shaking. "Hey, Shoe, I'm sorry, man. They grabbed me. I lost it. I told them you could prove I didn't kill Melnyk."

Davey Melnyk, Gussy's real estate agent and his supposed murder victim. Melnyk was discovered in his garage, in his running car, but it wasn't a suicide. The garage door and the door to the house were both locked from the outside.

Gussy is my best friend, my partner, the one person I can count on. He's far more interested in smoking dope and playing video games than murdering anyone. The police don't know that. His fingerprints were found at the site and he had motive—his real estate agent was going to kick him out of his retail marijuana shop on Broadway, probably to make way for his Russian friends. Not motive enough for me, though.

Problem was, my investigation had come up empty. Mackie couldn't get into the coroner's office. Some newly dead ghost biker staked out the coroner's office as his own turf and wouldn't let Mackie near the body. Dead people can be such asshats.

Mackie vanished, or turned invisible. I'm dangerously close to a sober state, and if either Boiko or Bondar have some kind of demon inside them, I need to see it.

"If you prove Gus innocent," Boiko says, "then fine. If not, we kill him. We kill you as witness. You stay quiet, I don't kill your mother. We want to be a nicer, kinder *Bratva*, so we give you chance."

Great, I have five seconds to prove Gussy is innocent or die.

"I'm telling you, I need to smoke a bowl," I say. "Then I can figure this out."

I crawl my way onto my La-Z-Boy and sit back, heaving for breath. Both mobsters stand in front of me, chuckling at my struggles.

Fat camp failures come back to haunt me. Damn them. I give them attitude I don't feel. "So, my Russian friends, why don't you want to wait for the courts to convict Gussy?"

Boiko hisses. "That is racist. We are not Russian. We are Ukrainian. And we have ways of dealing with scumbags who kill family."

Gussy stands next to my sixty-five inch Sony. He speaks up. "Dudes, I had no idea Melnyk was part of the Ukrainian mafia. No wonder he wanted to evict me. He wanted more of a cut."

"No," Boiko says, "he doesn't like you selling the drugs. He is good man. And you killed him. We get revenge."

"It wasn't me!" Gussy says, a bit too loudly. "Maybe he was cheating on his wife and some jealous husband got him."

"No, he loved Svetlana!" Bondar slaps Gussy into my TV. It wobbles, threatens to fall, but Bondar rights it.

"Is everything all right down there?" Mom calls from upstairs.

"Just fine, Ma!" I yell back.

"Do you want a tuna fish sandwich?"

"I want sandwich," whispers Bondar.

I glare at him. "No, Ma. I'm good. Thanks though." *Please don't come down here. Please don't…*

Footsteps recede above us as Mom retreats to her room to watch her stories. Thank Jesus.

Boiko motions for me to get on with it.

On the little table next to my chair, I take up Lancelot the

bong and load the bowl. A flick of my well-thumbed, stainless-steel lighter, and it's smoke through the water, fire in my skull.

Mackie appears and sighs approvingly at the contact high. Which is why she hangs out with me. Even in death, dope fiends can't let go.

Now that I'm buzzed, I see the sizzling crimson light clawing up the walls. The girls of Asmodeus are testing my warding sigil. Poor me. Poor them. Applying eyeliner with yard clippers must suck.

Aside from me, the living in the room don't see a thing.

I talk to Mackie as she floats over the Sony, her arms across her chest. "Was Mr. Melnyk faithful?"

Boiko and Bondar follow my eyes, their mouths slack in disbelief.

"Not a cheater, Daddy," Mackie says. "I went over and haunted the wife for a while."

I raise an eyebrow.

Mackie puts up a spectral hand, "No, not really haunted, but you, know, I offered the widow Svetlana a little comfort and support from the beyond. Like groovy, man. Melnyk wasn't great, but his sons loved him." Tears shine in her onyx eyes. "Like me. I wasn't great either, but my family loved me."

"Sorry, Macks." Good info, and I feel bad for her, but I need more. "Gussy, guys, I can't get access to the coroner's reports. Can you tell me anything?"

Gussy shrugs.

Bondar answers in deadpan, which somehow still seems to rage. "The body, it was blue color. I find him."

"Blue?" I nod at Mackie. "Hey, can you try and hit the coroner's office again?

"On it, Shoe. Don't know how you're gonna get out of this one." She vanishes.

"Who do you talk to?" Boiko asks.

"He can see dead people," Gussy spouts, blood on his lip from Bondar's backhand.

"All the time?" Boiko asks.

"When I'm stoned," I say. And I'm starting to feel like

myself again. Yes, I might be a morbidly obese pothead living with my mom in her basement, but I'm Shoe, dammit. And they are in my domain.

A little plan plays peek-a-boo with my brain. But it will involve me getting out of my chair. Better if I can think myself out of this mess.

Boiko and Bondar go back and forth in Ukrainian, blackened lips flapping. No idea if they're talking about us or not, but I take a moment to re-visit Lancelot and get another lungful while I wait for Mackie.

*Hurry, baby, hurry.*

"His body couldn't have been blue," Gussy murmurs. "I mean, what the hell is that about?"

"Actually," I say from my thinking chair, "it's totally possible. The color of a dead man's skin can be affected by carbon monoxide poisoning. Melnyk's car was found running. What shade of blue?"

"You know X-Men movies?" Boiko asks.

I nod.

"Bondar say it was blue like X-Men girl."

"Probably Mystique," Gussy mutters. Bleeding, turning pale, he slumps against the wall in his very blue leather outfit.

My heart shrivels into a prune, then a raisin, then evaporates. Now I know why the ghost biker is protecting Melnyk's corpse at the morgue. A spell put him there.

"Oh no," I whisper. "No. Man. No."

"What?" Gussy asks, so innocently. He has no idea.

My heart hurts and I shut my eyes for a moment. Then I grab my wireless keyboard and boot up my computer. The OS flickers onto the Sony.

"Turn that off!" Boiko and Bondar yell.

"Kill me if you have to," I growl. "But if you want to know who killed Melnyk, I need to run something."

"What are you doing, Shoe?" Gussy asks. But it's not Gussy.

I've known Gussy my entire life. We laughed milk out of our noses in elementary. He stood by me when the jocks

in high school lit my backpack on fire in the middle of the football field. Pig roast. That was the joke. Lost all my DnD books. Fuckers.

Bondar goes to put his beatdown on me, but Boiko stops him.

Mackie appears back in the basement. Her dark eyes sparkle a little because she has a big clue.

Too bad I already know it.

"Skinned?" I ask.

"Skinned," Macke affirms. Somehow she made it past the biker

"Get ready," I warn her. "I'll need you in a minute."

Bondar glances around. "Is ghost here now?"

"What do you mean skinned?" Boiko asks.

While I type, I'm grinding my teeth, miles beyond pissed off. "Hey Gussy, that's a swell leather coat. Where did you get it?"

Gussy shrugs. "Online." His forehead shines sweaty.

"And blue," I add. "Your boots and your coat are so very leather and so very blue."

"Holy shit." Boiko, the smart one, gets it. Or at least gets a part of it. "You evil son of bitch." He barks at Bondar, telling him what I figured out.

Control-F6 on my keyboard triggers my exorcism rite. As a good Irish Catholic, I'm pretty good at drinking beer, better at smoking dope, but best at exorcising demons.

My TV flashes a complex series of symbols. Latin booms over my speakers.

*Exorcizo te, omnis spiritus immunde, in nomine Dei.*

Gussy flings up his hands and his bowels let loose a storm of unholy stink.

Dense smoke writhes out of his body. The eyes of the living can't see it, but I do.

The smoke coalesces into a corporeal shadow, seeping evil, red eyes bleed open, so like the demon cheerleaders outside. A mouth of needle teeth opens and keens, "Wilson Shoemaker. Asmodeus sends his regards. Wasn't my blue suit divine?"

It laughs at the irony.

My sigils warned me but failed to keep Asmodeus's lackey out because I made allowances for Gussy's twisted soul.

Now, free, the demon raises hands like scorpion stingers. My sigil by the stairs explodes in a flash of fire. The sigil by the bathroom lights up. Then another and another. The odor of rotten-egg fills the basement. Boiko and Bondar, out of their depth and terrorized fishbelly white, throw their hands over their heads and cower.

Outside, the demon teens clack their clippers. If all my sigils go down, they'll be snipping off my important parts before the Ukrainians can do a thing.

The demon birthed from Gussy's twitching body lurches toward me with its scorpion hands.

Before it can sting me, Mackie latches on to it. The demon curls around to bite her, but she is too strong. In her pale, ectoplasmic fingers, she squeezes it with her bereft-mother fury. Melnyk lost his children because of the thing. And Mackie, rage full, sad Mackie, kills the demon thing in her righteous, dead-fingered grasp.

It squeals out of existence. Only my warding sigil by the patio door survived.

Gussy reaches out. He's back to himself. "I'm sorry, man. I'm sorry."

Wasn't his fault. I try and get out of my chair. Boiko shoves me back. Bondar circles a garrote around my best friend's neck. "You pay now. Sick fuck."

Boiko makes sure I don't get up. I close my eyes.

"It wasn't him," I whisper. "A demon killed and skinned Melnyk. A demon who was after me."

Only takes a few minutes. Gussy lays lifeless on the floor. Mackie is weeping over us. She's so broken up over losing Gussy, it's clear, I'm on my own.

Both Ukrainians pull pistols out of their coats and cap the barrels with silencers. "You witness now, Shoe. You come with us."

They want to dump my fat carcass somewhere else.

"No!" I shout in terror. They might kill me, but not before Asmodeus's demons get their chance.

Boiko and Bondar haul me up, but my legs don't cooperate. Still, they are strong enough to drag me toward the patio doors. I try to pull free until Boiko smacks my head. "Remember mother upstairs."

I go cold. Now that we're closer to the patio doors, the demon teens are there, laughing at me through their fangs. Clippers open and close. Open and close. Squeaking.

At the door, I fumble for a bottle of Axe spray and hope I've grabbed *Black Temptation*. I spray Boiko, then Bondar.

"What the shit?" Boiko growls.

Bondar sneezes. He slides open the door.

Before they can stop me, I lunge for the last warding sigil and draw a line through the bottom symbol, breaking the spell.

Then I snatch up *Black Chill* and douse myself.

Just in time. A clipper nips my ear. The floating demons bypass me to fall on the Ukrainians. Clippers chop off fingers, snip off noses, lop off ears, gouge out eyes. Blood sprays the patio door, the movie posters on my wall, me.

The thugs can't see what to fight against. Within seconds they're too paralyzed with agony from the chop-chop of rusty blades pruning them like Russian olive trees.

Excuse me, Ukrainian olive trees.

Once the cheerleaders are finished slicing and dicing, they whirl around the room. They shy away from me, thanks to the *Black Chill* spray. The leader howls, and the rest follow her out and into the night.

I redraw my warding sigil then slump to the floor, stinking of cheap body spray and blood.

"Shoe, are you okay?" Mom calls from upstairs. "You're so loud tonight?"

"Yeah, Ma, just fine. Sorry!"

"Keep it down. I'll make you and Gussy some tuna fish."

"Don't. We're okay."

But we're not.

Gussy. I crawl over to his corpse. I'm still breathing hard, and my heart feels like it's either going to explode or quit. I can't believe he's gone. He shouldn't have come back to my nightmare. My Tuesday.

Mackie floats by me. "You can go outside now," she murmurs, trying to find the bright side. "With the *Black Chill*, you can leave the basement."

"Yeah." My gut sickens at the idea. "But I don't want to."

# KAT RICHARDSON

## CARD SHARP

THE DESOTO CLUB ON SUNSET WAS HOTTING UP WHEN I arrived. I didn't see any sign of LA's finest turning a blind eye and a greased palm, so I went on inside the speakeasy, looking for a poker game and tailed by an invisible crowd of pissed-off dead guys. One of them had taken a swing at me during a riot a few days earlier, but the rest I'd only recognized from a photo in the papers. Freight handlers union organizers, all found together, smiling at the neck with no weapon in sight. Just bloodied playing cards scattered on the ground. Poor saps. None of these spooks was my doing, but I was the only guy listening, and that put me on the spot.

See: It's bullshit that "Dead men tell no tales." Ghosts always have some beef, but most of them can't tell it straight—they jumble it up and give it out in bits and pieces. They'll glom onto anyone who's connected, or anyone who can see them, and hound the unlucky schmuck until he solves their problem. Or dies. Personal spooks are different—they'll tell you everything, endlessly. The first ghost to ever give me a straight story was a guy I'd drowned by summoning saltwater into his lungs. You kill a man by magic, and he has the right to hang about and torment you—or your descendants—forever. Unless you manage to dispel his incorporeal ass, because you can't solve his problem short of going bughouse or eating a bullet.

Exorcising ghosts is a one-at-a-time job. So when this bunch turned up muttering about "poker," "DeSoto," and "Roberts," it seemed faster and easier to figure out their problem than try to snuff 'em individually. And there's always a poker game at the DeSoto Club.

Customers unconsciously moved away as they felt my spectral companions' chill. I skirted the dance floor and walked through the opulent main room and into the back room, where the bar was. No sign of anyone playing cards. Junior was issuing instructions to one of the bar tenders and I slipped into a gap on his other side.

"Danny in tonight?"

Junior forced a grin. "Hiya, Mr. Storm. Pop's in his office."

Daniel Bell Jr. hadn't inherited his old man's rugged features, much less his casual disregard for race and religion, and his smarts were on the same scale as his looks. But since the Crash in '29, it wasn't as easy to find customers with ready cash, much less a pile like I'd inherited, so Junior overlooked my Creole coloring. In the nine years we'd been friends, his father had never given a damn.

I gave Junior an inquiring stare and he leaned in to explain, "He's hosting a game upstairs with some high rollers."

"Anybody I know?"

He chewed his lip a moment. "Uh…Willie Dorrit, Emilio Torrega—"

"I thought you said 'high rollers.'"

"The rest are big fish: Keyne, Novicek, and some railroad mouthpiece from back east who's been in a couple times lately."

"What's his name?"

Junior shrugged. "I dunno. But he seemed hot on the good luck charm Torrega picked up in the bar." He winked at me. "Quite a dish."

I have a reputation for chasing skirts, but I usually wait for them to put on the for-hire light. In this case, it was the ghosts who lit up, getting noisy in my head and dropping

the temperature around the bar enough to start the nearest customer shivering. "Think they'd mind if I sat in?"

Junior moved to the house phone and chatted a bit before he answered. "Pop says you can come up if you brought your wallet."

Even with a card table set up, there was enough room left in Bell's luxurious office to swing a couple dozen cats around without knocking bottles off the bar. The ghosts spilled through the doorway after me. The card players shuddered unconsciously and a few glanced my way before the game continued. I recognized most of them. One of the two strangers at the table was a tall blond guy. The other was Torrega's hot number—a knockout brunette wearing a black silk dress that didn't hide more than a few freckles—but her escort wasn't paying her much attention.

Danny Bell spoke without looking up. "Nice of you to drop in, Storm. Thought gambling wasn't your thing."

"Not for money, usually—though in Willie's case, it won't be gambling." Fast cars, faster women, booze, coke, and black magic were my usual vices, but this would do if it got the ghosts off my back.

Willie Dorrit narrowed his eyes. He reported on some of my youthful follies back when he was more news hawk than lowlife opportunist. "Yeah, playing for a few Cs must seem downright puny. Tell you what, killer—if you lose, we'll take you out back and put a bullet in you. How's that?" He grinned like he meant it.

I wouldn't soil my knives on Willie, and I couldn't imagine anyone else would, either. I returned the cold smile. "Tempting. Especially if I get to offer you the same deal when I win."

He snorted and turned his attention back to the game. I went to the bar and built myself a drink. The water in the pitcher and the soda siphon welled toward me for a moment. I flicked it away before anyone noticed. I can manipulate or draw power from anything with enough water in it—

seawater particularly—but it's deceptive, fickle magic, and the landlubber ghosts were a persistent drag on my mind.

I lit a cigarette and drank while I waited for the hand to end. The ghosts hadn't been so polite. They circled the table, muttering, and irritated the male players into recklessness. But they didn't even raise goosebumps on the woman.

The blond man I didn't recognize won. He scraped in a pile large enough to pay the salaries of a couple of the dead freight handlers, plus bonuses. Judging by his snazzy New York suit and manicured hands, he was the fat-cat lawyer who worked for the railroad—the pot wouldn't cover his expenses for a week.

With the hand finished, most of the players left the table to freshen their drinks. Keyne and Novicek announced they were calling it quits and took off. I guessed a lot of the dough on the table arrived in their pockets. That left Bell, Willie, Torrega, and the strangers. Plus me and the ghosts—but they weren't taking up much space.

Bell fixed a hard stare on the winner. "That's more than enough to square your markers with me, Roberts."

*Poker, DeSoto, Roberts.* Now I just needed to figure the angle that would satisfy my phantom cohort.

Roberts chuckled, oozing patent charm. "Give me a chance to get ahead, Bell. I'm going back to Washington tomorrow."

"I don't care if you're going to Timbuktu. Dorrit persuaded me to let you play tonight, but if you think you're gonna keep on winning, you're a bigger bunny than I thought." Bell put out his hand and beckoned for the dough. Roberts heaved a sigh and started counting bills.

I studied the other players. Torrega twitched every time a ghost passed him by, though I knew he couldn't see them. He was a right guy, a little dim, a little desperate, but generally decent, so…what was he doing here? Willie went to brace him and muttered into Torrega's ear. I turned my gaze aside before Willie could notice it, and caught the lady in black looking me over. I smiled and she returned a long, slow smolder that reminded me of a cat making up its mind whether to purr or punish.

"Drink?" I was standing at the bar, after all, and I may be a son of a bitch, but I'm no heel.

"Scotch." The quirk of her lips wasn't really a smile and the little hairs on my body stood at attention.

I could see Bell and Roberts watching us, neither noticing the other's stare. *Roberts, poker, DeSoto. Bell, Willie, Torrega… and the lady.* It added up to something, but I didn't know what, yet. I turned to make her drink. "Not many women like Scotch—or poker. What else do you play?"

"When's the game's challenging enough, one doesn't play at it. And if the game offers no challenge, it's not *worth* playing." She accepted her drink with one elegant hand, and offered the other like a duchess. "Ivy Salazar."

"Marty Storm."

Her smile turned wicked.

"*Martin* Storm?" Roberts asked. "Of S & D Shipping?"

That broke the mood. I turned and headed for the table. "On my bad days."

"I heard you were injured in that riot the other day. Union playing rough with your company, too?"

"No. I was just in the wrong place. We've got no kick."

"Unlike your railroad," Bell added to Roberts. Rail and union had been at each other for years.

Roberts didn't rise to the bait, but he had the worst poker face I'd ever seen. I wondered how he'd managed to win enough to pay Bell off. But I didn't wonder for long.

The ghosts faded into the corners until the living sat back down to play, then the spooks started their weird circling again. I still didn't know what they wanted—revenge, salvation, something else?—but it wasn't a straight card game.

I felt a current of magic drifting along in the wake of every card dealt, and to my inner ear they snapped against the felt like gunshots. Bell and I both lost money steadily no matter what we held. The cheat was subtle, but it was still crooked. Bell wasn't paying it any mind though—he seemed more interested in Salazar than the crooked card game and that wasn't like him. Torrega continued to ignore the way Bell

ogled his good luck charm, while Roberts smiled a lot and watched Salazar and Bell like they were the floor show. Willie glared holes through me. The ghosts circled, whispering into our ears at every check, waiting for something they weren't clueing me into. So I waited too.

When it was Salazar's deal, the ghosts stopped on a dime and hissed. Kind of like the sound a sharp blade makes as it leaves its sheath. *Interesting.* I guessed the girl was a card mechanic, but why the spooks cared was still in the air.

The dead guy who hit me at the riot seemed to be the leader of the ghosts and he bent down to mutter into Torrega's ear. *Stooge.*

Torrega shivered, toying with his ante. He brushed at the ghost like a fly and then tossed his money in the pot with a shaking hand. As the cards were dealt, the dead guy whispered to him again. *It's goodnight, sucker.* Torrega gazed around, like he had the heebie-jeebies. He reached for his cards and my dead guy put his fist through him.

Color fled Torrega's face and the ghost shoved his hands down into Torrega's, who yelped as if the cards had cut him. He pushed to his feet in a panic and stood inside the dead guy's shade, going paler by the second. Then he backed away, fixing a wide-eyed stare on Willie. "I'm out."

I didn't think he was talking about the card game.

Salazar frowned at Willie and Torrega as Willie's face twisted up into something cruel. "You're out when I say you're out."

"Fuck you," Torrega spat and bolted for the door.

Willie reached for something under the table. Salazar shot her gaze to Roberts, didn't seem to like the fury slipping over his face, and flexed her hands on the deck of cards in front of her. Then she twisted her wrists and the cards sprang toward the ceiling like a fountain.

The pasteboards roared and glittered as they erupted from her hands.

"Shit!" Willie jumped up and knocked his knees against the table as he struggled to yank something hard and bulky from his trouser pocket.

The rest of us came up just as fast and loud. One falling card sliced open the back of Danny Bell's flailing hand like a knife. I threw a quick and dirty protection spell; all the liquids on the table splashed upward and knocked the cards back out of the air, limp and soaked, but only another magic-flinger would know I'd been responsible.

Bell shouted in surprise and cursed the whiskey that rained down and stung his cut hand as Roberts turned toward him. The ghosts crowded around Salazar.

*Cards sharp as goddamned razors.*

Willie went after Torrega.

Salazar watched him with a narrow glare. Then turned her eyes on me. She wasn't the only one.

The self-appointed steward of this ghost union stared me down from behind Salazar and put his big, incorporeal hands on her shoulders. The rest stood still and they all glared at me like suspicious fathers, degenerate skirt-chaser that I was.

*Jesus. She killed them, so why—?*

The pieces started slamming into place in my mind. I reached through the spooks, yanked Salazar to her feet, and hustled her into the hallway.

⁂

The sound of Willie and Torrega's running feet still rang on the staircase. Salazar dug in her heels once we were out of the office and I spun back around in the thick chill of the dead guys at our heels. She flicked her free hand at me. I barely caught the playing card that should have taken out my eye. It was cold with magic, and sharp enough to slice the web between my fingers. Blood oozed down my hand and the card went flimsy. "So it's not just a signature." I let it fall and clutched Salazar's shoulders. "The guys you killed seem to want me to protect you—"

"I don't need protection, *wizard*."

"Not a wizard—just a guy with a couple tricks up his sleeve and a lot of ghosts on his back." I shook her. Yeah, she didn't need my help, but someone else did. "What's the point of the game and who's your target?"

She brushed the last of her jujued cards against my neck. "Get your paws off me, or it'll be you."

"Gonna give me a shave like the guys at the freight depot? You think that'll work on me?"

The spooks spread out in the hallway like bums looking for half-smoked butts. Yelling and scuffling from the office demanded my attention, but the lady was a far greater threat. I needed her on my side, so I kept my gaze level and ignored everything else. "I haven't quite figured it, so, tell me quick: who's with the angels and who's for hell?"

"That'll be you, Storm. You smug prick." Willie and a tacky little nickel-plated .32 had come back up the stairs and were looking at us from the top step. "And don't think the dame's gonna help you. She's a darb with a straight razor, but there ain't room to hide nothing in that dress bigger than a dirty thought."

*He doesn't know...*and I'd never reach the flick knife in my own pocket before Willie drilled me.

Salazar shifted her hand holding the playing card. I narrowed my eyes at her in warning, then looked at Willie. "You're gonna shoot me? You said you'd wait till I was losing, Willie."

"You were losing soon as you queered my play." His grin was full of sharp, crooked teeth. "It'll look like a lover's spat— big, messy pity but..." He shrugged. "Cops won't look further than they have to. Hell, they'll probably give me a medal for pluggin' you."

I let Salazar go and turned, took a step forward, staying between her and Willie. There was no liquid in the hallway for me to cast a spell with. The ghosts weren't any help either, the useless sacks of ectoplasm. I only had one play.

"Nuh-uh," Willie grunted, twitching the gun. "I don't know how you get away with it, but you're not gonna bump *me* and walk."

"I didn't think you hated me enough to frame me for— what's it gonna be?" I asked. "Two murders or three?"

"Just Bell and the broad. Shouldn't have sat in, boy." He

wasn't referring to my age. "Torrega lammed it, so now I gotta improvise. And here you are, killer."

*Hate and money.* I shook my head as I shifted out of Salazar's way. "Always said you weren't worth dirtying up my blades." Salazar's card flicked past, just a blur and a swish in the gloomy hall. It sliced across Willie's wrist to the bone. "Never said I wouldn't use someone else's."

He screamed, the gun dropping to the floor. His hand flopped from severed tendons and blood sprayed. He might live, but I didn't have time to worry about it. I snatched the gun as Willie curled over his arm, keening, and Salazar and I rushed back into Bell's office.

Roberts and Bell were rolling on the floor. Each clutched the other by the throat. Salazar flicked her hands outward and every dry playing card left in the room sprang into her grip. She fanned them out and cocked one arm back. The ghosts hung just behind her.

I put my free hand up in front of her face as I pointed the gun at Roberts. "Hold it."

Everyone froze and looked at me.

"I assume Miss Salazar doesn't work cheap, so…was this a pay-off or a rub-out?"

Roberts staggered to his feet, leaving Bell on the floor. "How would I know? Ask Dorrit."

"Willie's a snake, but he's got no reason to knock off a bunch of union guys. You and your bosses do."

Bell coughed, rubbing at Roberts' fingerprints on his neck with one hand and groping the bookshelf with the other as he got up. "This one was into me for six Gs—so if he was hiring torpedoes to do the railroad's dirty work, he was paying with somebody else's money."

Now I got it. "Your money, Bell. Game was a set-up."

Salazar folded her lethal cards into her hands but didn't put them down. "Dorrit made the contract with me through a blind," she said. "When he realized I was a woman, he thought he could pull a fast one and change the terms. Rig the game, knock off Bell, and winner take all. Dorrit had Torrega bring

me, so Bell wouldn't connect me to him or Roberts. I smelled a rat, but I wanted my money."

I grinned at the ghosts crowding the room and then back at Salazar. "The greedy jackasses figured to let a little daylight through you and Torrega, then keep the haul." I turned to Roberts. "If I hadn't showed up, you'd have pulled your dirty tricks without paying a dime. I'll bet Willie even promised you'd split the loot."

"He wouldn't—"

Willie scraped himself up from the floor behind me. "Shut your yap, Roberts."

Half the ghosts surged toward him, half toward Roberts.

I looked over my shoulder. Willie was closer than I thought, and he lunged at me with something sharp and shiny in his good hand. Gun raised, I spun into him as ghastly cold enclosed us.

Cards whizzed past and I squeezed the trigger. The shot rang my head like a gong and Willie's dead weight pulled me down. I staggered back and looked around, wondering how the .32 had barked so loud.

There wasn't a ghost to be seen, but Willie was sprawled face-down on the floor. Roberts slid down the wall, sliced up like an Easter ham and leaving a red spray well below a bullet hole the size of a thumb. Salazar's hands were empty, cards strewn across the table and stuck into the plaster all around the mess Roberts made.

A hefty .45 smoked in Bell's hand. "Gimme the heater, Storm. I'll make it right." Bell laid his own gun down and looked at Salazar. "Way I see it, these two got theirs before they could croak me and rob the joint, so you got no cause to finish the job, do you, doll?" He glanced at me. "And I'm beholden. So I'm not gonna remember who else was here or what screwy shit went down. But you two gotta scram before Junior comes upstairs. He's stiff-necked, that boy. I swear to Christ, I don't know where his mother got him."

It was as good a deal as we'd get. I tossed Willie's peashooter on the table and hustled Salazar out the doors with me.

We made it to Sunset before there was any sign of trouble back at the club. I kept my arm hooked with hers as we slowed to a casual stroll.

"I'm out six thousand dollars," she said, her voice low and frosty.

"But you're alive, free, and the guys you blew down aren't holding a grudge."

Eyes narrowed, she chewed on that for a minute. "Why not? I'd expect them to want payback."

"Union guys can respect a good worker, but they can't stand a crooked boss. Willie and the company man got what they had coming. But, if another innocent had been added to your toll, the gloves would have come off."

"The 'gentlemen' from the union almost got you cut and stitched for murder."

"I think we've both skated on that before."

She gave me that long up-and-down again.

There was blood on my suit and I'd kept my hands in my overcoat pockets to hide the rest of the gore. I didn't know if she didn't care, or if it lit her fire. A shiver ran over me, and the hairs on the back of my neck weren't the only things rising. The lady was dangerous in *so* many ways. "Buy you a drink?" I asked.

"I suppose I have time to kill."

"Not me, I hope."

She chuckled. "Depends on how you play your cards."

# MARIO ACEVEDO

## TAKERS FIND GIVERS

I HEAD NORTHWEST ON THE PHOENIX-WICKENBURG HIGHWAY. I work to keep cool. Keep my foot light on the gas pedal. Keep my Chrysler Sebring easing through mid-day traffic, just another car rolling innocently out of downtown.

My mouth is so dry it hurts to swallow. I take a last pull from the water bottle in the console and toss the empty onto the backseat.

"Count the money," I tell Wynter.

He swipes his pointed, manicured fingernails across the screen of his Android. Who the hell is he texting?

I tell him again. He ignores me again.

"Goddamn it, I'm talking to you." I reach for his phone.

He pulls it away. "Jerry, what's your problem?"

"My problem? It ain't my problem. It's our problem." I yank the Cobra derringer from my pocket and wave it at him. "We just killed somebody."

"You killed somebody," he replies, his voice flat and controlled.

"You were there." I gesture with the pistol toward the backpack resting against his black patent leather, lace-up boots. "That makes you an accessory. I fry. You fry."

He snorts. *As if.*

Thick kohl eyeliner rims his pale green eyes, luminescent even in the shadow of the coupe's interior. He never wears sunglasses. His slim hands and bald head are so pale they seem

to glow against his black clothes. A tall, ruffled collar cups his neck. Underneath his velvet trench coat he wears a corset. Considering the heat, he should be sweltering, but I've never seen him sweat and his touch always remains cadaver cold. That's what you get when your partner in crime is a vampire.

His painted, black lips curve a bit.

I train the little pistol at his chest to let him know I'm not fucking around.

"If you're going to threaten me with that gun," he says, "at least make sure it's loaded."

*Oh yeah.* I emptied both of the Cobra's stubby barrels into Raul, double-tapping his fat gut with the .380 bullets. I shove the derringer back into my pocket.

Raul brought it on himself, the greasy bastard. For starters, the fucker ripped me off before, selling me X that was actually generic aspirin. He was talking shit about me and Brenda, then me and Wynter. Laughing as he called us a couple of *jotos*, then laughing again when I pulled the Cobra.

"Whatchu gonna do with that popgun?" He sneered. "*No tienes los huevos.*"

He learned I had plenty of balls when I capped him. He quit laughing and hit the floor, grunting and bleeding.

But Raul running his *cabron* mouth wasn't the only reason I shot him. It was about the backpack he left out in the open for Wynter and me to see. We'd gone to the *Llantera Superior* tire store to score Opana, and the teal blue North Face backpack looked way out of place among the Dunlops and Goodyears. So it was his stupid luck that I put two and two together and came up with…

"How much money?" I ask Wynter.

"Forty-two thousand, eight-hundred fifty dollars."

*Holy shit!* I take my eyes off the road only long enough to ask, "When did you count it?"

"I didn't have to. Raul told me."

"When?" The scene went down with Wynter and me getting let in through the back door, us doing the deal with Raul, me spotting the backpack, Raul acting like an asshole,

me seeing this as an opportunity to drop his ass. *Bang. Bang.* The bottle of Opana dropping from his hand and clattering to the floor. Me jamming it into my pocket. Me grabbing the backpack, zipping it open to find a stack of Benjamins smiling at their new owner. Wynter and me making tracks to my car. I didn't remember him talking to Raul.

Wynter says, "When I bent down and touched his head."

"Oh yeah." When Raul was bleeding out, Wynter crouched to search him and laid his hand on Raul's head. He must've used his vampire mind trick.

"Did he tell you anything else?"

"Nope." Wynter is back to swiping his phone.

Okay. No one saw us enter or leave the tire shop. One of the two security cameras covering the alley was busted, and the other sprayed over when someone tagged the wall. This being Saturday afternoon, we have until Monday before anyone finds Raul. We didn't touch anything or leave footprints so the CSI *pendejos* will have shit for clues. If it wasn't for snitches, the Phoenix PD would be batting zero against us homies.

I stare up the avenue, barely paying attention to traffic as I think about the money. Forty-two thousand, eight-hundred fifty dollars. That's a lot of *ficha*, enough to change a lot of things. I start making plans.

My phone vibrates. I tell Wynter to hold the wheel while I dig the phone out of my pants pocket. Since it's a burner, I haven't bothered to program any numbers. But I recognize Sergio's and put the phone to my ear. "Yeah?"

"Jerry, when-you-gonna-pay-me-my-goddamn-money-you-motherfucker?" The words shoot out the phone in *chola* rapid-fire.

I wince. *Shit.* Tina, my ex. How did she get Sergio's phone? I wince again. The usual way. Blowjobs.

I take the wheel and say, "I got your money."

"How much?" she blurts, suspicious.

"All thirty-seven hundred." I borrowed money from her to pay back what I mooched from Delia, my ex-ex, which in turn was to cover the loan from Xochi, my ex-ex-ex. And I owe my

current squeeze, Brenda, my share of our rent, three month's worth.

"Liar." Tina spits the word. "You know what your problem is, Jerry?"

I should hang up but I don't, or she'll be ringing this number for the rest of the goddamn day. Better to hear her out and get some peace afterwards.

"My rehab therapist says you're a taker, a motherfucking taker." She sobs. "And I'm a giver. You took advantage of me. You hear that?" Her voice rises, cutting as broken glass. "You took from me. Money. My love. My respect. My dignity."

*Dignity?* I roll my eyes. Her breath probably still reeks of Sergio's cock. I throw her a bone so she'll shut the fuck up. "I got your money, okay? You're going to get it."

"When?"

"Tonight?" I look at Wynter in case he's got other ideas. He shrugs.

"Tonight works," Tina says. "I'll be at Sergio's."

"See you there."

When the call ends, it's like a woodpecker has quit pounding the inside of my skull.

*Me, a taker?* I smirk. Damn straight and about time in my life. You're either a taker or a giver, and I'm tired of being a giver, a victim.

What to do with all of the money? Not much if I stay here. Word gets around that I'm squaring debts and I.O.Us, who knows what assholes will come out of the woodwork. And I have to consider Raul might've been holding that cash for some other *vato loco*, who will be gunning for it.

But if I leave? Then go where? Back to Riverside, lay low, and start fresh? Or San Diego? El Paso? Albuquerque? Denver? Seattle? Lots of options.

We pass under the Papago Freeway. The shadows from the twin overpasses flash over us. Dark. Bright. Dark. Bright.

I check the mirrors. Everything looks clear. I turn north on 19th Avenue.

Wynter's still on his phone.

"I could use some help keeping a lookout."

"We're fine," he replies.

"How do you know?"

"I just do."

A cop car cruises by in the opposite direction. My nerves tighten and my shoulders cramp into knots. I keep my head forward but track the car as it passes in the rearview. I imagine the light bar strobing red and blue, the car whipping around after us. But it doesn't. I watch it disappear into traffic.

"Told you," Wynter says, cool as death.

So, you ask, how the hell did I team up with a vampire?

A month ago we met at Ray-ray's place down in Chandler, when Ray-ray was still dealing scripts before the cops busted him. Among us *cholos,* Wynter looked like a grain of white rice on a plate of *mole.* Then, as now, he was decked out in heavy-duty Goth velvet as if he'd looted a Hot Topic. But he had the cash and everyone was creeped out by his freaky albino appearance, so nobody bothered him.

But when he got close, something inside me moved toward him like a compass needle swinging to a magnet. Like we were long-lost *hermanos.* On the way out I offered him a ride. By the time we made it to his tiny condo near the airport, my brain was vibrating like a tuning fork. I hadn't even touched the Oxycontin or the Percocet we scored earlier.

As my car idled in the dark parking lot outside his place, he said, "I want to show you something," and reached for my wrist. His frigid touch added to the weird appeal of his offer.

I watched, fascinated as he took my hand and brought it to his lips. Fangs sprouted from his mouth, but I didn't pull away. His sharp teeth sank into my wrist, easing through the skin with a small, sharp pain.

Then a chill started from the bite and flowed through me. It was like a blast of the best meth/heroin highball times ten and served ice cold. The sensation didn't last more than a few seconds and I relaxed against the driver's seat, the glorious buzz ebbing.

Wynter lapped blood from my wrist. He let go, pressed a

frosty hand against my forehead, and said, "Like a blast of the best meth/heroin highball times ten."

"How can you read my thoughts?"

"One of my tricks."

After that, I let him hang around, even took him to my place and introduced him to Brenda. He never told us where he was from, and we never asked. Brenda and I shared our stash of scripts in exchange for a delicious fanging. I didn't advertise to anyone else that he was a vampire; what did I have to gain? But should the secret get loose, I'll let *Mythbusters* tackle what Wynter was or wasn't.

I drive west to Maryvale, where Brenda and I share a one-bedroom rat hole in a Section-8 complex off Indian School Road.

I can't find any shady parking spots on the street. I text Brenda that we're right outside. As soon as we crack open the doors of the Chrysler, the cool air vanishes. Under the full glare of the sun, the Arizona heat gets its claws into me. I carry the backpack and walk beside Wynter, still amazed how he doesn't melt beneath all that black clothing. Sunlight doesn't affect him.

We head for the outside staircase. The heat blasts off the stucco like we're in an oven. I can't wait to leave Phoenix. Could I leave Wynter?

Forty-two thousand, eight-hundred fifty dollars split one way goes a lot further than forty-two thousand, eight-hundred fifty dollars split two ways.

The math cinches it. From now on, I'm flying solo as the king of takers.

The light is so intense that even with sunglasses I blink and trip on the first step. Wynter grabs my arm and with his free hand, keeps my head from banging against the wall. I straighten and thank him. Reaching the second floor, I see my door is ajar.

Brenda's waiting. She steps back and lets Wynter and me enter. Strands of dishwater-blond hair hang loose around her neck. I remove my sunglasses and lock the door. Brenda's

barefoot, and a muffin top sags between her white tank and cutoff jeans. A recent tattoo shines red and puffy from one shoulder.

Blinds cover the window, and since we're on the shaded side of the building, not much light peeks through. A coffee table sits between the TV and the sofa. Candles, a BBQ lighter, scissors, an ashtray, and cans of Diet Coke crowd the table. Brenda sits on the sofa and folds her big legs beneath her. I pause to consider her, this dump where we live, my life, and all the cash that has fallen into my lap.

She's been a good girlfriend and put up with a lot of my bullshit.

Oh well.

I look at Wynter. I'm going to miss the skinny bloodsucker.

Takers find givers. I'll leave these givers and find new ones.

Brenda asks, "What's in the bag?"

"Nothing much." To distract her I pull the bottle of Opana from my pocket and shake it. The pills inside barely rattle, muffled by cotton.

Smiling eagerly, Brenda rises and retrieves a box of syringes from the bedroom. Wynter follows. I sit cross-legged beside the coffee table, the backpack tucked between my knees.

Brenda kneels on the opposite side of the table and places the box between us. "Why don't you go first?" she offers. Wynter props his skinny ass on one of the sofa armrests.

"Wynter," I ask, "what about you?"

He shakes his head. He's like this sometimes, gets all emo and acts like he's too good to get high.

"What's on your mind?"

He doesn't answer, and I have better things to do than pry answers out of him.

Brenda uses the scissors to snip an empty can of Diet Coke apart and fashions the bottom into a cooker. I dump the load of Opana pills into the ashtray.

She lights a candle. I take a syringe, uncap it, and lay it beside the ashtray. Placing one of the Opana in the cooker, I

hold it over the flame like a tiny skillet. The pill starts to smoke and sizzle. The sight and sound is more appetizing than frying bacon. Wynter approaches. I'm sure he's changed his mind about indulging.

The pill splits open and liquefied Opana seeps across the cooker, like a drop of melted sugar. I set the cooker on the table and draw the Opana into the syringe.

Wynter crouches beside me and offers his hand. Giving him the syringe, I tilt my head to one side and expose my neck. Eyes closed, my nerves shrink around the spot where the needle comes to kiss me.

One prolonged sting—the pain is always worth it—and the needle withdraws.

I expect the rush to bloom though my body. Instead, it clangs into my head. My eyes pop open and the room swirls around me. I clutch at the coffee table but my fingers slide free. Losing balance, I fall backwards. The room keeps spinning. An acid taste makes me gag.

This isn't an opioid high, this is something else. My thoughts are clear but an invisible wall grows between my mind and the world.

Everything is distorted but I can make out Wynter, standing over me, a syringe in each hand. Where did the second syringe come from? What did he give me? Brenda's on her feet and pawing through the backpack.

I try to shout but my mouth and jaw have turned into rubber, and I can't form words.

Brenda takes stacks of money from the backpack and throws the backpack against my belly. It's still heavy with some of the cash. Money in hand, she leaves for the bedroom and returns with a cell phone. She sits on the sofa and makes a call, but her words slur together.

I squirm like an overturned turtle, unable to find the balance and strength to get upright. Time passes. Seconds? Minutes? I can't tell. The room keeps rocking and turning.

A distant knocking penetrates the puzzle of sensations.

Brenda drifts from the sofa toward the door. A moment later she retreats, two cops rushing past her, one white, the other black, both of them big smears of muscle and bad news.

She's shouting and what she says congeals in the haze. "That's him! He killed Raul Gonzales at the tire shop!"

I gape at her in disbelief. The cops pounce and flip me over. My arms are drawn back and steel cuffs lock around my wrists. Hands grope my pockets. The derringer is flung on the carpet, followed by my cell phone, my keys, the extra .380 cartridges. The black cop unzips the backpack.

Wynter says, "Jerry stole that money from Raul. I was there."

My mind boils with rage. That vampire asshole and that bitch Brenda squealed on me. *Snitches! Fucking snitches!* The words echo and echo to remind me that I'd been double-crossed.

Helpless, I flatten against the carpet. I am beyond fucked when I realize the empty cartridges remain in the Cobra, two clues that will link me to the slugs in Raul.

I'm hauled to my feet, but my legs can't hold me upright. The cops lean me against a wall, and they get busy squawking into their radios. Wynter steps close and his green eyes burn like flames.

My mind screams *Why, you fucking bastard? Why did you snitch on me?* but only drool slobbers from my mouth.

Wynter, that goth fang-banger motherfucker, brings his alabaster-white face closer. "From now on, I'm flying solo as the king of takers."

*Shit!* When I'd tripped on the stairs, he touched my head. He read my mind.

Wynter stands back, and Brenda clasps his hand.

They smile like a couple of takers.

WARREN HAMMOND

# THE COMBO

THE GUN FEELS STRANGE. EVEN UNLOADED, I FIND IT HEAVY and unnatural. Like a sledgehammer in the hand of a watch-maker.

Harlan is seated next to me in the cab of the parked Toyota pickup, and he chills me with one of his joyless grins before pulling the ski mask over his square head.

The realization of what I am about to do makes me shiver. Today, the eighth of August, I am about to rob my first and only bank.

Harlan checks his watch. "Six AM. You ready, Doc?"

For weeks now, ever since he found out I went to med school, he calls me Doc instead of Nick. He knows I hate it, but Harlan is an asshole, so he calls me Doc anyway. Never mind the fact that I never became an actual doctor. Didn't even make it through the first year before flunking out.

I look at the gun. "You sure it's unloaded? We don't want to hurt anybody."

"Emptied that bitch myself," he says as he tries to poke the hair jutting from the mask's left eyehole back under the knitting. "Ditto for my gun, just like you asked. Now you ready to break this pony or what? This mask is hot as hell. I feel like I got my head up a sheep's ass."

I breathe deep and close my eyes. Certain as I am my plan will be successful, I still need to hear the combo in my head. I need the numbers' familiar pattern to calm my fraying nerves.

The numbers don't let me down. They sing in my mind just like they have since I was a boy. Sing like a jingle at the end of a radio commercial. I used to think of the song as a bizarre soundtrack to my ho-hum life. A weird little earworm that repeats the exact same fourteen digits over and over and over.

A curiosity. Nothing more. A funny little trick of the brain that was easy to ignore and dismiss.

Until two years ago. Two years ago, the numbers—the combo as I think of them now—became an obsession.

"Hello? You in there, Doc?" asks Harlan. "You ain't goin' to rabbit-tail now are you?"

Rabbit-tail? Must every sentence out his hillbilly mouth involve an animal of some kind? I want to ask him, *where is this backwards swamp that oozes with your kind of redneck?* But I don't really want to know where he is from. An hour from now, after the job is done, I will sail my Catalina to Mexico and never see him again.

Harlan knocks on the dashboard, the sound prompting me to open my eyes. He points through the windshield at the bank standing a short way down the alley. "You said the manager would be in at eight. Best get a move on."

Annoyed by his interruption, I don't respond. He can wait until I'm good and ready. I want to relax a little longer so I close my eyes again and watch the numbers scroll along the stock ticker in my mind.

The combo brought me here, and I know with absolute certainty this moment has been predetermined. As has every single event in my life. Every last twist and turn has been carefully orchestrated to inch me closer to the destiny that awaits inside that bank.

Two years ago, I wouldn't have believed in destiny or fate or any other such nonsense. Two years ago, I was a lost soul, a med school washout despairing over a bright future burned to ash.

Now I know I was never meant to be a doctor.

You see, if I hadn't flunked out of med school, I wouldn't have gotten my job as a bank teller. And if I hadn't spent the

last two years stamping checks and counting money for those too stupid to use an ATM, I never would've known what the numbers in my head mean.

"So what is it, Doc?"

I open my eyes first, and then the truck door. The San Diego air is briny and glows with the first rays of dawn. I see nobody in the area, and I put on my own ski mask.

Harlan exits the pickup, and the two of us—guns in hand—walk alongside the parking structure. We pass cars owned by visitors of the hotel next door, and I can't stop myself from scanning the California license plates. The combo is there, the first few digits on a Chevy, the next few on a Subaru, and the remainder on a Honda. The vehicles are parked side-by-side so the numerals are lined up in perfect order once the letters are filtered out.

The synchronicity surges through my veins and makes me feel like I'm floating. Just like the first time the numbers appeared to me outside my mind. The first time they appeared in the real world.

That was the day I opened a bank account at this very branch.

I remember everything about that day: the ham sandwich I ate for lunch; the dent in the can of Coke I used to wash the sandwich down; even the way the clouds were arranged in the sky when I went into the bank.

I remember meeting branch manager Vanessa Washington with her red hairband, and her blue dress, and her gold wedding ring. I remember how the armchair had one uneven leg when I sat at her desk to fill out my application for a checking account.

"Here you go," she told me. "These are your temporary checks. You can use them until the personalized ones arrive in the mail."

I spotted it instantly. There, at the bottom of the checks was *the* number. The complete fourteen digits lined up in the same order they'd sung in my mind for so many years. I remember the way my throat closed up, and the way I had to cough it clear to offer thanks.

I went straight home afterwards and stared at the checks for hours. Yes, a few extra digits were tacked onto the end of my number, but still, what were the odds of finding all fourteen digits in exactly the correct sequence?

The next day, I walked right up to Vanessa's desk and applied for a job. The universe had spoken, and it called me to southern California's sixth largest bank chain. Two years later, I have my own card key, and right now, I use it to let Harlan and me through the door next to the loading dock. Quickly, I go to the touchpad to disable the alarm.

The alarm code is unique to me but I don't expect to escape without them reading the log and learning who took their money. Yet I wear the ski mask for the intimidation factor.

Harlan follows me silently to the end of the hall, where we wait for Natalia, the security guard. She will be coming to see why the door was opened, but she won't be worried since the alarm was disabled. She'll think it's one of her coworkers, and I suppose it is.

She rounds the corner, and my gun stretches for her forehead. Behind thick lenses, her eyes go wide first with shock then with fear.

"Hands straight up," I tell her. "And do not touch your belt."

She complies, her hands rising slowly above her head. If she recognizes my voice, she shows no sign of it.

I take the wireless alarm trigger from her belt, and then her gun and pepper spray. I tell her to hold her hands out straight so Harlan can use a cable tie to cinch her quivering wrists.

We lead her down the hall, stopping once to toss her weapons into her office and lock the door.

We enter the bank lobby. It's Sunday, so the bank is closed, but it's had a busy night. Harlan and I watched the armored trucks come and go since just after midnight. The bank chain's entire presence up in the greater Los Angeles area, twenty-seven locations in all, has been sold to another bank. Yesterday at noon, all twenty-seven branches closed their doors for the final time. Throughout the night, their vaults were emptied

and the contents brought here, where, starting in about two hours, the massive sums will be reorganized and redistributed.

Harlan tells Natalia to lie on the floor. With an effort, she lowers herself all the way down until she lies with her back resting on the tile in front of the deposit-slip stand.

"Make like a calf now," he says.

She seems confused for a moment before she raises her hands and feet in the air. Harlan uses a cable tie to connect one of her ankles to her already linked wrists. He laughs and looks at me. "Three legs just like a roped heifer, Doc."

Unable to keep her balance, she tips to one side and begins to sob. I feel bad for her, but I can't dwell. Not now. Not when I'm so close.

I turn to the vault and find forty-nine square feet of brushed steel reflecting back. The twin keypads flanking each side of the door stare at me, red lights beckoning. My smile goes wide under the ski mask as I imagine the piles of courier bags sitting behind that door. Never before has the vault been so full. My best guess is twenty million in cash.

All those zeroes dance in my head for a bit, soon to be replaced by *the* number. Fourteen numerals flashing in bright neon. I've deduced that the first four digits represent today's date: 8/8/16. Figured that out when I bought a cell phone contract a week after starting at the bank. The contract's expiration date? 8/8/16. The ten-digit phone number? I bet you can guess that by now.

I hear a thud and a yelp, and I spin around to see the heel of Harlan's boot driving into Natalia's kidney. I shout at him, and he laughs. "Listen to her moo," he says.

Her moaning stirs a sickness in my gut. "Cut the shit, asshole. Get the fucking truck pulled up."

Harlan heads for back door, and I toss him the keys before following. I let him out and watch through the window.

Poor Natalia. For her trouble, I resolve to send her a few grand in an anonymous package.

I watch Harlan follow the garage's shadow down the alley to the Toyota. Far as I know, his only skills are cleaning pools

and pocketing the homeowners' jewelry. It's a total kick in the ass to know that a man of such dumb cruelty is about to be rewarded with two million dollars, but the vault requires simultaneously entered dual inputs, which means a two-person job. No way around it.

For months, I had to sweat over who to bring in as my accomplice, but then the problem solved itself when I went to my mother's house to get her medication so I could mail the forgotten pills to where she was vacationing in Vegas. I walked into her bedroom and found the pool man rummaging through her dresser. If I had any doubts about his trustworthiness, they were put to rest when I read the twelve-digit RX number on the pill bottle. Combined with the two-digit pill count, it was a perfect match.

The Toyota's engine starts. The truck is a recent purchase of mine, bought for the sole purpose of transporting the money a half mile to the marina, where I live on my sailboat. Guess which fourteen digits you can find embedded in the pickup's VIN number? What are the odds of that? Probably about the same as being struck by lightning twice on the same day with winning lottery tickets in each hand.

Now you understand there is absolutely nothing random about the number that has long been seated in my mind. Each and every appearance it's made led me to this day. To this bank. To Harlan and even the truck backing up to the loading dock.

And at the center of it all is the vault that just happens to be packed with twenty million dollars on this one and only day.

I picture the fourteen digits in my mind, and I see them split into three groups. The first four digits represent this most serendipitous date, and make no mistake, the date is crucial because the vault's entry codes change daily. The combo's last ten digits stand divided into two five-digit codes, one for each of the vault's keypads.

I let Harlan back into the bank, and we return to the lobby to find Natalia still sobbing where we left her.

I stand before one of the keypads, and Harlan takes his position in front of the other. Already, I can feel the Mexican

sun beating on my shoulders. From Mexico, maybe I'll go on to South America. Someplace abundant with seafood and *cervezas* and *senoritas*.

I recite one of the five-digit codes for Harlan. It's the first time I've ever recited part of the combo aloud for another person.

He nods his readiness, and we both start to type.

But neither of us finish.

An alarm wails. I wheel around and see Vanessa Washington for only a second before she ducks behind the counter. While I'm slow to react, Harlan is already racing across the room.

Where did Vanessa come from? Must've entered through the front while we were in back.

My heart pounds. Five minutes, I think. That is all we have before the police arrive. I have to yell to be heard. "Forget her! We need to get this open now!"

Harlan jumps up onto the counter and pounces into the space where I usually stand when I'm on the clock. He has Vanessa by the hair, and he's pulling her my way.

I try to wave him off. "Forget her, dammit!"

But he drags her all the way across the lobby and tosses her to the floor by my feet before waving the pistol at her. "You twitch, and I shoot."

"Get in position," I tell him.

He does, and I recite his half of the code again.

He's punching buttons, and I rush to catch up. The two codes are entered, and I watch with trembling hands for the light to turn green.

It doesn't.

"Again!" I shout.

Frantic, I punch each of my five digits. So does Harlan. Nothing.

We switch places and try another time.

"What the fuck?" shouts Harlan. "You double-crossing me?"

I say I don't understand. And I don't. Seconds are ticking by, and I don't know what to do. My throat tightens like I'm

being smothered. I yank the ski mask from my head, and we try the combo one more time.

Nothing.

"Is that you, Nick?" asks Vanessa, her voice small.

"You were supposed to come in at eight," I say.

She wipes tears from her eyes. "I thought Natalia and I could get a head start."

I don't know what to say. I don't know what to do.

My eye catches movement. It's Natalia rolling over. She rolls some more, and the double doors swish open. Somehow she's almost managed to make her way to safety, and I think *good for her.*

The gun falls from my weak fingertips. Somewhere, I feel like the universe is laughing at me. But the numbers are still chanting in my mind. They chant loud and strong. Stronger than I've ever heard them. My skull vibrates with their power.

Harlan presses his gun against Vanessa's temple. "What's the code?" She tries to shrink away from him, but his aim holds steady. "The code."

"It's too late," she says, her voice cracking. "You can't get away before the cops arrive."

He kicks her.

I shove him away. "Don't touch her!"

He lifts his ski mask to show me his cold smile. He looks at Vanessa and says, "Give me the codes, or I put a hole through your brain."

She looks up at me, teary eyes begging the question *will he really shoot me?*

I shake my head. "The gun isn't loaded."

He turns the gun on me and says, "You sure about that, Doc?"

Before I can respond, the bullet slams into the cheekbone under my right eye. The hollow point flattens before busting through bone and entering my brain. Ripping with abandon through soft tissue, the slug impacts the back of my skull and blasts a piece loose.

I'm dead even before my legs begin to buckle, and I watch myself hit the ground.

Terrified, Vanessa helps Harlan open the vault, but he only gets one foot inside before the police burst through the doors. Harlan reaches for Vanessa in an attempt to hostage his way out, but she avoids his grasp, and Harlan takes a shot to the chest. He staggers, and then is riddled before he crumples to the floor, the tough bastard.

I watch Vanessa get ushered away, and I think *good for her*.

The next few hours pass slowly for me. Like I've been dipped in molasses then dropped into a pot of honey. I catch glimpses of myself every so often. Me getting photographed. Me getting stuffed into a body bag. Me getting placed on a seven-foot table of brushed steel.

I feel myself fading away. Somebody in green scrubs ties a tag to my toe. The date is 8/8/16. The case number? I think you already know.

# CHRIS HOLM

# THE GROUP HOME

ZACH STOUGHTON AND DENNY HULL HUDDLED IN THE DARK beneath a broken streetlight and eyed the tidy foursquare house across the street. Their breath plumed. The night air smelled of coming snow. Salt rime traced jagged patterns across the frost-heaved pavement. The weeds that pushed through the cracks during the summer were brown and dead.

Denny held a crooked cigarette to his lips with thumb and forefinger, his other fingers cupped around it to hide the glowing cherry from view. He'd found it on the sidewalk some blocks away, stubbed out but still broadly feasible, and picked it up as much for warmth as anything.

That's what he told himself, at least. Truth was, he'd gone too long without a fix, and he was getting desperate. His skin crawled. His hands shook from more than cold. He felt like he was gonna puke. The act of smoking calmed him some; the nicotine quelled his tremors and eased his roiling stomach.

"What tipped you to this place, again?" Smoke escaped his mouth as he spoke. Most of it wound up in Zach's face. Zach's nose crinkled in disgust, and he waved a hand to disperse it.

"I was lifting candy from the CVS around the corner—"

"Why?" Denny interrupted. "It's, like, three miles from downtown." In reality, the neighborhood was only a mile or so from the city center, but its endless residential blocks seemed a world away from the stoops and alleyways Denny haunted.

"What's it matter why?"

"Because I fucking *asked*, that's why."

Zach sighed. "The manager at the Main Street 7-Eleven caught me slipping a titty mag under my shirt and kicked me out. Said if I ever came back, he'd call the cops. I get arrested again, it'll be my third offense, and I don't wanna go to juvie… so I decided to branch out."

Denny nodded. He'd been to juvie twice and couldn't recommend it. Least he never had to worry about going back. They let him out a day shy of his eighteenth birthday. Next time he took a fall, he'd be headed to the state pen. "Okay, so you're at the CVS…" he prompted.

"Right. There I am, sizing up my options, when this wrinkled old biddy shuffles in. Tiny little thing. Looks to be a hundred. She's pushing around a walker with a wire basket on the front. Anyway, she picks up a fuck-ton of scrips and drops 'em in the basket, only she takes a spill on her way out the door. I was nearby, so I helped her to her feet and gathered up her stuff for her."

"Ain't you sweet. Your mama must've raised you right." Denny's words dripped sarcasm. He knew damn well that Zach's mother was a schizo junkie who spent most of Zach's childhood bouncing from institution to institution. She lost parental rights when he was six and OD'd not long after. Zach had no other family. That's how he wound up at the group home where they met. "This story circling a point?"

Zach scowled. "The point *is*, I got a good look at her scrips. She had a fortune in oxy—80's, not no bullshit 5's—and some bennies too, plus a bunch of stuff I've never even heard of. So I memorized the address on the labels and I've been scoping the place out ever since, waiting for the right time to make my move."

"What makes you so sure it's empty tonight?"

"Most evenings, there's a LeSabre in the driveway. A nightlight in the kitchen. A TV flickering upstairs. But when I walked past tonight just after sunset, the car was gone, the windows were dark—and as you can see, it don't look like she's come back since. Seems to me she's unlikely to come home

this time of night. She's probably off visiting her grandkids or some shit."

Denny looked at his watch. It was an analog Swiss Army model, too small for his wrist, with a cracked face and a fraying nylon band. A boy's watch, not a man's. He'd taken it from a snot-nosed brat new to the system years ago in return for protection.

As its softly glowing hands came into focus, Denny realized Zach was right. It was a little after 3AM. The decent people of the world were all asleep. Which meant they had the place to themselves.

"Okay," Denny said. "Now how about you tell me what I'm doing here."

"Weren't you listening? There's a fuck-ton of oxy in there!"

"Yeah, I heard you—but why cut me in when you could just as easily keep it for yourself?"

"Honestly?" Zach looked at his shoes. "The idea of breaking into the place alone at night kinda creeps me out."

Denny smiled, wide and predatory. "Aw. Is little Linus afraid of the dark?"

"Fuck you, dude. I've asked you not to call me that."

At fifteen, Zach was three years younger than Denny. He was quiet, shy, and slight of build. Life on the streets had hardened him some, but to Denny, he was still the skittish little newbie at the group home who trailed a dingy security blanket behind him everywhere he went and cried when he was first shown to his bunk. Denny's buddy Greg dubbed him Linus his first week. Unfortunately for Zach, the nickname stuck long after the blanket fell apart.

"Relax. I'm just teasing." Denny took a drag of his cigarette. His mouth filled with acrid smoke as ember met filter. He spat and pitched the butt into the street. "I'm surprised you didn't ask Trevor to come with you. Seemed like you two were always pretty close."

"Not *that* close," Zach replied, "and anyway, I haven't seen him around much the past few weeks. Look, if you're too chickenshit to do this—"

"Whoa whoa whoa. Let's not forget why you invited me to tag along tonight. If anybody here is chickenshit, it's *you*."

Zach smiled cautiously. "So you'll help me, then?"

If by *help you*, Denny thought, you mean *knock your ass out and make off with as much shit as I can carry*, then yeah. But what he said was: "Of course. What're friends for?"

They crossed the street and slipped into the yard. Frost gave the lawn a ghostly cast and made it crunch beneath their feet. To the right of the driveway was a tall hedge beneath which shadows from the distant streetlamps pooled. They kept close to it until they reached the backyard. Branches scratched like bony fingers against their threadbare winter jackets. Thrift-store nylon whispered secrets in response.

Denny reached the backdoor first and tried the knob. To his surprise, it turned freely in his hand. "Well, whaddya know," he said, grinning. "I guess today's our lucky day."

He stepped across the threshold. Zach followed and eased the door shut behind them.

At first, it was too dark for Denny to see much of anything. The only illumination came from the outside light bleeding through the gauzy curtains. The atmosphere inside the house was warm and close. It smelled heavily of potpourri, and underneath that, something else—damp, earthy, and unpleasant. A clock ticked. An appliance hummed. Denny's pulse throbbed dully in his ears.

As his eyes adjusted, he realized they were in a kitchen. It looked as if it remained untouched since the 1950s. White tile countertops. White appliances. Pale yellow cupboards with chrome pulls. Yellow curtains. A patterned yellow Formica table trimmed in chrome, and four vinyl chairs to match. A black and white checkered floor. The room was so clean and shiny, it gleamed in the scant light. It almost seemed to Denny like it was glowing, but he dismissed the notion as insane—and the subtle haloing at the edges of his vision as a symptom of his withdrawal. Still, it was astonishing to him that anything this dated could look brand new.

An open doorway led deeper into the house. To one side

of it was a wall-mounted rotary phone, yellow. To the other was a vintage Kit-Cat Clock, black with white accents—its eyes constantly scanning the room, its wagging tail belying its frozen smile and conveying irritation.

"We should split up so we can cover more ground," he said, less casually than he intended. The thought of an imminent score intensified his cravings. His head hurt. His mouth was dry. His clothes were drenched with sweat. "I'll head upstairs. You, uh, check things out down here."

Denny knew the prescriptions Zach saw were far more likely to be upstairs than down—in the master bedroom, maybe, or the master bath. Zach seemed uncomfortable with the idea of splitting up, but rather than object, he simply nodded.

"Good. Remember, the last thing we need is the neighbors realizing we're here, so leave the goddamn lights off, okay? I don't give a fuck if you get so spooked you piss yourself; you *do not* turn them on."

"Okay. Jesus. I got it."

"Attaboy." Denny clapped Zach on the shoulder. "And Linus?"

"What?" Zach replied testily.

"Good hunting."

Denny headed for the stairs. Drawers rattled behind him as Zach ransacked the kitchen. What that dipshit hoped to find in there, Denny had no idea—but as long as it kept him busy, Denny figured let him look.

His footfalls were deadened by a plush runner that ran the length of the hallway. Framed photographs graced the walls on either side—of family, Denny assumed—but it was too dark to make them out. Photos of various sizes lined the stairs as well, a hodgepodge of mismatched frames it probably took a lifetime to amass. He strode past them without a glance.

The first door he came to was the bathroom. Soft blue from tile to tub to furry seat cover, it smelled of floral air freshener and proved as tidy as the kitchen. As near as he could tell from the light spilling through the window, there wasn't so much as

a spot of toothpaste on the toothbrush holder, a fingerprint on the mirror, a single hair on the brush atop the vanity.

Denny opened the medicine cabinet and pawed through its contents. Aspirin. Toothpaste. Benadryl. Cough drops. Nail clippers. Not one goddamn prescription bottle to be seen.

He yanked open the cabinet beneath the sink. It was empty but for an open twelve-pack of toilet paper. There weren't even any cleaning products. Denny cursed and threw the toilet paper across the room. Rolls scattered when the pack hit the wall.

Opposite the door through which he entered was another—leading to the master bedroom, Denny supposed. He opened it and stepped through. What he saw made him stop short.

Nearest him, the room was more or less as he expected. Plush carpet beneath his feet. Framed photos on the walls, their subjects obscured by the reflected streetlights. Garish floral wallpaper and a comforter to match.

But as it approached the center of the room, the carpet grew threadbare. It vanished entirely before it reached the far wall, exposing stained foam padding and mildewed subfloor. The ceiling—smooth white overhead—was spiderwebbed with cracks above the bed. The wallpaper likewise bubbled and peeled, revealing water stains and holes through which old wiring showed. Even the bed itself faded to dun brown halfway across, as if one side of it were new and the other had been left exposed for decades.

He shuffled further into the room—hesitant, unsure—and was startled to realize he could see his breath. A fallen chunk of plaster crunched underfoot. He looked up and saw night sky through the gap it left behind.

It wasn't the only such hole. There were dozens. They became larger and more frequent as he approached the outside wall until, eventually, there was more sky than ceiling overhead. For a moment, Denny wondered idly how he failed to notice the roof damage from the street. Then he spotted the prescription bottle on the nightstand, and his idle wondering ceased.

The nightstand was on the side of the bed, where the room tipped toward decay. Its surface was bowed and dusty, its finish dulled by age. A lamp—its base cracked, its shade yellowed and moth-eaten—lay on its side atop it, as did a rusted old alarm clock that looked as if it hadn't worked for years. Denny barely noticed them. Once he saw that amber container—the only item in the room that exhibited the peculiar luminescence he witnessed earlier—all he could think about was his next fix.

The decrepit bedroom seemed to drop away as Denny staggered over to the nightstand, dropped to his knees, and snatched up the pill bottle. Its contents rattled like hard candies. Oxy, just as Zach promised.

He fumbled with the childproof lid. Impatience and cold rendered him clumsy. Or maybe it was more than that. Denny's extremities felt numb and tingly all the sudden, like that time last winter he'd fallen asleep on a park bench and gotten frostbite. A small, worried voice in the back of his mind told him something was seriously wrong—but it was drowned out by his overwhelming need.

Finally, the lid popped open. He shook the bottle into his open palm—but as he did, its strange glow guttered and died, and all that came out was a pile of ash. Black mold spread across the bottle like a cancer. The plastic crumbled in his hands.

The lamp on the nightstand flickered on.

Denny squinted in the sudden light. Then his eyes widened. The lamp—which, to his knowledge, he never touched—was now upright. The crack in its base vanished. Its shade was clean and intact.

And the tingling in his extremities had become a conflagration.

He raised his hands to look at them, and was horrified to discover wiring—its insulation braided red and white—running from the walls into his veins. He yanked at them, but they resisted, worming deeper into his skin like living things and burning like damnation. Wires disappeared up his pant legs, too, and burrowed into his calves. Their frayed

ends clawed at the insides of his blood vessels as they climbed upward, ever upward, toward his heart.

Denny grabbed the nightstand and forced himself to his feet. The effort required was astonishing. His arms trembled from exertion. His palms burned as if the nightstand were a hot stove, and the luster returned to its wooden surface, spreading outward from the corners where he placed his hands. The rust spots on the alarm clock receded, and it began to tick.

The framed photograph above the nightstand scraped against the wall as it straightened of its own accord. Denny saw himself reflected in the glass—gaunt, sallow, skeletal, and growing more so by the second. But, terrifying though that was, it paled in comparison to the realization that the person staring back at him from behind the glass was Denny himself, appearing much as he did now.

"Creepy, ain't it?"

Denny wheeled. Zach stood in the doorway.

"You shoulda seen the look on Greg's face when she ate him," Zach continued, and then he smiled. "Come to think of it, you can."

Zach disappeared into the hall and returned with a framed photo in his hand. It was of Denny's buddy, Greg—the one who dubbed Zach Linus all those years ago. In the photograph, he looked as if he hadn't eaten in weeks—eyes sunken, cheeks hollow, bone structure showing through his skin. His neck was corded with tension. His face was frozen in a silent scream.

Denny opened his mouth to speak, but he couldn't muster the breath. All that came out was a dry croak indiscernible from the rustle of wallpaper knitting itself back together and re-adhering to the wall.

"If I were you, I wouldn't struggle. It only seems to make things worse. Found that out the hard way when she ate Trevor. He was the first. An accident. Place was a wreck back then, overgrown and long abandoned. We broke in looking for somewhere dry to sleep. Trevor decided to tag the place while we were here. She didn't take kindly to it. Anyway, I tried to remove the wires, and damn near turned the poor guy inside-

out in the process. His picture's in the downstairs hallway, right over the spot he tried to spray-paint."

Denny's shinbones snapped like dry twigs and he collapsed. His world went wobbly around the edges.

"That's when she started speaking to me. A whisper at first. Now, she's all I can hear. She said she would look after me, make a home for me—for all of us—but in return, I had to keep her fed. Truth be told, it ain't easy. This lady's got one hell of an appetite."

Denny's vision failed. He felt his eyes dry up in their sockets. Beneath him, the subfloor sprouted fresh padding and new carpet.

"One last thing before you go," Zach said. He knelt beside Denny and took his desiccated hand. Zach held it gently for a moment. Then he broke it off at the wrist. It made a papery sound like stepping through a wasp's nest. The dying boy convulsed in pain. "I think I'll take my watch back now. I sure as shit don't need your protection anymore."

# CHRISTINE GOFF

## AFTERWORD

*While the old adage that crime does not pay might well be true,
crime has nevertheless been the foundation for an entire genre
of fiction for over one hundred and fifty years.*
—*John Scaggs in* Crime Fiction *(Routledge 2005)*

*Blood Business* was presented to me as "crime fiction with a touch of the macabre." Intriguing, I thought, but what exactly does that mean?

As Scaggs points out, there are many ways to approach the study of crime fiction. One can catalog the books by their endless number of sub-genres, leading Scaggs to mention categories from "amnesia thrillers to the whodunit," or one could take the more historical approach.

While many folks credit Edgar Allen Poe as the "father" of the detective genre, Scaggs cited an observation by esteemed mystery author Dorothy L. Sayers. In her 1928 introduction to *Great Short Stories of Detection, Mystery, and Horror,* Sayers identified four stories she felt sparked the genre: two from the old Testament, one from Herodotus in the fifth century BC, and one drawn from the Herculean myths. Scaggs quotes her as saying, "In the story of Hercules and Cacus the thief, Cacus is one of the first criminals to falsify evidence...in order to mislead his pursuer."

Scaggs then moves forward to *The Newgate Calendar.* Originally a monthly bulletin of executions, produced by

the Keeper of Newgate Prison, this collection of cautionary tales of actual prisoners and their demise was first published in 1773. In these stories, perpetrators of criminal deeds are captured, tried, and punished. Scaggs theorizes the popular demand for these bloody and shocking accounts are due to the violent crimes of the 17th Century. Citizens, readers, wanted to see criminals get their just due.

As time marched on into the Age of Enlightenment, Gothic novels came into being. These stories are characterized by "the disruptive return of the past in to the present." In a time of transition from pre-Enlightenment to post-Enlightenment, people craved stories that reflected on the social and intellectual tension of the times.

Up to this point, what readers wanted could be considered noir—a type of literature where the heroes were of questionable—indeed often despicable—character with little hope for redemption.

Then in 1828, Eugène François Vidocq, a convicted felon—who later founded the Sûreté Nationale (the French police force)—became a criminalist. After Vidocq retired, he published a memoir that inspired Edgar Allen Poe, Victor Hugo, and Balzac to shift from telling stories focused on the bad guys to telling stories of the detective hero. The modern detective novel was born.

Traipsing through the historical context of crime fiction, one can't help but note how the mores of society influenced literature through the ages. Sir Arthur Conan Doyle introduced Sherlock Holmes, the analytical eccentric, and his sidekick, Watson, who embodied the middle-class morality of the time. In the 1920s, Agatha Christie ushered in the Golden Age with her traditional puzzle mysteries, while Ellery Queen and Rex Stout presented works with the notion of fair play.

It was during this time that hard-boiled detectives and modern-day noir emerged in America, the writing influenced by westerns and the gangster culture of the era. In the hundred years since hard-boiled novels appeared, they have morphed into books that encompass and reflect the gender,

ethnic, and cultural differences of our world. And more and more sub-genres of crime fiction have emerged—historical mysteries, science fiction and fantasy thrillers, horror, geezer-lit mysteries, romantic suspense, medical thrillers, cozies, PI, police procedural, psychological suspense, steampunk mysteries, graphic thriller novels, etc.

Macabre crime fiction, then, would be: crime fiction touched by the macabre—gruesome and horrifying; of, pertaining to, dealing with, or representing death at its grimmest, ugliest worst. Synonyms to macabre include: gruesome, morbid, unearthly, hideous, shocking, and weird. Plus it's worthwhile to note that the origination of the word macabre is French (remember Vidocq). We've come full circle. In *Blood Business*, we're back to noir, with a disturbing twist!

# SEAN EADS

# THE ASH OF THE PHOENIX:
## REMEMBERING EDWARD BRYANT

GRIEF OFTEN TRIGGERS MEMORIES NOT DIRECTLY RELATED to the person lost. Ed Bryant's death caused me to recollect two lectures from a high school English class. This might seem odd considering I graduated in 1991, approximately sixteen years before I knew Ed in person.

Or perhaps not, if you understand I *met* him in 1988, in the most vital way any author wants to be encountered—through his or her work.

Or when you realize the lectures I recalled centered on two of the world's great writers, John Keats and Henry James.

Fitting company for Edward Winslow Bryant, Jr.

Like so many fortunate people, my association with Ed began with an invitation to join one of his critique groups. I met him in the spring of 2007, so our friendship lasted just shy of a decade—more than enough time to appreciate the man's good qualities, but a pittance compared to those who enjoyed his company far longer. Even as I write this, Facebook fills with posts of heartfelt tribute to Ed, and I find myself pouring over an astonishing array of accompanying photographs that show a man so vastly different from the Ed I knew. Compared to those who knew him professionally and personally for thirty or forty years, what qualifications do I have to properly reminisce about Ed Bryant?

Nevertheless I'll do my best.

Let me say that Ed's death, though upsetting, did not shock me. He was beset by health problems of increasing magnitude, mostly related to his Type 1 Diabetes, and there were several times I visited him in one hospital or another and left in despair. Typical thoughts were: *This is going to be the end,* or *Ed's just not going to bounce back from this.*

Ed surely would be the first to snicker at the phrase *bounce back*, especially in regards to the nasty tumble he took in August 2014—within days of his birthday, no less—that shattered several vertebrae and left him with both extreme physical and psychological trauma. I sat by his hospital bed the next day, deeply anxious for some magic wand I could pass over his body as he writhed from a pain that overpowered the morphine drip. At that moment, it seemed his life's soundtrack was doomed to be played out on the Casio keyboard noises of the machines keeping watch over him.

I did not think he would survive.

Ed, however, had a different notion. He went through physical rehabilitation that included him wearing a plastic two-piece carapace that made him look quite a bit like a Geriatric Mutant Ninja Turtle. Since the carapace was white, Ed thought it made him look a bit like an egg. Somewhere there's a photo of Ed in that carapace with plastic horns attached to his forehead. *A deviled egg.*

Classic Ed Bryant.

And so I come to the first memory his passing evoked. One of the most notorious legends in Western literature surrounds the death of John Keats. He was a Romantic poet, practically guaranteeing he'd die young. And so he did, expiring from tuberculosis in 1821 at the age of 25. Several notable colleagues, like Percy Shelley, nevertheless believed it was unfavorable criticism of his poetry that killed Keats. Shelley said as much to his friend Lord Byron, who reacted with extreme skepticism, even mocking the notion publically in *Don Juan*. Nevertheless, the belief that Keats died from the stress of negative reviews persisted and grew over the years, nearly becoming an article of faith.

John Keats. What a dainty little snowflake.

After telling us this improbable but fascinating story one day in English class, my teacher then reassured her students that none of it was true. In fact, far from being the epitome of fragility, accounts of Keats' autopsy revealed a man who by all accounts should have died many months sooner. Here was a poet with an iron will to continue living. Coughing up arterial blood day upon day, he kept going when others began to doubt.

And dammit, so did Ed Bryant, whose body of work evokes many fine descriptions, none of which include the word *delicate*. When a story demanded it, he marshalled moments of shocking violence and biting sarcasm that are completely alien to his personality. But warmth, wry humor, and a healthy appreciation for the absurd will always be the hallmarks of Ed's work. One of the great testaments both to the power of Ed's personal perseverance and his strength as a writer was his ability to mine medical setbacks for storytelling gold. "Styx and Bones," (1999) a lacerating, kinky tale of revenge through witchcraft, originated from Ed's real experience of waking up helpless after his shoulders broke in his sleep. And one of Ed's last published stories, "Marginal Haunts" (2015) from the *Nightmares Unhinged* anthology, stems from the terror he endured during his back injury.

Not just surviving all these health scares but using them as grist for the storytelling mill as well?

What a stoic old badass Ed Bryant was.

But he was far from a stoic writer.

He once offered an amusing scenario for his death when he opened the preface to his short story collection *Particle Theory* with the following:

> At intervals I indulge the fantasy that someday I will be discovered lying dead in a gutter with crumbs of Ko-Rec-Type on my fingers. What will the coroner's report say? "He wrote short stories. He didn't write enough novels." The conclusion will be that I perished of starvation.

Typical Ed Bryant humor here. But his preface concludes with lines that become so much more poignant in hindsight:

*I am essentially a writer of the 1970s, hoping to continue on as a writer of the 1980s...I suppose I am an optimist—on good days. And maybe they won't find me dying in the gutter...*

*I'll persevere to the 90's.*

This brings me to my second memory from high school. Different teacher, different year. We're about to read *The Turn of the Screw*. It's the fall of 1990, I'm a senior, and my love of all things horror knows no equal. So of course I'm psyched to be reading what's supposedly one of the greatest ghost stories of all time.

By this point, I'd been a Stephen King devotee since 1984. My favorite story? "The Mist." It appeared in 1980 in an instantly famous anthology called *Dark Forces*. My father, likewise a fan of horror fiction, had the book on his shelf, but I never bothered with it until I learned about the King connection. This would have been around 1988.

After finishing "The Mist," I decided to give the other contributors a try. And what a staggering list of writers to enjoy! Ray Bradbury, Joyce Carol Oates, Theodore Sturgeon, Robert Bloch—to name a handful. Anyone who could hold their own among these worthies must be counted as great.

Ed Bryant was among the twenty-three geniuses I met over the next week as I explored every page of that anthology. Some, like Bradbury, I knew well. Others, like T.E.D. Klein, made an electrifying first impression.

Then there was Ed.

Ed Bryant who, at the time *Dark Forces* appeared, was heading for his second straight Nebula Award and would emcee the 1981 Hugo Awards on roller skates. He was Mr. Science Fiction Writer.

And I met him in an anthology of horror stories.

"Literary critics sometime separate Henry James's career

into three stages," my high school teacher intoned in her introductory lecture. "Like kings, they call these periods James the First, James the Second, and James the Third." She explained these separations were justified by notable evolutions in style and subject matter, concluding that in some cases a writer can change so dramatically over time that it's difficult to imagine how the aging author of one novel could ever have been the young author of another. How had the man who wrote *Daisy Miller* become the man who produced *The Turn of the Screw?*

It's definitely oversimplifying to section a writer's development into rigid phases. Neither artistic nor personal development happens so precisely. But writers *do* change, often dramatically, and thinking of those distinctions as strict delineations has its uses.

So in that sense I think it's fair to call the writer and the writing I'll always associate with Ed as belonging to Edward the Second. Or in more contemporary parlance, Edward 2.0. In light of what he wrote in his preface to *Particle Theory*, you might say I met 1980s Ed.

Put plainly, I met Ed the Horror Writer.

Which isn't to say there weren't dark elements to the science fiction he produced in the 1970s. His first collection, *Among the Dead*, proves otherwise, and Ed will always be a writer difficult to categorize. But I think it's safe to say he found his storytelling interests turning increasingly to horror throughout the 1980s. After reading "Dark Angel," Ed's contribution to *Dark Forces,* I soon encountered his work again in Skipp and Spector's *Book of the Dead* zombie anthology. Once again, it was actually the promise of a new Stephen King story—"Home Delivery"—that reeled me in.

But it's King Edward the Second who utterly ruled *Book of the Dead* with a story that must be one of the bleakest, sickest, most bombastic tales ever composed. I'm referring of course to "A Sad Last Love at the Diner of the Damned." This is a story that *Goes There.* By that I mean you read page after page of it, so stunned that by the end your thoughts boil down to: *Wow. He went there—didn't he?*

Yes.

Yes, he did.

Ed's horror fiction in fact goes a *lot* of places, and I for one enjoyed the ride. And I vividly remember, as I slogged through *The Turn of the Screw*, how much I wished the guy who wrote the cool zombie story had written it instead of Henry James. Because the guy who wrote the cool zombie story knew how to entertain. Henry James meanwhile was just an American trying to be more British than the British.

I wish I'd recalled that particular memory when Ed was still alive. I think it would have amused him. But the sad fact is I didn't think anything more about Henry James *or* Ed Bryant for another fifteen years. I certainly didn't know Ed lived in Colorado when I moved out to Denver from Kentucky in 1999 and began a career as a librarian, surely the trench warfare of literacy. It was one of my library co-workers, discovering our mutual interest in writing, who invited me to her critique group.

"You'll really like it," she said. "It's run by Ed Bryant, and he's won the Nebula Award twice."

I perked up at the impressive credentials, and the name seemed vaguely familiar. But I've never been a big reader of science fiction. After some debate and doubt, I accepted the offer and attended a meeting. Everyone introduced themselves, and when Ed finally spoke—he almost always went last—I quickly realized I was in the presence of the writer whose stories *went there*.

"Oh my God," I said. "You're *that* Ed Bryant!"

Everyone laughed, and over the years the phrase *You're that Ed Bryant* became a private joke for our group. I began to read much more of his work and appreciated the scope of it. But above all I was staggered by the sheer number of people he knew as friends, and the inexhaustible anecdotes and facts he could drop into any conversation. I submitted a story in advance of that first critique group meeting, figuring if I was going to do attend I might as well take the full plunge. Ed opened his comments by saying, in that wonderfully deep

and calm voice of his, "Sean, this is the most literary chainsaw massacre I've ever read."

I have no idea if he meant that as a compliment or not, but I sure took it as such. And I've yet to hear a remark about my fiction that I prize more highly. Ed championed both my writing and my career as a writer. He offered an important blurb for my second novel, *The Survivors.* On more than one occasion he arranged readings and signings for me. He counseled me about book contracts and clauses. As so many people can attest, his friendship extended far past the literary life. When I was traumatized by a home robbery, he called to ask me how I was doing and we talked about feelings of safety. I live alone. He lived alone. He knew my psychology.

Ed gave more than he ever got back. I used to fantasize about signing powerful blockbuster book deals that would give me the ability to erase his financial worries forever. Very few people can inspire that level of devotion, but I believe many people felt that way toward Ed. I hope I was able to help in other ways, lending him use of my house to store materials, offering him rides, getting a bite to eat with him. These things seemed good enough at the time.

In hindsight, not so much.

So here we are—you, Ed, and myself—sitting down to talk in this little space at the back of a crime fiction anthology. Are you encountering Ed's work for the first time? If so, it might be useful to apply my teacher's lecture on Henry James a step further to Ed's career and suggest that you're really meeting Edward the Third. I never thought about Ed as a crime or suspense writer, but the evidence is clear. Just as the 1980s saw him largely abandon science fiction for horror, I think the argument can be made that Ed made another transition to mystery fiction. Once again, the shift appears to approximate a ten-year itch. As the 1990s approached, Ed began producing stories like "While She Was Out," filmed as a movie starring Michelle Pfeiffer and produced by Guillermo del Toro just a few years ago.

I won't belabor the point further with all this Edward I,

II, and III talk. In the end, there's only Ed the writer and Ed the person, and I'm one of the many who knew both. The man who vowed to persevere into the 1990s did a hell of a lot better than that, against unfavorable odds. Ed wasn't found lying in the gutter with crumbs of Ko-Rec-Type on his fingers. He died peacefully at a home he cherished. Those who loved him wish it could have been put off a few years longer. But the writer continues through the stories left behind, fading and brightening in turns, sometimes falling into obscurity, other times subject to delightful rediscovery. One of Ed's most famous collections is *Cinnabar*, a cycle of stories about a city at the nexus of time. I like to think that Ed lives in Cinnabar now, and he greets you whenever you open his books.

Seek him out.

The road to Cinnabar continues…

# ABOUT THE AUTHORS

**PAUL GOAT ALLEN** has been a genre fiction book critic for the last twenty two years, working for companies like *PW, The Chicago Tribune, Kirkus, BN.com, Goodreads,* and *BlueInk.* He has written more than 8,500 reviews and interviewed hundreds of writers. He has published stories in a variety of genres and works as an adjunct faculty member in Seton Hill University's Writing Popular Fiction program. He lives in New York.

**SHANNON BAKER** is the author of the Kate Fox mystery series (Tor/Forge). Set in the isolated cattle country of the Nebraska Sandhills, Kirkus says, "Baker serves up a ballsy heroine, a colorful backdrop, and a surprising ending." She also writes the Nora Abbott mystery series (Midnight Ink), featuring Hopi Indian mysticism and environmental issues. Shannon makes her home in Tucson where she enjoys cocktails by the pool, breathtaking sunsets, a crazy Weimaraner, and killing people (in the pages of her books). She was voted Writer of the Year by Rocky Mountain Fiction Writers in 2014 and 2017. Visit Shannon at www.Shannon-Baker.com

**PATRICK BERRY** is an author and professional puzzle constructor whose work has appeared in *Harper's, The New Yorker, The Washington Post,* and numerous other publications. He's written several puzzle books, including a how-to book on crossword construction, and he has regular puzzle columns in *The New York Times Magazine* and *The Wall Street Journal.*

**EDWARD BRYANT** was a Nebula award-winning author that helped bolster The New Wave movement of science fiction. The ongoing theory that it was a severe neuro-chemical event that switched him from writing sizzling science fiction to mildly unsettling horror still hasn't been overturned. Ed wrote a few decades' worth of short fiction, nonfiction, Hollywood stuff, and the occasional novel. He lived in Denver, Colorado, preparing *On the Road to Cinnabar,* a huge retrospective of his life's work. Ed passed away February 10, 2017. This book is dedicated to his memory and the profound impact he had on genre fiction.

**BETSY DORNBUSCH** is the author of several fantasy short stories, novellas, and novels, including the *Books of the Seven Eyes* trilogy and *The Silver Scar*, which is forthcoming from Night Shade Books in 2018. When she's not writing or speaking at conventions, she reads, snowboards, and goes to concerts. Betsy and her family split their time between Boulder and Grand Lake, Colorado.

**SEAN EADS** is a writer and librarian living in Denver, Colorado. His second novel, *The Survivors*, was a finalist for the 2013 Lambda Literary Award. His latest novel, *Lord Byron's Prophecy*, was a finalist for the Colorado Book Award and the Shirley Jackson Award.

**WARREN HAMMOND** is a Denver-based author known for his gritty, futuristic *KOP* series. By taking the best of classic detective noir, and reinventing it on a destitute colony world, Warren has created these uniquely dark tales of murder, corruption and redemption. *KOP Killer* won the 2012 Colorado Book Award for best mystery. Warren's latest novel, *Tides of Maritinia*, released in December of 2014. His first book independent of the *KOP* series, *Tides* is a spy novel set in a science fictional world. Always eager to see new places, Warren has traveled extensively. Whether it's wildlife viewing in exotic locales like Botswana and the Galapagos Islands, or trekking in the Himalayas, he's always up for a new adventure.

**JASON HELLER** is an author, journalist, and Hugo Award-winning editor whose books include the alt-history novel *Taft 2012* (Quirk); the Goosebumps tie-in *Slappy's Revenge* (Scholastic); and the nonfiction book *Strange Stars* (forthcoming from Melville House). His writing has appeared in *The New Yorker*, *The Atlantic*, *Rolling Stone*, *Pitchfork*, *Entertainment Weekly*, *Weird Tales*, *Clarkesworld*, Tor.com, and NPR.org. He's also the co-editor of the Hex Publishers fiction anthologies *Cyber World* and *Mechanical Animals* (forthcoming). He lives in Denver with his wife Angie, and he plays guitar in the post-punk band Weathered Statues.

**ANGIE HODAPP** has worked in language-arts education, publishing, and professional writing and editing for the better part of the last two decades. She is currently the Director of Literary Development at Nelson Literary Agency in Denver. She and her husband live in a renovated 1930s carriage house near the heart of the city and love collecting stamps in their passports.

**CHRIS HOLM** is the author of the *Collector* trilogy, which blends crime and fantasy, and the *Michael Hendricks* thrillers. His first *Hendricks* novel, *The Killing Kind*, was named a *New York Times* Editors' Choice, a *Boston Globe* Best Book of 2015, and *Strand Magazine*'s #1 Book of 2015. It won the 2016 Anthony Award for Best Novel, and was also nominated for a Barry, a Lefty, and a Macavity. His second *Hendricks* novel, *Red Right Hand*, garnered starred reviews from *Library Journal* and *Publishers Weekly*, Best New Thriller nods from *Barnes & Noble* and the UK's *Daily Express*, and was named a *Boston Globe* Best Book of 2016. Chris lives in Portland, Maine.

**GARY JONAS** is the author of more than twenty books spanning a variety of genres. He's best known for the *Jonathan Shade* urban fantasy series, and is currently writing *The Half-Assed Wizard* series. He lives in Oklahoma.

# CONTRIBUTORS

**STEPHEN GRAHAM JONES** is the author of sixteen novels, six collections, and two or three hundred stories. His most recent books are the horror novella *Mapping the Interior*, from Tor, and the comic book *My Hero*, from Hex Publishers. Stephen lives in Boulder, Colorado.

**TREVOR JONES** was a writer and herpetologist from Baton Rouge, Louisiana. An expert in venomous snakes, Trevor did academic research as well as consulting work for the FBI. He enjoyed writing as a hobby but never took it seriously until his late twenties, when he began co-writing stories with noted children's author Nikki Barringer. Unfortunately, he passed away in 2016. "Straight to the Top" is his first published work.

**CAT RAMBO** lives, writes, and teaches atop a hill in the Pacific Northwest. Her 200-plus fiction publications include stories in *Asimov's*, *Clarkesworld Magazine*, and *The Magazine of Fantasy and Science Fiction*. She is an Endeavour, Nebula, and World Fantasy Award nominee, and her first novel, *Beasts of Tabat*, was a Compton Crook Award finalist. Her most recent books include *Hearts of Tabat* (novel, WordFire Press), *Neither Here Nor Here* (collection, Hydra House), *Alternate America: Steampunk Stories* (collection, Plunkett Press) and the updated edition of *Creating an Online Presence for Writers*. She is the current President of the Science Fiction & Fantasy Writers of America (SFWA). For more about her, as well as links to her fiction and online classes, see www.kittywumpus.net.

**MANUEL RAMOS** is the author of nine novels and one short story collection. His first novel, *The Ballad of Rocky Ruiz* (1993), was a finalist for the Edgar® award from the Mystery Writers of America and won the Colorado Book Award in the Fiction category. His published works include *Desperado: A Mile High Noir* (2013), winner of the 2014 Colorado Book Award in the Mystery category, several short stories, poems, non-fiction articles and a handbook on Colorado landlord-

tenant law, now in a seventh edition. He is a co-founder of and regular contributor to La Bloga, an award-winning Internet magazine devoted to Latino literature, culture, news, and opinion. *My Bad: A Mile High Noir*, a follow-up to *Desperado*, was published in 2016.

**KAT RICHARDSON** is the bestselling author of the *Greywalker* paranormal detective series, and the science fiction police thriller *Scattered Objects* coming from Pyr in late 2017 under the pseudonym K. R. Richardson. She lives in Western Washington, and is an accomplished feeder of crows.

**AARON MICHAEL RITCHEY** is the author of six young adult novels and numerous pieces of short fiction. In 2012, his first novel, *The Never Prayer*, was a finalist in the Rocky Mountain Fiction Writers Gold Conference. In 2015, his second novel, *Long Live the Suicide King*, won the Building the Dream award for best YA novel. His epic sci-fi western series, The Juniper Wars, is available now through WordFire Press. The second book, *Killdeer Winds*, was nominated for InD'Tale Magazine's best YA speculative novel of 2017.

**JEANNE C. STEIN** wears two writing hats. Under her own name, she writes the national bestselling Urban Fantasy series, *The Anna Strong Vampire Chronicles*, and as S. J. Harper, she writes *The Fallen Siren Series*.

**MARK STEVENS** writes *The Allison Coil Mystery Series,* set in The Flat Tops Wilderness of western Colorado—*Antler Dust, Buried by the Roan, Trapline,* and *Lake of Fire*. Three of the four books were finalists for the Colorado Book Award; *Trapline* won. Kirkus Reviews called *Lake of Fire* "irresistible." Mark is currently president of the Rocky Mountain Chapter for Mystery Writers of America and hosts a regular podcast for Rocky Mountain Fiction Writers (RMFW). He was the 2016 RMFW Writer of the Year.

**CARTER WILSON** is a *USA Today* and #1 *Denver Post* bestselling author who explores the depths of psychological tension and paranoia in his dark, domestic thrillers. His novels have received critical acclaim, including multiple starred reviews from Publishers Weekly and Library Journal, and he's the winner of the Colorado Book Award, the International Book Award, and the National Indie Excellence Award. His highly anticipated fifth novel, *Mister Tender's Girl*, will be released in February 2018 by Sourcebooks Landmark. He has also contributed short fiction to various publications, and will be featured in the R.L. Stine young-adult anthology Scream and Scream Again, releasing Halloween 2018 by HarperCollins. Carter currently lives outside Boulder in a spooky Victorian house.

**ALYSSA WONG** lives in North Carolina. She was a finalist for the 2016 John W. Campbell Award for Best New Writer, and her story, "Hungry Daughters of Starving Mothers," won the 2015 Nebula Award for Best Short Story and the 2016 World Fantasy Award for Short Fiction. Her fiction has been shortlisted for the Hugo Award, the Bram Stoker Award, the Locus Award, and the Shirley Jackson Award. Her work has been published in *The Magazine of Fantasy & Science Fiction, Strange Horizons, Nightmare Magazine, Black Static,* and *Tor. com,* among others. Alyssa can be found on Twitter as @ crashwong.

**DEAN WYANT** is a forty-year resident of Colorado with a decade of retail bookselling experience and a deep network of author contacts. His short fiction has appeared in *Nightmares Unhinged, Found* and *Thing.*

**ALVARO ZINOS-AMARO**'s book of interviews with Robert Silverberg, *Traveler of Worlds,* was a Hugo finalist. His more than thirty stories and one hundred reviews, essays and interviews have appeared in magazines like *Asimov's, Analog,*

*Lightspeed, Nature, Clarkesworld, Tor.com, Galaxy's Edge, Strange Horizons, Lackington's, Farrago's Wainscot* and *The Los Angeles Review of Books*, as well as anthologies such as *The Year's Best Science Fiction & Fantasy 2016, This Way to the End Times* and the Hex anthology *Cyber World*.

## ABOUT THE ARTIST

**AARON LOVETT**'s work has been featured by Dark Horse and published in *Spectrum 22*. His cover art for the *Denver Post* bestselling horror anthology, *Nightmares Unhinged*, inspired season two of AMC's spinoff series, *Fear the Walking Dead*. His art can also be found in various video games, books and comics. He paints from a dark corner in Denver, Colorado.

## ABOUT THE EDITORS

**MARIO ACEVEDO** is the author of the bestselling Felix Gomez detective-vampire series, which includes *Rescue From Planet Pleasure* from WordFire Press. His forthcoming book is a middle-grade science-fiction novel, *University of Doom* (Hex Publishers). He edited the Colorado Book Award Finalist anthology *Found* for the Rocky Mountain Fiction Writers (RMFW Press) and contributed stories to award-winning anthologies *Nightmares Unhinged* and *Cyber World* (Hex Publishers). Mario lives and writes in Denver, Colorado.

**JOSHUA VIOLA** is an author, artist, and former video game developer (*Pirates of the Caribbean, Smurfs, TARGET: Terror*). In addition to creating a transmedia franchise around *The Bane of Yoto*, honored with more than a dozen awards, he is the author of *Blackstar*, a tie-in novel based on the discography of Celldweller. His debut horror anthology, *Nightmares Unhinged*, was a *Denver Post* number one bestseller and named one of the Best Books of 2016 by Kirkus Reviews. His second anthology,

*Cyber World* (co-edited by Jason Heller), was a Colorado Book Award Finalist and named one of the Best Books of 2016 by Barnes & Noble. His short fiction has appeared in The Rocky Mountain Fiction Writers' *Found* anthology (RMFW Press), *D.O.A. III: Extreme Horror Collection* (Blood Bound Books), and *The Literary Hatchet* (PearTree Press). He lives in Denver, Colorado, where he is chief editor and owner of Hex Publishers.

# ACKNOWLEDGMENTS